B+T
io|u|i2

W9-BSG-632

NO LONGER THE PROPERTY OF
BALDWIN PUBLIC LIBRARY

STEALING FROM THE DEAD

FORGE BOOKS BY A. J. ZERRIES

The Lost Van Gogh
Stealing from the Dead

STEALING FROM THE DEAD

A. J. ZERRIES

A TOM DOHERTY ASSOCIATES BOOK

NEW YORK

BALDWIN PUBLIC LIBRARY

This is a work of fiction. All of the characters, organizations, and events portrayed in this novel are either products of the author's imagination or are used fictitiously.

STEALING FROM THE DEAD

Copyright © 2012 by A. J. Zerries

All rights reserved.

Edited by James Frenkel

"December 1963 (Oh What A Night)"
Words and Music by Robert Gaudio and Judy Parker
© 1975 (Renewed 2003) JOBETE MUSIC CO., INC. and SEASONS MUSIC COMPANY
All Rights Controlled and Administered by EMI APRIL MUSIC INC.
All Rights Reserved. International Copyright Secured. Used by Permission.
Reprinted by Permission of Hal Leonard Corporation

A Forge Book
Published by Tom Doherty Associates, LLC
175 Fifth Avenue
New York, NY 10010

www.tor-forge.com

Forge® is a registered trademark of Tom Doherty Associates, LLC.

Library of Congress Cataloging-in-Publication Data

Zerries, A. J.
    Stealing from the dead / A. J. Zerries.—1st ed.
        p. cm.
    ISBN 978-0-7653-2717-8 (hardcover)
    ISBN 978-1-4299-8828-5 (e-book)
    1. Women detectives—New York (State)—New York—Fiction.   2. Holocaust
survivors—Fiction.   3. Claims Resolution Tribunal—Fiction.   4. Conspiracy—
Fiction.   5. Fraud investigation—Fiction.   6. Serial murder investigation—
Fiction.   7. New York (N.Y.)—Fiction.   I. Title.
    PS3626.E77S74 2012
    813'.6—dc22

2012017238

First Edition: August 2012

Printed in the United States of America

0   9   8   7   6   5   4   3   2   1

For Al, who made life a glorious adventure

ACKNOWLEDGMENTS

Morgan and Zach, Ed and Peggy Strauss, Leo Guthart, Michelle Wetzel, Carole and Frank Fischer, Michael and Dolores Jannuzzi, Chris McDaniel, Doctor Frevola and the exceptional staff at Harborside Veterinary Hospital, Paul Scherff, Bill James, Saundie Roethel, and dearest Zeus . . . in gratitude for your support during the darkest days.

STEALING FROM THE DEAD

CHAPTER **ONE**

Greta wasn't the only one who heard the music.

The beat seeped into the Seventh Avenue express as it slowed for the Ninety-sixth Street station, and even the bleariest early rush hour passengers were tilting their heads and squeezing their eyes shut, trying to place it.

When the doors parted, it slithered in like a woman in a rumpled party dress, mascara smeared, hair a mess: a tango, predatory and voluptuous, lust thinly disguised as music.

At least twenty people were gathered in a loose circle near the middle of the platform, drawn by the boom box breathing out piano and bandoneón and bass. An eleven- or twelve-year-old girl in a school uniform, cheeks flushed, tore herself away and ran for the departing uptown train. Greta slipped into her place.

All eyes were on the two dancers in the center: a man in tight black pants, his redheaded partner in a miniskirt and clingy glitter sweater. Though meticulously choreographed, their routine's every feint, advance, and retreat still gave off the heat of a spontaneous erotic skirmish.

A swooning dip accompanied the song's end, and the man bent his partner so low that her long hair fanned out, flamelike, over the concrete floor. Only then did Greta catch on. It wasn't a couple at all, but a man and . . . a tango dummy. She had a pretty Macy's mannequin face and a stuffed body, like a Raggedy Ann doll—except Raggedy Ann never had D-cup boobs. Her flared mini showed off a small waist, a literally well-padded derrière, and willowy legs sheathed in black fishnet stockings. The dancer had skillfully kept her crude, mittenlike hands out of sight, clasped in his; clear plastic bands attached her black patent leather shoes to his ankles, so she'd never fail to follow his lead.

Applause broke out—for the dancer, for his partner, even for the clever deception. When the man and his life-size doll took their bow, he copped a feel, she slapped his face, and he pulled back, surprised and wounded. Dollar bills dropped into the basket that sat next to the boom box, another train pulled in, a new song began, and on they tangoed.

The rhythm made it impossible to walk away without moving to the beat. Strangers were grinning at one another, half-dancing up the subway stairs.

Greta, unsmiling, wondered about her life so far, and how much of it resembled the dummy's.

CHAPTER **TWO**

The Twenty-fourth Precinct shared a single building with the FDNY's Engine Seventy-six and Ladder Twenty-two. Directly across West 100th Street were neighborhood outposts of the Public Library and the Department of Health. To the side were playgrounds and an AstroTurf soccer field. Back in 1964, some whiz of an urban planner must have heard the siren song of the prepackaged Community Hub of the Future:

Want to read a book or play some hoops? Get a blood test? Report a fire? Snitch out your noisy/nosy neighbors? Just one stop can do it all—your neighborhood's municipal services center!

As Greta walked inside, a mix of coffee and aftershave wafted from the door to the right, the precinct commander's office. At least five men in suits blocked her view of Quill, and vice versa. She hurried in the opposite direction, where a stairwell lined with urine-yellow tiles led to the second-floor squad room. Detective Russell Kim, her young partner, stood up and grabbed his jacket as soon as he saw her. No matter how early she got to work, Kim always made it there first.

"Good morning. We just caught a DOA on One-hundred-and-fourth Street," he said. His perfect, English-as-a-second-language enunciation always sounded dubbed, like an actor in a foreign film. Maybe you had to be Korean to see the subtitles running across his chest. He waited for Greta to grab what she needed from her desk and followed her out.

———

A uniform car was parked outside the small apartment building on 104th Street. Ninety years past its prime, its classic limestone façade had been reduced to disintegrating fluted columns and a crumbling portico. The garbage at the curbside, painstakingly stacked and separated for recycling, made the building look shabbier than its own trash.

3C was one of the few doorbells in the vestibule with a name: P. Kantor.

The apartment door had a peephole and three locks. A rookie recently assigned to the precinct admitted Greta and Russell into a short, narrow foyer. The kitchen was to the right, the bedroom to the left, and directly ahead, through an open archway, was the living room. It was so small that every piece of furniture seemed to be touching. Two narrow windows looked out on the rear wall of what appeared to be an identical building on 103rd Street, the space in between hardly wider than an air shaft. The thin, nearly spring sunlight didn't stand a chance of breaking through the room's fuzzy predawn grayness.

One step forward brought the single chair and small table tucked just to the right of the arch into view. A teapot and a dessert plate with an arrangement of Pepperidge Farm cookies—Chessmen and Milanos—sat in the center of the table. A cup and saucer, distanced as far as possible from the chair, didn't make sense until Greta looked down.

On the floor, a white-haired woman lay parallel to the right wall. Apparently, she'd collapsed onto her side, tipping over her chair as she fell. One hand clutched the front of her housedress at mid-chest. Her eyes were open, registering a terrible surprise. Greta guessed the woman was in her eighties. While she wriggled her fingers into her plastic gloves, she briefly pondered the mystery of where elderly ladies could still find printed cotton housedresses in 2005.

"Who called her in, Betlinger?" Greta asked, thankful that her eyes could still make out the rookie's nametag at ten paces without glasses.

"She was supposed to meet a friend at a restaurant last night. Never showed up or answered her phone." Besides being strangely garbled, Betlinger's speech was annoyingly slow. "So the friend came here this morning and made the super open up. He was the one who called."

By the time he finished parsing his way through all that, he'd given up his attempt to conceal the braces glinting in his mouth. Wondering what grade he was in and how he made it past the school metal detectors with his gun, Greta asked, "And the friend? Where is she now?"

"Downstairs in the super's apartment, with Officer Alvarez." After a long swallow, he added, "Another old lady. Crying like crazy. We had to get her out of here before we had two of them down on the floor." Halfway into a grin, he remembered his braces and clamped his lips together.

Russell hurriedly asked, "Have you spoken to any of the other tenants yet?" It had taken Kim only a few weeks as her partner to become adept at rapid interceptions between Greta and people who didn't bother to think before speaking.

Betlinger didn't have a chance to reply. Roulier, the Patrol Sergeant, had let himself in. "What's up?" he asked, not waiting for an answer. His eyes darted around the room. "How come the ambulance isn't here yet, Betlinger?"

"We just got here ourselves," said Kim. "Haven't had a chance to look around yet." Greta stepped to the middle of the archway, clearing Roulier's view of the corpse.

After a two-second glance, he responded, "Hell, I could have called this one in. Saved you the trip."

First the kid, then the sergeant. Callous remarks, casually tossed off about an old woman who'd died all alone in a sunless apartment so cramped it didn't need a corpse to resemble a coffin. The sergeant, unapologetically crass, must've walked through scenes like this so many times that they'd thoroughly desensitized him, like some cop-Novocain that permanently numbs the brain's Compassion Zone. As for the rookie, probably jittery from his first time around a dead body. Credible excuses, if any were needed at all, yet the two of them had Greta's indignation simmering. She quickly turned away, her nose nearly hitting the glass doors of the china cabinet that jutted from the corner opposite the table.

So far, she'd avoided whatever was supposed to jump out of the dark and grab a woman when she turns forty. Well, it had just pounced, but instead of scaring her, it was really pissing her off.

Here in 3C, she was attending a sneak preview of her own Final Curtain. Like a high-speed fast-forward, the female Caucasian under the table had momentarily morphed into a future Greta Strasser, DOA—Dead, Old, and Alone.

P. Kantor was Greta's very own Mirror, Mirror, on the floor.

Only after several deep breaths did the contents of the china cabinet actually register. Except for a few cut crystal wine glasses, it was filled by a set of dishes. The empty center spot on the middle shelf was just about the size of the teapot. The pattern was a wide border of pink cabbage roses with a gold rim, matching the cup and saucer and cookie plate on the table. Porcelain or bone china—Greta had never known the difference—it definitely fit the pretty, old-fashioned Sunday Best category.

Like the rest of the apartment, Kantor's bedroom was tidy. Kim wandered in after Greta, and they both examined the low navy pumps and roll-on shoe polish lined up on a flattened brown supermarket bag. The shoes had an even, light shine. Kim opened the narrow closet, exposing clothes jammed in tight. A hook on the inside of the door held an outfit arranged on two wire hangers: a striped silk blouse and a sky-blue wool suit. "That would work with those shoes she polished," said Greta.

"Goes back pretty far, doesn't it?" Russell asked.

The suit was completely lined. The blouse's stripes matched up perfectly at the seams. "Not necessarily pricey, but the details—definitely vintage." She'd spent enough time sorting through thrift shop racks for undercover getups to add, "Late Fifties, maybe early Sixties."

"My grandmother still has clothes like that." A couple of weeks back, Kim had confided to Greta that he was torn between his desire to live on his own and his filial duty to remain with his parents until he was married. His grandmother was also part of the household. "Last fall, my mom took her shopping for a new dress to wear to my cousin's wedding. They went to a lot of stores until they found one that fit and was the right color and price. Then, all of a sudden, my grandmother refused to buy it—and she wouldn't let my mother buy it for her, either. She kind of freaked out. Nearly ran out of the store."

"How come?"

"The only explanation she gave was, 'What if I only live long enough to wear it once, to the wedding? What if I don't even live long enough to go?' You know, like a new dress would be tempting fate."

Greta could anticipate the grandmother's buildup—transcending all cultures—to her final jab, the Pity Punch: *"And if I do live to go, who will even notice? Nobody!"*

"Has she gone shopping since?"

"Nope. Not for clothes, anyway." He sighed, then looked around at the bedroom's unadorned walls, night table, and dresser. "This is just like the living room, isn't it? Not a single photograph. No mementoes, no souvenirs. Doesn't tell you a thing about her."

"It's like Kantor moved in years ago, but never lived here at all," Greta agreed. "Except for those dishes."

After checking out the bathroom, they passed back through the foyer. Roulier was perched on the edge of one of the armchairs, writing up his report, his wrist flying back and forth across the page like a shuttle. He didn't look up when Greta slipped back through the archway.

That teapot, and the time it would take to brew tea in it—in striking contrast to the sergeant's haste—had drawn her back to the table. A rose bloomed on its lid, and bowed longitudinal lines swirled down the sides. For the first time, Greta took note of the little blue Tetley Tea tag—no, that was *tags*, one overlapping the other. She studied the cup and saucer, also too delicate to run through a dishwasher. And the gold border made nuking them in a microwave a risky prospect.

Russell was already in the two-burner stove, table-less kitchen. A shelf on one wall served as the only work counter and also held the apartment's single concession to the last quarter of the Twentieth Century: a small microwave. Next to the sink, an upside-down white mug had long since dried in a dish drainer. Reaching up, Russell opened a painted metal cabinet. In easy reach on the bottom shelf were plain white dishes and three more mugs, the kind Kmart sold in a boxed service for four.

"That doesn't make sense, does it?" she asked, pointing at the washed mug. Without giving Russell a chance to reply, she returned to the living room.

Squatting down, Greta took a closer look at the body. Average weight, maybe five-four, but big-boned, with wide hips. She guessed she'd been strong for her size when she was a young woman.

Greta wanted to check for a wedding ring, but Kantor's left hand and wrist had been trapped underneath her torso when she fell, leaving only part of her forearm and elbow in view. Because she was pressed so close to the wall, she'd remained balanced on her upper arm and shoulder. At the lowest visible part of the forearm, Greta noticed a dark mark. "Kim," she asked, "did you notice any prescription medicine anywhere?"

"No. Just a big bottle of aspirin in the bathroom."

"That's all I saw, too." A prescription drug would list the name of P. Kantor's physician. Unless either the super or her friend could give them contact numbers for family members or the dead woman's doctor, the ambulance team would transport the body to the Office of the Medical Examiner, same as a suicide or murder victim.

Only a few feet away, the sergeant, now in the middle of a call, was demanding to know why he was being held up on 104th Street. All she knew about Roulier was that he had a nineteen-year-old son who'd been caught with drugs so many times the kid had run out of slaps on the wrist—a judge had put him away for five years. She didn't even want to think about a cop's kid in prison. It had to be eating Roulier up alive, had to be the reason he kept racing around, as if that could make his son's sentence go by faster. She felt sorry for him, but saw no reason to like him.

Dreading the feel of cold flesh through her gloves, Greta used the housedress's right shoulder to gently rock the body. She was blocking Russell's view, and doubted he'd noticed her shiver when the rest of the mark came into view. She twisted to one side, so he could see the five-number tattoo.

"Concentration camp?"

Greta nodded.

That explained why Kantor had no photographs. Not one baby or a single smiling high school graduate, no 1940's soldier boy or lace-and-lilies wedding photo, no hand-tinted portrait of mom and dad. When they gave you that number, they'd already taken everything else.

"Betlinger," she asked without looking up, "what's her first name?" They owed her that, the dignity of a full name. More than what was next to the doorbell.

"Paulina." He pronounced it *Paw-lina*.

No, it had to be *Po-lina*. Lovely, but old-fashioned, like her china.

Greta shifted her gaze, in search of a wedding ring. But that, of course, would have been confiscated, too. Paulina Kantor's left hand was slightly cupped, the pad of the thumb against the top of the index finger. Just before Greta began to straighten, something white just above the thumbnail caught her eye. "Hold on. There's something . . ." She bent closer to examine a tiny scrap of paper with a ragged edge: crescent-shaped, it conformed to the edge of a fingernail deeply ridged by age. "It's a piece of paper, sort of caught under her thumb. Did you see any paper like that around when you came in, Betlinger?"

"Not that I noticed."

"Think. Maybe a newspaper?"

While Betlinger shook his head, Russell said, "That looks too white for newsprint."

"Probably. And it looks like the rest of it, whatever it was, was torn away. So where the hell is it? The rest of the paper?" After a careful release of Paulina Kantor's shoulder, she searched the floor under the table and checked the seat of the second chair. "Come on, guys, can we find a piece of paper with a corner or an edge missing somewhere in this apartment?"

Suddenly, a large pair of black shoes confronted her. "What kind of paper, Detective Strasser?" Roulier asked from above.

While Kim and the uniform scrambled to find any kind of match, she filled in the sergeant as she backed out far enough to clear the table and get to her feet. "Several things here don't add up," she concluded. "This lady was supposed to meet her friend for dinner last night. We don't know exactly when, but since senior citizens tend to eat early, I'm assuming it was sometime around six or seven." Greta gestured toward the bedroom.

"She picked out what she was going to wear, even polished her shoes. Why have tea and cookies before you go out to eat?"

Roulier took no time to reply. "Ever been to a nursing home, Detective? Most of the old people there can recite their address and phone number from seventy years ago, then draw a complete blank if you ask them where they are. So she picked out her clothes. Five minutes later, those plans for supper—gone with the wind."

Greta shot back, "Okay, Sergeant, let's say she *did* forget, and was in the mood for a cup of tea—oh, and this could just as well have happened earlier in the day—why not just grab the clean mug that's sitting in the kitchen, nuke the water, dip in a teabag, one-two-three? But no, she went to the trouble of taking out her best china—and the teapot, no less. Why would she do that, just for herself?"

"Maybe she didn't think she was alone," he countered. "You know, one minute, nobody's home, the next minute, you've got company."

In the meantime, Kim and Betlinger had returned from their search, empty-handed. "But the paper," Russell broke in, "how could it be ripped away, unless . . . ?"

"Precisely," Greta nodded. "That's where I'm at."

All the floating, scrambled inconsistencies coalesced. Like an old-fashioned telegraph with its pasted-down strips of words, they'd assembled themselves in coherent order.

"Miss Kantor had a visitor," she said decisively. "Someone she considered important enough to invite in, make a little fuss over. Good china, cookies, brewed tea. Maybe she showed her guest a paper she had in her possession, or maybe she was looking over something that person brought along. At some point, that paper was ripped out of Miss Kantor's hands. Was the visitor responsible for her death? Possibly. My bet is that his or her cup and saucer were carefully washed and returned to their place in the china cupboard. So whenever the cops did show up, it would look like the old lady was home alone and a little dotty—a quick slam-dunk. But that's only because the mystery guest didn't know about the dinner date. And certainly didn't notice the snip of paper."

"But doesn't she look like she had a heart attack?" Betlinger asked.

"That very well might be—technically," Greta replied. "But there are at least two drugs I know of that can stop the heart. Hopefully, we'll find out more in the autopsy." She pulled out her phone and started for the door. "I'm calling this in as a crime scene. Let's get out now—we've already trampled over enough to drive the techs crazy."

At a standstill at last, Roulier was perhaps no longer holding on to his Alzheimer's theory so resolutely, but neither was he ready to accept the tempest over the teapot, either. He barely nodded when Greta said, "Detective Kim and I will be in the super's apartment, Sergeant." Turning to Betlinger, she added, "While you're waiting for the techs, you might as well start canvassing the other tenants. I'll send up your partner to assist." Shifting her eyes toward Roulier, she added, "Be thorough—don't rush any of them through it."

CHAPTER **THREE**

The super had a wiry build and steel wool hair tied back in a ponytail. Dressed in jeans and a faded black T-shirt with the Stones' trademark tongue, he immediately volunteered that his name was Pete, had been taking care of the building eleven years, and knew everyone. He spoke in a Slavic stream, the accent so thick that undivided attention was required.

"Miss Kantor she real great old lady, clean, nice, live here God knows how long time," he'd informed the detectives before they took a single step into his apartment. The layout was the same as 3C's. "Always with the 'Hello Pete!' she was and she need something she write little note—not call to yell at three a.m. because one bulb in hall burn out like some bastards, believe it no kidding. Very sad see her dead on floor but at least she go like that." A finger snap clarified his point.

Someone sized like a ten-year-old was sitting on Pete's living room sofa, feet not quite reaching the floor. A box of Kleenex was on the cushion next to her, a glass of water before her on the coffee table. "Here you meet her friend Mrs. Hermann," Pete continued, "also nice old Jew lady." He shot a look at his watch. It, too, had a Stones tongue. "Garbage cans out too long after truck picks up, bastards give ticket—I get ticket, you fix?"

"No, that's the Department of Sanitation," Greta replied. "Go ahead and take them in. Just don't leave the area." After a step toward Mrs. Hermann, she turned back to Pete. "Did you know if Miss Kantor was under a doctor's care?"

He shrugged and shook his head.

"How about relatives? Anyone you were supposed to call if—" She raised her eyes, looking past the ceiling, all the way up to 3C. Again, Pete's response was negative. "Last question: When you went up to Miss Kantor's apartment this morning, how many locks did you open?"

"One lock to open."

"How many keys for her apartment do you have?"

After a quick glance at his watch, Pete replied, "More, not sure, but come see here my keyboard." In his foyer, there was a large Peg-Board with key rings for the twenty-four apartments. Each was tagged with an apartment number. Pete picked out a key ring in the third row. It held three keys. "Always I use first the key for doorknob lock then turn knob. Must try after each key. Keep track or go nuts with six-lock assholes."

"The doorknob, that's the kind you push in and twist while you're inside the apartment?" Pete nodded, and she asked Kim, "You noticed the other two?"

"Yes, both dead bolts." Kim and Greta exchanged a nod, acknowledging the need for a key to turn the tumblers when leaving 3C. He turned to Pete. "Was that unusual, only that one lock secured?"

"Tenants leave apartment, lock all. At night, lock all. Daytime maybe one lock not so unusual." Pete put 3C's keys back on their hook. "But Miss Kantor I think she lock all. All the time."

Apparently a much perkier octogenarian than her friend had been, Mrs. Hermann was in a pale yellow nylon running suit and a bouncy pair of cross trainers. Both were at least ten years out of date, but nevertheless good indicators that there wasn't a single housedress in her closet. Her thinning hair was dyed light brown, teased, and sprayed hard enough to deflect a slug from a .45. Only a thin stain of lipstick remained on her lips; she kept rolling them in over her teeth, pressing them together, to hold back the sobs. Her eyes were puffy and red-rimmed from crying.

"Poor Paulina," she sighed into her Kleenex, as she wiped her eyes.

"We have a few questions for you, Mrs. Hermann," Greta began, after introductions. "First, what time were you and Miss Kantor supposed to meet for dinner?"

"Same time as always . . . six o'clock."

After a quick affirming look at Kim, Greta continued, "And how long did you wait for her?"

"But I already told this to the policeman! Now *you're* asking? Two *detectives*?" Mrs. Hermann's voice was tinged with the suspicion of a crime show aficionado.

"Miss Kantor lived alone," Russell explained, "so we need a little more information about . . . we need some help about who we should contact."

"*Contact?* You mean *relatives*?" Flattening one palm against her cheek, she rocked her head as if she had one hell of a toothache. "Not one. Not in this country . . . not anywhere. All murdered in the war. Terrible. I know it for a fact. Paulina and me, we were pals for over fifty years."

"Long time. You met in Europe?"

"No, no. We met when we worked together at Ohrbach's on Thirty-fourth Street. I sold girls' dresses—girls wore dresses then, nearly all the time—and Paulina worked in the office. She was one of the bookkeepers. I used to tell her that if she'd cooked the books, maybe Ohrbach's would still be in business." Mrs. Hermann brightened briefly at the memory before adding, "She had friends—very few left now—but no family. And of course, there was always the gang at The Hungarian Club."

"The Hungarian Club?" Russell's eyebrows shot up, playing her along, "Does that mean I can't join?"

"Oh, years back it used to be strictly Hungarian, but no more. It's a private club, but the restaurant is open to the public. The food isn't fancy, but it's delicious. You'd swear it's homemade." Finally catching on, she added, "Sorry. Homemade schnitzel, dear, not sushi."

Smiling right through the unintended slight, Kim got the club's address and phone number. "Did you and Miss Kantor meet there for dinner often?"

"Every two weeks or so, we'd get together, except if I was visiting with my son's family, or with one of my daughters." Her eyes welled up. "See how lucky I am? I have three children, seven grandchildren."

Greta guessed that those grandkids kept her on her toes enough to prevent her from slipping into the classic granny mold—ironic that the solitary Paulina Kantor was the one who fit the sentimental, white-haired stereotype. After Mrs. Hermann finished blowing her nose, Greta asked, "Can you tell us the last time you saw her, and if she appeared to be in good health?"

"Well, I spent some time at my younger daughter's home on Long Island . . . so that would make it three weeks ago. As far as good health, Paulina wasn't a complainer, but after all, she was eighty-four. Neither of us was running the marathon. I'll tell you this, though," she said, wagging a finger for emphasis, "every day of the year, without fail, Paulina went out for a walk—well, except when there was ice. You have to be careful with the hips."

"So I hear, yes," said Greta. "Do you know if she was under a doctor's care for any type of health problem?"

"If she was, she didn't tell me."

Greta went back to the night before. "So last night . . . your first thought wasn't that she was ill?"

"I didn't know what to think. Paulina usually showed up early, so it didn't take long for me to start worrying. I waited about half an hour, then I telephoned her. There was no answer, so I figured she was on her way, maybe it was the crosstown bus caught in traffic. I waited a little longer, and meanwhile the club filled up with people who spend the winter in Florida that I hadn't seen for months. They sat down with me, and we ordered dinner, but I kept looking at the door for Paulina." Mrs. Hermann crumpled up her tissue. "To be honest, I wanted to go to her place when we finished, but by then it was dark, and I was afraid to go all the way over to the West Side and back."

Russell gave her an understanding nod, the cop confirming that you can never play it too safe in the big city.

"I kept trying Paulina's number when I got home, over and over. I don't have to tell you I didn't sleep a wink. I came here first thing this morning, ringing her doorbell. Then I saw the super sweeping off the sidewalk, and I grabbed him. Such a shock it was, seeing her like that!" Her hand flew to her chest—either in grief, or to simulate her friend's final gesture.

Russell handed her the glass of water, and she took a few sips.

Greta paused; there was no way to get around the next question. "Mrs. Hermann, we noticed . . . on her left arm."

Mrs. Hermann's mouth contorted as she whispered in another language, unmistakably a curse. "None of us can imagine what it was like for the people who walked out of those camps! Think about that, to be someone like Paulina, all alone in the world, no family or home left to go back to. Your last memory of your neighbors is them hanging out of their windows cheering the Nazis while they rounded up the Jews." The thought made her cross her arms defensively over her chest. "My family came to America in 1933, when I was nine years old. My mother and father kept up the traditions, spoke Hungarian at home. Paulina's family hoped things would change . . . but it only got worse. Well, they weren't the only ones living in a dream world."

Greta did some quick math. Paulina Kantor would have been in her early twenties back then. "I've been calling her Miss Kantor. Was she married?"

"Yes; I didn't want to correct you, but it was *Mrs.* Kantor, a married woman with two little children. The SS grabbed them away from her as soon as they got off the train. Her husband was on crutches from a trolley accident, so he was of no use to them, either. Old people, babies, anyone they couldn't squeeze the blood out of with hard labor, those the Germans got rid of immediately.

"Paulina said that every morning she woke up in that place, she prayed to God to let her die. This she told me several months after we met—somehow, we both hit it off together, you know? That day we were having lunch, and it came out how she lost everyone. She broke down, and I couldn't stop crying either, and everybody was staring at us. After that, she never mentioned it again, and, naturally, neither did I." Mrs. Hermann brought her hands together and twisted her wedding ring "My husband, Nate, may he rest in peace, we both tried to introduce Paulina to nice fellows, but she refused to even meet them." She shook her head, perhaps to demonstrate how adamant Paulina Kantor had been. "Plenty of men and women we knew, refugees from Europe, got together after they came here. They married, had children. It's not a sin to start over. Widows, widowers . . . you know, life goes on. But Paulina—" She put her hand over her mouth and spoke through her fingers. It reminded Greta of how people watch a horror movie with their fingers over their eyes. "Both Nate and I had a feeling she didn't want to be with a man because . . . because of whatever the Nazis did to her in the camp."

A grinding cramp wrenched Greta's insides, even though her period was weeks away. "So as long as you knew her, Mrs. Kantor was pretty much on her own?"

Mrs. Hermann pointed up. "That apartment upstairs—it's nothing to write home about, but it's rent-controlled. If not for that, she never could have managed to make ends meet."

Greta said softly, "That set of china up there looks like the only thing Mrs. Kantor splurged on."

"Oh, finding those dishes made her so happy!" Mrs. Hermann exclaimed, smiling for the first time. "Can you believe, it was the same pattern she had as a bride! She found it under the El!"

"The El?" asked Kim.

"The old East Side elevated line. The Third Avenue El. Long before your time," Hermann explained. "It was ugly and blew soot and made the street dark, so you didn't exactly find fancy stores under the tracks. I think they tore it down in the Fifties. Anyway, one day, Paulina saw that set in one of those hole-in-the-wall places—service for eight and a half. Back in Hungary, she had service for twelve, but even half of eight and a half wouldn't fit around that little postage stamp of a table. The crook asked for thirty bucks, but he was happy to get fifteen. Oh, how she loved those dishes!"

"She used them?" Greta probed. "There weren't just for display?"

"Sure, she used them—for company, like when Nate and I came to visit. She was very proud of them."

Kim smiled back at her, then changed course. "You said she had friends . . . what about people who weren't exactly friends?" Hardly a smooth transition, and Mrs. Hermann was no fool.

"What's not a friend? You mean an enemy?" She drew back onto the sofa, apprehensive.

Russell did a quick save. "That's in the rule book, Mrs. Hermann. We have to ask that."

Wary but relieved, she replied, "No enemies. Paulina was very sweet-natured. I couldn't have asked for a better friend. It's a crime that she had to die like that, all alone."

CHAPTER **FOUR**

"Detective Strasser." Lieutenant Geracimos' big frame filled his office door. "I need to see you. Now."

Nick Geracimos, who'd been dubbed Geronimo about five seconds after he entered the Police Academy, was the Two-Four's head of detectives. With his silver hair, sloping shoulders, and truck-sized spare tire, the lieu was a very old fifty-five. When Greta was transferred to the precinct, he'd immediately let her know that Hank Strasser was his first partner. "He was a good man, a good cop." Respect and regret tinged his voice, as if twenty-nine years hadn't passed since her father was gunned down. But his tone warned that there wouldn't be any warm reminiscences today.

Like the crowd in the town square back in the days when a public hanging was one of few entertainment options, the detectives in the squad room perked up. With rolling eyeballs, they exchanged bets on how long she'd dance on the rope. To her relief, Geracimos took a step back as she entered and shut the door.

He gestured for her to sit down. That was good, too. But after he settled down behind his desk, he tilted his chair all the way back and stared up at the ceiling, as if he needed guidance and strength from above. "How long you been on the job, Greta?"

"I just passed nineteen and a half years."

He nodded. "Not too long ago, I reached twenty-nine. My wife can't wait for me to retire. And you know what? Neither can I. What about you?" Before she could answer, he bolted straight up and locked eyes with her. "Don't even think about thirty, Greta. Think about how you'll manage to hang on by that thin and fraying thread of yours for the next six months."

"Are you hinting that I won't get a party?"

"You think it's funny? Quill has you in his scope. I don't know why, only that it isn't for anything you've done on my watch. But in order to be fair, I checked up."

Checked up? The real reason Quill hated her would never be in any file, but just in time she stopped her arms from crossing defensively over her chest. There was no controlling the sweat that was leaching out under her blouse, hot and cold at once, like a fever breaking. Fucking Quill.

"How shall I phrase it?" Geracimos asked, with exaggerated delicacy. "The knack you have for antagonizing your superior officers?"

"Okay, I've burned a few bridges," she admitted.

Incredulous, he shot back, "Looking at it like that, you're a goddamn serial arsonist! You've been transferred so many times, the city's running out of precincts!"

She couldn't help smiling—that was the very reason, when she found out that she'd be under Quill's command, why she hadn't been able to ask for a transfer from her transfer.

"Look, your dad saved my ass more than once," the lieu confided. "I owe him to keep an eye out for his only child. But you're making that pretty hard to do."

"Lieu, Kantor was no DOA!"

"C'mon, I told you this morning it sounded over the top to call in the crime scene crew. And what turned up? Crumbs. Literally, a few useless crumbs."

She couldn't refute that. A sprinkling of cookie crumbs on the floor near the one standing chair was the only indication Mrs. Kantor might've had a visitor before she died.

"Nothing on prints so far," Geracimos continued, "so all we're left with is the tenants. Any leads?" He rolled his chair as far back as he could, providing plenty of room for all the suspects she didn't have.

"Not yet," Greta replied. No one had buzzed anyone in, or spotted a stranger in the building before or after the approximate time of death. Like the super, they all had pretty much the same opinion of Mrs. Kantor: a nice, quiet old lady who kept to herself. "But not everyone was available. I'm going back this evening. And I'm waiting on some items that were sent to the lab."

"A pot of tea and a piece of paper? What happened to the poisoned apple?" He sighed. "I sent you your techs. In case you didn't notice, I held back on the homicide squad. But while you and Kim spent most of the day MIA, we had more calls than we could handle. I was juggling like crazy, and Quill put two and two together. He's only half as stupid as he looks. I wound up with an earful—the difference between initiative and cheap showboating, tight budgets, blah-blah-blah. You getting this, Greta?"

"I put you in the seat under the pigeon nest today. I'm sorry, Lieu."

"You're on the homestretch, kid. Be careful not to throw it all away."

The next morning, while her train passed under the East River from Brooklyn to Manhattan—like every day for nearly three and a half years—Greta tried to shut out the bridge to the north.

For her, the bridge was The Day and The Day was the bridge.

She'd fought her way west over its roadway, struggling against a tide of frantic, fleeing people. Thousands of faces rushed at her, dodged around her . . . disembodied faces, streaked with smoke, disfigured by their personal preview of hell. But her fiercest battle was with her own dread of what might be at the other end . . . cracks in the pavement racing toward her, expanding, cracking, rupturing under her feet . . . no west exit ramp . . . nothing but a sheer cliff of broken concrete and twisted cable . . . far below, the river flooding over where Manhattan used to be.

The bridge, of course, had remained intact, none of its grace or strength or triumphant embrace of the river diminished. But that imagined jagged precipice and watery abyss would always be more real to Greta than the scenes of the crumbling towers that replayed endlessly on every TV around the world.

Greta blinked back at the train's flickering lights. The river's unbearable pressure bore down on the arch of the subway tunnel, on the roof of the train, on the top of her skull, until her heart no longer beat on its own, but pulsed with the throb of its current.

She'd returned to Mrs. Kantor's building the evening before to question the people who were away earlier in the day. Nothing had turned up. With the autopsy scheduled for the afternoon, she felt a twinge of guilt about hoping it would prove that Paulina Kantor had indeed been murdered.

Ultimately, it didn't matter whether that hope was in the interest of justice or the confirmation of her suspicions. Three strikes and Greta was out: Nothing had come of the crime scene, the neighbor interviews, or the autopsy. Old age was, it seemed, the villain that had stopped Mrs. Kantor's heart.

Kim had opted out, leaving Greta as lone witness to the poor woman's final indignity—her naked body exposed to the scrutiny of strangers in a bright and frigid room.

Before she left the Office of the City Medical Examiner, Greta checked the paperwork. The body was to be released to a funeral home in the East Eighties—but who had made the arrangements? She had to return to the Two-Four to fill out the DD5 form on Kantor, but no one would know if she made a stop along the way. Hadn't Crappy Craig, her ex, called her a bulldog? Affectionately at first, when he thought her tenacity was cute, as "my little bulldog." Acrimoniously later, whenever she didn't agree with him (which occurred with increasing frequency, right up to signing the divorce papers), as "you fucking bulldog."

A memorial service was being held in Chapel One, and a young man with a carnation in his lapel pointed Greta to the business office.

A woman with her back to the hallway was standing before a credenza, slowly unpacking a Bloomingdale's Big Brown Bag, carefully sorting through framed photographs and sports trophies, less mindful of their history than of her manicure. She held a small glitzy dog collar at arm's length for a moment, then dropped it over the bat of a tarnished Little Leaguer statuette.

Greta coughed, held up her shield, and introduced herself as the woman turned toward her. Under the soft, indirect lighting, it was hard to tell if she was, like Greta, in her early forties, or if she had a great plastic surgeon. Lately, affluent women in the city appeared to hover at either twenty-six or forty, excluding other ages in between or beyond. "I'd appreciate some details about Paulina Kantor's service, please."

"I don't believe she's even here yet," the woman said apologetically.

"I know—I just came from the autopsy. I need information about who made the arrangements." A nameplate was on the desk. "Celeste Gordon—is that you?"

The woman nodded. "Actually, Mrs. Kantor met with my late father-in-law in 1982. She paid for her own funeral in advance." In response to Greta's quizzical look, Gordon explained, "At the time, it still hadn't quite caught on. But even the most modest service and burial—like Mrs. Kantor's—have more than doubled in cost since then." Celeste Gordon steepled her fingertips together, hands-in-prayer mode. "It's becoming more and more popular to preplan," she added, easing into the presentation. "Our preplanners—generally people who live alone, or without family nearby—are asked to designate at least two people to contact us." That set Greta's brain scrambling for two designees of her own. "We send out postcards annually, requesting information updates. Mrs. Kantor's friend called us yesterday." Gordon stepped to her desk and referred to a folder. "A Mrs. Hermann. We immediately contacted the Medical Examiner's office." Tilting her head to one side, she asked, "Was anything . . . amiss?"

"No," Greta replied quickly. "Thanks, Mrs. Gordon, you've answered all my questions. By the way, that prepayment—"

"Preplanning," Gordon corrected.

"Right. Does that include a newspaper obituary?"

"It does, and we'll have it in the papers the day after tomorrow—plenty of time before the simple memorial service Mrs. Kantor requested."

Before Greta could ask, she added, "Sunday, at one."

Sunday was damp and overcast, cold enough to snow. The precinct felons, ostensibly staying home to warm in the glow of their hijacked HDTVs, made it easy for Greta to slip out of the Two-Four.

She signed the book at the chapel entrance, not only out of respect, but to boost the scant number of mourners. Pete the Super was clustered with three women, and Mrs. Hermann was at the center of a slightly larger group. Still looking spry in a dark pants suit, she broke away to hug two women who'd walked in just before Greta. When she caught sight of Greta, she waved her over.

"Oh, you have a good heart, Detective Strasser." Standing, she was even tinier than expected, barely four-ten in heels. "Where's that nice Chinese kid?"

"Detective Kim sends his respects," Greta lied. "He's at a concert he bought tickets for last summer." If Mrs. Hermann wanted to think that detectives made a habit of showing up for DOA funerals, no harm done.

Mrs. Hermann introduced the two ladies as friends from the Ohrbach's days, then added, "Layette and men's shirts, but they both jumped ship for B. Altman's—like that store would last forever." All three, smiling sadly, shrugged their shoulders.

"And those people you were just with? Are they from Ohrbach's, too?" Three men and five women, they might have been a little younger, but not by much.

"Oh, no. They're from The Hungarian Club—remember?"

"Sure, 'like homemade.' I plan to give it a try."

"I'd invite you to join me there, but this whole thing with Paulina . . . I've got to get away."

"That's understandable," said Greta. "A visit with one of your children?"

"My younger daughter. I'm taking the first train I can catch to the Island, and I haven't made plans for when I'm coming back. She wanted to attend the service, but it's *her* younger daughter's tenth birthday. They're holding the cake just for me."

"That's lovely, Mrs. Hermann. Believe me, you've done more than most relatives would." That summoned up an approving chorus from her friends.

"If the tables were turned, Paulina would have done it for me, I guarantee you. Look over there, you see those ladies with the super? All tenants from the building. I just met them myself. You know what they told me? When their kids were little, if their babysitter didn't show up, or maybe they had to run out for an emergency, they could always count on Paulina to keep an eye on them. She never took a dime to do it." Standing on tiptoe, Mrs. Hermann whispered up to Greta's shoulder, "Imagine how hard that had to be—wondering what her own two children would be like at the same age. So sad, so sad."

A man in a blue suit and a yarmulke strode up to the lectern at the front of the chapel. He introduced himself as a rabbi who, although he had never met Paulina Kantor, had learned how she'd suffered during the war. Either Mrs. Hermann had passed that along, or a funeral director had alerted him to the unmistakable SS tattoo.

In an incongruously silky Dean Martin voice, the rabbi chanted a prayer for all those murdered in the Holocaust, and one for Paulina Kantor herself. A short pitch for peace and understanding was followed by a psalm. Mrs. Hermann read a poem in English and Hungarian, the rabbi said another prayer, and the service was over.

Greta shook hands with Mrs. Hermann and Pete, nodded briefly at the others, and turned to leave. In the same instant, a man at the rear of the chapel hurried toward the door. His face was already turned away, so all she could make out was that he was medium height, gray-haired, and dressed in a Burberry-style raincoat. She was positive he wasn't one of the few men at the memorial. His haste made Greta take off after him, but when she reached the sidewalk, he'd vanished. Up the street, a bus was lumbering from the curb into a traffic lane, and the light went out on the roof of a taxi pulling out right behind it.

The small gathering was still milling around in the chapel when she reentered the funeral home. She checked the guest register. Her signature was the last one on the page.

CHAPTER **FIVE**

Late that afternoon, Greta surfaced at Grand Army Plaza, her home subway stop in Brooklyn, and hurried along Eighth Avenue to Montgomery Place. Halfway up the single-block street, her hand automatically went to the small silver whistle she wore on a chain around her neck. A few brownstones from home, she blew.

The pitch was too high for human ears, but it brought a black-and-tan Doberman to the nearest of the three windows that formed a bay on her floor. With her ears peaked up like goalposts, front paws on the sill, and deep chest thrust forward, Greta's big girl was ready for a run.

Molly had a basket full of chew-bones and toys, but those windows were her own Dog Channel, providing continuous live coverage of cars, bicycles, pigeons, cats, pedestrians, and, most riveting of all, other dogs. If Greta ever moved, she'd have to machine-sand and repaint the claw-gouged sills. But selling was something she'd never even consider, not after what she'd gone through to hold on to the apartment.

Years ago, after she kicked out Crappy Craig, he'd demanded that they sell and split the proceeds—even though he'd put up barely a third of the down payment. Outraged, Greta resisted until his smarmy lawyer finally threw in the towel. He allowed her to repay Craig's contribution in the form of a ten-year second mortgage—gouging her on the interest rate. But since smaller apartments on less desirable streets were currently selling for five times the original price, Greta had no regrets. Nevertheless, the pleasant prospect of writing her ex's final check in July was diminished by the prospect of not knowing where—or if—she'd be employed in September.

Except for after-school or summer jobs, the NYPD was the only employer she'd ever had. Geronimo might see no option for her other than retirement, but on that issue, she was at war with herself. The scary part was not knowing which was worse: suppressing everything she'd learned on the job just to hold on to her job, or handing over her gun and her shield . . . a surrender that, with only the slightest nod from Quill, would irrevocably lock her out of the NYPD. He was the last person she wanted to force her decision, but either way, the bastard won.

In the waning light, Greta and Molly jogged up the block, crossed Prospect Park West, and took off down the broad promenade that ran along the park's stone embankment. Pedestrians and other runners gave them a wide berth. A big Doberman and a woman running full-out together had that effect, especially when neither was smiling.

Greta was the fourth generation of her family to serve in the Department, but no one was left to advise her. Long before she was born, both her great-grandfather and grandfather had made it to retirement, but neither lived more than two years after. Her father had died in the line of duty when she was twelve; not coming home from that last patrol was the only time he'd ever let her down.

As for her mother, as soon as she found out that Greta would be entering the Police Academy after her college graduation, she announced that she was moving to Florida. "You just flushed four years of college down the toilet, and you think I'm going to hang around and wait for you to get shot? Put on that damn uniform, and you are on your own!" was her only good-bye.

Of course, Bram was the one—the only one—who could have talked her through to the right decision. After all, planning the future together is one of the things engaged couples do best . . . until one of them dies. Greta doubted the NYPD retirement forms would have an option for the

Marital Status limbo she was in: not widowed, but subject to the same unpredictable and unrelenting cycles of grief-anger-emptiness.

About nine that evening, Greta was on her sofa, shuffling the Sunday paper, searching for anything that could distract her from the Paulina Kantor affair. In retrospect, it could be viewed as a desperate attempt, fueled by premenopausal hormones, to prove that her detection skills were still as sharp as ever—with the opposite result. She started another re-sifting of the papers when the phone rang.

"Strasser," she said, curt enough to keep the agita from seeping through.

Someone was breathing on the other end.

Greta snapped, "You have two seconds. Then I'm hanging up."

"No," a man said, "please stay on. It's just that I'm not sure I have the correct person, and if I don't, I apologize for disturbing you." He sounded uncomfortable, like a good actor reading a bad script.

"Who are you trying to reach?"

"The G. Strasser who attended Paulina Kantor's memorial this after-noon."

The papers slipped from Greta's lap as she straightened up. This time, she was the one who said nothing.

The man finally said, "Obviously I'm mistaken . . . so sorry."

"I was there." G. Strasser was exactly how she'd signed the guest register.

A deep breath, then a tentative "Are you a relative of the deceased?"

A scam, that's what this has to be, some kind of scam. They find out who attended the funeral, contact the relatives, sell them something sentimen-tal and worthless, like a cup of dirt from the cemetery. Except it's from a backyard in Jersey.

Greta stood and started pacing back and forth. "And if I am?"

"Then could you kindly tell me if any other relatives were at the ser-vice? Or perhaps some who weren't able to attend today?"

Now that's one truly accomplished scam artist—looking for referrals before he even sells her The Lord's Prayer in a frame shaped like a Star of

David. If I tell him I'm not Jewish, he'll switch to a pitch for a picture of Jesus autographed "Good Luck, Your Savior."

When she didn't reply, he added, "I've contacted most of the people who were there. If you are a relative, you're the only one so far."

Nope, the only potential mark. "I don't see why—"

"Excuse me, Miss Strasser," he cut in. "Could I please meet with you, as quickly as possible?"

"Hold on. You're an absolute stranger, and you expect me to—"

"There's so much to tell you. But not over the phone."

"Well, tomorrow, then," she said reluctantly, wishing it could be that very night, that very minute, the quicker to nail a con artist depraved enough to prey on the newly bereaved. "After work."

"Where, Miss Strasser?"

The more he pressed, the more difficult it was to control her irritation.

"Actually, I was planning to go to The Hungarian Club. Tomorrow, at six-thirty."

CHAPTER **SIX**

At the point in Central Park she estimated to be equidistant from both Quill and the Deathwatch Telemarketer, Greta tucked her straight blond hair under a curly brown wig and slipped on glasses. Keeping up a brisk pace, she continued east through the park, intending to arrive at The Hungarian Club well in advance of her Sunday night caller.

Quill's payback agenda was intensifying. Twice, she'd been called from her desk to search a woman in the tank because (or so Greta was told) no other female officer was available. Both times, she had to breathe through her mouth and curse plastic glove manufacturers for not making their products longer—opera length, at least. The two encounters only renewed her belief that people who walk around with a putrid crust on their bodies really don't give a damn about the gender of the cop searching them. On her way back upstairs, she overheard another of Quill's boys looking for her. She raced to the bathroom and, with a smile, held the door for the patrolwoman who exited as she entered. After enough time had passed for the frisk to be assigned to someone else equipped with tits and a gun, she left for the day.

The address she had for The Hungarian Club apparently belonged to a street-level French restaurant. Confused, Greta paced back and forth in front of the building until she spotted a small brass plaque. Resembling a historical marker more than a sign, it was engraved *The First Hungarian Literary Society*. Close enough. The door next to it was unmarked and locked, but it had a doorbell. Greta was buzzed right in, and she found herself in a vestibule filled by a steep, narrow staircase. While a surveillance camera blinked above her head, she climbed the stairs, stopping to examine the framed pictures that lined the walls—mostly annual group photos of members. The further back they dated, the more formal the poses and clothing became. Some had been taken more than a hundred years before, the ladies in evening gowns with trains, the gents in tail coats. On the second floor, just past a propped-open kitchen door, she entered the dining room, a large space with windows facing 79th Street.

Half the tables were set up for supper with red or green tablecloths, but at six-fifteen, only three had diners. Low-key and sleepy, it was the perfect place for a meet-and-greet-and-arrest with Funeral Fred. When the hostess led her to a table in the middle of the restaurant, Greta demurred in favor of the dais by the windows, where four small tables afforded a full view of the room. She took a chair facing the entrance.

At six-thirty, a small crowd, all senior citizens, suddenly gathered at the door. In a wave, they surged into the dining room, shouting greetings while they claimed tables like the Oklahoma land grab. Mrs. Hermann had mentioned that many of the members wintered in Florida, and it was a snap to pick them out, tanned or not. As if they were still in Boca, the men wore bright blazers or cardigans; the ladies' suits and dresses— watermelon, kiwi, mango, and pineapple—were a tropical fruit salad.

One man remained by the door. In his late sixties or early seventies, he was at least ten years younger than most of the men in the room. He was about five-nine, Greta's height; another similarity was that they were the only ones in the restaurant in dark suits. As the hostess pointed out her table to him, Greta glimpsed Sunday's tan raincoat draped over his arm. Slight of build and markedly agile, he threaded his way through the tables like a man extraordinarily light on his feet. Was she looking at a seasoned con artist spry enough to make one more quick escape, or a silver-haired man who still had some great dance moves?

He stopped directly in front of her and bowed deeply from the waist.

Greta had no idea how it had happened, but her right arm was fully extended, and her hand was in his. "Miss Strasser, thank you for meeting me. My name is Theo Appel." Another bow, this time from the shoulders. "May I join you?"

She hadn't picked up his trace of an accent on the phone, so faint it was hard to pin down. "Isn't that why we're here?"

As he sat down, he began, "I'm very sorry for—"

Before he could finish, the waitress swooped in with menus and asked if they'd like a drink. "Non-alcoholic," the woman explained, "because we don't have a liquor license. Members bring their own, but there's a liquor store right down—"

"No," Greta cut in, "I'm fine with an iced tea, please."

Appel ordered the same, and picked up where he'd left off. "I was about to tell you how very sorry I am for your loss. I neglected to say that last night." His eye contact was strong, and the blue eyes conveyed sincerity and solicitude.

Greta glanced down. If she hadn't spent all night perfecting her scam-the-scam-artist script, she might be wavering.

Tentatively, he asked, "Were you related to Mrs. Kantor? Last night, you didn't say."

"Great-niece. On my mother's side."

He frowned slightly as he considered her reply, something Greta wasn't expecting. "Any other relatives, who weren't able to attend the service?"

"No. No other relatives."

"Do you recall if your great-aunt ever mentioned a relative—a father, father-in-law, uncle, any relative at all—with the first name Hershel?"

Appel studied her face while she pretended to summon up snippets of adult conversations overheard by an uninterested little girl. "I think so . . . maybe," she said at last.

"I'm not sure how to ask this, but did your aunt—"

He was drowned out by new arrivals, members who turned up the decibel level by calling out to friends across the room and dragging chairs along the floor to wedge in at their tables. Apparently, few had come for dinner: One big, bright handbag after another yielded up pencils, pads, and packs of playing cards. Ladies with arthritic knots on their fingers were dealing with the flash of Atlantic City croupiers.

"Did your aunt," Appel resumed, "mention anything about . . . a bank account?"

Bingo! Up until that, the guy had made a little polish on the brass go a long, long way. "Mr. Appel, did you ever meet my aunt?"

Just as the iced tea arrived, he replied that he hadn't had the pleasure.

"Well, if you had, the last thing you would've asked about is a bank account."

"Miss Strasser, I didn't mean a . . . a *local* bank." Hunching forward, he spoke in a lower, more confidential tone, despite the growing din. "I meant a bank in Europe. To be specific, a bank in Switzerland."

"Oh, *that* bank!" Greta barely suppressed her mounting anger. "The one with the crystal chandeliers and mahogany paneling and the numbered accounts? With the safety deposit boxes in the marble vault, three stories underground?" *I saw that movie, too, asshole.*

He drew back in his chair, confused by her answer, her surge of hostility, or both. "I didn't mean any specific bank. What I'm concerned about is if she acted for her family . . . if she recently submitted a claim for family funds deposited in a Swiss bank."

"Her family, Mr. Appel? Murdered in concentration camps. All of them."

"I . . . yes." The contradiction of a great-niece's survival had momentarily escaped him. "I'm not surprised to hear that. Sadly, that's the very reason I'm here." Reaching into his inside coat pocket, he pulled out a folded sheaf of papers. "I believe her husband's or father-in-law's name might be on the 2005 list. The updated CRT list."

"CRT?"

"Claims Resolution Tribunal. It was set up for Holocaust victims, to help them settle claims against the Swiss banks. The class action suit, the Global Settlement."

"Hold on," Greta interrupted. *Was he the front man for an entire network of predators? Or a candidate for a soup-to-nuts psychiatric screening at Bellevue?*

But Appel was on a roll, moving their glasses, unfolding the papers. "It was on the Internet, there were ads in newspapers." He was running his index finger down a page, not looking up. "Here it is. Hershel Kantor." He rotated it and tapped the name.

In a sudden, noisy about-face, excited Hungarian Club members were pushing back to the entrance. A man and woman in their eighties had just walked in with a couple in their twenties. Despite the vast age difference, there was a strong family resemblance between the two men—presumably a grandson. The young man held an infant in his arms. Club members, both men and women, quickly had them surrounded.

Appel, following Greta's intent gaze, looked back over his shoulder. Fear and delight seesawed back and forth on the baby's chubby face, until he settled on a two-tooth sunbeam. A collective, joyous *"Ahhh!"* rose up, followed by congratulations in English and what had to be Hungarian: a perfect example of the camaraderie Mrs. Hermann had said the otherwise solitary Mrs. Kantor enjoyed at the club.

When Appel turned back, his eyes were glistening. "A fourth generation," he said softly. "A blessing . . . and also the truest measure of what so many of us lost."

Stalling, Greta sipped at her tea, still unable to pin down Appel as the world's slickest geriatric hustler. But whatever his game, it was time to end her own masquerade. She reached for her shield. Clasping it so no else could see, she held it right under his nose. "Detective Strasser, NYPD. I'm no more related to Paulina Kantor than you are. And now I want to hear why you're so damn interested in her and her bank account."

Appel stared at the shield for a long time. "Are you really a detective?"

"A detective who came here to arrest you, Mr. Appel—or whatever your name is."

His hand flew to his chest. "Arrest *me*? On what possible charge?"

"Running a scam. Preying on grief-stricken people at their most vulnerable."

"Ah. A one-woman vice squad!" He raised his eyebrows. "So . . . you think I'm a crook?" He sounded amused, as if she'd mistaken him for a latter-day Clyde Barrow or Willie Sutton.

Greta, usually able to read people with ease, was having a tough time figuring the guy out. "Let's say I'm definitely considering the possibility."

"My wallet's inside my jacket . . . okay?" He didn't wait, just reached in and produced a small billfold. He withdrew a few plastic cards from one of the leather slots and shuffled their order. The first he held up was a New York State Driver License for Theodore Appel. "Valid," he said, pointing at the expiration date. He replaced it with a Visa card, followed by an AARP card. "So are these." He handed over a fourth card for a closer look. In the photo, his hair was sandy brown, his face fuller. "No longer any good for getting me into the building—I've been retired for a while. But it's proof that I once worked there."

Behind Appel, people were flitting from table to table, laughing, chatting over the card players' shoulders. She'd been to weddings where people didn't have half as much fun. The First Hungarian Literary Society was anything but a quiet place where seniors met to compare antidepressants. A bad enough miscalculation, but nothing like mistaking a spook for a swindler. The card in her hand was a Central Intelligence Agency ID.

"I wasn't a cloak and dagger agent. But I did work there for thirty years. You can check me out." He suppressed a smile as he added, "The only crimes I ever committed were sanctioned by the U.S. government."

"Whether I buy this or not," said Greta, with a nod at the card as she handed it back, "why the urgency to establish a link between Hershel and Paulina Kantor?"

"To be honest, I suspect far more than I actually know. I've been to the police several times. Because I need more than a minute to explain my concerns, they either lose interest or conclude that I'm suffering from full-blown dementia. They shove paperwork at me, I fill it out, and it's in the wastebasket before I'm out the door. You might be on the verge of arresting me, but it's a small price to pay—you're the first member of the NYPD I've actually been able to talk to. As for your Hershel-Paulina connection, there are intricacies I haven't come close to figuring out, but there's one thing I'm sure of: Murder is involved. And Paulina Kantor's murder isn't the first—it's the latest."

Using both hands, she lifted off her glasses. She was too late to conceal the jolt he'd given her, but she needed a moment to recover.

"I believe that's sparked your interest," he said softly, "but I need your help even more."

"Okay. I'm listening."

"I've been linking up names on the CRT list—most recently, Mrs. Kantor's possible relative—with obituaries. Then I hunt for the details."

"What kind of details?"

"Age. Cause of death. Possible concentration camp survivor. Number of survivors, or mourners—if any. Along those lines."

His words hurtled Greta back to Apartment 3C, grainy air shaft light percolating in, the outline of the woman she herself might become chalked on the floor.

After he put away his wallet, Appel whispered, "Have I trapped a member of the NYPD into listening . . . in the course of her attempt to entrap me?"

She waved her hand, a signal to keep going. "Who's on the list?"

"People who were, and I quote, 'a victim or target of Nazi persecution' who made deposits in Swiss banks between 1933 and 1945. The majority are Jews. There are also Romani—a more polite word than Gypsies—Jehovah's Witnesses, homosexuals, and the mentally or physically handicapped. During that period, a trip to Switzerland for such a purpose was extremely dangerous. But that was outweighed by the Swiss banks' reputation as safe harbors. They were known for safety and confidentiality."

"Numbered accounts . . . no names to give away whoever owned them."

"In theory. After the war, some Holocaust survivors straggled back to Switzerland. The concentration camps were so efficiently operated, many of them couldn't even dream of happiness like that." He gestured back toward the door.

"The four generations."

"Thank you for understanding. Yes, Detective Strasser." He took a deep breath before he continued. "So these depositors walked back into those safe Swiss banks. Right to the survivors' faces, the bankers either denied the accounts had ever existed, or refused to pay on inactive accounts whose time limits—meaning any date convenient to the circumstances—had expired."

"What happened if surviving relatives went?"

After a sharp intake of breath, Appel replied, "The banks demanded to see a death certificate."

"A death certificate from a concentration camp? How the hell could they expect—?"

"They didn't," Appel said dryly. "That was the point. The banks employed every subterfuge imaginable. They insisted that all the Jews in Europe combined hadn't deposited more than fifty thousand dollars in Switzerland during the entire twelve years leading up to 1945."

"No accounts, no money," Greta whispered in disbelief. "How did they get away with it for so long?"

"In Switzerland, Detective, the banks have always had their own charters, their own rules and regulations. They weren't accountable to the government. When they chose to band together, they wielded incredible power. International challenges started right after the war ended, but every time the Swiss banks came to the bargaining table, they managed to stall. Another year became another decade. The decade became a half century."

"What—who—put an end to it?"

"An odd couple if there ever was one—Senator D'Amato of New York and Edgar Bronfman, then the president of the World Jewish Congress. D'Amato was on the Senate Banking Committee. The hearings he ran exposed the Swiss banks, shamed them in the eyes of the world. Finally, a reparation program was set in motion. You don't recall reading about it?"

"Maybe," Greta replied. Reading the newspapers hadn't become a daily habit for her until 9/11. "Mostly I remember that D'Amato was a feisty guy. So he was the one who finally nailed the banks?"

"That he did, back in the Nineties. It took several years more, but the dollar amount put on the Holocaust accounts was $1.25 billion."

"Fifty thousand dollars to that? You tell me—was that considered a fair amount?"

"Fair?" He sighed deeply. "Can anything about the Holocaust ever be called 'fair'? Certainly not to all the people who died before the banks paid out a penny."

"What happens to the money if the people on that list don't survive to claim it?"

"It's slated to go into a general fund."

"Controlled by the Swiss banks?" asked Greta.

"Absolutely not! None of it can be reabsorbed by the banks."

Greta picked up the list. "You said they put ads in newspapers and on the Internet." She gazed out at the room, where the combined age at every table had to be at least five hundred years. "I'd like to take a poll of how many seniors in this room go online." She riffled through Appel's pages. "What do all these X's stand for?"

"What I just told you about the banks' power, their arrogance, and the creation of the fund—that's all fact. The X's are my attempt to make sense of . . ." He shook his head. "No, first please understand that the names on the list are the *account holders*—the people who *opened* a Swiss account."

"Back between 1933 and 1945."

"Correct. The typical depositor of the era would be a male—an established businessman or industrialist, doctor, lawyer . . . possibly even a banker himself."

"At least a hundred and ten by now," Greta calculated. "And that's not even considering the odds he had to beat just to make it through the war."

With a nod of acknowledgment, Appel resumed. "So back to your question about those X's . . . From what I've started to work out, they're the heirs of the original depositor. Usually children. Children who'd now be quite senior senior citizens."

"So it's their obituaries . . . the X's are all dead."

Appel's eyes held hers for a long time. "How did Mrs. Kantor die, Detective?"

"No asphyxiation, no blunt trauma, no sign of injection punctures. I attended the autopsy. Natural causes. A heart attack."

He sat back in his chair, very still. When he spoke again, his voice was scratchy, as if he'd swallowed a pill without water. "Nearly all my X's died of a heart attack. The only accident was a fall down a flight of stairs. Whenever I can dig a little deeper—someone who'll get on the phone at a funeral home or synagogue or club or union mentioned in the obituary—I discover that these deaths all occurred at home, when the deceased was alone."

"That translates into 'without any witnesses.'"

"Yes. And I believe someone *is* around. Tell me . . . was there any sign that Mrs. Kantor had a visitor the day she died?"

The paper scrap . . . the teacup . . . And what was it that Mrs. Hermann had said about the china her friend found under the El? Only service for eight and a half, while back in Hungary, she'd had service for twelve? Twelve. That didn't necessarily make her incredibly rich, but maybe her husband's family . . .

Maybe Paulina Kantor didn't find out about the fund. Maybe someone found her, instead.

Finally, she answered, "My partner and I were the only ones who suspected she wasn't alone. But the autopsy officially closed the case for him." *And I wasn't about to drag a good kid like Kim through the shit trench Quill has ready for me.*

Appel held out his left wrist, as if he were about to check his wristwatch. Instead, he unbuttoned his shirt cuff and pushed it and his jacket sleeve up as far as they'd go. Five numbers were tattooed on his wrist. "You can call this an official cause of death, too. A weapon designed to kill the spirit, or the soul, or whatever that thing is, like a cosmic computer chip that makes you want to keep on living. So let's stretch it a little. I'm as officially dead as Paulina Kantor officially died of a heart attack."

CHAPTER **SEVEN**

"Those will give you the basics," Appel said, after hurriedly jotting down half a dozen Web sites. "Follow the links, and before you know it, you'll be just as paranoid as I am." They exchanged contact information and planned to meet the following Friday evening.

Unexpectedly, Lieutenant Geracimos called Greta into his office late Friday afternoon. "You just caught the bike thing downtown," he said. Though not apologetic, his tone had a whiff of don't-shoot-the-messenger. "It's their time of the month again. Union Square." Averting his eyes, he added, "You're ordered to report in the bag."

A blue Post-it Note, GET RB, was stuck to the wall behind the lieu's head, and staring at it beat counting to ten. Was a suspect with those initials today's top priority? Was it a reminder to call about a report from ballistics, or to stop at the deli for roast beef on the way home?

Greta's RB was the Rotten Bastard Quill, letting the other shoe drop.

Just holding back on the assignment until the latest possible moment was spiteful enough—the Critical Mass Bike Ride always took place the last Friday of each month. But Quill was pushing this all the way to malicious with the specific order for a detective as experienced as Greta to show up for parade duty in uniform—the aforementioned "bag."

Her focus returned to the lieu, who was shuffling papers on his desk. That RB of his definitely had to stand for retirement benefits.

"I'd better get changed," she said.

"Yeah, go ahead." The relief in his voice indicated that whatever reaction he'd braced for from Detective Strasser, it was not compliance.

The women's locker room was unoccupied. Greta banged her locker door as hard as she could. Then she kicked it, right where Quill's balls would be if he were standing in front of her.

What pissed her off the most was not being able to meet with Appel. The online searches he'd sent her had revived her suspicion that Paulina Kantor was indeed a murder victim. Appalled by how little she knew, she'd been glued to her computer every evening, as addicted as a pre-teen gamer. Only Molly's long snout coming between her eyes and the monitor—a silent reminder that their bedtime walk was hours overdue—broke her concentration.

As the cyber-labyrinth grew progressively darker and more complex, it invaded Greta's dreams. Sometime before dawn that morning, she'd bolted up in bed, wishing for the impossible—to unlearn it, all of it.

Appel didn't answer his phone, so she left a message, promising to reschedule.

After she pinned up her hair so it wouldn't stick out under her hat, Greta reached for her uniform. Back in her undercover days, she'd started stowing most of her cop stuff in her locker, in case any of her "dates" succeeded in tracking her back to where she really lived. The dry cleaner's plastic wrapper was dusty, and the fabric felt unpleasantly limp. Thinking back, she'd arrested someone on a bicycle only once—a Staten Island kid with raging acne, who'd keyed her patrol car while she was writing a parking ticket. She'd been a rookie then, and in a much crisper uniform.

Greta doubted that particular juvenile delinquent would have grown up to be a participant in what Geronimo called the "bike thing." What had begun as a monthly protest against car pollution blew up during the 2004

Republican National Convention with the arrest of nearly two-hundred-fifty bikers. Far from the heavy-metal, Nazi-helmeted, hog-straddling types, these were bikers of the leather-alternative, acoustic guitar variety—Sixties activists magically reconstituted by sips of their ever-present bottled water.

Since then, the monthly Critical Mass Ride had escalated into a nasty sparring match. The city, citing disorderly conduct and marching (albeit on two wheels) without a permit, sought an injunction against promotion of the ride. The cyclists responded with preride rallies that condemned NYPD arrests and bicycle confiscations.

Bikers approached a rally from multiple starting points, text-messaging to evade the police; when it was over, they'd fan out again. Police scooters, motorcycles, cars both unmarked and marked, and vans did their best to thwart them. The city maintained that arrests were justified because the bike-clotted streets impeded emergency vehicles. Overhead, a 9.8-million-dollar NYPD helicopter, video-equipped to read a license plate from a thousand feet, hovered above the cyclists. (That earned the bikers unexpected support from a surprising number of couples enjoying rooftop sex while the ride took place below.) On the ground, Critical Mass's volunteer First Amendment lawyers tracked the police. They accused the cops of creating panic among the bike riders by forcing them into life-threatening situations. The city countered that the cyclists who recklessly ran red lights and headed into oncoming traffic did so to avoid arrest.

Just past seven, word was radioed along that the Critical Mass rally in Union Square was over. Undercover cops disguised as cyclists were now en route with the ride, reporting in on cell phones. As usual, CM bikers were scattering to draw police away from their largest contingent, which was headed south on Broadway. At Broadway and Astor Place (where Greta was positioned on the southeast corner), they were expected to turn east. After Astor's three short blocks, they'd cross Third Avenue and head to the after-ride party scheduled to take place at a St. Mark's Place church.

As soon as they came into view, Greta and a handful of cops would alert the police operation at the other end of Astor, sequestered in the deepening shadows behind Cooper Union. The hulking nineteenth century institute stood with the impregnable calm of an island fortress before the constant two-way traffic of Third Avenue. Reasoning that only crazed kamikaze bikers would run the Astor-and-Third light, the NYPD was poised for the eastbound riders to stop there on red. Out of nowhere, a phalanx of unmarked cars would rush in to block them from crossing, while scooter cops would race out of the holding area and surround their rear. Escaping to the church and demanding sanctuary would not be an option. Greta's small detachment would join the principal unit at the intersection as soon as the main body of bikers passed through, to assist the arrest-fest.

Not quite D-Day, but a carefully planned operation, nevertheless.

From her position in front of the corner vitamin store, Greta fixed her eyes north on Broadway. Suddenly, her peripheral vision picked up a sizable influx of pedestrians surging from the east. She turned right to check them out. No placards or bullhorns, just briefcases and bags: another trainload of working stiffs who'd made it through another week. Only dogged determination had hoisted them up the subway steps.

A quick glance north, then across Broadway, where a uniform leaned against the wall of an underground parking garage. Plainly bored, fidgety, and easily distracted, the guy was in serious need of a cop game-face refresher course. Quill himself couldn't have paired her up with anyone less professional.

Behind the twitchy cop, the garage's twin bays gaped like bottomless cave mouths—the in/out ramps were so steeply inclined, only the taillights of a car that had just pulled in were still visible. Before Greta looked away, three buffed, bumpy bowling balls rose up from the entrance ramp. Bobbing into view, they became the shaved heads of three African-Americans. As their broad shoulders and swinging arms materialized, it was their belligerent, synchronized stride—far more than the shaved heads—that triggered Greta's positive ID of the man in the middle.

She'd been looking for him for a long time.

The tallest of the trio, his gang name was Viper Xtreme, or VX—about as far as you could get from Ernest Flowers. He was the current leader of a gang that went way back in the Two-Four. VX had a rap sheet long enough to be broken into chapters. He was last seen the day he spotted a rival gang member dealing on his turf. With utter disregard for where that transaction was taking place—across a playground packed with little kids—VX fired his .38 at the interloper. Greta and Kim responded to the anonymous 911 and rushed into a playground that was completely deserted except for an unconscious five-year-old and his hysterical aunt. A girl of only ten, she swore through her sobs that she'd never taken her eyes off little Tyrel, never saw who shot him. One second, she'd pushed her nephew up on the swing; the next, blood was running from his head.

While the unlucky boy lingered in a coma, Greta and Russell managed to track down nearly a dozen adults who'd been in the playground that day. Outraged as they were by the shooter's recklessness, no one could be persuaded to describe him, no less speak his name. And even though they didn't vary on how the rival dealer had been dragged into a car that sped away, no one recalled a single physical detail about him, either. Or his rescuers, or their vehicle.

A break came on a door-to-door while they questioned a woman in bubble-gum pink sweats whose body filled her apartment's doorway. Somehow, her little girl managed to scoot between her ankles and out into the hall.

"Tell them, Mama!" her daughter screamed, and there was genuine terror in her squeaky voice. "Tell them it was that Shiny-Head Man!"

"You get back inside, Kayla!" With astounding speed for her size, her mother scooped her up.

Before she could clamp her hand over Kayla's mouth, the kid got out, "Mama, the lady asked who shot Ty—"

While the girl squirmed to get free, the woman's eyes darted back and forth along the dingy hallway and the stairs above and below. Through clenched teeth, she uttered the first half of a curse: "That boy—*that* was an accident." What remained unsaid was clear: "Anything that happens here won't be an accident—and it'll be on your heads."

Shortly thereafter, word got around that the every member of VX's gang had shaved his head.

Whatever had prompted this dirtbag to resurface was unclear. Certainly, if VX had known about Critical Mass and the huge police turn-out, he would've picked any other evening, any other place. Nevertheless, here he was, less than fifty feet from Greta, striding across Broadway. Beyond, two blocks north, the Critical Mass vanguard appeared, already merged into the left lane. VX and his buddies were now opposite her on Astor, strutting past the long storefront of the Gap for Women. Greta stepped off the curb and crossed the street, her eyes locked on the three men. As if they'd all caught sight of her in the same instant—that perfect, intuitive synchrony again—the collective badass attitude vanished.

The uniform—Quill's goddamn mandated uniform—had robbed her of any element of surprise. If she'd been in plainclothes, no way they would've reacted—or, for that matter, even noticed her.

Far off, she heard whirring—the first of the bikers. "Ernest Flowers," she called out, "stop right there!" His cohorts were doing a slow fade, but VX-Flowers was her primary concern. He appeared calm—too calm—and kept walking. Greta had no doubt that the .38 he'd used to shoot Tyrel had been tossed in the Hudson and replaced with another weapon before the boy's ambulance arrived at the hospital. Her fingers flexed restlessly over her own holstered gun.

A biker whipped between them, inches from Greta's chest. As she instinctively retreated a step, he blasted "Get your dumb cop ass back on the sidewalk!" over his shoulder at her. Suddenly trapped in a blur of spinning spokes and Day-Glo spandex, the safest thing she could do was freeze. For a moment, her sight line cleared enough to pick out VX, not more than ten feet away, now also in the street. His focus wasn't on her, but on the approaching bikers. After letting a few pass, he reeled back and coldcocked his selected target so hard a perfectly vertical spray of blood shot skyward when the poor guy's head snapped back. Because he didn't fall off fast enough, VX gave the handlebars a violent shake.

Another wave of cyclists blocked VX again, but they immediately began veering to either side or braking hard to avoid his latest victim, who by then was sprawled motionless in the middle of the street. In no time, they were getting slammed from behind by the rest of their contingent.

Greta grabbed her radio, but the cop at the other end couldn't hear a word she said over the cyclists' fury and agony.

Before she could repeat her urgent request for backup, a lone rider emerged out of the rapidly mounting pileup of mangled bodies and bicycles—the only one pedaling away from the fray, in the direction of Broadway. Shiny-Head Man, ripped out of little Kayla's fears and looming larger than life, was aiming his stolen bike at Greta. Her only escape from his head-on assault was a swift pivot left. As soon as she turned, her left shin exploded with pain. All at once, the radio went flying, a body thumped down at her feet, and Greta stumbled forward onto it. Disoriented, she had no idea if she was sprawled across the same cyclist who'd razored into her leg, but whoever landed beneath her had done VX an invaluable favor.

Rising on one elbow, she could see the thug doing a wheelie onto the sidewalk. "Flowers, halt!" Greta yelled, but she couldn't even hear her own voice over the pandemonium in Astor Place. No sign of her radio, but the bike lying next to her appeared pretty much intact. Clenching her teeth, she righted herself and the bike together, took a deep breath, and threw her leg over the seat. Her left trouser leg was already wet with blood.

From the roadbed came a muddled, "Hey! Where you going with my bike?"

"I have no idea," Greta muttered, as she wobbled down the sidewalk after VX. Pedestrians in their path were jumping back, plastering themselves against the storefronts.

Flowers was easy to spot, so big he looked like an adult squooshed down on a second grader's dirt bike. His arrival at the corner coincided with a break in the Critical Mass procession; without even stopping, he was able to zip off the sidewalk and cut left onto Broadway. Greta, who had to wait for an opening, was poised to commandeer the radio of the cop in front of the parking garage, but he was gone.

While she unbuttoned the pocket that held her cell phone, a split-second chance to dart out presented itself, and she took it—unavoidably cutting off an extremely angry clot of bikers.

When the hell was the last time she was on a bike, anyway? Sure, one of the things you never forget is how to ride a bicycle, but that doesn't make you Lance Armstrong when you hop back on.

A quick reach for the phone was ruled out by her death grip on the handlebars. Further down Broadway, VX had edged into the right lane. Greta, desperate for a rearview mirror and directional signals, willed her right hand to become unglued, extended her arm, and flapped it up and down. A horn honked, but she made it across as VX turned right onto Waverly Place. He was going the wrong way on a one-way street, but anyone cold enough to fire a gun between playground swings had been going the wrong way his whole damn life.

On the north side of Waverly, a taxi pulled away from the curb just as Greta came around the corner. Luckily, her turning skills hadn't fully returned: her drift was so wide that the cabbie, accelerating to beat the light across Broadway, didn't run her over. Only her right calf made contact with his fender, so the sledgehammer wallop balanced out the chain saw gash in her left shin. Somehow, both legs kept on churning.

Up ahead, she saw trees—Washington Square Park. VX passed Mercer, then hooked a left onto Greene, another attempt to shake her on a one-way wrong-way. Besides oncoming traffic, Greene Street presented another menace: a bit of Olde New York, it was still paved with ancient cobblestones. Inside her pelvis, all the body parts so finely detailed and labeled on the big chart in her gynecologist's examination room were being jolted loose.

Meanwhile, VX, who obviously had steel balls, was widening his lead, going so fast he never saw the pothole up ahead. It swallowed enough of his front wheel to throw him—he went flying into the path of a small truck careening around the corner. Swerving to avoid him, the driver had no choice but to crunch over the bike. Although he was no longer in control of his vehicle, he didn't slow down, putting Greta at risk virtually anywhere in the roadway. Forced to veer into the narrow gap between two parked cars, she barely escaped. Behind her, the truck kept on going.

Near the end of Greene, VX staggered briefly, accelerated to a run, then made another left turn. Greta, maneuvering back into the street, had to wait for a car to pass.

VX had a shot at escape.

When she turned, she caught sight of Broadway again, two short blocks ahead. VX was running on the sidewalk, with only one block between him and the intersection. As she skipped the bike onto the sidewalk of the same block, the traffic light up ahead was green, about to flip red. He'd never make it across. Even if it was a short light, she had him. No matter how fast he ran, she was the one on the bike, steadily gaining.

Near the corner and just ahead of VX, a blonde in a bright blue coat had just pushed out a heavy exit door. Using her back, she held it open while a wheelchair rolled out. Slumped to one side, a small person with long blond hair was operating the chair. The woman was smiling down at her, talking. Neither of them noticed VX's approach.

Running hard, not missing a step, he seized the wheelchair and whirled it around to face Broadway. Pushing with both hands, he raced toward the busy thoroughfare.

CHAPTER **EIGHT**

For a split second, the woman in the blue coat stared down at the empty space before she spun around. Like Greta, all she could see was VX—his outsized frame completely blocked the chair. As his unthinkable purpose registered, she took off after him, screaming, arms flailing. One of her high heels skidded out to the side, and she lost her balance, avoiding a fall only by grabbing for the door handle of a parked car.

Greta squeezed the brakes, swerving and barely avoiding her.

"Help—my daughter! Please!" the woman cried, when she realized a cop was in pursuit.

Greta had another twenty feet to the corner, but with his long-legged stride, VX was already there. No heart, and he ran so goddamn fast.

The screech of brakes came first, then the horns, then the endless repetitions of metal crumpling and glass shattering. In no time, the stench of gas, brake fluid, and burned rubber fouled the evening air. The intersection was an ugly conga line of rear-ended vehicles.

Something was lying in the middle of the intersection; Greta jumped off her bike and ran toward what was left of the wheelchair. Thrown at least ten feet farther, the girl—no, as Greta hurried to her, she saw that she wasn't a child, but a tiny woman in her early twenties—lay far too still. Greta spoke to her. She was unresponsive, but still breathing. As she pulled out her cell phone, the girl's mother caught up, running in stockinged feet, crying, "Abby, oh, my baby!" Her knees buckled at the sight of her daughter's injuries, and Greta caught her just in time to prevent her from collapsing onto her child. Tightly cradling the woman in her arms—to both comfort and restrain her—Greta whispered, "Your daughter's still breathing. I'm calling EMS. Hold her hand, talk to her, but be careful not to move her." Sobbing, the mother nodded, and Greta released her.

As the call went through, she glanced south down Broadway, the way VX had gone. By now he'd already vanished into the swiftly darkening streets. After her urgent request for an ambulance, she reported his description, his direction, his horrific act.

Somewhere to the south, he was loping along effortlessly, his total lack of conscience not the least of his appalling crimes.

When Greta turned back, the mother had lifted her child's head onto her lap, and was stroking her forehead. No cop rulebook she'd ever read about moving a critically injured person applied to one already so severely handicapped. "The ambulance is on its way" was the only consolation she could give.

A man stood by the open driver's door of a Jeep, the vehicle closest to the wheelchair. When he saw Greta staring at his grill, he moaned, "She came out of nowhere! I hit the brakes, but her wheelchair . . . Did it like, go out of control?"

Instead of answering, she questioned him about who and what he'd seen, but all he gave her was that he'd been looking straight ahead, concentrating on driving.

Greta glanced back at the sidewalk. The only person on the corner was a pale young woman in a sweatshirt and jeans. A long, tube-shaped canvas bag was slung over her shoulder; perhaps she was an art or architecture student. Her shoulders heaved with silent sobs. Greta pointed at her, then at the intersection, then at her own eyes. The young woman nodded: a witness. Greta pointed her way again, jabbing at the air twice: *Stay there, please.* In response, the young woman slipped her bag off her shoulder and settled down on the curb to wait. A nod and thumbs-up were Greta's heartfelt *Thank you.*

Maybe a block away, an ambulance bleeped; its team of paramedics was already running toward them. As if on cue, the streetlights sizzled on, and Ninth Precinct cops swarmed in. An unmarked pulled up, and their commander eased his big frame out of the rear door. The vertical lines etched in his cheeks deepened into furrows as Greta reported how VX had hijacked the wheelchair and as she listed the charges against him in the Two-Four. Motioning at the ambulance snaking through, he asked, "Detective, do you need a medic? Your trouser leg is ripped, and you're bleeding."

"It can wait."

As the girl was lifted into the ambulance, her mother ran back toward the wheelchair, but a uniform body-blocked it just in time. "No, no," she insisted, "her chair is everything, my daughter can't get around without her chair!" Despite all the anger and wreckage VX had wrought on that short stretch of Broadway, a hush fell over the crowd while a paramedic wrapped an arm around the woman's shoulders and steered her inside the ambulance. The silence remained unbroken until the doors slammed closed and it pulled away.

The precinct commander resumed, "The Two-Four isn't exactly around the corner, Detective. How long were you in pursuit? And why didn't you have any backup?"

"I made him on Astor Place, sir. My radio was knocked out of my hand—lost—so I just took off after him."

"Astor Place?" His head tilted back slightly. "Were you working the bike thing?"

"Yes, sir." Greta braced herself, anticipating a Quill-grade explosion.

Instead, he asked, "What the hell was this Flowers mutt doing downtown?" Then he answered his own question with "Garbage like that had to be up to no good. Okay, Strasser." He waved over a woman only a few feet away in a black knit coat, like a long cardigan sweater. It made Greta realize how cold she was, and she did her best to suppress a shiver. "After you talk to Detective Mercado, we'll get you a ride back to Cooper Union."

"Sure, but I've got an eyewitness waiting on the corner."

The three of them walked over to the young woman. Head down, the chief listened carefully to her statement.

———

When Greta was returned to the Critical Mass command center, about a dozen people in bike garb were lined up under guard, facing Cooper Union's thick stone walls. They kept glancing over their shoulders, protesting while their bikes, tagged as evidence, were transferred into a police truck. Not much of a haul, taking into account the motorized force that had been waiting to pounce. Greta guessed they were the lead bikers who'd swerved around her. No sooner than they'd been caught in the net, the flow of detainees must have ceased—either warned off by cell phone or rushed away by ambulance. Apparently, Greta had made her inaudible request for backup at the same time the brass was trying to figure out the reason for the sudden cutoff.

After several inquiries, she was directed to report to four gold-braid honchos. It was obvious that not one of them heard a single word of what she told them about VX; she'd just singlehandedly ruined an operation they'd had in the works for months, and they were mightily steamed.

One, an Uber-Inspector, summoned the other three into a huddle. The group wasn't quite out of earshot, and Greta patched together that he'd been contacted by the Ninth's PC.

His description of their conversation was met with "Shit! That only makes it worse!" and "For Christ's sake, if she'd only made the damn arrest, we wouldn't be here arguing about damage control!"

They buzzed back and forth until the inspector broke from the group. His name tag read Sullivane, and Greta figured he'd spent half a century explaining, "Like Sullivan, just with an 'e' at the end." He reached into his tunic for his card and held it at arm's length. "Detective, when you get back to the Two-Four, fax a copy of your DD5 to this number." After a pause, he curtly added, "You acted in the line of duty. In the future, I suggest you confine it to your own precinct."

Greta spent the next few hours at the NYU Medical Center ER. The line—mostly hostile, bloodied people dressed for the Tour de France—seemed endless. By the time her leg was treated, the rest of New York was waking up to Saturday morning, but she was still stuck somewhere in Friday night. Out on First Avenue, a man at the nearest bus stop battled with the wind to keep his newspaper open. Even so, it was impossible to miss the huge front page headline that perfectly explained "damage control":

CRITICAL MASS MESS!

Back at the Two-Four, where she was slated to report for work in two hours, Greta stretched out on a bench in the women's locker room, worried about Molly. Claudia Ross, a neighborhood teenager, had fed and walked the Dobie the evening before, but it was far too early to call and ask the girl to fill in for her again. Knowing that the creaky door would alert her when the first patrolwoman arrived for duty, Greta dozed off, sure that she was quickly becoming the top contributor to Claudia's college fund.

She hadn't even entered the date on the DD5 report when her phone rang. Quill was on the other end, demanding, "Strasser, what the hell did you fuck up now?"

"Sir?"

"Don't 'sir' me! Why did I get a message from an Inspector Sullivan at Police Plaza about the MIA detective I loaned out for that bike thing? How is it possible to screw up parade duty? All you have to do is stand on a street corner—one thing you're well qualified for!"

"Captain, I don't know when that message came in, but it was all straightened out. In fact, I'm writing up the DD5. Ernest Flowers showed up on Astor Place. Remember, VX—the playground shooter?"

"Of course I know who Flowers is," he snarled.

"Sir, I couldn't let him walk. When I approached him, he resisted arrest. Then he assaulted a cyclist, and I pursued. That wasn't known immediately, due to a communications failure, but when I returned to the command center, Inspector *Sullivane*," she emphasized the proper pronunciation, "stated that I acted in the line of duty."

After a brief silence, he said, "Strasser, because something goes wrong every time you leave the precinct house, I'm assigning you to your desk. Effective immediately, and indefinitely. That way, we'll all be spared from what you see as acting in the line of your damn duty." No good-bye, just a click. Not a single inquiry about the felon at the top of his precinct's most wanted list.

After finishing her DD5, Greta sent Theo Appel an e-mail:

> Hi,
> Hope you got my message about having to work last night. I'm beat. How about 5:00 tomorrow afternoon—working again—unless you have other plans? Where is up to you—I picked the last place, remember?

Almost immediately, he replied:

> New developments during the last few days, so no problem. In fact, tomorrow works better for me.
> Can you come to my place to take a look at what I've got so far?
> Regrettably, I am old enough to be trusted with your honor. Besides, you carry a gun.

CHAPTER **NINE**

Appel lived on the seventh floor of one of the prewar apartment buildings that ran along West End Avenue in a nearly unbroken line. The exterior and small elevator lobby were undistinguished, except for being extraordinarily well maintained.

He was waiting for her by an open door at the end of a long corridor, looking dapper even in a blue button-down shirt and chinos. After a quick handshake, he hurried Greta into the entry foyer and locked the two deadbolts and chain—an excess of caution, considering a cop had just walked in.

"A blonde," he said, as he turned to face her. "At the Hungarian Club, I suspected you were wearing a wig. So . . . is this the real you?"

The question, though unmistakably cordial, made Greta hesitate too long. *Maybe once it might've been reduced to that . . . wig on–wig off. But even back then, could "real" have been so . . . static? Wasn't it more elusive . . . more fluid—or at least have the potential to be?*

The moment for any reply was lost; Appel broke the silence by inviting her into the living room. At the center, two small streamlined sofas, chrome-and-black leather, faced one another across a pale oriental rug, separated by a glass coffee table. Under other circumstances, she would have detoured directly to the window, where a slice of the Hudson sparkled under the low, westering sun. Instead, she was transfixed by the reason the room had no TV, no bookshelves, no credenza or cupboards: the five giant posters dominating the walls.

In every one, a woman transcended the paper space; her essence, un-containable, flowed out, beyond the glass and gilt of the frame. Greta slowly rotated, taking in the posters one by one. "They're all the same woman, aren't they?" she whispered. "At first, I thought they were life-sized . . . but *she's* larger than life . . . or maybe it's the way she was painted. All by the same artist, right? What about that one?" She gestured toward a poster with the woman in a cream-colored gown and cape, leaning back against a balcony railing. The sky behind her was lavender, dotted with silvery stars. "I don't know French—what's it about?"

"They all advertise plays starring Sarah Bernhardt," Appel explained. "Actually, you picked out my favorite, *The Lady of the Camellias.* Years later, the play was made into a Greta Garbo film. Hollywood shortened the title to *Camille.*"

"I've seen *Camille*—bad girl sacrifices all for love, still drop-dead gor-geous while she drops dead of TB."

In fact, she'd seen just about every film Garbo ever made. Her cop nick-name back when she worked undercover was Garbo—not only because she was a Greta, but because her unofficial job description at the time boiled down to playing one role after another. Other cops joked about her obsessive approach to her phony identities—the way she spent hours scouring stores for the right clothes and makeup, all the speech and act-ing classes she signed up for—as if they didn't know that the smallest slipup could be fatal. Entrapment wasn't so much of an issue at the time, and her cameos as Angie/Mandy/Cindy in Big Hair, micro-minis, and Miracle Bra cleavage succeeded in locking away plenty of shitheads whose parting shot was always some variation of "I'll get you, you bitch, who-ever the hell you are!"

Is this the real you?

Unfortunately, predivorce Crappy Craig couldn't handle the endless jibes from their fellow officers:

Heard your wife's tits were dusted for fingerprints last night.

Is it true your old lady made that arrest in the middle of a blow job?

He demanded that she ask for another assignment, even quit the Department if the request was denied. The truth was, he'd always been a jealous bastard, even before her Garbo days, when she reported for work in shapeless uniforms and crepe-soled oxfords. Hypocrite that he was, he made a habit of soothing his wounded machismo by fucking as many real-life tarts as he could.

Greta knew all about Garbo. She was a woman who'd quit while she was ahead—she left Hollywood when she was barely four years younger than Greta, still good-looking, and sharp enough not to hang around until some studio head or Quill-type decided to axe her.

Moving close to the poster's protective glass, she pointed at a word underlined with a flourish. "The artist's signature, right? Is it pronounced like what they serve at Starbucks?"

"Close. That's mocha—he's Mucha." Appel made it sound like *moo-ka.*

"Moo-ka. Are you a fan of his, Mr. Appel? Or of Bernhardt?"

"Oh, both, equally. Mucha's posters of Bernhardt made his career, and they also transformed Bernhardt into a legend. Eventually his style—Art Nouveau—fell out of favor. It stayed at the bottom of the art market dust heap for decades. Estelle—my late wife—put this collection together before his work was rediscovered in the Sixties. She would have been thrilled by your enthusiasm."

Greta slid down onto the closest of the sofas. A new angle on Appel had suddenly presented itself. "Your wife . . . did she pass away recently?"

His reply was a rushed, "No, no! There's absolutely no connection between Estelle and the fund! Neither of us had a single relative with enough money for a one-way train ticket to Switzerland, no less to open an account." He sat down heavily across from her, minus his usual grace. "No, this . . . investigation of mine stems from the passing of two old friends. Their names were Abe and Dave."

Briefly, he held his left wrist aloft, although well-pressed broadcloth now concealed the tattoo. "The three of us were all similarly decorated by the SS, but we didn't actually meet until we made it to New York. Abe and I were enrolled in the same school in the Bronx in the late Forties—designated as 'war orphans.' That makes us sound like children—but even then, it was tough to remember what it was like to be a child.

"We went to high school together, then NYU—the old uptown campus. After that, the two of us pretty much drifted apart, but we kept in touch by catching a few games up at Yankee Stadium every year. Our first game of the spring—I'm not sure if it was fifty-eight or fifty-nine—we were able to meet early enough to catch batting practice. Out of the blue, Abe said, 'I went to Europe during the winter.' All along, I'd thought he was like me, a dedicated amnesiac-in-reverse."

"Instead of trying to remember—?"

"Trying to forget. Precisely. My immediate reaction was to ask if he'd gone nuts, but I just kept my eyes on the batter." Appel leaned forward, elbows on his knees, as if Mantle had just stepped up to the plate. "I knew that Abe's mother and father were gassed right after they arrived at Auschwitz. What I didn't know was that he wasn't their only child. That day he told me that when the SS rounded them up, they put him and his parents on one train, his sister and two older brothers on another. He'd been trying to find his siblings ever since.

"He said that he'd written hundreds of letters. Sent them to every country in Europe, to Israel, to Canada, to this organization, to that refugee committee. The few that bothered to write back had no record of any of them. But he had one last thing to go on: a Swiss bank account his father opened before the war. Abe wrote to the bank several times. He got bubkes—do you know what that means?"

"No, but the way you say it, it sounds pretty nasty."

"Bubkes is worse than nothing—it's nothing with a grudge. But Abe didn't give up. His new theory was that maybe his brothers and sister were having no better luck at finding *him* than he was at finding *them*. Maybe they'd already been to the bank. So, if the account was closed, cashed out, that could be interpreted as *good* news—you see?"

"A sign that at least one of them was alive?"

"Exactly. So every penny he could save went toward that trip to Zurich. The first person he spoke to at the bank literally pointed to a corner, and told Abe to wait there—like a disobedient child. After more than an hour, another bank employee walked up and said two words: 'Death certificate.' As soon as Abe explained why that was impossible, the banker insisted there was no such account. Abe was confused—why had this man asked for a death certificate in the first place? But instead of confronting him, he told the banker that he didn't care about the money . . . his primary reason for traveling so far was to find out if any of his relatives were alive.

"The banker's answer was that no one could have withdrawn money from an account that never existed. Then he threatened to call the police and have Abe arrested if he didn't leave immediately. That was more than enough to convince Abe that the bank—not his sister or brothers—had closed the account. More accurately, confiscated everything in it—the same way the Nazis had confiscated everything. Imagine . . . all those years of clinging to hope . . . only to find that your entire family is dead."

Appel swallowed hard, and Greta noticed how tightly his hands were fisted. "But even stealing from the dead wasn't enough for the bank—they'd pushed it even further, determined to wipe out any evidence that his family had even existed. Abe said he didn't know where the words came from, but he screamed them right in the banker's face: '*Arrest me? How can your police put handcuffs on a ghost? On the son of a ghost? On the brother of a ghost?*'"

Suddenly, golden light panned over Mucha's posters, intensifying the color and thrusting Bernhardt's outlined figure forward—an eerie, nineteenth-century version of 3-D. After one brief, dazzling minute, the setting sun exited, stage west, to New Jersey. Appel fell silent. Perhaps he, like Greta, was considering the elusive line between optimism and self-delusion.

"Switzerland," Greta murmured, as the first shadows filled the room's corners. "Up until a few days ago, I would've played back the basic tourist baloney—the Alps, expensive watches, trains that run on time."

But the very first thing would have been That Word: bright as a neon beer sign, it blinked in a dusty, undisturbed corner of her mind, plugged in decades before by a relentless Social Studies teacher whose name, paradoxically, she couldn't recall.

"And *NEUTRAL*," she added. "Switzerland's famous neutrality."

"Swiss gold was never neutral," said Appel.

Greta knew exactly what he meant. "From what I found online, the Swiss banks had to be rooting for Germany to win. No matter how much money and property the Nazis stole, it was never enough to pay for their war—and the Swiss banks held the note."

Only a few nights before, Greta had read about the huge loans the Swiss banks had made to the Germans. When Wehrmacht Panzers destroyed everything in their path, when the Luftwaffe bombed Allied troops and cities, it was the Swiss who'd helped to finance that destruction. "Double dealing—hiding behind phony neutrality—that's low enough, but then I came to the part about how the war in Europe might've ended at least a year sooner if the Swiss banks had stopped pumping gold to Hitler."

"At least a year," Appel echoed, "making it impossible to estimate how many soldiers—on both sides—wouldn't have died, how many civilians wouldn't have been bombed, how many people in concentration camps wouldn't have been gassed or shot or starved to death. Most of forty-four, part of forty-five . . . the body count has to be in the millions."

"I bet that never kept a single banker awake at night." She shook her head in disbelief. "What the hell happened, Mr. Appel? Why didn't the Allies put them on trial with the rest of the war criminals?"

"What happened, Detective, was Stalin, the Iron Curtain, the Cold War. America wanted the Swiss banks on its side, not on the USSR's. Trials like Nuremberg for the bankers? Pursuing that path—vengeance, exposure of the financial support they gave Hitler—could have pushed them right into the arms of the Russians, just as cozy as they'd been with the Germans."

"I like that. You make them sound like sluts with money. So the Swiss held that Soviet card for fifty years. . . . Meanwhile, all the challenges about the Jewish accounts never went anywhere. Okay, I get it. Like a dear friend of mine used to say, 'Politics is a huge, tangled ball of string, bigger than the world itself.'"

"She's a pretty smart friend."

"He. Yeah, he was." Without acknowledging Appel's questioning look, she plunged right ahead: "So in the Nineties—no more Berlin Wall, one superpower—Senator D'Amato and Bronfman finally had some leverage against the Swiss banks."

"More kicking and screaming followed, but the fund was established . . . at last."

A brief silence followed, broken by Greta's sudden apology: "Sorry—you were telling me about Abe, and I interrupted you."

Appel got to his feet and asked, "White or red? I need a little help for what comes next."

"Too serious for white."

Greta followed him into a bright kitchen-dining area that had been renovated for an accomplished cook. As if he read her mind, he said, "Estelle's design. Sometimes in my sleep, I smell bread baking . . . better than any perfume." He busied himself with the wine, and when Greta lifted her glass and toasted Estelle, he squeezed his eyes shut. "Three years and two months ago . . . outpatient for a routine procedure . . . complications . . . gone."

They sat down at the table, the wine bottle between them.

"The last time Abe and I were supposed to get together," he resumed, "was at one of our Yankees days—that tradition continued for decades. I was running late, rushing out the door, when the phone rang—it was Abe. He said, 'Theo, I didn't think I'd get you before you left. I can't make it.' I asked if he was sick. He laughed—never something Abe did much. 'No, but listen to this! I just got a call about my family's Swiss account!' That was the first time he'd mentioned it in nearly fifty years.

"That evening, I phoned to find out what happened. No answer. No answer the next morning. I went to his place, pounded on the door. I called the police. We found his body on the sofa, leaning to one side. Right next to the phone on an end table."

"Was that all he said? That someone had just phoned about his family's Swiss account?"

"Yes. Upbeat, excited—not the typical Abe at all. My impression had been that he was heading right out to meet someone. From what I saw, it looked like he'd said good-bye to me one second, and had a heart attack the next. That was the official cause of death. Compared to most, Abe led a solitary life, but that morning—I never saw anyone look more alone."

Greta tried to block the image of Paulina Kantor's staring eyes, her hand clutching at her housedress, the unlikely teapot on the table above.

"So you don't know if he made a claim or not?"

"Certainly not from the look of things." Briefly, Appel's mouth tightened into a thin line. "Remember, I was unfamiliar with the process at the time. And still was when I lost my other friend, Dave." Appel sat back in his chair—Dave had to be a far more agreeable memory than Abe.

"We met at my first real job after college—a small graphics outfit in midtown. A week or so after I started, the temperature hit ninety degrees, and the office air-conditioning went on the fritz. We all took off our ties and rolled up our sleeves. Dave points at my wrist, and says, 'Look! Another former guest of the SS! What did you enjoy more, Appel? The food or the service?' That was Dave.

"Same as with Abe, we stayed in touch. Estelle and Dave's wife, Hannah, also clicked, and the four of us would have dinner together maybe four or five times a year. A couple of months before their thirty-fifth wedding anniversary, Hannah died of a cerebral hemorrhage. Several years after that, their only child, who was living in Miami, went from HIV-positive to full-blown AIDS . . . whatever medicine he was on, it stopped working. Dave flew down to take care of him, but the kid didn't hang on too long."

"Not even bad luck . . . no luck," Greta observed.

After a deep breath, Theo continued. "Dave inherited his son's condo, instead of the other way around. I guess the warm weather helped him decide to stay. The last time we spoke, he told me he was working forty hours a week: twenty at Home Depot, twenty at the beach—working on his tan. Said you couldn't find two better spots to pick up chicks."

Greta couldn't help smiling. "He sounds like a perennial teenager."

"Sure, but a teenager who never got over his son, and was still in love with his wife." Appel turned his head over his shoulder, looking back, but not at anything in the room. "When Dave missed a few days at work—well, you can guess the rest. He'd collapsed in his kitchen. One of his neighbors called me with the bad news."

"Heart attack?" Greta asked.

"Of course. And now I have to backtrack to a night all those years ago, when the two of us were working late on a rush job. I don't remember how we got into it, but Dave started talking about when he was a kid in Poland, and how his father whispered some numbers into his ear, then turned around and whispered into his brother's ear, too. He made them swear they'd keep their numbers secret from one another. Knowing Dave, I waited for the punch line. But no, that was what happened . . . a father trying to be fair to each of his sons."

"A father who also believed in the natural order of things—that both his children would outlive him."

"I see you've guessed the rest, Detective. Each set of numbers was half of a Swiss bank account. Only Dave survived. Without a complete account number, and no idea of the amount his father deposited, or the date, he assumed contacting the bank would be futile. Even with that sense of humor, he was nothing if not a total realist."

Both Appel and Greta were jarred by a phone ringing in the kitchen area. As soon as Appel answered, he grabbed a pad and pen. Figuring it had to be someone calling back about one of his X's, Greta signaled that she was returning to the living room.

After revisiting the Muchas, she wandered to the windows. A corner apartment in a corner building, the first window looked out at the side street; the second and a fraction of the third window were blocked by a studio-sized room or apartment atop the sixth floor roof of the adjacent side-street building (close enough to make out a brilliant green baseball diamond on a big flat-screen TV). But that remaining three-quarters of a window was fortuitously two stories above the rooftops of two facing brownstones on Riverside Drive. Lights were already twinkling on the Jersey side of the Hudson. She returned to the second window, eyes on the game, until Appel called her back.

Despite having refilled their glasses and switched on the kitchen lights, he appeared distraught. "New information?" she asked, as she returned to her chair.

"Unfortunately, yes—more of the same terrible pattern." He looked down at his wine glass, very still.

When he finally lifted his gaze, she let him know that her silence wasn't entirely empathetic. "Mr. Appel, you haven't been totally honest with me about your friends."

He didn't blink. Nor did he protest. Maybe he'd been testing her, a tidy reversal of their roles at The Hungarian Club.

"I've studied the fund Web site," she continued. "It's pretty straight-forward—how it operates, the time limits, all that. A first list of names was published back in 2001, and that deadline's long expired. The second list came out this January thirteenth, and it excludes everyone on the 2001 list, as well as any names not listed—simply put, if you're not on the sec-ond list, there's absolutely no way you can file a claim. The deadline for applications is just a few months away. After that, the door is slammed shut on everyone, forever." Appel was listening intently, his face a blank. "You mentioned that you and Abe met at Yankees games. Since as of this afternoon, the team's still playing down in the Grapefruit League, that means he died last year. Did Dave also die in 2004—or at least before January thirteenth?

"You're a good detective," said Appel softly. "Go on."

"I'll take that as a yes. I'll bet that the Claims Resolution Tribunal needed a year at the very least to compile its final list—a list months from going public when your friends died. How about telling me when that was."

"Abe in July, Dave in August. You have no idea how incredibly relieved I am that you see what I see, Detective."

"To tell the truth, Mr. Appel, the little I do see has me baffled. You told me that someone phoned Abe about his family's Swiss account. The only good news that could come out of that—and you said he sounded atypi-cally happy—was hearing he had a chance to claim his inheritance. If he was killed, it was six months too soon."

"He and Dave were the first black X's."

"I understand you have those obituary-to-CRT list matches. But last summer, the list wasn't the only thing missing—there wasn't even a claim form. So how the hell did this work?"

Appel lowered his head. "Other than assuming that whoever pirated the list pirated the prototype applications, I have no idea."

Greta realized too late that her growing impatience was humiliating Appel. Not only had she been pressing him too hard about timing, but that surely wasn't the only issue out of whack. After a long pause, she asked in a whisper, "Mr. Appel, please tell me what first alerted you that something was wrong. How did you become involved?"

"I saw the list in the paper on January thirteenth," he murmured. Slowly, he lifted his head. "Instinctively, I searched for Abe and Dave. Of course, the terrible irony of how they might have missed out on their inheritance by months after sixty long years made me hope I wouldn't find their names. Then there they were, right on the page, in black and white. For days, every thought I had was about my friends. Then my attention drifted back to the list itself. Regardless of all its good intentions and righting of wrongs, I began to view it as a threat. I saw a dangerous, open invitation to identity scammers. I guess I'm an old geezer with too much time on my hands. By the end of the month, I'd gone past identity theft, all the way to outright murder."

Greta thought for a while, frowning. "The only way I can make sense of when your friends were killed is that a number of deaths—sorry, but it's going to be the closest word I can come up with—were *stockpiled* in advance. Saying it out loud sounds damn cold, but stockpiled they were, as many as possible, so applications could be submitted immediately after the '05 list was printed back in January. And I have no doubt that the killers will keep multiplying your X's, right up to the very last minute they can get a July thirteenth postmark stamped on an envelope. Then they'll disappear forever. And anyone who tries to stop them will be up against the same damn clock."

Appel broke the long silence that followed. "It has to be an insider . . . as much as I hate to suspect someone on the Claims Resolution Tribunal."

"The CRT is in Switzerland, Mr. Appel," Greta shot back.

"Where else, since the bank documents are located there?"

She threw up her hands. "Exactly. And that necessitates constant interaction between the CRT and the banks." He started to speak, but she kept the thought rolling: "Assume every one of the lawyers who make up the CRT is a saint. What about the paralegals, the researchers, the administrative types who work for them? What about the cleaning people? The security guards? The window washers? How many are imported, how many are . . . Swiss?"

"Greta—may I call you Greta? And I would like you to call me Theo, please."

"Since I'm not here on official business, Theo, that's fine with me."

"Well, Greta, there's more. Quite a bit more."

CHAPTER **TEN**

"Before this goes any further, there's something I have to tell you." He propped an elbow on the table, cradled his temple with one hand, glanced at her briefly, then—for the first time—deliberately avoided eye contact. "The data I compiled during the last few days . . . I'm afraid this damn scheme we're up against has turned me into a hacker."

"You? A hacker?" Greta asked, half in disbelief, half teasing. "I always thought a hacker was a kid who locked himself in the basement with computers and Doritos . . . kind of a teenage troll."

"I'm not joking, Greta. Those 'new developments' I mentioned in my e-mail? They're not Google searches. I've breached so-called 'secure' networks and mined them for links, patterns—any small details that might add up to a clue." When he finally met her eyes, a knot of concern was visible between his eyebrows. "And, to my regret, I never once stopped to consider how that could compromise you. If your involvement comes to light, I'll have seriously endangered your career."

Barely suppressing a smile, she put up a hand to stop him. "Congratulations, Theo! You're the only person in all five boroughs who thinks I have something that even remotely resembles a career. Not only that, I've never heard of any law against having a glass of wine with a hacker. And by the way, is that a skill you picked up working for the government?"

"Yes . . . no! What I meant is yes, I was never even in the same room with a computer before I was recruited. But Greta, are you quite sure that you—"

"Don't worry about the NYPD." *I'm already in the shitter, breathing through a straw . . . but at least it's my own damn straw.* "Did you say the CIA *recruited* you? Were you in the military, or some secret government—"

"No, nothing like that. I never served in the military, never held a gun in my hand. To tell the truth, no one could've been more astounded than I was when they approached me. I was working at a small design firm that turned out sales promotion pieces—stuff the big ad agencies didn't want to be bothered with: store displays, annual reports, brochures, posters.

"At the time, a poster I'd designed was on the walls of every subway station in the city. The artwork was a huge three-dollar bill, the headline something along the lines of 'Anything but XYZ brand is as phony as this.' Remember, this was the pre-computer Stone Age, when everything was still done by hand. I faked the bill's watermarks, the typefaces, the Treasury Secretary's signature, added creases and wear to make it look like a bill that'd been in circulation. A portrait of Aaron Burr was in the middle—another forgery, but the artist was no longer around to take me to court. I got a real kick out of watching people on the platform looking at it up close.

"A man in a suit tracked me down, asked me if I did the subway ad. For a moment, I thought he was from Madison Avenue, about to hand me my ticket to the big leagues. Then I looked at his card, and I was sure I was going to be arrested—imagine the déjà vu moment you gave me back at The Hungarian Club! But instead, the CIA had seen my potential as an in-house forger. As well as an auxiliary company counterfeiter."

"You mean . . . like papers for the agents? IDs for the spooks?"

"Passports, driver's licenses, government and military and student IDs, press passes, library cards—you name it, I faked it. Part of my training was studying the work of real-life master forgers. A lot of them were serving time, so they'd all made mistakes I could learn from. Once I got started, it was very intense, very challenging, and often incredibly tedious. But you could never do less than your best, because real lives depended on those phony documents. I doubt anyone would've told me if anything had gone awry, but I think—I hope—I had a respectable success rate. After all, they didn't kick me out. I made it through the Cold War, and then some. Retired after thirty years."

"By that time, you were doing most of your work on a computer?"

"All of it. Looking back, it's hard to believe that none of today's applications existed when I joined. Eventually, it became apparent that the day would come when computers would put my particular expertise out of business, so I took the old 'If you can't beat 'em, join 'em' approach. I even helped develop a few programs that compressed days of work to a single mouse click. They're still in use—even though they must've gone through at least a thousand updates by now."

"So all those years you spent creating phony identities were what formed your initial reaction to the CRT list—suspicion that it exposed every name on it to identity theft?"

"That's right—phony heirs, phony claims. But my background should have alerted me to what it really was much sooner. I blame myself for that." He pushed back his chair. "If you have no reservations about proceeding, I'll show you where I'm at so far."

Greta had already noticed the laptop a few steps away on a kitchen counter. Appel booted it up while he slid their wine glasses out of the way, then placed it in front of her. He took the empty chair to her left and dug a flash drive out of his shirt pocket. As he leaned toward the side port, the little cartridge suddenly took on all the menace of a loaded gun. "No—don't," she shouted, startling him so he snapped back. "Whoever you're hacking, can't they hack you right back? Track you right to this computer? To this apartment?"

"Undoubtedly, and without that hackee even having to put down his bag of Doritos—which, by the way, I happen to like. I alternate between Cool Ranch and Nacho Cheese. However, this particular computer has never been out on a date—never had an Internet connection. It's not even registered. So either with or without this little gizmo," proclaimed Theo, as he inserted the flash drive, "we're perfectly safe." He raised his eyebrows. "Now that we've each had our genuine bouts of concern for the other . . . shall we continue?"

"Sorry. Cops see very smart people put themselves in really stupid situations all the time, and . . . crime happens. Go ahead."

"I'll preface this by saying that what you're going to see is completely out of my league—I never could've gotten this far without my former protégés pointing the way. They've taught me far more than I ever taught them."

Greta sneaked a sideways glance at Theo. If the part he'd played in rebuilding her self-confidence was any measure, those protégés surely felt similar indebtedness to this charming and compassionate man . . . exceeding any help they could offer in return.

A solid wall of text popped onto the screen. "Those are banks, locations, amounts, time in, time out. Believe it or not, it's only a portion of a single check's trail, after the payout left the U.S."

"I guess I shouldn't ask about how you locked on that particular check."

"We . . . I . . ." Theo's eyes widened slightly, his Pinocchio moment. "Let's say I . . . came across the routing number of the CRT's bank, as well as their account number. At this point, few checks have been issued. All were initially deposited in U.S. banks. No red flag went up until the money was wired out of the country."

"So the domestic deposits were probably legit?" After a nod from Theo, she anxiously prodded, "And the funds that are wired out? Can you tag them? Stop them?"

"Arrest them? Cuff them?" he shot back with a half smile. "Observation only, Detective—if you don't want it to blow up right in your face. Basically, a security password needed for remote access to a financial computer network—from a branch office, or an employee's hotel room, or home—is hacked. Copy the data, then run like hell. Our first attempts failed; the latest is incomplete, but promising." He pressed a key, and a grid appeared on the screen, then became the background for a map. "This is a graphic of the check's trail, after the money left the United States. Is this part of the world familiar to you?"

"It looks like the Caribbean."

"It is indeed. Home to those delightful islands synonymous with 'money laundering.'" Suddenly, a green line popped on the monitor. Jerking and weaving, it inexactly retraced a segment of its trajectory. "What you're watching," Theo explained, "is money flipping in and out of banks. Next, a strategy designed to camouflage the amount." The line divided into multiple hairlike filaments; when only about a third had merged together again, the screen froze. "Blocked," Theo sighed. "As you can see, this isn't far enough along to follow it to its final destination—or, more likely, destinations."

"Quite a journey for one check."

"I'm ashamed to admit," Theo whispered, "that the first time I saw this breakthrough, I was terribly excited by the technology." He shut down the laptop, snapped it closed. "I'd lost sight of what that green line represents."

"A murder."

"A murder which might have been committed two or three months ago, possibly longer, but a murder, nevertheless. Somewhere out there, a heartless and extremely cunning bastard—possibly a whole squad of them—is committing one after another. But first, he somehow manages to con his way into his victim's home, and goes on to draw out all the horrific personal details required by the CRT application. Next, he not only secures a verifiable signature, but irreplaceable supporting documents. If he's not a master hypnotist, how the hell does he do it?"

Greta glanced down—her left thumb and index finger were pressed together so hard, the skin beneath the thumbnail was white well past the quick. "Paulina Kantor had a tiny bit of paper—a corner of what turned out to be ordinary printer paper—caught between two fingers. One side was jagged, like it was ripped right out of her hand. It could've been a page of the application. Maybe she became suspicious, and tried to grab it back."

"Too late, just like all of this," Theo murmured. "I'm afraid the fund deadline will come and go before a single life can be saved."

A long silence followed, until Greta said, "What you're doing—chasing the money trail—is perfectly logical. You don't want the pot of gold at the end of the rainbow, just the son of a bitch who's holding it. But have you considered working it from the other end, as well?"

"What do you mean?"

"Turn it around—try to figure out who their next target will be before they strike again. Catch the killer just as he's about to strike, and you've got a chance he'll give up the guy with the gold."

"You see a way to do that?" He sounded somewhere between hopeful and desperate, but definitely ready to spark to any new possibility.

"Me? You have me confused with those ladies who wear a turban and gaze into a crystal ball. You're the one with access to all the computer guys and programs."

"The list . . . twenty-one hundred names . . . it's not that big a database."

"Slow down—just like you warned me, those are the names of people who *opened* the Swiss accounts, sixty or seventy years ago, not the people we have to locate today. Sure, the last name could match a father to a son. But what if the family name was misspelled coming through immigration, or Anglicized? What if a child was adopted, name changed? Plus, you run into all those issues and more when you try to contact a married daughter or granddaughter."

"The thieves who steal the few years these people have left of their lives—*they* manage to find them, don't they?" Theo asked bitterly. "If they're able to find matches to the list, what's stopping you?"

"Inside information, Theo. They have it. I don't."

"Not true! You already have something to start with—a very strong victim profile. I know it all too well." Theo held up fingers as he went along. "One, age. These thugs are looking for someone old enough so that death by natural causes doesn't raise questions—not much of challenge with my contemporaries, I'm afraid. Two, few heirs—if any at all."

"Like Dave and Abe," Greta agreed.

"Three, location. A densely populated area with a sizable Jewish community—the lone Jew in rural North Dakota doesn't fit the profile." Theo addressed her questioning look by adding, "Besides New York and Miami, I have heart attack obits in Los Angeles and Chicago."

Drawn in, Greta added, "All right, four: this person can't be a standout in any way—basically, a face in the crowd. And five, a man or woman who lives alone: no roommates, no assisted living facility. A senior citizen like that is likely to stick to a limited routine, with predictable comings and goings. Easier to observe, easier to tail, easier to . . ." With an apologetic glance at Theo, she let it hang in the air.

"You can say it," Theo said softly. "Easier to kill. Go on."

"Number six really should be number one: the size of the victim's pay-out check."

Theo shook his head. "The amounts were never published. The biggest break they got was all that extra time when some insider smuggled out an advance copy of the list and the application."

"Doesn't that depends on how *in* the insider is?" Greta frowned, not convinced. "Okay, let's go ahead, assume our profile parallels their criteria for selecting a victim. How do you see the killer getting in? A phone call first, like with Abe?"

"Even the wariest Holocaust survivor could be thrown off guard by hearing his father's name. But to open the door to a stranger like that—"

"All sorts of emotions have been stirred up by that call, Theo. And I'm sure the killer arrives in record time—before that vulnerability fades. The old 'I'm right in your neighborhood,' or 'I'm calling from my car.' Don't expect the victims to be as skeptical as someone in your line of work. Come on, who'd be more distrustful than you?"

Raising his eyebrows, he countered, "Here's looking at you, kid."

"Okay, we're tied." She smiled briefly, then sat back and closed her eyes. "How the hell do we turn it around?" After a while, she said, "It's zero-tech and obsolete, but we've got to start somewhere."

"If it saves one life, it's a stroke of genius."

Greta reached into her jacket for her notepad and pencil. "Abe's death occurred last July, in New York; Dave's in August, in Miami; Mrs. Kantor's, March, New York." After scribbling out thirteen little squares for July 2004 through July 2005, she marked two *NY*, one *MI*. "The victims you found through obituaries—I need months and cities. You have another New York or Miami?"

"Miami, December. A strong 'probably' for November in New York. Los Angeles was February; Chicago, January." Before Greta had all those month-boxes marked, he blurted out, "What do you have?"

"Hold on, Theo! Do I look like one of your damn computers?" Head still down, she reported, "Starting last July—your friend wasn't necessarily the first, but the earliest we've got—seven victims through March. I'm missing September and October, and I'm using that November New York. At least a murder per month."

"Adequate time to stalk the victims?"

"Assuming they were prescreened to lead uncomplicated lives. But you must have been hitting the online obits like crazy, Theo, because—let me just double-check." Her finger tapped over the boxes before she turned the pad toward him. "A case could be made for a cycle that goes like this—" Using her pencil as pointer, she recited, "New York, Miami, Chicago, Los Angeles, New York, et cetera. Your next murder is slated for Miami in about three weeks."

"That's remarkable! Why didn't I see that?"

"Theo, if not for you, we wouldn't even be here today, no less considering a next step. Maybe tomorrow I can—" Hitting her forehead with a flat palm, she cried out, "Damn! I totally forgot! I'm chained to a desk—maybe forever. I won't be able to make a move!"

"A desk? A detective good as you? Who'd ever—?"

Putting up a hand, she explained. "The precinct commander. Quill."

"For what possible reason?"

"Because he can, for starters. But it goes way back, Theo, and it's nothing like the sweet memories you have of your friends. Ten years ago, I went through a nasty divorce. My husband was the one who cheated. I followed the rules up to the minute I was legally single again. After that, I was . . . driven to get even.

"It was mostly with cops—we hung out at the same bars, there was at least a fifty-fifty chance I wouldn't go home with a pervert, and—most important—I knew it would get back to my ex before I even made it to the shower." A flush raced from her cheeks to her neck, but she kept going. "I believed that if I remained uninvolved emotionally—totally detached—that would *empower* me. I also convinced myself that the disconnect would give me a lifetime warranty against ever getting hurt again. How stupid was that?"

"Not stupid . . . if your goal is to not feel anything at all."

"Well, my most detachable moments were spent with Quill. I couldn't wait to break it off, and I didn't think the sparks were flying for him, either. But he kept phoning me, and I finally told him no more, it was over. Instead, he started following me. No matter what shift I was working, when I got home, I'd see him across the street, watching my windows. I knew that if I reported him for stalking me, I'd catch all the blame—unofficially, of course—for sleeping around in the first place. Then, one morning, he wasn't there. I was incredibly relieved, I felt so free . . . until I got to work.

"One rule I had was to stay away from married men—I'd spent too many nights waiting up until my own husband waltzed in. Quill told me that he'd been separated for two years, and he never mentioned kids.

"I found out that he'd lied to his wife about working lots of overtime—the time he spent watching me—and they'd had a big fight the night before, about why all those extra hours weren't showing up on his paycheck. She took the baby—almost three, the youngest of four kids—and went for a drive on the Interboro Parkway. It was a rainy night. That's a narrow, twisting, dangerous road even if it's sunny and you're sober, and she was so drunk she forgot to buckle the baby's car seat. She was the only survivor, but the tree she hit left her as smart as a can of V8. Her mother had to move in to take care of her and the three older kids. She has to hate her son-in-law even more than her son-in-law hates me. Not a good idea to write all that down as a reason why you desperately need a transfer to another precinct. So I'm stuck." Met by Theo's silence, she blurted out, "I don't expect you to . . . sorry."

"Shhhh! Listen to me, Greta!" His voice was low and steady. "There's this misconception about people who survived the camps . . . that we were so thoroughly purged by our horrific experience, we somehow achieved a higher moral state. The truth is, the survivor is defined by those who didn't survive. The objective of a concentration camp is to starve its prisoners—not only of food, but of basic humanity, so that no bond or kindness can matter more than a piece of moldy bread. Whatever you have to do to stay alive leaves you feeling dirty—down to your very core, for all the rest of your life." He took her hand and gave it a gentle, fleeting squeeze. "I can't judge you. I can't judge anyone. But this I know: You are a good person, a dear friend, and one smart cookie."

"I wouldn't be here if I didn't think of you in exactly the same way. And because of that, I'm extremely uneasy about what you're doing. These people are murderers, Theo! What makes you so damn—" She threw up her hands, searching for the word. "So damn *cavalier* about what you're doing? Once they have you cornered—wherever you do what you do—how the hell are you planning to escape?"

"Ah—projecting a 'cavalier' demeanor is half the battle!"

With a bit of a swagger, he crossed to a hall closet just beyond the kitchen and returned with a vintage leather briefcase. It had straps and a taped-over handle, but it was deep enough to accommodate the two laptops stacked inside. "Do you have any idea how many public places there are all over the city where a person can go online? I work for a while, move to another part of town, switch computers. I've never hacked in the same locale twice. My preferred mode of transport is the subway, but I hopscotch around by foot, bus, taxi, even the occasional pedicab. I'm always on the lookout for stalkers. And if you were the hackee racing into a public library hot on the path of a signal, wouldn't a silver-haired septuagenarian be the last person you'd suspect?"

"Why not just start the new approach on the list? When it comes to the risk factor, there's no comparison."

His eyes crinkled, but the rest of what she took for a smile was suppressed. While he busied himself closing the briefcase and replacing it in the closet, Greta grasped what was going on. This might be the first time in Theo Appel's life that he'd willfully undertaken any such risk . . . and it came after three decades of supplying others with the means to put their lives on the line on a daily basis.

As he reentered the dining area, he said, "I have some people in D.C. who'll be very interested in your cycle of cities and murders. I'll get in touch with them first thing tomorrow about the best way to trace the names on the CRT list. I'll also keep on the obits, to verify the rotation. That should keep me busy."

She bit her tongue just as she was about to push Theo to promise that he'd stop hacking. Instead, she asked him to call her the next evening and gathered her things, explaining that she had an early morning on desk duty coming up.

What she didn't tell him was that the day after that was her day off.

CHAPTER **ELEVEN**

Greta's head popped up from between the two mounds of paperwork on her desk. Russell Kim was holding up a 2003 prison photo of VX in one hand, and the Photoshopped shaved-head version in the other.

"Good job," she said with a nod.

The day after Critical Mass, Geracimos had called a noon meeting with as many detectives as he could pull from open cases. Greta, after giving them a detailed briefing on VX's actions downtown and fielding their questions, had watched them stream out, headed for the streets. Kim looked back over his shoulder as he left with his newly assigned partner, Manny Cepeda. She was the only detective left behind, still assigned to desk duty.

The lieu, leaving to resume his day off, stopped at the sight of Greta surrounded by a roomful of empty desks. Telegraphing his powerlessness, he lifted hands pressed together at the wrists before stomping out.

That evening, Russell had called her cell, an angry rasp in his voice. "What he's doing to you . . . Three words: this situation sucks."

"That means a hell of a lot to me. Three words back: *Don't get involved.*"

Now, as Kim slipped the photos back into his pocket, she asked, "Any progress on VX's two buddies from Astor Place?"

"We have a tail on one. The street buzz is that the other beauty skipped to Baltimore. He has a sister living there—clean, no record, but nobody's seen her since Saturday night. The cops down in Maryland are following a couple of leads from her neighbors. Thankfully, the VX rule of silence hasn't reached across state lines."

"What do you think? Is VX with her and her brother?"

Kim bent forward over her desk, close enough for her to see the irreversible lines fatigue was etching on his young face. "Something's just happened . . . bad news, bad enough so people might start to open up."

"That has to be the little boy. Tyrel."

"They just took him off life support."

Greta flashed back to their intensive care unit visits.

Tyrel's mother never left, keeping a constant vigil over her comatose five-year-old; immediately after the shooting, Kim and Greta had introduced themselves to her as the detectives assigned to her son's case. They'd also approached everyone in the rotation of visiting family members, friends, and neighbors. Like the mother, they were distant: minimal eye contact, grudging hellos, no good-byes.

"Damn it! Why aren't they *angry*?" Russell had fumed after their third visit. They were standing in front of the ICU elevator bank, and he'd started to pace back and forth, his usual composure gone. "Why aren't they totally pissed that we don't have VX and his whole scumbag crew locked up? I'd be going crazy, knowing the animal who shot my son—my grandson, my nephew, my little boy's best friend—is right outside on the corner, dealing. Like nothing ever happened!"

Greta had remained very still, her eyes on the elevator's progress from floor to floor, but aware that some of Tyrel's visitors were queuing up behind them. "I think I have a good guess," she answered. When a nurse hurried by, she jogged after her and asked something in a tone so hushed, only the nurse could hear.

After the elevator emptied on the main floor, she'd jabbed a button for one of the lower levels. When the doors parted, she and Kim followed the arrows labeled PATIENT ACCOUNTS.

The PAID CASH stamp they'd been shown at the cashier's window had to be just as sharply imprinted on Russell's memory as it was on her own. Neither said a word until they were back in their car.

Before Kim turned the ignition key, he'd asked, "He shoots the kid in the middle of a playground, then shows them what a great guy he is by paying the hospital bill?"

"He's a worm," Greta sighed, "a worm with an undeniable flair for community relations."

"I keep remembering what it felt like to be a kid on a swing," Russell was saying. "Seeing nothing but my own sneakers and blue sky."

After a long silence, Greta replied, "This won't be the first time I've warned you about how this job can eat you up."

"It's the same as if the bastard sneaked into the ICU and pulled the plug himself."

"Kim, it scares me when you read the instant message passing through my head—the one I didn't send you because I want to keep my cynicism all to myself."

About seven-thirty that evening, Theo called her cell. She was relieved to hear his voice. "How'd it go with your guys in D.C.?"

"Remarkably well! I have the tools I need. I can't wait to get to work!"

"I'll be there in less than an hour."

"No, no," he said quickly, "these new applications . . . I haven't finished downloading all of them, and at my advanced age, the concentration it takes to learn something this complex takes double—sometimes triple—the effort."

"I doubt that, but don't let me keep you. Good luck and—oh, I almost forgot! I'm going to be on different shifts all this week, but the scheduling isn't firmed up yet. How early can I call you in the morning, to let you know? I don't want to wake you, in case you're up working late tonight." After she clicked off, she returned to her shopping.

After an early run with Molly and a quick breakfast, Greta dressed—a major undertaking, because it involved squeezing into layer upon layer. Fortunately, the weather had obliged by turning cooler: her final outfit was a man's bulky thermal-lined flannel plaid shirt-jacket (distressed and smudged to look well worn and heavily padded across the shoulders), jeans, and work boots. She pulled a Bud Light baseball cap low over her brown contact-lensed eyes and arranged an inch or so of her dark wig to straggle out over the back of her collar. With a canvas Klein Tools bag over her shoulder, she took the subway to Theo's stop in the Two-Oh Precinct, two stations before her usual stop in the neighboring Two-Four.

Just about seven o'clock, she positioned herself behind a van parked diagonally across from his building's entrance. It was fifteen minutes before he claimed his "infernal internal clock invariably" woke him, no matter when he went to sleep. Her face obscured by a copy of the *Daily News* folded to the sports section, she kept an eye out for other watchers. At seven forty-five, she called Theo, who gave her a sketchy but enthusiastic review of the new software. She was equally sketchy about possibly having to work overtime, but said she'd call to see how it was going before leaving her desk.

The locals heading for work crested by eight and ebbed within the next half hour, so that two nannies pushing carriages were the only people on the street when Theo emerged at eight forty-five. His raincoat was loosely belted over a dark gray suit, and his leather satchel was at his side. He looked left and right, but the only caution involved had to do with jay-walking. She gave him a one-block lead, then followed him back to the Eighty-sixth Street station.

Theo exited at Forty-second Street, took a short, brisk walk to Bryant Park, found a seat, and wasted no time going to work on one of his computers. Confused, Greta scanned the park until she realized that he wasn't the only person using free wireless access—just the only one without at least one earring. To his credit, Theo looked up and to his right with regularity; he'd selected a spot with no view of his screen from either his rear or his left. Nevertheless, he was totally exposed, and for nearly an hour she found herself battling the urge to snatch his computer, drag him to a cab, and rush him uptown to the relative safety of his home.

His next stop, the Science, Industry and Business Library, was seven blocks away, on Madison Avenue. The night before, she'd had a minor panic attack when she discovered there were forty-four branches of the New York Public Library in Manhattan alone, all offering wireless connections. She never doubted for a moment that Theo would hit one of them. From afar, she watched as his briefcase made it through the checkpoint, but she was sure her bulky canvas bag would have to be checked. Since she knew exactly where he was headed, she backed away and strolled casually down the block, walking like a guy until she rounded the first corner onto Thirty-fourth Street, where she tossed the balled-up shirt and hat into the first trash receptacle she came to. As she turned right again, onto Fifth Avenue, she fluffed the hat-hair look out of her wig and slipped on nerdy glasses. The trickiest part involved switching her boots to low black loafers—even leaning against the apron of a loading dock on Thirty-fifth Street, she had to struggle to keep her balance. By the time she made it all the way around to the main entrance on Madison again, she was a bookish, dark-haired, dark-eyed woman in a black blazer, black sweater, and jeans schlepping a big black tote bag.

The Salomon Research Reading Room was on the lower level. To enter, she had to pass the B. Altman Delivery Desk. At warp speed, the day of Paulina Kantor's memorial service rewound in her head, right to the moment when Mrs. Hermann introduced the two Ohrbach's friends who'd "jumped the ship for B. Altman's." This library, she suddenly realized, had taken over the building that once housed one of New York's greatest department stores—"greatest" to Greta, at any rate, but not because of anything that might've been sold inside.

Every year when she was a little girl, Altman's huge arched windows framed an elaborate, old-fashioned Christmas display that was the first stop in the Strasser family's holiday pilgrimage to Rockefeller Center. Walking between her mother and father, Greta, dazzled by an overload of tinseled glitz, usually made it to the rival Lord & Taylor windows a few blocks uptown, but she invariably wound up on her father's shoulders long before they got to the skaters gliding around the rink under the tree.

Only a few minutes before, so absorbed by her switch into her second persona of the day, she'd skirted Altman's Fifth Avenue façade without the slightest stirring of memory—a betrayal, if even in a small way, of the man who, along with Bram, her fiancé, had meant more to her than anyone. She silently cursed at how she'd let a piece of the rapidly melting personal ice floe she occupied break off and drift away.

Theo was totally engaged with his second computer, typing in spurts, tensing when he hit a wall, tilting his head as he attempted alternate strategies. After an hour in an environment where signs warned that computer data could be "captured by anyone within three hundred feet," Greta was beyond twitchy. Suddenly, Theo hunched forward, scrutinizing his screen. A flurry of keystrokes, and his flash drive was safe in his suit jacket, his computer shut with a hint of triumph.

Good, solve this damn thing, so you aren't captured by anything within three hundred feet!

Clearly, Theo had planned his route with care: a cup of coffee stretched out over an hour at the wireless Herald Square McDonald's, followed by only twenty minutes at an Office Depot near Times Square. Greta's tension ebbed a bit when he headed down a flight of subway stairs—at least he was leaving midtown. It was nearly three, and the day had warmed enough for him to carry his raincoat and for Greta to feel comfortable after she'd peeled down to her final disguise—a not quite crew-cut platinum blonde in a filmy poncho, mini, and patterned tights that steered more looks to her legs than to her face.

Her radar still hadn't picked up on anyone tailing Theo, particularly on a day when he'd obviously progressed on his money trail quest. At first she thought taking the shuttle and getting on the Lexington Avenue line was a diversionary maneuver, but when he rode past the transfer points that could return him to the West Side, she was puzzled. He got off at Ninety-sixth Street and walked west. For the first time that day, he stopped in the middle of the sidewalk, put down his briefcase, and let his arms dangle—certainly he had to be fatigued, after schlepping two computers all day, but something in the gesture also hinted at surrender.

Less than a minute later, he was on the move again, and eventually headed north on Fifth. This part of the avenue was an enclave of Old Money co-ops—no free Internet likely. A number of the buildings had ground-floor maisonettes—offices with private entrances. Visitors could enter right from the sidewalk, without having to pass through the main lobby. Brass plaques indicated that most of them were medical practices—not surprising, since Mount Sinai Hospital was only a few blocks north. Theo stood squarely before one of those doctor's doors, rang the bell, spoke into an intercom, and was immediately buzzed in.

About half an hour later, a couple in their fifties walked out, the man steadying the woman by the elbow, their expressions grim; the woman had a silk scarf tied around her head, and no eyebrows. As soon as they were out of sight, Greta rang the bell, asking if this was the dentist's office. When she heard the reply, she tried to say "Sorry," but her mouth had gone dry, and a swallow felt as if she had a razor blade stuck in her throat. Half-blinded by tears, she barely made it across Fifth Avenue, where she stumbled onto one of the benches that lined Central Park's outer perimeter. "No, this is an oncology practice," reverberated in her ears.

Theo's going to get good news, or at least hopeful, operable, treatable news . . . maybe he had an annual physical, and the blood test got screwed up . . . he's not going to walk out of there like that poor woman in the scarf. . . .

During the next two hours, five patients left the doctor's office, but Theo had been the last patient of the day to enter. It was nearly five-thirty, and a damp chill was creeping out of the park. She rummaged for the black blazer in her tote bag, and slipped it on beneath the poncho. A woman in a red coat and white nurse's shoes emerged from the office, the only one who checked the door to make sure it had locked behind her. Theo came out ten minutes later, his face difficult to read from across the avenue. For a moment, she thought he'd spotted her when he stepped out into the roadway, but he was hailing a cab that had just come around the corner. Jumping up, she sighted another taxi heading down Fifth, but a junker pulled out, blocking her and her raised arm from the cabbie's view. Several minutes passed with no luck, and she could have walked through the park, but the backseat of a cab would make the rest of changing back to Strasser mode much easier—she'd already ripped off the tight platinum wig and let the disposable lenses live up to their name. Rush hour would die down, she'd call him, and he would lie to her about what he did that day, and she would lie to him.

She phoned a few blocks from his building, her ears straining for any sort of tell in his voice, but Theo was his usual jaunty, gentlemanly self. When he turned serious with, "Greta, there's something you should know," she braced for the worst. But to her surprise, he blurted out, "I cheated today. The damn money trail—I couldn't resist one more try. I had this hunch—I fear that has the ring of Gamblers Anonymous, does it not?—anyhow, it seems to have paid off! I'm anxious to tell you, but not over the phone."

"I've just officially been unchained from my desk—how about right now?"

"What a long shift! If you're not too exhausted, by all means, do come by."

Once again, they sat side by side at the long table, watching the housebound laptop come to life. Whether brave, accepting, or in denial, he certainly was energized by his day's hacking.

"Remember those wild money trail splits we saw? All that money flying around eventually did funnel into a single Caribbean branch bank . . . except not all at the same time."

"So it's all staggered . . . or timed?"

"That's it. And when it comes out, it splits again, but in the next phase— and this is where the clouds part and the sunshine blazes through— eventually *half* of the original amount reenters that bank a second time. Not into that Caribbean branch, but into the bank's center of operations."

"You mean corporate headquarters . . . a main branch?"

"Yes! The end of the line! And I'm close to verifying that the other half of the money ultimately winds up in one other bank. All that way, all that circumlocution, just to go fifty-fifty."

"Which two banks?"

"I've confirmed one—as I said, I'm close on the other. I doubt you've heard of either one—I never did. They're relatively small—we're not talking Citibank here. But even though they're both international, I can't find them operating in New York or anywhere else in the USA. I want to learn more about what they're up to, and why they've partnered with one another. Getting involved in this exposes them to phenomenal risk, but what were the odds," he smiled, "that they'd encounter the Strasser-Appel trip wire?"

"Listen, Theo, you already know what they're up to—they're murdering people like Dave and Abe all over the country! You've already built a credible enough case—let the government take it from here."

Theo smiled, then sighed deeply. "I'm very troubled by what I've found, but I'm nearly there. It will make the case go from 'credible enough' to damning. Damning is what I want for all the unimaginable suffering they've caused. And I won't need more than half an hour online."

"Then at least let me go with you. Promise me, please, that you'll wait until my shift ends tomorrow afternoon—" That visibly troubled him, and she suspected that the problem was an entire day passing with his work stuck on pause. "Scratch that. I have an early start again—I can take a lunch break at eleven. How's that?"

"Perfect . . . but are you sure it won't—"

"Theo, I wouldn't have suggested it otherwise. Just don't go out until I get here."

"A beautiful young blonde with a gun offering to protect me? Who could possibly refuse?" He got up and grabbed a set of keys from a counter. "I'll take the elevator down with you—I completely forgot to pick up my mail today."

Greta glanced away. So the news had been bad, after all. He'd been all alone on that cab ride home, and he'd rushed upstairs only to be even more alone. Yet here he was, determined to nail the bad guys to the wall. She hoped he'd be just as determined to fight back against whatever the oncologist had found.

Downstairs, he walked her to the entrance, they shook hands, and she headed for the subway. When she reached the end of the block, something made her look over her shoulder, but no one was there.

CHAPTER **TWELVE**

When Greta arrived at Theo's building the next day, he was already waiting in a cab, dressed in a suit and tie, briefcase hugged to his chest. "We'll save some time this way, the sooner to deliver you back to the shackles of your desk."

Barely past where West End Avenue turned into Eleventh, the driver pulled up in front of a Lexus showroom. Shaking her head in disbelief, Greta followed him into what was designated as The Lounge, the poshest place she'd ever seen for people to cool their heels in while their cars underwent an oil and lube. There was tea, coffee, TV . . . and wireless access. "You do have a knack for finding these places," she said under her breath. Five customers were already in The Lounge, multitasking so furiously that they never glanced up at the new arrivals. Theo typed away while Greta fended off a salesman and a service manager who wanted to make sure they were being taken care of. After only twenty minutes, he said softly, "Let's go now, please."

"Problem?" Greta asked an unusually silent Theo as soon as they flagged a cab.

"Blocked . . . something atypical . . . it couldn't have been anticipated. I'll speak to the guys, but . . . I'm sorry I dragged you down here."

"Nothing to be sorry about. If it didn't feel right, leaving was better than sticking your neck out."

He paid the driver and gave him more than he had to in order to get Greta back to work ASAP. Before she could refuse, he was heading into his building. That afternoon, just before her shift was up, she called to ask if she should stop by.

"Thank you, Greta, but there's nothing new. Actually, I just got back—I had to take care of some business—without my computers or going online."

Greta closed her eyes, picturing Theo walking into the oncologist's office again. "Were you able to get in touch with your D.C. guys?"

"They're working on it. Think a Grand Canyon–sized firewall."

"You sound tired."

"A bit. We'll talk tomorrow—or sooner, if they manage to figure it out."

The next morning, shortly after Greta checked in with Theo, a mini-crime wave swept through the Two-Four. Just before four, he called to ask if she could stop by.

"It's kind of backed up—is five-thirty okay?" Just after five o'clock, as she collected her gear, the lieu blocked her way, pointing to the floor—straight down to Quill's office. "We still have a log jam, Strasser," he explained. Her protest was cut off with, "Hanging in is *highly advisable*."

She called Theo, but he wasn't picking up. Luckily, Claudia Ross, the teenager who walked Molly right after school every day, was at home. "Can you go back a little after six, and take her for another walk and feed her dinner?" When she hung up, she could hear the ka-ching in the kid's college fund—by now she probably had grad school covered—but at least Greta was free to worry exclusively about Theo.

Not until seven (after covert attempts to contact him every twenty minutes), was she able to sprint down the piss-yellow cinder-block stair way. After a near-collision with Cepeda, she caught sight of Kim, trailing by a landing. He touched his watch—surprised to see her there so late.

"Russell," she whispered when she got closer, "do you guys still have a car signed out?"

He called up to Cepeda that he thought he'd left his notebook on the front seat. Without a word, he led her to one of the Crown Vics outside the precinct house.

"I need to get to West End in the eighties, really fast—can you help me out?"

He made straight for the driver's door. Once they were around the corner, Kim put the red light on the roof and hit the gas. As he raced the final leg down West End Avenue, dusk thickened into night. From eight blocks away, the glow coming from somewhere near Theo's corner stood out like a beacon in the dark. It could have been Con Ed digging up a street . . . a pothole repair . . . a movie crew . . . or . . .

As the gap narrowed, the lights became headlights and flickering roof lights, and the massed vehicles they belonged to became NYPD blue-and-whites. Their haphazard parking angles indicated they'd all raced up from different directions . . . to a crime scene. Suddenly, Russell was neck and neck with a speeding Emergency Services truck.

Staring straight ahead, Kim asked, "Is that why you—?"

"No, no—I didn't know anything about what we're seeing, Russell." Feeling for her shield, she said, "Drop me off a block away. Get back before anyone notices you're gone."

"Who's going to notice? Manny? Guaranteed he's still on the phone with his main squeeze. He calls her first, then the wife. I've got half an hour before he catches on I'm not in the room, no less the building."

"Remember what I told you the other night? *Don't get involved.*"

"Damn it Greta, I've never seen you like this before . . . what the hell's going on?"

"I'm late to meet a friend. No one you know. Thanks for the ride."

Before the Vic came to a full stop, she was out of the car and running. "I hope your friend's okay," he yelled after her. She lifted an arm in thanks.

From the corner, Greta saw the ambulance crew dash between two uniforms who were sealing off the side street just beyond the patrol cars. Greta rushed up and flashed her shield, but before she could ask what was going on, one of them turned slightly to answer his radio, exposing the medics as they dropped their gear and knelt beside a man sprawled on the sidewalk. His silver-haired head, barely an inch from the curb, was turned away. Blood seeped out from under it, running straight into the gutter.

Through the blur of tears, she tilted her head back and looked up at Theo's apartment. In profile, a patrol officer stood at one side of the open window, writing in a notebook, while a cop in a suit, careful to avoid the sill and frame, was leaning out, probably studying the trajectory taken by the body on the sidewalk.

Neither of them could guess at the incongruity below: a man of such elegance—of mind, of character, of bearing—so brutally and awkwardly splayed and broken. Just outside that window, the essence of that particular abundance of grace had to be hovering, lost and bereft. It might be saved from disintegrating, dissolving, dispersing into the night air— but only if it had the luck to find another Theo Appel to inhabit. Greta knew that such a man didn't exist.

"—not until the jumper here—" the cop was reporting. Her head snapped around. As much as she wanted to set him straight, she put on the brakes, willed calm into her voice and told the other officer, "I have to talk to whoever's in charge."

"Detective Navarro," he said, pointing up at the suit. "I'll let him know, Detective—I didn't catch the name."

A few seconds later, Greta heard an annoyed voice blurt out, "What's she want?"

"Tell him I'm a friend of Mr. Appel."

Navarro was crossing through the entrance foyer when Greta approached the uniform posted at Theo's door. A man about her age, Navarro's posture was flawless, his spine stretched to gain every possible quarter inch above five-seven. The navy pinstripe suit had been expertly tailored to his frame.

Behind one of his perfect shoulder pads, Greta caught sight of the posters in the living room. She searched Sarah Bernhardt's faces, as if they could somehow replay the violent act that had taken place before them.

Greta handed Navarro her card as part of the introductions. "I heard our neighbors in the Two-Four had a rough day."

Greta nodded. "I've been worried about Mr. Appel. I was supposed to meet him earlier, but that had me stuck past my shift."

"'Worried'? Was he depressed? Physically ill?"

Possibly all three . . . but Theo would never have asked her to stop by if he had intended to . . . no, not even if his guys in Washington told him it was a dead end. "Why are you treating this as a suicide?"

"Well . . ." He looked pointedly at the open window. "Except if you have something to change my mind."

"He was in the middle of a project—totally caught up in it, very excited."

The last phrase activated a little tic in Navarro's right cheek, a human smoke alarm. "And your relationship to Mr. Appel, Detective?"

"We were friends." He was studying her, trying to figure out how old she was, surely already aware of Theo's age. She gave him the most withering look she could muster, and added, "Nothing beyond that. Initially, Mr. Appel contacted me about a case I'd worked."

"Related to that project that had him so 'excited'?"

"That's right." She hesitated, reluctant to get into an explanation of the Holocaust Victim Assets Litigation. "Research he was doing on his computer. Computers, that is."

"Computers?" Navarro's interest was piqued. "What kind? Where?"

"The three laptops. One's usually in the kitchen, either on a counter or the table. He had a briefcase with two more that he kept on the floor of the hall closet—right behind you. I don't know about the rest of the apartment."

With a flourish, Navarro swung open the closet door. Nothing was on the floor except for a pair of galoshes and a small upright vacuum. "This is the way we found the closet. No computer in the kitchen . . . and *we've* been in the rest of the apartment—the bedroom—no computer anywhere."

"Those computers—" Greta began, and the rest spilled out, rapid-fire: "They've got all the proof you need to see that Theo Appel didn't jump out any window!" As far Navarro was concerned, she'd just run off the rails. But the look on his face wasn't all that had made her stop short—she had it wrong. The kitchen computer was clean, and Theo was computer-savvy enough to wipe his searches off the other two. Everything was on the flash drive, and she suspected he used several as backups.

"Look," she began again, "Theo was investigating a scam with big money at stake . . . every time it was put into play, someone was murdered. Just a couple of days ago, he pinpointed one of the—" She choked down *banks*. "One of the two perps."

"And you think they traced him to his computers, whacked him, and left with the computers?"

"They were smart enough to find him, and smart enough to make it look like a suicide."

"Who?"

"He didn't tell me. He was trying to wrap it up. Like I said, I was late. But actually, we don't need the computers . . . it was all on a flash drive."

"A flash drive," Navarro repeated.

"A memory storage device. It looks like—"

"I know what one looks like. This seventy-something guy, into three computers and flash drives . . . impressive."

"He usually kept one in his shirt pocket. But I'm sure he backed it up on several others. A key to at least one of his killers is on a drive somewhere in this apartment—guaranteed."

Navarro didn't say anything for a while. "If you weren't a detective, you'd be out the door by now. You know that."

"What?" She glared at him. "Just another hysterical female?"

"Come on, don't pull that sexist shit. I didn't say that . . . mean that." He frowned, and studied his shoes. A good choice with the suit, black leather monk straps, definitely with lifts. His shoes told him to back off. "Wait here." Without urgency, he entered the living room and caught the attention of a tech working on the open window.

The tech shook his head at whatever had Navarro asked him, shot a covert look at Greta, glanced at his watch, and said, "Soon as I'm done with this."

"He'll recheck," said Navarro. "And I'll ask the EMS team to go through Appel's pockets. I'll tell them you're leaving now."

Bristling, Greta turned sharply, then turned back. Navarro was already walking away, radio in hand. "One last question. The other two windows . . . were those blinds down and closed like that when you got here?"

"Down and closed," his voice drifted back.

"Every time I was here, they were pulled all the way up. I could read the scoreboard on that neighbor's TV, so imagine how easy it is for that neighbor to see everything going on in here. If I was going to throw Mr. Appel out a window, it definitely wouldn't be done with built-in witnesses. I'd be sure to lower and close the blinds—just like you found them."

CHAPTER **THIRTEEN**

Two days later, Greta was holding on to the overhead subway railing, re-running everything that had happened since Theo's murder. Absorbed, nothing like her usual watchful self, she hadn't taken note of the other passengers, either standing or sitting. Suddenly, she felt a light tug at her right sleeve. A round-faced young woman in an oversized gray sweater was staring up at her through thick-lensed glasses with retro pink frames.

"Lady, you want my seat?"

"Your seat?" Greta repeated. "Why?"

"You're like . . . crying."

During the last forty-eight hours, with great effort, she had pushed down her grief and her anger, but nothing could stop the tears. "It's only an allergy," she mumbled, "spring—all the pollen." For effect, she sniffled. "But thanks. Thanks a lot."

How many thousands of trips had she taken on NYC Transit? A couple of times, she'd witnessed seats given up to extremely shaky octogenarians or women who looked ten months pregnant. Never before had anyone ever offered her a seat. If she'd just elicited such pity from a perfect stranger, how unhinged did she look?

At the next stop, she hurried out and entered another car, squeezing into a corner that afforded relative privacy.

———

People with wet hair were running down the subway steps to escape the rain, and Greta searched her briefcase for her latest black telescoping umbrella. Conforming to the same wretched standards of its countless predecessors, three of its spokes twisted as soon as she opened it. The steady spring drizzle didn't have much wind behind it, but to protect against a sudden gust, she held the umbrella low, close to her head, hoping it wouldn't turn inside out before she reached home. As she trudged along, she played back Navarro's call. No good morning, just "No flash drives. No computers."

That was exactly what she'd expected to hear, along with his unsuppressed vindication.

"But we e-mailed back and forth!"

"That doesn't establish that he had a computer—sorry, *computers*—in his apartment. But let's put that aside, Detective. We found a prescription bottle in his bathroom. The prescribing doctor is a GP. When he finally took my call, I squeezed out—and these guys plead the patient-privacy thing like they're taking The Fifth—that your friend saw him for his annual physical in February. After his blood test came back, Mr. Appel got a referral to an oncologist. He had two appointments with the oncologist. The second was two days before he committed suicide." After a long interval during which Greta didn't—couldn't—reply, he asked, "You there, Detective?"

She croaked out, "What arrangements were made?"

"We found one of those fireproof strongboxes in his bedroom closet. His will was inside, so we were able to get in touch with the law office that prepared it. We confirmed that one of the partners is the executor."

"Who's the lawyer?"

"I see no need to share that with you, Strasser. What I will tell you—before you ask—is that there won't be a service, just a cremation." After adding a curt, "That's it," he cut the connection.

Greta could practically hear how hard Navarro would've slammed down the phone if he'd been on an old-fashioned handset. As of yet, no one had come up with a better way of informing someone that she (or he) was the biggest pain in the ass that he (or she) had ever met.

Barely ten minutes later, Lieutenant Geracimos had barked out her name and a summons to his office.

"Let me guess," she began, as they both sat down. "You just got a call from a detective in the Two-Oh."

"What don't you understand about desk duty, Strasser?" A package of gum was on his desk, the brand nonsmokers buy smokers to make them quit smoking. He seemed oblivious to how fast and hard he was chewing. "It's so simple: You come to work, you go home. You can do whatever the fuck you want to do at home, as long as you report in the next day. In between—" He abruptly stopped chewing, and the next sentence shot out, one word at a time: "You . . . are . . . not . . . NOT! . . . to . . . fucking . . . freelance . . . in . . . another . . . fucking . . . precinct!" With a tilt of his head, he posed the question, "And why . . . WHY . . . is that?" Before she could reply, he continued, "Because when you do, it creates a monster fucking headache for ME!"

"I'm sorry, Lieu, but—"

"That guy, Detective—what's his name?"

"Navarro."

"Right. Just imagine if, instead of calling me, Navarro had called *him*!" As he had the week before, he pointed to the floor, rather than giving breath to Quill's name. "Look, Greta, VX was your case, and the way you went after him downtown—if it'd been up to me, you'd be heading up the squad on that. Instead, you got yourself shafted in a political shit storm. Unjustified, sure. But guess how it plays when the story is told by—" This time, he only glanced down. "In *his* version, you fucked up a humongous Police Plaza sweep. And rained down disgrace, embarrassment, et cetera upon the Two-Four."

"And here I go again, Lieu, with a call from the Two-Oh. I'm a serial disgracer."

Geracimos waved his hand. "The last time you were in this office, I made it clear that no one is a bigger threat to Greta Strasser than Greta Strasser. Oh, and by the by, this Navarro thinks you're dangerously nuts.

While his people did a search *you* demanded—sound familiar?—it occurred to him there was a possibility that you never even *met* the jumper. Like you spend your free time looking for patrol cars with their flashers on and yellow tape, and wander into other precincts' crime scenes." After a deep sigh, he acknowledged, "Okay, I know you're not that weird. But you've got to agree that it's not all that hard to see where he was coming from."

"First of all, Theo Appel wasn't a jumper. Second, he was my friend."

The lieu craned his head back just a little, examining her face. "He and that DOA old lady with the tea and cookies last month—they had something in common, right? I mean, besides being senior citizens?"

"Both were Holocaust survivors. Both were murder victims."

"This is the second time you've tried to prove that. But you have no evidence, no witnesses, not even a suspect. What's changed?"

"The last time I saw Mr. Appel—the *homicide* in the Two-Oh—he'd discovered that there were two . . . organizations . . . involved in a string of homicides. He was on the brink of wrapping it up, about to share the names with me. In fact, I was supposed to meet him the day I was stuck here so late."

"While the bad guys pushed him out of a window . . . and then vanished with his computers." He opened his empty hands, "Come on, convince me you've got *something*, Greta."

"Only that they've got some kind of network targeting more seniors—Holocaust survivors who are eligible to receive payment from a Swiss bank fund. They kill at least one a month, apparently in four rotating cities. A pattern."

"Really?" He sounded genuinely pleased. "Not just New York?" When she shook her head, he observed, "And since they just did the cookie lady a few weeks back, no murder is scheduled in New York for a while? Nothing imminent?" An affirmative nod made him smile. "Not anything to indicate that the next victim will necessarily be a resident of our very own Two-Four?"

"No. The next strike could happen anyplace in the metro area."

"Good. In that case, I hope you'll be reassured that, besides you, we have over thirty-six thousand other cops in other precincts who'll vigilantly guard their senior citizens against those rotating perps."

"Come on, Lieu! I'm not—"

"No, *you* come on, damn it! Greta, unfair as it is, you'll be stuck on desk duty right up to the very last day of the five months you have left. I'm not a betting man, but it's a sure thing you'll get your first countdown memo by next week—the reminder that your retirement paperwork has to be submitted at least thirty days in advance." He stood, clearly as uncomfortable as she was, and waited for her to make a hasty exit.

"That's it?"

"My neck only goes out so far."

With her hand on the doorknob, she said softly, "I've got to stop and wonder if, historically speaking, the Department has been more protective of its dirty cops than of its hypothetically crazy ones."

She couldn't hate Geracimos. Or, for that matter, even blame him. For the rest of her shift, she sat at her desk and tackled her paperwork, trying to keep herself together.

Then the girl had offered her that seat on the subway.

As she turned onto Montgomery Place, Greta just wanted to hit the sofa and go numb. Shaken and depressed over Theo, frustrated by her inability to complete the investigation that had been so important to him, pissed about her job, confused about the future, she was just about depleted. A 100-watt bulb, burning like a 25. Not as bright, not as useful, definitely not as hot.

Once again, just as when she was on the train, she realized she hadn't been paying enough attention to her surroundings. Nearly home, and she didn't have her whistle ready. After juggling her briefcase, handbag, and umbrella, she fished it out from under her jacket and sweater and blew her hello.

Molly didn't appear in the bay.

Greta gave it another try. The window remained a blank reflection of the colorless sky. Suddenly, a trace of red, a dull glow, appeared about where Molly should have been, but higher. From years of surveillance, she knew what someone taking a drag on a cigarette looked like. Her mind raced while she did her best to maintain a steady, unremarkable pace. It could've been nothing more than an odd reflection—a brake light, maybe a red vehicle. She held the umbrella even lower, so it pressed on the crown of her head, and looked back over her shoulder. If any traffic had passed, it would be slowing down for the stop sign at end of the block, waiting to turn right onto Eighth Avenue. There were no cars in the street. Nothing close to red parked nearby. That glimmer was something she would have ignored . . . if Molly had been there.

Someone was in her apartment.

Whoever that person was, he was on lookout for someone to walk up the stoop. For now, Greta was just another black umbrella passing by, plodding up the slope of Montgomery Place. As soon as she was out of sight, she began to run, wheeling left onto Prospect Park West. A short block of one apartment building and a handful of houses, then left again, down Carroll Street. Near the end of the long block, she ran into the cement courtyard of a brownstone and jabbed the doorbell next to the heavy wrought-iron gate of the basement apartment.

A dead bolt flipped behind the inner wooden door, instantly releasing the yelps of fighting kids and a whiff of roasting chicken. "Claudia, did you forget your keys *again*?" Greta recognized the voice of her dog walker's mother. Annoyed, she continued, "If you lost them, this time you're pay-ing the locksmith to—" Her scolding stopped short as soon as she saw Greta, who'd stopped by on previous occasions, either to drop off a check, a forgotten textbook, sweatshirt, or—right on target—keys her teenage daughter had left behind.

"Is Claudia home, Mrs. Ross?"

"After she walked Molly, she went to a friend's house to work on a school project." Ross glanced at her watch. "I'm expecting her home for supper in"—she consulted her watch—"about twenty minutes."

The woman's answer had triggered all sorts of alarms, but Greta tamped any reaction down to a tight little nod. "Okay if I come in?"

"Sure." Mrs. Ross's eyebrows rose, but she immediately took one half-step back, allowing just enough room for Greta to enter; it was an economy of space practiced by those who'd experienced one home invasion too many.

Greta kept on walking down the hallway, toward the rear of the apartment. "You have access to the garden, right?" Off to the right, in the living room, two twin boys, about ten, were in a fierce struggle over a video game joystick. "And I have to borrow a ladder, the tallest one you have. Right away. Please."

Confusion and fear spread over Ross's face. "Is Claudia—?"

"This is about my building—I have to get inside right away. No one was home . . . I rang all the bells," she lied.

"The ladder—it's in the cellar," Mrs. Ross said, ducking into a doorway under the house's main staircase. Soon a small grunt, followed by the grate of metal against concrete, drifted up from below. Meanwhile, Greta tried to estimate when, between the time Claudia had walked Molly and her own return home, the intruder entered her apartment.

Claudia's mother was banging an eight-foot aluminum ladder up the worn stairs. She passed the top of the ladder to Greta. Because the hall was so narrow, they had to angle it back and forth a couple of times to get it out. Ross pointed ahead, and they entered the kitchen, warm and fragrant from the oven. Even in her rush, the snug, cozy room pulled at Greta; more than anyplace she'd been in a long time, it was a real home.

In the next room, the twins' bedroom, Claudia's mother motioned to put down the ladder while she turned to unbar a metal door. Reality, in the form of the chill rainy evening, pushed in. "I know you're a police detective," she whispered. "I'm getting worried—should I be?"

"This isn't a police matter, Mrs. Ross." Greta deposited her briefcase, purse, and umbrella in a corner, next to the boys' crumpled book bags. "Thanks," she said. "I'll be back with the ladder to pick up my stuff as soon as I can."

"Wait," Mrs. Ross said. "The rain—at least take this." She handed Greta a Yankees hat that'd been draped over a bedpost. Greta pulled the door closed behind her and hustled the ladder toward the rear of the small garden.

Wasting no time, she pushed stacked flowerpots away from the east corner of the garden and leaned the ladder, still folded, against the fence.

The Ross yard had cyclone fencing not quite eight feet high, and she clambered up the ladder to survey the patchwork of backyards between Carroll and Montgomery. Six separated her from her own building, and no two of their fences were alike. In the fading light, she considered the next-door Carroll Street fence, but its arrowhead finials screamed vaginal impalement. The one after that looked ready to cave in—with a soaking wet hundred twenty pounds on it, collapse was guaranteed. In comparison, the closest three fences separating the Montgomery Place yards—as far as she could see in what had turned into a downpour—seemed a safer choice. Holding on to the top of the ladder for dear life, she angled up her butt and sat on the cyclone corner, on a diagonal. After a deep breath, she loosened her death grip on the ladder and transferred her hands to the fence. Reminding herself that it wasn't all that far to the ground, Greta straddled the fence and, after a struggle to control the ladder, rested it parallel with the fence top, swiveled it around, lowered it, and used it to climb down. Five to go.

Every house seemed to have lights popping on. The ladder scraped and clinked on the garden's flagstones, and her shoes squeaked from the puddles she'd already waded through, but the heavy rain muffled nearly every sound. The slate sky was darkening; her black pants suit, completely saturated, would provide perfect camouflage by the time she scaled a few more fences.

After only three steps up the ladder, a dog began growling and barking on the other side of the vinyl fence panel it was tilted against. Fractured and fuzzy in the deluge, light spilled out over the adjacent yard. Greta pressed herself hard against the cold metal rungs, as if that could make her disappear. Even with her shield, if she was discovered anyplace outside the Ross yard, there'd be far too much explaining to do. Inches away, a man's voice pleaded, "Come on, Chippy! Too wet for park-y bye-bye—do it quick for Mommy, then yum-yum!" The snarls ceased, and the dog, more interested in dinner than Greta, earned a relieved "Good boy!" A door slammed shut, and the light went out. Wetter than she'd ever been in her life with all her clothes on, Greta carried on with even greater caution, her vigilance doubled by the possibility of another Chippy, only bigger, quieter, and not as easily distracted.

With each consecutive breach of Park Slope's rear defenses, Greta clung to the hope that the key component to tackling the grand finale of her miserable, sodden garden tour would still be where she'd seen it last. Absolutely crucial, it had her detouring back diagonally to the Carroll Street side, to the house directly behind her own.

Two days before, the morning after Theo's death, the weather had been unseasonably warm. For the first time since November, Greta had carried her post-run coffee out onto her terrace. The plastic flaps of the dog port thwacked open, and Molly wandered out after her, but she ran to the iron railing as soon as she heard voices below.

Three men, their work clothes and tools identifying them as masons, stood in the backyard of the Carroll Street yard, waiting for a batch of mortar to set. The neighbor's redwood table and bench set had been pushed up against the fence, away from the house. In their usual place was a scaffold, secured by hooks that curved over the edge of the roof, and, lined up next to it, an extension ladder.

Molly, who must have spotted them the previous day and judged them too far to pose a threat, found a sunny spot and stretched out. Soon, two of the masons were pointing bricks on the scaffold, while the third moved the ladder to work on another section of the wall. He untied the rope that secured the upper extension in its lowest position, then ratcheted it up about five feet—not even close to as far as it could go. And as far as it could go, every last inch, was essential to Greta's plan.

Now, surveying the scene through the rain, she saw the redwood table was still next to the fence. Greta made the four-foot drop onto it easily enough, accompanied by a loud squoosh from her shoes. To her relief, the ladder was also in place. Even telescoped down, it was roughly four feet longer than Mrs. Ross'. Not only the extra length, but a heavier grade of aluminum made it much more difficult to maneuver. If she dropped it, the crash would alert the entire neighborhood, even the son of a bitch smoking all the way in the front of her apartment. Struggling, she moved the unwieldy beast along, lifted it onto the table, propped it against the fence, and gingerly tilted it down into the next yard . . . her building's yard, at last.

With her head tilted back, Greta searched for the edge of her terrace, but it was absorbed by the soupy night. Excluding a few grand mansions, Park Slope's brownstones measured an average eighteen to twenty feet across, sixty feet long. A number of them had extensions in the back; often included with the original construction, they were not always, as the name implied, later add-ons. Conforming to the building's width, most extensions were two stories high and added an extra twenty feet or so to the length. On the garden floor, the extra four hundred square feet could have been divided into a laundry room and servants' quarters; the parlor floor, a brownstone's most ornate, gained a generous space for entertaining. Greta's terrace, ringed by a wrought-iron railing, was the roof of her building's extension. Judging by where the third mason had been working, there was a reasonable chance the ladder could reach it.

The garden floor had only two barred windows at the rear, and thankfully their inside shutters were tightly closed. As soon as the ladder was propped up against the wall between them, hopefully directly beneath one of the terrace's balusters, Greta untied the thick knot of rope that held it closed. The rope ran through a pulley wheel, and she'd observed how the mason had used it to adjust the height. Just as he had, she put one foot on the bottom rung, and tugged on the rope. Hooks on each side—they reminded Greta of lobster claws—ratcheted up, grabbing progressively higher on the lower frame while the ladder's extension rose. The clicks were noisy, and she worked as fast as she could, then froze at intervals, expecting a neighbor's angry protest any minute, but none came. Angling out the lower ladder became more and more of a struggle—she wasn't only grappling with an increasingly unsteady fifteen, then twenty, then twenty-four foot ladder, but was wrestling it into position in stealth, during a monsoon.

After the pulley rope was completely played out, she stood on the second step and gave the ladder a test-shake. The wobble wasn't a hell of a lot worse than she'd anticipated, but the higher she went, the less she trusted the narrow, slippery rungs.

When she'd cleared the garden floor's windows, she once again reached inside her jacket. Next to her racing heart, her hand was shockingly cold. She pulled out the whistle and blew for Molly. While she was at work, Greta left the dog port's interior cover ajar, in case Molly had to use the terrace as an emergency dog run. Molly would hear her whistle, and in seconds, she'd be bounding out, barking at Greta's strange new way to come home, barking at this new game.

All she heard was the wind and the rain.

Unprotected by the barrier of garden fences for the first time, she became aware of how much the storm had intensified. It blew from the east, barreling across one of New York City's largest open spaces, the Great Meadow of Prospect Park. One particularly strong, howling gust had the ladder trembling.

The parlor floor extension had four windows at its rear. They had no bars, because it was a logical assumption that no one would be stupid enough to attempt an entry through them. Under the dripping bill of the Yankees cap, Greta's eyes came up on a plane with the windowsills. Luckily, the room—used as a living room—was in shadow. Twenty feet away, partially opened sliding doors led into the brownstone's former library, which was directly below Greta's bedroom. Joy and Hal Littlewood, the parlor floor owners, used it as a combination dining room–home office. She could see Joy, in profile, sitting at the table, eating. She stopped to pass a serving dish to an outstretched hand—the second snug and cozy scene of the evening from which Greta was excluded.

If Greta couldn't see Hal, it was a good bet he couldn't see her, but she was determined to make getting past the Littlewoods' windows the fastest segment of her climb. She dragged herself up the increasingly shaky ladder, reminded of how the top step of pigmy six-foot ladders had decals warning DANGER! DO NOT STAND OR SIT! Here she was, close to three stories up, nearly out of rain-slicked rungs, scared shitless of making the wrong move—any move at all—until the wind quieted down. With the slant of the ladder, her face was close to the brick wall. Doing her best to hold her center, she reached one tired arm up over her head. Her resolve began to waver as she touched more brick. Down came the arm, up she stepped onto the next-to-last rung, her stomach on spin-cycle.

Probing with her right hand, she finally made contact with the terrace edge—relieved, but not exactly overjoyed. No easy stepping off the ladder onto home plate. Like too many of her teenage blind dates, the ladder was much shorter than she'd expected.

Her fingers explored the concrete above her head. In her mind's eye, she pictured the space between the balusters, positive they weren't that far apart. Nothing to her left, but at the extreme right of her range, they curved—gloriously—around a support bar. Holding on for dear life, she willed her other hand off the ladder and searched left. Again at the outermost limit of her reach, her fingertips barely closed around a second baluster. Arms spread like that—not the easiest way to haul your body up, but at least there was that top rung to push off on, for that final move onto the terrace. In protest, her toes curled around the rung she was standing on, but she pulled up fast, with a ferocity she didn't think she had left. Before she knew it, one foot was on the top rung, then both were on the edge of the terrace, her torso bent back like a limbo dancer. Gradually working her hands up the balusters, she grabbed the railing, straightened, and stepped over it.

More than anything, she wanted to lie on her belly for a while, panting. Instead, she crouched down and ran for cover behind the fireplace chimney that rose above the terrace. Shivering, she pulled the whistle out one more time, and blew as hard as she could. Even if Molly was locked in a closet, or trapped in the bathroom, her girl had to hear it now. Even if she couldn't get out, at least she'd know Greta was on her way.

Greta pulled off her shoes, then took her Glock from its holster. Edging out from behind the chimney, she ran along the railing, then flattened against her terrace door. Slippery in her wet fingers—she had nothing to dry them on—the doorknob took several tries. She walked into her bedroom.

In total darkness, her feet moved over fabric that shouldn't have been there. She felt buttons, kneeled down. A blouse, jeans, a scarf . . . her clothing, strewn all over the floor. She dried her hands on what felt like a pillowcase, tiptoed around books, shoes, CDs, picture frames—the room had been thoroughly tossed. Wary of crunching over anything, she slowly crept into the narrow hall that ran between her kitchen and bathroom, her trouser socks gliding silently toward the living room, the Glock steadied in both hands. Cigarette smoke wafted toward her. Crappy Craig was a smoker, and it had taken months to get rid of his nicotine stink.

At the end of the hallway, just where she could see across to the bay window—Molly's window—she stopped short. Illuminated by the streetlamp a couple of houses down, a figure was silhouetted against the glass: tall and broad in the shoulders, positioned for the optimum view down Montgomery to Eighth Avenue. He was shifting his weight from one foot to the other. He'd been waiting for her a long time.

As Greta tiptoed over the doorsill dividing the hall from the living room, a large splinter of wood that hadn't been there before caught her sock. She tried to work it free, but the wet fabric held on and her sock began to rip. Low as it was, the sound made the guy at the window whirl toward it.

As he came around, she shouted, "Police! Don't move!"

Instantly, a soft pop! sounded, followed by a flash, dazzling and intense. She hadn't expected the guy to start shooting right from the get-go. *Why expect this piece of shit to follow any rules?* Pure reflex was behind the burst she got off while she made a dive for the floor and flattened. There were more bubblelike pops—the son of a bitch was using a silencer—more blinding explosions of light. Bullets were flying over her. The shooter's vision had to be at least as messed up as hers—all starbursts trailing flames.

The pops stopped, and she felt more than heard feet running over the parquet floor. Fast as she could, she crawled backward, retreating from the living room. The front door banged open, and light flooded in from the main hall. Meanwhile, the shooter, still a blur, had yet to run all the way across the room. The good news was, instead of coming at her, he was also headed for the door. The bad news was there were two of them. Sure enough, Greta heard a pair of heavy feet pounding along the hall, followed by another pair stomping by. She hoisted herself up and raced back toward her bedroom, actually sprinting right alongside them—only the wall between the building's main hall and her open galley kitchen separated them.

Each of the brownstone's floor-through units had a front and rear entrance door, and, given how the staircase switch-backed, anyone mounting the stairs would pass Greta's bedroom door first, then continue up to the top floor by passing her living room door at the front. These guys were making a dash for the street. While she opened her locks, their shoes shuffled around, slowing for the U-turn on the landing at the top of the staircase. They were already clomping down toward the parlor floor when Greta moved from her doorway to the landing, gaining a direct view down the stairs. A man in a black leather jacket was halfway down. His large torso completely blocked any view of his accomplice, who was only a couple of steps below him. The staircase wall was wainscoted, with an upper molding wide enough to brace Greta's arm— the last salvo hadn't exactly left her rock-steady, and she needed all the support she could get. Assuming a shooter's stance, she yelled down, "Freeze, assholes!" Her voice betrayed her with a trill, a tremble, but she was as primed as she'd ever be.

The intruders were only a few treads from the lower landing. Resembling a little balcony, it overlooked the vestibule door, straight ahead. On the left, it was framed by columns; three stairs led down to the parlor floor. The leather jacket turned toward Greta, arm lifted, head slightly tilted back, the gun in his hand. This time, it was Greta who fired first, her finger locked down on the trigger while the impact knocked him backward. The recoil lifted her arm, but she kept on firing, correcting while the polished banister chipped and splintered around her target. Staggering backward, he went right over the balcony railing, headed for the parlor hallway's marble floor.

Whether or not he was out of commission, someone else was down there.

Greta hugged the wall as she crept down the stairs, gunfire still roaring in her ears. She rapidly shifted her Glock back and forth, between the place under the balcony where Leather Jacket had landed and the base of the stairs, where his accomplice had to be. As she edged around the landing, blinding light washed over the balcony area, exposing her. Instinctively, she returned to shooter stance. Just as quickly, the light receded—the curtained glass vestibule door swinging shut. The splash of light had come from the entry area's high-wattage ceiling fixture. Beyond, the tall, glass-paneled outer door also started to close, forcing in a cold gust that raised goose bumps under Greta's wet clothes. The second man was gone. But determining whether or not the man she'd shot remained a threat had to be her next move.

Glock leveled, Greta peered over the balcony. Even though the body sprawled out below was motionless, she moved down the steps and around the base of the staircase with extreme caution. With her gun held to the back of his head, she crouched down to feel for a pulse. No pulse . . . and no gun.

A radiator startled her with a metallic bang and steamy hiss, driving Greta to her feet—her ears were working again. She spotted something, maybe fifteen feet from the body. The floor's black and white pattern provided the perfect camouflage for his gun, which had skidded farther than she'd expected over the smooth marble. She walked over and bent to pick it up by the silencer. Suddenly, a click sounded just above her head. She froze until she realized she was next to the Littlewoods' front door. Again, she yelled, "Police! Don't move! Do not open your door!" Two faint voices, in muted disagreement, filtered through the door. The Littlewoods had been in their apartment less than a year. Neither would know she was a cop unless another resident had told them. The lock snapped shut.

Greta got to her feet. Both assailants were faceless to her, and she wanted to see at least one of them, to get some kind of clue as to what the hell was going on.

Blood had begun to eke from the dead man's torso, shockingly red against the floor. During his fall, his cap had slipped forward, covering his face. To avoid blood-soaked socks, Greta balanced carefully and pushed it back with the tip of her toe. She was looking at a young black man, probably in his mid-twenties, whose face she'd never seen before.

Something nagged at her, something that made her look up at the banister to estimate how far he'd fallen—only three or four feet, at the most. His cap was tightly knit, like a navy watch cap, with a snug fit. One more nudge with her toe, and she immediately understood why it had slid so far—his head was shaved perfectly smooth.

"Son of a bitch bastard!" she whispered. "You're one of his!" An uncontrollable rage fanned up inside her. Her first thought was to run out the front door and down the stoop, but she knew no one would be there. The second man—maybe VX himself—was once again long gone.

She called 911. The dispatcher told her the Seven-Eight was already on its way to her address. Was it the Littlewoods who'd placed the call? Or neighbors who'd heard shots through the common wall in the brownstone next door?

Here she was, making waves in yet another precinct, and these were definitely gathering into a tsunami. What had the lieu said, a million years ago, this morning? "Do whatever the fuck you want to do at home, as long as you report in the next day."

Okay, Lieu, I'm at home.

CHAPTER **FOURTEEN**

"I brought up your paper," said Schuyler, the lead detective from the Seven-Eight. He'd already taken off *The Times*' blue plastic sleeve and shuffled the sections around, so that she received it with the Metro section on top.

A moody color photo dominated the front page, a rainy night scene of double-parked patrol cars and people under umbrellas crowded in front of a brownstone. Yes, *her* brownstone, with yellow crime-scene tape stretched across the stoop.

"Metro isn't so bad," Schuyler said over Greta's shoulder, as she scanned the article. "Only cops who get killed or arrested make the front-front page." He'd gone home and changed, probably caught an hour or two of sleep. Like the night before, the fresh clothes still looked two sizes too big for him.

Greta hadn't slept at all, and she was still in the sweats she'd changed into, long after her rain-soaked clothes had completely dried on her adrenaline-charged body.

The night before, the Seven-Eight detectives had put her through the drill. She'd danced the dance she knew so well, taking not a single false step, careful to be just as patient and noncommittal as they were. But after giving her statement over and over, she began to suspect that the VX protégé actually had shot her, and that she'd landed in her own personal hell, stuck in the parlor floor hallway forever, never to be allowed to go up to her apartment. All the while, the techs had relentlessly measured and photographed. Somewhere in their pile of Baggies was Greta's Glock, as well as the silencer-fitted .22.

She didn't have to go upstairs to know that Molly was gone. All she had to do was replay the guy at the window, turning, firing. Like his mentor with Tyrel on the swing and Abby in the wheelchair, he wouldn't think twice, especially about shooting a dog who could give him away with a single bark.

When Greta finally entered her apartment, more techs were prying the last of the .22's bullets out of the wall. During the attack, there hadn't been enough light or time to register that, like the mess on her bedroom floor, the living room was a wreck. Her sofa was slashed and upended, cushions and pillows and books and CDs scattered everywhere. Close to the door, the floor was stained with wiped-up blood. And there was a puzzling florist's box, the kind used for long-stemmed roses, leaning in a corner.

It had been Schuyler who guided her toward the bathroom.

Molly was lying on the bath towel the killers must have used to carry her from the doorway. Her utter stillness tore at Greta, even more than the blood. When she kneeled down beside her big girl, someone had briefly rested a consoling hand on her shoulder, but she hadn't looked up to see whose hand it was. Bending to kiss the top of Molly's head, the void next to her—where Molly should've been, brushing against her, leaning lightly against her side—felt enormous.

From somewhere that seemed miles away, Greta heard a growing commotion, voices shouting back and forth:

"Christ—is that the kid?"

"What kid?"

"The missing kid! That was the last call that came through before—"

Disoriented, Greta got to her feet. Not that far away at all, the voices were coming from her bedroom. Tearing herself away from Molly, she glanced back through the open door, where a knot of cops and techs who'd bunched up around the closet broke apart, letting Schuyler pass through.

When he emerged, a person in jeans and a hoodie, blindfolded and gagged, was cradled against his chest, struggling against the duct tape binding both arms and legs. Carefully navigating his way through the piles of debris on the bedroom floor, the detective spoke reassuringly to the thrashing form, which he then gently lowered onto Greta's bed. As soon as he eased off the blindfold, the head writhed from side to side, desperate for him to remove the gag as well.

Greta screamed, "Oh my God! Claudia!"

Schuyler glanced toward the doorway, shooting her a questioning look. Immediately after spitting out a wadded-up cloth, Claudia Ross was sobbing, "I'm sorry, Greta! I'm so sorry! They . . . they shot Molly! I loved Molly, Greta! She was such a good dog!"

Procedure abandoned, Greta ran across the room. Schuyler hesitated, then stepped aside while she hugged Claudia to her. "We both loved Molly," she whispered, "she was the best." Sighing, she eased the girl back, propping her against the pillows. "Let me get you out of this." She set to work peeling away the tape pinning back the teenager's arms, then stopped abruptly. "Claudia . . . did they hurt you?"

"They scared me," she answered, "but they didn't hurt me like what you mean. No, I just hurt all over from being tied up."

"What did they say to you?" Schuyler asked, as Greta concentrated on the tape again.

"Only one of them talked. The one who tied me up. He said that if I gave him any trouble, he'd kill me . . . like the dog." Claudia turned back to Greta. "They were going to kill you as soon as you walked in, and there was nothing I could do! And I kept thinking that they were going to come back and . . ."

"Nobody's coming back," said Greta, stripping back the tape from Claudia's jeans. "It's over," she lied. He was out there. VX was out there.

To shake the numbness away, Claudia stretched her arms and did a few flutter kicks, then stared at her watch in disbelief. "Oh my God! My mom will be going nuts! It's tomorrow!"

As they listened to Schuyler notifying Mrs. Ross that her daughter was safe, and that a car would be dispatched to ferry her to her daughter, Claudia began to tremble. Besides all the pain, fatigue, and fear she'd endured, the realization that this night might've had another ending had pushed to the surface. Schuyler was ready to resume his questioning. Greta wanted to remind him she was just a kid, but Claudia surprised her by responding immediately, the words coming so fast, she was nearly out of breath when she finished. Greta suspected they were hearing something equivalent to mind-bulimia . . . the teenager's desperate attempt to purge her memory of everything that had happened.

The account she gave was Classic Push-in:

Claudia had walked up the stoop and unlocked the front door with the set of keys Greta had given her. She entered the vestibule, and, just before the front door was about to swing shut, a man with a florist's box barged in behind her. She had one quick look at him: African-American, black leather jacket, knit hat, tall. All at once, he dropped the box—right where it would keep the front door wedged open—and wrapped one arm around her, clamping his hand over her mouth and lifting her off the floor. He ordered her to hand over the keys. After he used them to unlock the vestibule door, he moved her into the hallway. They waited there several seconds, until she heard the front door open. Reaching back, he opened the vestibule door, then half-carried, half-dragged her up the stairs. Someone else was right behind them. Claudia could hear Molly barking.

When they got to the landing, he asked her which door was the one she used, and she pointed to the front—the only apartment door she had a key for. He handed her back the keys and ordered her to unlock it. She wondered at that—he'd opened the vestibule downstairs—until she realized that now he had a gun in his hand. With Claudia between him and the door like a shield, he threw it open and immediately shot Molly dead. He shoved Claudia inside, barely avoiding Molly's body. The other man stepped in right after them.

Straightaway, he swooped down on Claudia from behind with a blindfold. As soon as it was tied, the first man let go of her mouth, and she opened it to scream—giving his partner a perfect opportunity to ram in the gag. Moving fast, they worked in tandem, taping her wrists behind her, taping her thighs together just above the knees. After warning her,

"No trouble, or you get what the fucking dog got," the first man—she recognized his voice—threw her over his shoulder and carried her toward Greta's bedroom, at the back of the apartment.

He threw her down on the bed, leaving her there while she heard them moving furniture and ripping and breaking things all over the room. Things shattered in the kitchen and bathroom, then it was quiet. She was carried across the room, tossed on the floor, kicked back against a wall. A door closed, and she was left alone for nearly nine panicked hours.

Schuyler asked her what they looked like, and Claudia again described the man Greta had shot. As for the other man, she hadn't seen or heard him at all. That didn't matter to Greta. She knew exactly what VX looked like.

A few minutes later, when Claudia's mother rushed in, Greta wasn't sure what to expect.

She'd learned that Mrs. Ross hadn't contacted the cops until Claudia failed to return home for dinner—after a call to the friend she was supposed to be studying with. The precinct radioed a description to the cars on patrol—but all they had was a teenage girl in jeans and a sweatshirt, missing for a couple of hours. And shortly after that, there was the distraction of all hell breaking loose on Montgomery Place.

With a furtive glance at Schuyler, Greta watched the mother-daughter reunion, bracing for Ross to start hammering her with recriminations about how she'd needlessly and intentionally exposed Claudia to danger. Her eyes darted his way again when Mrs. Ross wrapped Greta in a breast-crushing hug and sobbed out her thanks for saving her daughter. If she hadn't made a connection between Greta's need for a ladder and her daughter's absence when she called the Seven-Eight, Mrs. Ross certainly was making one now, assuming that when Greta walked out into the rain with her ladder, she not only knew that her daughter had been kidnapped, but was determined to risk life and limb to rescue Claudia—with or without the help of the Seven-Eight.

At that point, Greta was pretty sure, a suggestion for the way his precinct commander could present the incident to the press was forming in

Schuyler's head. The Metro headline, "Kidnapper Dead in NYPD Rescue of Park Slope Teen" had a heroic ring.

Just as the Rosses were leaving, Greta took off the Yankees cap and gave it to Claudia's mom. "How about if we work out an exchange—this for my stuff? The police officer who drives you and Claudia home can bring it back." She paused for a moment. "The ladder—that might take a little longer—okay?" Mrs. Ross's response was to tear up and clutch both Greta and Claudia to her bosom.

For once, no one was going to accuse Greta of being delusional. From Claudia's statement, it was clear that VX's crew had found out where she lived, that she had a dog, that a teenager walked the dog after school every afternoon. Thankfully, Claudia had been spared—the alternative was something Greta never would have been able to live with. As for shooting Leather Jacket in self-defense, she felt no remorse. Greta didn't have to close her eyes to see Molly waiting by the window. No remorse at all.

"Thanks for the low profile," Greta said to Schuyler, as she folded up *The Times*.

"Hey, thank *you*. For now, there's just a tad of a misconception—let's call it a misinterpretation—by all the papers. You know, about the precise meaning of 'a detective *from* the precinct.' Live here, or work here? We're certainly not going to make an issue of it if the media makes the Seven-Eight look good. And I doubt the Two-Four would want it to read like they're so ineffective against their own mutts that they've graduated to opening branch offices in other precincts." He studied her. "How you holding up?"

"I'll tell you as soon as I have a cup of coffee. Want some?"

"I've already exceeded my three-cup limit, so why not? Black, one sugar—if you've got it."

"Sure." Turning to grab two mugs, she said, "I kept forgetting to ask—what was with the flower box? Just a cover for walking up the stoop?"

"Oh, it wasn't empty. But the stuff inside wasn't anything you'd want to get on Valentine's Day. Lots of duct tape, gauze, cloth for the blindfold and gag. And considering how they trashed this place, I wouldn't be surprised if they used it earlier, ringing doorbells, checking out if any of your neighbors were home."

"Got anything on the gun yet?"

"Twenty-two caliber, four-inch barrel, pistol target ammo. Government issue, used in Vietnam. It's considered a pro gun for assassins. Minimal power."

Greta understood right away. The less force to propel the bullets right through the body, the greater the potential for internal damage. "In other words, Molly didn't stand a chance."

"He wasn't counting on you having one, either." Schuyler took the coffee Greta held out to him. "Like I told you, we need you to hang in here for another round—the Two-Four was already notified."

"I figured." Seeing Quill might be the last thing she wanted to do, but Internal Affairs was hardly a pleasant alternative.

CHAPTER **FIFTEEN**

When she was done, Greta counted up the big black trash bags. To her surprise, there were eleven, and every one full.

Not until the afternoon of her second day home had she been given the green light to tackle the aftermath in her apartment.

Since the night of the shooting, she'd come to believe that the mess was an attempt by VX to make an execution look like a robbery gone awry. Molly, the only loss that mattered to Greta, was nothing more than collateral damage to him. What little jewelry she owned was still concealed in the toes of a pair of retired running shoes, with sports socks stuffed in as camouflage. Her five-year-old laptop was smashed, but it had been developing a habit of slowing down and shutting itself off, tech-Alzheimer's disease. As for the rest, all the senseless strewing, slashing, and smashing gave her an excuse to finally confront a mound of tired clothes and objects that no longer held any particular value or meaning. All of it seemed to belong to some other Greta Strasser.

When she walked into the Two-Four the next morning, the desk sergeant gestured that she was to report directly to Quill's office. Greta was prepared.

She didn't knock, just walked straight in. "You want to see me?" If her tone was crisp, if she was projecting confidence, those acting classes back in her undercover days were really paying off.

"*Want* to see you?" he asked. "No, I never want to see you, except the day you walk out the front door of this house for good."

Through a thin smile, she replied, "Then I'm afraid you're going to be disappointed." Uninvited, she slid into the chair directly across from him.

In the years since their brief time as an item, he'd gained at least forty pounds, most of them from booze. His eyes appeared flatter and smaller, the light remaining in them diminished, as if sopped up by his spongy cheeks. "*I'll* be disappointed? No, I don't think so. I command this precinct, Strasser."

"I command my own self-respect," she shot back, "and I want to know why—"

Pushing back from his desk, he feigned amazement. "Did I hear you right? Did you just claim to have self-respect?"

Disregarding him, she forged ahead. "Why are you doing everything possible to keep me from performing my duty?"

"You can't do your duty if you consistently ignore the importance of—"

"What? Mindless paperwork?" To keep her rising anger from getting in the way, she hissed through clenched teeth: "Nothing is more important than getting VX off the street. My partner and I worked that case. Was I supposed to stop and ask you for permission to pursue when he was only a few feet away from me on Astor Place? That's not even taking initiative—that's just plain instinct. It's being a cop, doing my job. Being chained to a damn desk is not!"

Quill's little eyes rolled upward, as if he'd heard it all before. "We're not getting anywhere. You can go back to that same desk right now. And stay there."

"If you're so concerned about the precinct, why shut down a detective who should be out there, lowering your stats?" Before the shaky façade crumbled, she cocked her head to one side and raised her eyebrows. "Isn't that the CompStat crown all you PCs run after? 'Oh, my murders are down, my felonies are down, but how many precincts are lower than mine this year, this month?' Tell me, what's your vendetta against me accomplished, other than exporting VX to the Seven-Eight?"

That had caught Quill off guard. Now he was paying attention.

"Right now," Greta continued, "the Ninth and the Seven-Eight, besides worrying over their own numbers, are watching them go up—thanks to another PC's failure to contain a one-man crime wave in his own precinct. I didn't turn up on my own for March's Critical Mass. You assigned—"

Quill's upper lip rolled back. His neck swelled over his shirt collar. "You have no right to question any assignment I make!"

"A detective in a uniform on parade duty? You won't find a single cop, not even one of your kiss-ups, who wouldn't call that punishment. You and I both know exactly why you did it, and it wasn't over a request for some techs to check out a potential crime scene. What you're doing is counterproductive, unwarranted, and *personal*. It's also twisted—you're trying to shift the blame for what happened to your kid and your wife fourteen years ago onto me."

Quill jumped out of his chair and bounded across his office, slamming the door, which she'd intentionally left ajar. He wheeled around, snarling, "You fucking cunt! You whore! Get my family out of your damn cesspool of a mouth!"

Strangely calmed by his outrage, Greta asked, "When you come right down to it—then and now—nothing's really changed much, has it? I mean, it's still that same creepy control thing of yours—whether it was stalking me back then or doing your damnedest to squeeze me out now. All I wanted was to be rid of you—I begged you to leave me alone. I even considered filing a report, until I realized that would only turn around and bite me in the ass—like if your wife heard about it and kicked you out. If that happened, I'd never lose the nightmare standing outside my home every damn day."

"Get out!"

"I'm not going to let you grind me down for what happened to your family. You can't kick me out. You can't force me to retire. And as long as I don't break any law, you can't dictate what I can and can't do when I'm off-duty." She moved toward the door. "Don't you see where you're going? If VX succeeds on his next attempt, and I wind up dead . . . compared to you, I'll be the lucky one."

Just before Greta entered the detectives' squad room, she realized that she'd been so fixated on convincing Quill to put an end to her desk sentence, she hadn't given the slightest thought to the type of reception she'd receive from her peers.

In the process of becoming the cop who'd eliminated a member of VX's gang, she'd also alerted them that VX possessed not only the determination, but the ability to ambush any one of them at home. In the role of her teenage dog walker, they could easily substitute their own spouse, child, sister, or brother.

Kim had been the only one to contact Greta, checking to make sure that she hadn't been hurt. When he asked, "How'd they get past your Doberman?" all she could reply was, "I can't handle that yet, Russell." Neither he nor Manny Cepeda—Kim still called him his "temp" partner—was in the squad room, and she guessed they'd already left on a call.

One detective, a veteran known for being taciturn with everyone, including his own partner, leveled an appraising look at her. "Good job, Strasser," he said matter-of-factly. The rest weren't exactly holding up *Free Greta!* signs, but she received scattered thumbs-ups, two Vs-for-Victory, and a high-five. And not a single how-many-blowjobs-to-get-your-shield? look from any of Quill's boys.

Lieutenant Geracimos was on the phone, but he crooked a finger for her to come in, then motioned her to close the door. When his call ended, he said, "We're working on your loaner gun."

"Thanks."

"Your dad would be proud of you, Greta." His tone said that he was, too. But before she could get a word out, he added, "You're still assigned to your desk." Again, he pointed down toward Quill's office. This time, he added, "What an asshole."

While she was walking back to her desk, the phone rang. It was Schuyler.

"How is it, finally back at work?" he asked. "Returning hero?"

"Better than I could've hoped for, but that could change at any minute." Silence hummed on the line far too long. "Schuyler?" Greta asked.

"Yeah. Still here." More silence. "Look, I know you've been through a lot. I was thinking, maybe we could get together for a couple of drinks, maybe dinner. I don't necessarily mean tonight. When you're feeling up to it."

Closing her eyes, Greta tried to remember how long it had been since her vow to never, ever, have anything to do with another cop outside work again. If anyone seemed like the type who really meant dinner—on the first date, at least—it was Schuyler. After all, he didn't work in her precinct or squad, which was how it had gone before: jerks trying to outdo one another, lying about all the ways they'd done her, like kids trading baseball cards, gaining instant acceptance into the I-Fucked-Greta-Strasser-Club. Had Schuyler asked around and found someone whose partner's cousin said he'd slept with her? Did it change things that neither she nor Schuyler would ever see forty again? All that, plus he'd seen her at her absolute worst—soaking wet, filthy, physically exhausted, and in the collection basket of the cross-cut emotional shredder.

"Greta?" he asked.

"Let's make it a definite rain check," she said, not sure if she meant it or not. "After I've worked my way up to being better company. Thanks for the offer."

At the end of the day, Greta and Kim met at a coffee shop. She asked him to fill her in on what had been going on in the precinct, even though it ultimately didn't amount to much more than VX's obvious return from Baltimore. "No one's sighted him. No buzz about the missing member of his crew, either."

With the high level of fear that VX generated, she doubted any snitches would come forward, but she put out the word anyway. After work each day, she canvassed the neighborhood for hours, stopping people and asking questions. More people than she could count had either clammed up or cursed before they hurried away. No one had slithered out from the shadows to bargain for a favor, a twenty, or both.

Quill couldn't order her to go directly from her desk to her home, especially since home was where she'd come so close to being executed. Without Molly, there was no need to rush back to Brooklyn. Nightly, she'd wrap up her extracurricular investigation over coffee with the beat cops. Never before had she been so tuned in to the pulse of a precinct, and never before had she encountered such a wall of silence from its citizens.

CHAPTER **SIXTEEN**

Just before midnight, Greta turned onto Montgomery Place. Molly was gone, her lookout window blank. In her thoughts, Theo, with a silvery aura, glided through his own flickering black-and-white movie.

The empty spaces they'd left behind had edges sharper than broken glass.

She was halfway up the stoop, headed for the wrecked apartment that was no longer a home, when a click sounded. The bright vestibule light made her an easy target, and she lunged into the half-shadows of the stoop's side wall. She hovered on the edge of a broad stone step, her replacement Glock in both hands. Slightly crouched forward to minimize her silhouette, she kept the gun lowered between her knees while she scanned the street.

Close by and low enough for only Greta to hear, a man's voice said, "Detective Strasser, I have to speak with you." It came from a dark sedan parked directly below her, the driver's door ajar—the source of the click. A man was walking around the hood. "I have ID," he said.

"I don't care who you are or what the hell you want. It's midnight. Get back in your car and take off."

"You left work hours ago. I've been waiting here a long time. How else do you think I got such a choice parking spot, right in front of your building?" As soon as he stepped onto the sidewalk, she let him see her gun. He raised his hands and let go a "Whooooa! I'm one of the good guys!"

"Not as far as I'm concerned." A little late for a member of the press to be snooping around, unless an unfriendly snitch had pointed out some of the woollier parts of the Seven-Eight's account.

"Look, you can call Detective Schuyler to verify—I was with him all afternoon."

That helped—except it almost instantly raised the possibility of another type of threat. "Are you from IA?"

"This isn't a police matter. And that's all I'll say out here on the street." She straightened up a bit, to get a better look at him. Acknowledging her intense scrutiny, he very slowly lifted his plastic ID card to eye level, as if she had the binocular vision to read it, compare it to his face and confirm his identity.

What Greta saw was a man in a baggy dark suit, somewhere between thirty and forty, heavy stubble sprouting on his cheeks, dark circles under his eyes. He looked too worn out to make a fast move.

When he said, "Just take a look, okay?" it had the cadence and exasperation of "Who needs more grief today?"

She held out her left hand, and he trudged up the two bottom steps. Once she had the photo ID, he retreated back down to the sidewalk, purposely planting himself where she wouldn't even have to take aim to shoot him. In the photo, he looked considerably more alert. The name with the face was Thomas M. August. If the card was genuine, he worked for the FBI.

Not relinquishing her grip on her weapon for a piece of plastic, she asked, "What's this about?"

He lifted his head to the left and right, a reminder that they could be overheard. "Your intruder of last week is—was—a person of interest. The rest has to be discussed in private, not out here. Can we go upstairs?"

"Absolutely not."

"Schuyler and I went over all the crime scene reports and photos. Your apartment was thoroughly trashed. I'm sure that under normal circumstances you're fastidiously neat. So—?" He glanced up, toward Molly's window.

"Uh, uh. I've had too many visitors lately." *Why a Fed? Was VX oper-ating on a level beyond what anyone imagined?*

"Then how about my car?" he persisted.

Going for the person-of-interest carrot, she got to her feet, her gun still trained on him, and took one preliminary step down. He went di-rectly to his vehicle's front passenger side door and grabbed the handle, but she shook her head. "*You* sit there. I'll sit right behind you. I want to see your hands at all times."

He got in first, twisting around so that his hands spread over the backrest of the front seat. "Before you vaulted your way over the back-yard fences that night," he began, "your Doberman was shot right in-side your apartment's front door. Sorry for your loss—I'm a dog lover, too. And the girl who was locked in your bedroom closet—her name is Claudia Ross."

None of that information had been in the papers. And because Claudia was a minor, her name couldn't be published. Greta offered no response.

"So . . . how did you know the dead man?" Casual, as if they were swapping the names of mutual acquaintances at a dinner party.

"Know him? I never saw him before."

"Then who do you believe was responsible for your attempted murder?"

"If you really were with Schuyler, that's all on record," she shot back.

"From *you,* please, Detective."

Like someone swearing on a bible in court, she stated flatly, "My partner and I have been after the leader of a drug-trafficking gang for months—Ernest Flowers, street name, VX. The guy I shot was one of his."

"How did you determine that?"

"Physically, a head that could double as a bowling ball. Psychologically? This guy crawled out from under the same rock as VX. I also believe VX himself is the man who got away. Unfortunately, I never got a look at him. Neither did Claudia. And so far, no one's come forward to ID the dead guy. That's typical of the type of maneuver VX would—" She stopped abruptly. "You know how you look?"

With a weary half-smile, he shrugged his left shoulder up past the front seat.

"Like you know a hell of a lot more about what's going on here than I do. How about clueing me in?"

"Thought you'd never ask. The guy you shot was part of a group my team's been investigating. We were notified through his prints. Then we met in person, so to speak—at the morgue. He's our guy, all right. You were correct about no one coming forward to identify him—there hasn't been a single inquiry. That's part of the reason we've held off on the release of his name."

"I don't get it. He's your guy for *what*?"

"I couldn't tell Schuyler that, and I can't tell you. What doesn't work for us is why *you*? Why a *cop*? We've been tracking him for quite a while, and we can't come up with a reason why this guy would break into your apartment. Sorry to trash your theory, but the only sure thing is that nothing's come up to connect him to VX."

"Then who the hell is he?"

"I'm not at liberty to tell you any more. We need your help, though, to find some kind of thread . . . assuming one exists. I'm requesting that you visit our office tomorrow morning. Then we'll be able to share some sensitive information with you, and—"

"Sounds like a sensitive way to say 'Don't be late for your interrogation.'" He raised one of his exposed hands in protest, but she quickly added, "Hey, I'm almost looking forward to it. The way things are going, being cross-examined just might be the most fun I'll have in the next few months. But there's a little problem. I'm not—"

"You're under an open-ended order to remain in the Two-Four—not the precinct, the precinct *house*—during all of your shifts."

"You know that?"

"We not only know about the situation, but my boss gives you high marks for every action you've taken that's pissed off your precinct commander. Just think of him as the anti-Quill."

"That's a hell of a lot of forgiveness. Don't tell me, let me guess—does your boss also moonlight as Jesus?"

"Detective Strasser, how many cops would hop on a bicycle and chase a prick like VX through downtown traffic? Or have the guts and determination to do what you did on this block—during a storm, no less—or the smarts to figure out how to do it in the first place? You think on your feet, you're unafraid, you have a strong sense of duty. Your record in undercover was amazing. Plus, you were a first responder on 9/11."

"That's a hell of a lot of digging. If you'd gone a little deeper, you'd know that all I did was direct traffic and drive some brass around."

"You weren't on duty that day. You ran through Brooklyn and over the Brooklyn Bridge to get there."

"Nobody knows about that," she whispered.

"Maybe somebody who was running east noticed you were the only one running west."

"I was running for one person. None of that do-good stuff applies."

"Strasser, don't play armchair God. There's no ranking of selfless acts. You ran there for one man, but you hung in for three days, until you were ordered to go home. You lost Bram Archer, North Tower. You two had set the date to be married at City Hall on Friday morning, September fourteenth, 2001. Eight friends had been invited to join you at your favorite restaurant in the West Village for a wedding lunch. You were the only one who showed up. You were exhausted and filthy. You ordered Archer's favorite meal and stared at it for two hours."

Behind them, a siren raced along Prospect Park West and trailed off. A young couple, walking unsteadily, came up the block, carrying a large cardboard disc between them. It held a half-eaten birthday cake, some candles still stuck in the frosting. August turned when he heard their slurred singing, and they watched as the pair repeatedly pretended to almost trip and drop the cake. After they passed, Greta put her gun back in its holster.

"You'll never forget," he said softly, "and neither will we." After a while, he added, "You're familiar with the JTTF—the Joint Terrorism Task Force?"

"Sure, about a zillion young cops want in on that. That's you?"

"That's us. We're called 'The Front Line on Terrorism,' but that sounds like the end of a TV commercial. You'll understand more tomorrow. I'll pick you up as soon as we clear it with Quill."

"You make it sound easy. Good luck."

CHAPTER **SEVENTEEN**

"He's being a total asshole," said August.

"Like the last person who called him that, you're being kind. Didn't I warn you?"

Greta had given August her cell phone number the night before, so no one on a precinct line could listen in on their conversation. It was nearly noon, and she'd been expecting his call for hours.

"As soon as I mentioned your name, he said 'No way!' and hung up. I've been trying to call him back, but I can't get past the desk sergeant. I could get my boss to turn the screws, but if he's already making your life hell, probably not the best move."

"I'm done at four. I'll take the train," Greta volunteered.

"You know my car. I'll be at 100th and Broadway. I'll fill you in on the way."

Once they were headed downtown on the FDR Drive, August asked Greta what she knew about the JTTF.

"I think it started here in New York—half FBI agents and half NYPD detectives. Makes you think of oil and water."

"Right—ten each, back in 1980. The basic concept is that local cops and nearly forty government agencies can be tapped for the JTTF. We're nearly four thousand strong and operate in a hundred cities. Fifty-six field offices, run by a Special Agent in Charge—a SAC. In New York, L.A., and D.C., there's another layer on top—Assistant Director in Charge. But he's given my direct boss, SAC Folkestone, complete autonomy on our assignments so far."

At Federal Plaza, he took her up to a conference room. Two men walked in immediately after them, carrying folders. Right from the start, Greta got the vibe that August was a person who'd not only earned their respect, but was also (though he certainly hadn't described himself as such) their team leader. First to be introduced was Agent Dell Rice. If his size hadn't been the first thing she noticed—he was tall and wide, big enough for a college linebacker, not quite a pro—it would have been his head. An African-American, Rice's was shaved and shiny. Despite the immaculate white shirt and conservative tie, that head instantly summoned up VX—had August quoted her comments of the night before verbatim? But a smiling Rice gave her hand a strong, friendly shake, leaving all bones intact. The other agent, Eric Brauner, was a dour six-footer with close-cropped hair and the military bearing to go with it. Only slightly less uptight than he appeared, he indicated a sideboard with coffee and sodas, and brought her a Coke.

As soon as they were seated, August passed Greta a folder of her own. Inside, a prison photo of the man she'd shot was right on top.

"Our subject," August began, "is a homegrown Brooklyn scumbag who spent more than half of his short time on earth as a guest of the New York State Department of Corrections. As I've already told you, Detective, the first thing we verified was whether he and VX or any of VX's gang could've met in the can. No paths crossed."

Uncomfortable in every way, Greta shifted in her chair before looking Rice straight in the eye. "The way I linked this guy to VX sounds like classic racial profiling. But VX has plenty of motive for going after me. This guy—he apparently took a lot of time and trouble tracking me down and planning the break-in, so it's hard to believe he had me mixed up with someone else." She turned to August. "Have we finally gotten to the point where I find out who the hell he is?"

"Born in seventy-nine, named Parlance Lewis," August replied. "Put away in juvie when he was fourteen. Shot another kid in the head."

Greta leaned forward. "Fourteen? You're talking about sealed records."

"Well, sometimes we peek. Anyhow, not even a month after he was no longer a youthful offender, he was sent to a real prison after he was caught hijacking a truck that'd already been hijacked. You can imagine how unpopular that made him with the mob. But as his record bears out, he turned out to be much better at killing than at stealing. You see, until he met you, Lewis was lucky. Never got a single murder indictment—and by the way, there were *three* separate cases—which we believe points to a strong possibility he got away with even more. His rep in prison was that he was not to be messed with."

"Exactly what we're up against with VX," Greta observed grimly. "The fear factor."

"And that had to be what made him such an attractive recruit."

"Recruit for what?"

"Conversion to Islam. He was sucked in during his latest stint upstate. Parlance becomes Akbar, who, the same day he gets off the bus from Attica, reports for work at a car service. Just off Church Avenue, close to Flatbush. You familiar with the area?"

"Sure. It's lined with stores that make Kmart look like Saks Fifth Avenue. Always busy, always lots of people on the street. Very . . . international. A car service?"

"As a front, it's pretty ingenious—provides cover for more than one activity. Just for starters, they're involved in cigarette smuggling. You familiar with that?"

"Sort of. Drive far enough south to get a ridiculously low tobacco tax, drive back north and sell high. Except there's some kind of limit on how much you can bring back."

August nodded to Rice, who explained, "Three hundred cartons. Sixty thousand cigarettes. They stick on phony state and city tax stamps and discount them to lung cancer candidates—the tax here in the city is three bucks a pack. But gas, tolls, meals—even if you sleep in your car, it makes you wonder if the trip's worth it, right?" At Greta's nod, he spread his burly arms out wide. "Now imagine an entire van packed with those three-hundred-carton maximums, each bought at a different outlet. I should point out that as soon as you go to sixty thousand and one cigarettes, we're talking a federal crime."

"But that would be the ATF's department, right?" Greta asked.

"Good question," Rice replied. "Actually, I was with Alcohol, Tobacco, and Firearms before I joined the JTTF, and the answer is yes, it would be in their purview—except that this little car service does something with the profits that takes the enterprise to an entirely different level."

Greta put up a hand. This was like one of those dreams where she wound up taking the final exam in a class she'd cut all semester. "Wait for me to catch up, please. Parlance Lewis, aka Akbar . . . what's making me think wasabi, but not sushi?"

Brauner supplied the answer. "Wahabism. After crude, Saudi Arabia's runner-up export. Radical views are a big hit when it comes to prison proselytizing."

"Death to America crap?"

August looked at her approvingly. "You're not only there, you've jumped ahead several squares. The car service wires the cigarette profits overseas, to Islamic charities. And those charities front for organizations that provide food, medicine . . . and terror. It's the Marlboro Man on a camel, holding a rocket launcher. One of the biggest cigarette rings— based in Michigan—was shut down hours before it could wire Hezbollah nearly two million dollars."

"Jesus."

"Wrong religion. But that stepped it up to a Joint Terrorism Task Force investigation. What makes our friendly neighborhood car service particularly interesting is that it's like the United Way—it spreads the tobacco money around. So far, two of their favorite charities have had their assets frozen by the government. Tracking where their donations go gives a new spin to 'Charity is its own reward.'"

"Is that enough of a wash for you to let them keep on smuggling?" She took the glimmer of a smile that passed across August's face as a yes. "You said that's one of the things the car service provides cover for. What's the other?"

"You're a good listener," said August. "Eric, go ahead."

Brauner leaned forward. After Rice, his speaking style was clipped. "Dream Ride Car Service is open twenty-four/seven. It consists of the owner, a night dispatcher, and twelve to fourteen drivers, depending on the day and shift. It's a front for a sleeper cell run by the owner and manned by six of the drivers. Parlance-Akbar was the seventh. At present, only the cell guys go on the tobacco runs. We suspect that some of the others are going through a vetting process. The Dream Ride fleet consists of rusted-out sedans and vans—all clunkers. They're constantly being bought and sold."

"Amazing that any of them ever make it all the way to JFK and back," Rice interjected, "but the charm has to be that pine tree deodorizer hanging from every rearview mirror."

Without missing a beat, Brauner continued, "Their other activity is surveillance. We've been doing random checks, to get a handle on what the cell drivers watch when they're not driving south. First of all, they're selected for virtually all the calls with a Manhattan destination. After they drop off their fares, they drive to stakeout locations: the Stock Exchange, Times Square, Grand Central, Penn Station, the Brooklyn Bridge, the Metropolitan Museum. If they're not blocking traffic, the cops will let them wait for a limited time. They make them move on when their nonexistent fares don't show. We've taped them covertly making sketches, taking photos, using the stopwatch function on their Casios. TV-grade spy crap."

"Ambitious targets."

Brauner nodded. "*Extremely* ambitious, especially for these guys. But right from the start, they've been alternating them with others that don't appear to offer either a high body count or any strategic significance. Martyrdom and The Next Big One don't mesh with a one-family house in Forest Hills, a three-story building in Bensonhurst, a small apartment building on the Upper West Side, or even the Lexus dealership on Eleventh Avenue."

Suddenly, Greta shot to her feet.

"What's the matter?"

August sounded far away—a strange rushing filled her ears. "Hold on—just give me a minute," she said, holding up a hand. But far from regaining her composure, she blurted out, "They killed Theo—Theo Appel! And Mrs. Kantor! That apartment building—was it on 104th Street?"

Brauner shot a look at August. All three agents were nodding, eyes glued on Greta.

"Damn it, stop staring at me like that!" She paced back and forth behind the conference table, working it out, talking more to herself than to them. "Careful as Theo was, they still managed to track his computer. After I visited him, they followed me home, figuring he'd passed me information. No reason for them to suspect they were tailing a cop." She sat down again, and, beginning with Paulina Kantor's death, recounted all that had happened during the brief time she and Theo had been acquainted.

Some time later, a confounded August put his head in his hands. "We were each piecing together a jigsaw puzzle that'd been cut in half. You put your side together, we did ours. But neither side made sense without the other." He ran his fingers through his short dark hair. "Everything you've told us . . . it's—"

"Diabolical," Greta cut in. "Boil it down—these crazies are killing Holocaust victims to fund another attack on this country, and I'd rather slit my wrists than sit at a desk all day while they do it!"

"This didn't exactly start out as a job interview," August replied, "but you should be onboard, ASAP. If we're going to stop them, your input's essential. You should meet with my boss, SAC Folkestone, but first, I'll do my best to outline what you've told us. Dell, contact D.C. and find out who helped out Theo Appel with the software."

Greta felt her cheeks redden. "Will someone wind up in hot water for that?"

"I hope not. This is one of those cases where the ends more than justify the means." He got to his feet. "I'm on my way upstairs. Brauner will drive you home."

"That's not necessary."

"Our guys have been following you since we found out the late Akbar paid you that visit. Now that we understand the connection, your security's even more important. Don't get pissed off at me for saying this, but your desk duty made it a lot easier." With a sheepish grin, he added, "I'll call you later, right after Folkestone and I have our talk."

"Folkestone wants to meet you tomorrow," August began, "it's looking very good."

"Thanks. What about Quill?"

"We checked him out. He's an old-school Irish cop with an old-school drinking problem. According to one source, he's a distant relative of some union leader who shut down the city's entire transit system about forty years ago—a true story of misplaced authority in the hands of a megalomaniac. Apparently that gene was passed along to your precinct commander. In the old days, that helped to get up the ladder at the NYPD—a perennial drinking buddy, lots of union rah-rah, a control freak. Hey, what do we need terrorists for, when we've got pricks like that?"

"Well, that prick is my boss."

"I'll be at the Two-Four tomorrow at nine o'clock."

August called her cell right on time. "I'm just getting out of my car, so come on down from your ivory tower. He's expecting me."

"How'd you manage that?"

"The bait was you—that you're needed downtown ASAP. No details. He thinks you're in big trouble."

August, semi-neat and focused, entered the lobby area the same time as Greta. The desk sergeant shot up when they both headed for Quill's office. "Appointment," August said, without breaking stride.

After a cursory glance at August's credentials, Quill scowled up at him. He remained seated behind his desk, ignoring August's outstretched hand. "What the hell's she done now?"

"Enough to be integral to one of our ongoing investigations. Enough for the Special Agent in Charge to request her transfer to our team, effective immediately."

Through a tight, icy smile, Quill asked, "Transfer? To your 'team'? That means jackshit to me. You think you can waltz in here and take one of my detectives just on your say-so?"

"Captain, let's not beat around the bush. I know that Detective Strasser's been taken off her active cases, and assigned to desk duty—indefinitely."

"There're two good reasons for that: incompetence and poor judgment."

"Then letting her go shouldn't be much of a sacrifice for you, should it?"

"Don't get cute with me. You're talking like you have some authority in this office. You have zip."

Absorbing the punch with equanimity, August replied, "I'm not here to argue—" His torso jerked suddenly, and he reached into his jacket for a phone set to vibrate at defibrillator strength. "Excuse me, I have to take this," he muttered, after reading the caller ID. Greta saw his thumb hitting a speed-dial button.

As soon as August began speaking in muffled tones just beyond the office door, Quill leaned toward Greta. Little white specks foamed up at the corners of his mouth as he hissed, "I've tried to get rid of you, but you're worse than the clap. No other precinct wants a washed-up, can't-retire-fast-enough whore."

"Hey, you're talking about your own little club," Greta shrugged. "That's your reward for doing such a great job of bad-mouthing me all over the Department."

Before she could add that she wasn't opting to retire, he thundered at her, "You will go upstairs—and stay there! That's an order!" Suddenly, his eyes shifted behind her, toward the office door.

He had to be staring down August. Greta didn't bother to turn around, expecting him to reproach Quill, starting with you-don't-even-speak-that-way-to-a-three-year-old.

Instead, as if Quill's outburst hadn't happened, the agent spoke with newfound respect. "Captain Quill, couldn't we start over again and try to work this out?"

One glance at his shoulders, slumped with failure, made Greta want to run out of Quill's office, out of the Two-Four, out of her own life.

"Isn't there anything we can do to change your mind?" August sounded so plaintive, she couldn't bear to look at him.

"Absolutely not," said Quill. Swollen with defiance, he added, "There was never any question that I would even consider it." His eyebrows lifted slightly at August's failure to grasp that he'd been summarily dismissed.

"But it's a security—" August plodded on, making Greta squirm.

"Bullshit! Done! Don't waste another minute of my time!"

August began to beg his case yet again, but the direct-line phone on Quill's desk, the one that didn't go through the desk sergeant, jangled.

"Quill here," he said curtly. A pause, then a polite, "Yes, of course I'll hold." Putting his hand over the mouthpiece, he growled, "This is a private call." He jabbed a "Get Out" finger at the door.

Shaking his head in defeat, August turned. Greta did the same.

Behind them, his tone attentive and respectful, the PC was chirping, "Quill, sir! What can I do for—"

Even halfway to the door, Greta heard the clear burst of anger—the actual words were indistinguishable—that exploded from the phone. She glanced back in time to see the color drain from Quill's face, leaving his nose a terrible magenta against a deathlike pallor. His body had gone rigid. The fury on the other end didn't abate. Looking up as if wishing for a miracle, Quill realized that he wasn't alone, and swiftly swiveled his chair around. His turned back was no longer a sign of arrogance, but retreat.

Greta turned back to August. He winked at her. Stunned and impressed by what had turned out to be a bravura performance, she gave him a stealth thumbs-up.

The tirade came to an end, but it took a while before they heard Quill's chair creak around. "Stop!" he ordered. They kept on going until "Come back" barely squeezed out between clenched teeth.

As he turned, August reached into his jacket again. This time he withdrew folded paper and a pen. A shaken Quill watched as he strolled back and spread the paper on his desk. "What's that?" he asked, sounding as if he'd nearly been strangled.

"Oh, that's the release form," August replied breezily. "You have to sign and date it. Now." Head down, Quill complied without a word. "Thanks for your cooperation, Captain. I'd like to point out that the little box for

'Term' is checked 'indefinite.' As was Detective Strasser's desk duty." He refolded the form, pivoted on his heel, and strode toward the lobby.

Greta stared at Quill, eyes wide. She raised one hand to her mouth, as if shocked by all that had happened. Then she winked, pursed her lips, kissed her fingertips, blew the Fuck You directly at Quill, and took her time walking out of his office.

When she caught up with August in the lobby, she asked, "Who was that?"

"I don't know for sure," he shrugged. "But my bet is on the commissioner."

"Any advice?" Greta asked August. Garrett Folkestone was on his way downstairs from a meeting, and they'd just settled into the chairs facing his desk.

"Sure. Never think of yourself as an outsider—forget NYPD, FBI. Investigators like you, analysts, SWAT experts, linguists—we're all JTTF."

"That's excellent advice, Strasser." A gray pinstripe suit stopped at the side of her chair, left hand extended, the other leaning on a T-topped cane. "Gary Folkestone. Welcome."

Since he was well over six feet, she didn't get a good look at his face until she stood up herself. Momentarily confused about which hand to offer, she hesitated until he grabbed her right and shook it briskly. A thin white scar ran from his salt-and-pepper brush cut down the entire length of his right cheek. He had bright blue eyes, but she suspected that the vision in the right one had been compromised in some way connected to the scar. For a man who used a cane, his perfect bearing had to be a feat of will. He didn't seem quite old enough to be a Vietnam vet, or young enough for Desert Storm.

"Thank you," Greta replied. "I can't wait to get started."

"I understand that you were concerned yesterday about Mr. Appel's former colleagues getting into trouble . . . 'hot water,' I believe you put it. Well, it turned out that only a day before your friend was murdered, he e-mailed them some modifications he'd come up with—called them 'little tweaks to the program.' They turned out to be a major breakthrough for the group working money laundering in D.C. Pardon the pun, but it's a wash—all has been forgiven. Did you contribute to the software revisions?"

"Me? I can barely cut and paste. No, that was all Theo. My only contribution was the pattern—the city rotation—and believing in Theo Appel."

"Leave out the 'only'—thank goodness you did. And I understand you really stuck your neck out when it came to Mrs. Kantor. August, tell Strasser how much that unfortunate lady was worth."

Wondering about their source on that particular leak, like Parlance Lewis's sealed youth records, she held her tongue.

"Over a million dollars," reported August.

Like a slideshow, Mrs. Kantor's threadbare apartment, with all the blank spaces where family mementoes should have been, flashed through Greta's mind. "It's difficult to connect that to . . . to the way she was forced to live."

"I brought it up only for comparison—how much more lucrative it is for these bastards than smuggling cigarettes." Folkestone shook his head sympathetically.

Hesitantly, Greta brought up a concern triggered during her meeting with August, Rice, and Brauner: "I have a question, but I'm pretty sure that my zero security clearance will prevent you from sharing any kind of answer with me."

"Try me."

"Will your computer people be replicating what Theo turned up?"

"You sound apprehensive—why?"

"Theo obviously triggered some sort of Internet alarm. Whoever was smart enough to move all that money in such a helter-skelter blur was able to trace that alarm back to Theo's computer. What worries me is, if they discover a government agency is on to them, they might end the whole damn operation. There aren't that many weeks left before the CRT's July thirteenth deadline, so why risk getting caught when they can just walk away? If that happens, we lose them forever."

"We've had the car service under surveillance for months," said August, slowly shaking his head, "and they have yet to pick up on it."

"Of course," Greta countered, "but who's to say those guys on Church

Avenue are the ones who caught on to Theo's hacking? Sure, they're working together, but the computer geeks might not even be in this country."

"Strasser has a valid concern, Tom," said Folkestone. "And it points to Dream Ride Car Service being part of a much bigger, much more sophisticated setup than we imagined. Now those oddball, small-potato surveillances finally make sense."

August nodded. "All along, they were the ones that really mattered, while those landmark, Grand Central Station–type locations were nothing more than distractions—mixed in to keep the jihad juices flowing. The drivers—and maybe even Big T. himself—took the bait."

With a quick aside to Greta, Dell Rice explained, "Big T. is Tariq, Dream Ride's owner."

"They believe that their reconnaissance is vital, that they're laying down the groundwork for the next big attack on America," August continued. "That keeps them focused on glorious martyrdom."

"They were being played," Rice sighed, "and, consequently, so were we."

"To sum it up, someone combined a sleeper cell actively involved in a cigarette smuggling enterprise with an agenda that has them scouting for the Holocaust scam," mused Folkestone. "Quite a hybrid."

August sparked to the idea. "Keeps them busy, pays the rent, generates more of those charitable donations. By the way, Strasser, the tsunami the end of last year? All that terrible devastation? You have any idea how many charities sprang up all over the world? I'm being generous if I tag two out of three as the real deal. See how that fits the template of the Holocaust scam? The bastards we're up against feed on human misery."

"Couldn't have put it better," Folkestone said. His eyes went to a dossier in the center of his desk. Flipping to the last page, he signed it with a flourish. "I guess it's time to bury Strasser in paperwork. Why don't you get them started on it downstairs, Tom? Give us a few minutes."

When August closed the door, the SAC asked, "Strasser, do you know what a veneer is? Literally?"

An easy question, but she carefully thought out her answer before she spoke. "A very thin layer of expensive wood applied over an inferior wood. Like a veneer of mahogany over pine, or even plywood."

"Say you know a guy who always looks haggard. Sort of sloppy. Sometimes you'd swear he's a head-nod away from falling asleep. But if that same guy consistently manages to be ten steps ahead of what everybody else is thinking, what's a good way to describe him?"

"A veneer in reverse?"

"Thank you. Tom August is one of our best. Like you, he came to us as a detective, but first and foremost he was a real street cop. In his time, he was the most decorated cop ever in the city of Philadelphia. His first assignment with the JTTF was in Seattle—remember that millennium plot? And like you, he's always ready to go above and beyond the call. Which, by the way," he smiled, "we never reward with desk duty."

CHAPTER **EIGHTEEN**

"How much fun was that?" August asked, as the elevator doors closed. It was just past 10 P.M.

"Well, at least they ordered sandwiches," Greta replied. "One fundamental need fulfilled." She yawned. "It's going to be hard not to fall asleep on the subway home."

"No subways for a while. I'll drive you."

"Thanks, but how else do I get to work tomorrow?"

"That won't be a factor. We didn't have a chance to discuss that part yet."

"Oh shit! You're not going to tell me—"

"Subways and home . . . neither are advisable for now. Our team works out of a location that's not too far from the car service. After you pack up what you need, I'll drive by Dream Ride on the way . . . to orient you."

With Greta's hastily packed suitcases in the trunk, August headed for Grand Army Plaza. Even at that time of night, negotiating the five o'clock to two o'clock section of the traffic circle around the memorial arch to get onto southbound Flatbush Avenue was dicey. "Houdini must've planned this layout," August muttered, "just to make us appreciate how he always managed to escape alive."

Instead of turning chilly, the spring night remained surprisingly warm, and they both rolled down their windows. "Big T. will still be at Dream Ride," he said, angling his chin toward the time display on the dash. He's there from five-thirty a.m. to midnight, seven days a week. In between, he sleeps and watches satellite TV in a studio apartment—Al Jazeera, all the way. Anyhow, he has nine distributors for his cigarettes. The way he schedules drop-offs is pretty haphazard—he matches them up to the customer calls coming in. A cell driver drops off a trunkload of cartons, then picks up the fare. Saves on gas."

"All in Brooklyn, then?" Greta asked.

"So far as we've observed. We don't have the manpower to follow every car all the time. The exception is Fridays, when we're on Big T. like Krazy Glue. First, he brings the tobacco smuggling cash—pardon me, the charitable donations—to a halal butcher shop on Coney Island Avenue. From there, it's eventually wired to Islamabad. Next, he goes to his mosque, two blocks down. Synching this routine with prayer time—the schedule's online, like the weather forecast—we've been able to get an agent inside the butcher store shortly before T. shows up. The action's always the same: T. passes a CVS drugstore bag over the counter and says, 'Your wife left this in the car.' The butcher grunts. Some weeks, T. goes to pray several times."

"What kind of monitoring are you using?" Greta asked. They'd been driving along the eastern border of Prospect Park; when the park ended, so did the faint scent of trees and grass.

"We're tapped into their phones and car radios. Nothing to do with any of the cell drivers' surveillance has ever come through. No mention of you or Appel, either. We have a camera in a window air conditioner right across from Dream Ride, and it's surprising how few people go into the office. One of the drivers picks up T.'s meals. He calls the guy on the radio, tells him what he wants."

"So not even delivery guys?"

"Nope. We've covered all that stuff."

"Does that narrow it down to the mosque? He's meeting someone there?"

"We're guessing that his contact is one of at least a hundred-plus other guys who leave their shoes at the door." He switched on his right directional and turned onto Church Avenue. A few blocks west, he turned right again. "On the right, four doors in," he said, gliding by a storefront attached to a small garage. Two Dream Ride cars, one a faded blue and one a faded green, each at least ten years old, were parked outside.

"Even seedier than I expected," said Greta.

August made a series of turns, bringing them back for another pass. "The three-story building directly across the street—that's our air conditioner."

Greta craned her neck to look up. "Super vantage point."

Again, they drove past. "Except for bad weather or Friday and Saturday nights, there's usually a car or two hanging around waiting for calls all night. That's how they get away with such a small garage—it's a twenty-four-hour business."

"The city never sleeps," said Greta, stifling another yawn.

Within minutes, they had entered a quiet residential section, a mix of aging apartment buildings and single-family homes. August double-parked in front of a neat two-story house with a landscaped front yard and positioned an NYPD card on the dash. An alley separated the home from a small apartment building. He and Greta each took one of her bags, and she followed him down the alley. Immediately after August pressed a bell next to a solid metal door, they were buzzed in. "Sorry, it's six flights up—we have the whole top floor, but we never use the elevator. As far as the other tenants know, we're not here."

The stairway was narrow and poorly lit, and the door on each landing was padlocked. "I hope these aren't the fire stairs," said Greta.

"No, the fire stairs are wider and brighter . . . and unlocked. This passageway was intended solely for the original owner, a married man and father of five who didn't want anyone to see him sneaking up to visit his girlfriend. No one else lived on the top floor—her apartment and the three others were all connected."

"Wow, a love nest!" Greta stopped to shift her suitcase from one arm to another. "They sure don't build them like they used to."

"Every time I finally make it to the top, I swear I hear him yelling, 'Honey, I'm home!' and then collapsing. Anyway, the honey's apartment is our main work area. From there, we access the main hallway. The other apartments are for staff."

As they approached the door at the top of the stairs, it swung open.

"Hi, I'm Stan," said one of the two men at the door. "Chris and I monitor the Dream Ride surveillance. We work under threat of being sent back to Best Buy if we screw up. All right to call you Greta?"

"Sure," she replied, shaking hands.

Stan, slight of build and in his late twenties, could have passed for a mildly hyper adolescent. Chris was an African-American with hair just long enough to be braided into cornrows. Once they were inside, he told August, "Zinah's doing whatever chicks do to get set up for Greta." He took a long look at the team leader. "You driving back to Jersey tonight?"

"Right after the introductions. Kindergarten fair tomorrow, but I'll be reachable. You'll see me early afternoon."

August led Greta out into the common hallway, and knocked on the farthest apartment door, which was slightly ajar. It led directly into a living room furnished in pre-Ikea safe house mode. A woman hurried toward them from another room to the right. She was several inches shorter than Greta, at least a decade younger, and had the dark, almond-shaped eyes that peered out from chadors in news photos. That effect was pretty much canceled out by a wiry body dressed in jeans and a T-shirt.

"Welcome, Greta. I'm Zinah. Tom calls me the team's resident linguist and cultural go-to." They shook hands while she explained, "I translate radio transmissions and phone calls. My English needs lots of work, and I welcome corrections, please. We are the only two women, so I moved us into the two-bedroom apartment, if that is okay."

"Absolutely. Sorry I wasn't here to help out," said Greta.

"No problem," Zinah replied. "Tea? Or best to sleep now?"

"Thanks, but I'm pretty beat," Greta replied.

She caught Tom August looking on from the door, smiling as if he knew they'd hit it off.

Sleep came fast and deep, until a dream snapped Greta straight up in bed, her hand searching wildly for the place Bram had just been—the scent of his soap was still in the air, the warmth still lingered on her shoulder where she'd been cradled by his right arm. Of all the dreams she'd had of him in the last four years, it was the most real.

On September 11, 2001, he'd had an early meeting at his office in the World Trade Center. About seven-thirty, Greta, who had the day off, accompanied him downstairs. Ready for a run, she and Molly headed for the park, Bram for the subway. When twenty feet or so separated them, she pivoted around to glance back at him. At that exact same moment, he'd turned as well, a man in a dark gray suit and crisp white shirt. His hands went to his tie, and he pretended to adjust the knot, raising his eyebrows as if he'd never set eyes on her before, and really liked what he saw.

Later, while she was enjoying a second cup of coffee on her terrace and soaking up the late summer sun, a woman cried out sharply, either in shock or in pain. Running to the railing, Greta yelled out, "What's wrong? Who screamed?"

A female voice, not necessarily the same woman, called out, "Turn on your TV!"

They were already replaying it over and over when Greta turned to the news channel. Overwhelmed by shock, grief, outrage, she immediately grasped that thousands of people, if not already dead, were about to die. The towers had not yet fallen, nor did it occur to her that they might. Without hesitation, she hit the street and ran toward the Brooklyn Bridge, through that terrified, dust-covered army in retreat. Her mind created the bridge-precipice, and her mind told her to keep on running, right over it. By then the air was thick with the stink of a plastic pot handle melting over an open flame.

Her first assignment was moving civilians from the scene and guiding those injured or in shock toward medic stations. Obsessively, covertly, she kept phoning Bram over and over . . . even after she learned that his office was in the middle of the floors where the first plane went in. She knew the conference room had no windows. Literally, he never would have seen it coming. Figuratively, no one else had, either.

When she finally returned home, on what was to have been her wedding day, she bought a copy of *The Times* at the Grand Army Plaza newsstand. From then on, she read the paper daily, searching for understanding in black print on white paper. Even bin Laden hadn't expected the towers to fall. Now, nearly four years later, arguments still festered about the inadequacy of the towers' design, as if any architect or engineer or builder could have conceived of a plan so evil.

The next morning, viewing the surveillance tapes, Greta became acquainted with the cast of characters at Dream Ride. The cell drivers appeared to be a uniformly humorless group in their twenties, every one a serious smoker—no surprise, considering all that tax-free tobacco. Five were black-haired, with nicotine-oak complexions; all of them looked as if they shaved once a week, but never in the last day or two.

Pointing at the remaining cell driver, who was a compacted version of Parlance-Akbar, Stan said, "This guy was born in Queens, first name James, also a prison recruit. His mother's a big-hat church lady who, as they say, hath cast him out. That happened when he walked in the door and told her she was to address him as Allahrakha and that it was time she traded in the hat for a hijab."

"I never thought about a situation like that," Greta whispered. "Wow."

Chris called to her from his station, a grin spreading across his face. "Good one, isn't it, Greta? Fresh out of prison in his little crocheted beanie, and he starts right in, fresh-talking his momma? Orders her to cover up in something submissive? Give yourself a running start, stupid, you got a rolling pin aimed at your head!"

Greta reached out and high-fived him. "And don't expect anything for Christmas!" Turning back to Stan, she asked, "Are the rest from Pakistan?"

"Only two for now, besides Big T. See those two in the windbreakers? Hold on—this shot's closer." Hitting rewind, he returned to an earlier day, the same pair carrying a small stack of take-out Styrofoam clamshells into the car service office. "The one with the glasses is Guda, known here as The Cheese. His buddy is Daud—The Dud." Rolling forward, he froze a frame of two men dressed in the type of faded green jackets that were once a staple of army-navy surplus stores. "This pair is Palestinian. They don't even get along with each other. That guy's a Syrian who replaced a Saudi who left the States two months ago—forget that, it'll only confuse you."

"Too late," Greta smiled.

Besides the hidden camera aimed at Dream Ride, another had been set up across from the main entrance of the mosque T. attended. Greta noted that he always entered and exited alone, never pausing to socialize with any of the other worshipers. Not a visual standout among the rest, she initially needed help picking him out. T. was in his late thirties, medium height, his graying beard full but short, apparently self-trimmed with a pair of blunt scissors. Most often his shirt was a three-button collared knit, all buttoned up. In cooler weather, he also wore a dark sports jacket. Long hours in the office had earned him a sluggish gait and a sloping gut. His scruffiness had something belligerent about it, like a person who refuses to use deodorant. Greta was sure a Speed Stick had never found its way into T.'s medicine cabinet.

August returned while they were still reviewing mosque tapes. "The mosque is the one off-premises constant in T.'s life. We've narrowed it down as the only place where he could meet or be contacted by some kind of controller."

"You've tried getting someone inside?"

"Way back. They'll all have their heads down to the floor, praying, but as soon as a stranger walks in—you know, someone without a third cousin or a brother-in-law's brother inside—he's on their radar before they come up for air. We figure we're better off on the outside, not spooking anyone. The problem is—as you can see—it's a popular mosque, so there's usually a good crowd whenever T. attends. We try to isolate the guys whose visits line up with his, but we can't rule out anyone switching between Western and Middle Eastern clothes, changing beards, wigs, glasses—" Cutting himself off, he asked, "Hey, why am I telling this to a master of disguise?"

"And the women are separated from the men?"

"At all times. Forget a woman."

"Okay, so I'll take a crack at the tapes." She couldn't keep the resignation out of her voice.

"Look," he said, "I know we're up against the time thing. I've spoken with Folkestone. One more Friday at the mosque to identify the controller. If that doesn't happen, we're finalizing a plan that will go into effect within twenty-four hours after T. walks out of there."

"Why does that sound like you're going to pick him up?"

"We are . . . in a way."

Gesturing toward the door, she nearly pushed him out into the hall. "Do that, and the entire network will immediately cease to exist!"

"Greta, go back to your own rotation theory—the four cities. If nothing's coming up in New York for another two months or so, there's a good chance the controller's out of town, setting up the next hit in Chicago or L.A. or Miami with another cell leader . . . another T. Folkestone and I both agree that this is the optimum time."

She was shaking her head vehemently. "That doesn't make sense."

"You will love this plan. There's a one-in-a-billion guy who can make it work like a charm, and he's already on his way. You've got to trust me on this."

Greta, though tempted, found she could not stare down the weary-looking guy who'd not only rescued her from Quill, but also had instantly transformed her into a valued member of his team. Never before had she been part of a squad or special unit that operated with such evident mutual respect. She paused briefly, aware she was about to say something that, little more than a day ago, she wouldn't have dreamed possible: "Okay, I trust you."

CHAPTER **NINETEEN**

"Everyone, say hello to Harry!" August called out, ushering a new face into the surveillance room.

He'd been off-site most of the two days since his discussion with Greta about T.

The crew greeted Harry with the same friendly intros Greta had received. In return, Harry gave them each a bright smile, but not a single word in reply.

August, who'd obviously neglected to mention the newcomer was a mute, continued, "Harry will need our full cooperation all around, although he'll be working primarily with Zinah." Turning to her, he asked, "You and Stan isolated those specific conversations yesterday, right?"

"Oh, yes. Thirty-one there were," she reported, stealing a glance at Harry. Clearly, she was unsure of his role in the operation. "T. made those calls twice a month, like a working clock, second and fourth Tuesday."

Harry turned to Zinah. Keeping to a whisper, he spoke for the first time. The language was unfamiliar. Zinah's fingertips flew to her heart in surprise. Her answer, apparently in the same language, seemed tense and guarded. As if he were kindling a small fire, Harry managed to get a conversation going between them. Gradually, Zinah became animated, even laughed. Although totally clueless about the nature of their conversation, everyone listened intently. Near the end, a bitter, resigned look crossed Zinah's face, and she held up three fingers; Harry's reply was hushed and sympathetic.

When their talk ended, Zinah turned to August. "His accent!" she marveled. "You have no idea how authentic . . . it is truly amazing!"

In a distinct British accent, crisp and classy, Harry replied, "Quite reassuring, Sergeant Hafeez, to hear that from you—many thanks!"

Zinah's nod confirmed that she'd been an Army pick for the JTTF, prompting Greta to ponder what type of government entity could have a Harry to loan out. The man obviously could speak Zinah's native tongue flawlessly, although his looks bore no link to Pakistan. He wore a lightweight suit that was nearly the same pale straw shade as his straight hair. Several times since his entrance, he'd absently brushed a lock of it off his forehead, away from large, extraordinarily round gray eyes that locked, with guileless curiosity, on whatever or whoever came into range. That stare, combined with his child's smile and slight build, could be unnerving. But Greta couldn't help liking him.

"Well then, shall we begin?" he asked Tom August expectantly. "I'm rather anxious to get to work."

"That'll be great, Harry. But after such a long flight, I thought you'd like a chance to . . . you know, to get comfortable first."

Chris said, "Yeah, look around. Us guys aren't exactly GQ. I can take you right back to your apartment, if you want to change."

With another sweet smile, Harry ran his hands down his lapels. "Hey, thanks, but I'm cool with this."

Everyone in the room froze. Harry's answer had been delivered in Chris's deep, ultra-mellow voice, rippled through with the cadences of Harlem.

Stan's head snapped toward Chris. "Hey, I didn't know you can throw your voice! Awesome!" Suddenly confused, he caught himself. "Wait a minute—did you?"

In Stan's voice, Harry cut in. "Yes, *my* lips were moving! How awesome is that?"

"That, my friends," beamed August, "is a perfect demonstration of

Harry's gift. On this entire planet, there might be a hundred people with his ability to catch languages. But he's one of only four who can also mimic a voice so spot-on in any one of them."

"'Sorry, it's six flights up,'" said Harry-as-Tom, pretending to mop his brow. "'We have the whole top floor, but we never use the elevator.'"

August broke up, along with everyone else. As fascinating as she found Harry, Greta kept silent, not looking forward to her turn.

"I wish I could borrow your talent for my English," Zinah said. "Where I grew up, girls spoke only the village dialect."

"You'll get it. English is a very difficult language to master," Harry-as-Zinah consoled her.

"Wow, you do chicks, too!" exclaimed Stan.

"Pardon me, ladies," he said to Zinah and Greta in what might—or might not—have been his own voice. "Yes, Stan, I do—whenever such good fortune presents itself." Again, that beatific smile. "But right now, I'm rather keen on listening to those tapes, please."

Friday at the mosque came and went, without any progress toward identifying T.'s controller. As the surveillance team watched T. disappear out of frame, August asked, "Harry, will you be ready to launch tomorrow morning?"

Since Harry's arrival, Greta had learned that although English was Pakistan's language of business and diplomacy, Urdu was considered its lingua franca—the country had so many distinct regional languages, Pakistanis depended on it to communicate with one another. Since T. and his brother did almost as much grunting as talking in their taped conversations, Greta wondered if Harry had enough to work with to nail their local dialect. Nevertheless, he answered Tom without hesitation. "Oh, I'm quite ready. I could do it right now." It was the pleasant Brit voice, brimming with the enthusiasm of a little kid ready to hit the sidewalk on his new Christmas tricycle—the blizzard howling outside would only add to the fun.

"Great, but don't forget that it's all timed to the flight. We have to wait until tomorrow."

Later that afternoon, Greta had returned to her bedroom for a ten-minute break when her cell phone rang. Kim got right to the point: "I'm trying to go along with the communications blackout, but there's a new case linked to VX." He was almost whispering, but it turned out to be more for anger management than privacy.

Doing her own best to sound neutral, she replied, "Thanks for keeping me up to date."

"The guy VX was trying to shoot when he hit Tyrel . . . I'm sure you remember that all we had on him was that he's in the Blu-Steel Gang."

"That's changed?"

"VX's crew grabbed his girlfriend when she left school yesterday. A ninth-grader."

"So somebody spotted them?" The only upside could be that someone at last had come forward and called the cops.

"Not that we know of. Not one call came in."

"Then how do you know—?"

"Because they carved 'VX's' all over her face and breasts. And beat her and gang-banged her."

Greta held back a moan. "Are you with her? In the hospital?"

Without a reply, Russell continued, "They took their time, because it had to be after dark when they dumped her in the middle of the street, naked. A uniform car almost ran over her body. She'd already bled out . . . multiple hemorrhaging from blunt head trauma and crushing trauma in the pelvic region."

Greta felt unsteady, blind to everything but the image of the girl sprawled in the street.

Russell, sensing her agitation, resumed. "I canvassed after we finished at the scene, and I decided to wait for the Medical Examiner's report before I called you. God, Greta, it's terrible!" Greta heard him stop to take a deep breath. "Fifteen years old. Five feet and one half inch. Estimated weight, ninety-seven pounds. Consuela Cristina Martinez. Never had a chance. Her attackers all wore condoms, but they couldn't hide their DNA."

"You think VX was one of them?"

"We're assuming he returned to the city just before he tried to kill you at your place."

Greta had to scramble to set him straight. "Keep that no more than an assumption, Russell. Remember, I never got a look at that second guy."

"I hear you. But if VX isn't actually here, he's doing a good job of pulling strings from wherever he is."

"So the precinct's bracing for a response from Blu-Steel?"

"The funeral arrangements haven't been made yet. But it goes without saying it'll be closely watched."

"Russell, you and Manny have to get inside."

"He can pull that off, but I might be the only Korean there."

"She was in high school. You could be one of her teachers, or a guidance counselor. Get inside, find the boyfriend. If he's dealing drugs, he might even be the person paying for the funeral. Stick to him like glue. VX winged him in the playground and killed his girlfriend. People will console him. If anyone has a motive to find VX, it's him."

"I'll do my best."

"I know you will. I'll call you."

Just as Kim began to say good-bye, he caught himself. "As long as I broke phone silence, you should know that a Detective Schuyler from the Seven-Eight has been trying to get in touch with you. I told him you've been reassigned. Undercover. He said if you ever called me, I should remind you about a rain check. Does that make sense?"

With a shiver, Greta realized that, besides Kim, Schuyler was the only person who gave a damn about where she was and how she was. And that might be only because he wanted to get laid. "Yeah. Just tell him it didn't come with an expiration date."

On Saturday morning, a call was placed to T.'s cell phone. Chris and Stan had been able to alter the caller ID on T.'s screen to make it look like a call originating in Pakistan.

T. answered on the second ring.

Later, Harry would translate their conversation:

"What's wrong? Why are you calling?" T. immediately demanded.

Harry had whirled a finger, a signal for Chris to saturate the connection with phony static and cable hum. Harry asked, "Tariq? Is that you, Tariq?"

"Yes, yes, it's me, Rashid." His tone was a mix of worry and impatience. "Are you calling about our mother?"

Rocking one arm across his chest, Harry cued Chris to insert the clip of the wailing infant that had punctuated so many of the brothers' previous conversations. Mimicking Rashid in one of his nasty turns, Harry snapped, "Stupid woman, get that child out of here!" Expertly, Chris made the baby's cry trail off. "Yes, Tariq. Mother . . . she's very ill."

T. took a deep breath before he spoke again. "As she has been for two years, brother."

"The new doctor says now her condition is complicated by"—Harry's signal was a finger pointing up, and an ear-splitting burst of static cut off a word—"failure."

T. jumped in, "What did you say? What kind of failure? Heart? Kidney?"

As if T.'s questions hadn't come across the line, Harry-Rashid plowed ahead—"but little can be done to stop the"—three fingers up, and three electronic pings cut him off again—"home as soon as you can," he pleaded. "She cried your name, Tariq . . . and she can barely speak! I will be staying with her at the clinic, so don't call, just come!"

Harry's index finger slashed across his throat, and Chris made a hard cut to end the call.

Tense and expectant, the crew sat bolt upright. Only Harry leaned back, lazily stretching out his arms and cracking his knuckles, while a broad grin spread across his face.

Less than a minute later, an outgoing call was made on T.'s cell phone. A woman's chirpy voice answered, "Hello, Horizons East Travel Agency, Daliya speaking. May I help you plan your next trip?"

Whistles, cheers, and applause, all directed at Harry, shattered the silence in the surveillance room.

"I need a ticket to Karachi," said T.

"When will you be departing, sir?" Daliya asked.

"Right away. Today. Family emergency."

After an exasperated, how-many-times-have-I-heard-this-before sigh, she replied, "Sir, it's very late—I have to put you on hold, please, while I check with PIA to see if they have a cancellation. How many people? Round trip?"

"One person, round trip, open return—just get me on the next flight!"

Several minutes passed before Daliya returned. "Thank you for holding. They have several openings in business class. At present, three seats are available in Economy Plus."

"What? No Economy?"

"Sir, it's highly unusual that they have any Economy Plus openings at all so close to departure time—9:05 p.m., by the way. If you want me to secure a seat while one's still available, I'll need your credit card number, Mr.—?"

"No credit card. Cash. Hold one seat. I'll be there in less than five minutes."

"Please don't forget to bring a valid passport and your—"

T. clicked off and disappeared into Dream Ride's back room. A few minutes later, he made a radio call.

"That is Daud who answers," said Zinah, identifying one of the two Pakistani cell drivers. "T. asks if he dropped off the fare at Methodist Hospital. Yes. T. tells him—not so polite—to get right back." She listened, then rapidly translated, "T. tells Daud to check that he has his key, because he will lock the office. Daud has his key. T. puts him in charge of phone and radio calls until he returns."

Fifteen minutes later, Greta, wearing bronzer, a hijab, and sunglasses, was browsing in a discount store across the street from the travel agency. Perhaps fifteen minutes more passed before T. emerged from Horizons East. He paused to jam a brightly colored folder into his sportcoat's inside pocket, then hurried down the street. Greta held up a pair of toddler-sized sneakers, shook her head at the price tag, and walked out. Predictably, T. was heading straight back to Dream Ride. Greta, stopping once to glance at a display window, kept him in her sights. At the last corner, she rummaged in her purse until she received confirmation that the air conditioner–camera was once again focused on its star player.

When she returned to the sixth floor surveillance quarters, August filled her in: "The first thing he did when he got back was to radio all the drivers to let them know Daud would be temporarily in charge for about a week. Then he radioed Guda, the other Paki, to pick him up at his apartment at six-thirty and drive him to JFK."

Just after 5 P.M. August led Greta and Zinah to a small unmarked room at JFK's Terminal 4. Agents Rice and Brauner were already inside. Well-groomed as usual, they made the perpetually crumpled August appear closer than ever to the brink of exhaustion.

Two hours later, a team surveillance camera captured Big T. climbing out of a battered Dream Ride car at JFK, a carry-on bag over his shoulder. Guda popped the trunk and walked around to hand him a medium suitcase. At that moment, a man who'd just eased out of a yellow cab—Rice—stopped on the curb, barely two feet away, tinkering with a briefcase latch that refused to stay closed. His mike picked up what passed between T. and Guda. Back in the room, the sound feed was translated by Zinah:

"Guda asks, 'Not even the one that's set up for tomorrow?' T. says, 'Cancel it. No more trips south. No deliveries to the distributors. No action until I'm back in Brooklyn.' Even without translation, you surely hear how much T. resents Guda thinking he can do his job."

August gave a small sigh of relief. "Loud and clear, and that's good for us . . . very good. It gives the five of us a green light to concentrate on Big T., and while the cat's away, the guys on the sixth floor might open up a bigger window on the other cell drivers."

". . . while the cat's away?" asked Zinah.

"The mice will play," explained Greta.

Between Brauner and Rice, they received constant audio reports of T.'s progress through Terminal 4. The PIA flight would depart on time; after stopovers in Manchester and Lahore, it was scheduled to arrive in Karachi Monday at 1:05 A.M.

On his way to the security checkpoint, T. passed a bank of pay phones.

For a split second, Rice reported, he hesitated, then kept on walking. His only stop was at a shop where he bought a pack of gum. Forty-five minutes later, he finally reached the head of a long, snaking security line. He put down his carry-on and presented his papers.

The rest went according to plan:

As soon as T.'s name was entered in the system, the processing agent received a prompt to press a concealed button.

Instantly, a man in a blazer zeroed in on T. "Sir, we need to speak with you for a moment, please." With a reassuring smile, he added, "Don't worry, you have plenty of time before your flight."

Coming from out of nowhere, two more men promptly scooped up T. and his carry-on. He might as well have been pressed between two Zero King refrigerators on roller skates as they swiftly transported him away from the security checkpoint area. T. briefly attempted to resist, but failed to make either of them break stride. Still flanking T., they came to a stop before an unmarked door. From behind, another pair of men took their places, and marched T. into a darkened room. It appeared to be empty, but the moment the door closed behind them, something pierced the side of his neck. He bucked, his torso briefly arched back, and then he went limp.

"He's out," reported Brauner.

"Bring it around," instructed August.

Minutes later, Brauner opened another door at the back of the room. Two men dressed as EMS workers rolled in a gurney, lifted T. onto it, and pushed it into a waiting ambulance. Brauner and Rice followed them, closing the vehicle's doors from inside.

CHAPTER **TWENTY**

"Can't beat tailgating an ambulance," August observed, after killing the engine. They were somewhere in the vicinity of Long Island City, in a dead end section too derelict to still be called an industrial park. As they stepped out of their vehicle, he advised his passengers to take care where they walked.

The warning was an understatement. Greta and Zinah followed him around the side of an old warehouse, picking their way through an obstacle course of rusting oil drums and rotting skids overgrown with the tall, bristly weeds that thrive in toxic dirt. When they came to a dented steel door, he ran his fingers along the corrugated siding, feeling for a slot. It swallowed his key card and belched it back out. The door slid open.

Once they passed through a littered room with peeling walls, the facility no longer resembled the exterior. Tom led them down a long hallway into a room with new carpet and a half-dozen swivel bucket chairs grouped around a large monitor. On the opposite wall, a buffet table waited with sandwiches, soda, and a coffee urn.

Brauner, tie still firmly knotted, walked in and announced, "He'll be coming to in a few minutes." He flipped on the monitor and dimmed the overheads to a synthetic twilight.

Onscreen, T., his head lolling to one side, was on an uncushioned straight-backed chair. Facing him on a diagonal, a much more comfortable chair awaited his interrogator. Just out of reach, but visible to T., was his carry-on. Muffled background sound came up gradually: a mix of airport announcements, canned music, conversations that approached and trailed off, and, intermittently, the whine of jet engines.

"I almost smell the jet fuel," said Greta.

"He actually *can*," said Brauner, pointing at T.'s image. "Just a waft every now and then, through the climate control. It's going to get so sticky in there so fast, it won't take ten minutes for him to feel jet-lagged."

Rice walked into frame and took the waiting chair. "Okay, Tariq, let's get started!" he shouted, full drill instructor mode.

T.'s eyes flew open. Startled and disoriented, he tried to focus on the large black man. "What happened?" he demanded. "What did you do to me?"

"You don't remember? When security brought you to the door, you tried to run. One of them had to restrain you—no big deal. The sooner we get through, the sooner you can go on to the PIA gate. What's the purpose of your trip to Pakistan?"

"My mother . . . she is dying. If I don't make this flight, I will not see her alive."

Rice leaned back into his chair. "Why should I believe that?"

T.'s face darkened. "What kind of man would say this about his mother if it was not true?"

"You'd be surprised what I hear in here."

"That is the talk of liars. I speak the truth."

"Good, then we'll only be here a few minutes. Who helped you set up the operation with the cigarettes?"

"Cigarettes?" T.'s thick neck compressed downward, like a turtle in retreat. "I don't know what you're talking about."

Rice laughed. "Come on, Tariq! You're The Cigarette Man. Your crew's gone to the Carolinas so many times, I'll bet they're praying with a Southern accent."

"You have picked up the wrong man. I am a victim of ethnic profiling." He rattled off the two sentences as if they'd been memorized for just such an occasion.

As Brauner had said, the upsurge of heat and humidity came on fast; T. was already blinking at the sweat running into his eyes. Rice swiped at his own brow with a folded white handkerchief. But T. kept to his story, insisting that all he did was manage a car service. Rice leaned on him, peppering his questions with warnings: his PIA flight was boarding; its final call was being announced; he had the authority to hold the plane on the runway.

T. parroted back his ethnic profiling mantra. He checked his watch when it pinged the hour at 9:00 P.M., five minutes before takeoff—the actual time was nearly midnight. During the following fifteen minutes, he kept glancing at his wrist. When the next jet on the soundtrack roared by—signaling his last chance to get out of the country—he entered an even more resistant phase.

"T.'s tougher than I gave him credit for," said Tom after several hours. "Rice is good, but our boy Tariq is definitely up on his interrogation technique. We'll put it to the test when he's introduced to Stanton."

Two guards came onscreen. They cuffed T.'s hands behind his back and pulled a hood over his head. The monitor went black, then T. appeared again as he was prodded forward into a cramped, harshly lit room. As soon as its chill closed in around him—the cell's temperature was about fifty degrees lower than the sham airport—he began to shiver uncontrollably. The cuffs, his watch, and his clothes were removed.

"Like a manatee, but hairy," observed August. "A reminder to spend my next day off at the gym."

Zinah's head was lowered, but Greta didn't look away from the bloated man responsible for Theo Appel's murder.

Stanton, the JTTF interrogator, stood by while T. was pushed down onto a chair bolted to the floor. Made of metal, the chair itself was refrigerated; since it didn't melt, it was worse than sitting on an iceberg.

Brauner groaned. "That dude is shriveled for life."

T.'s wrists and ankles were secured in cuffs attached to the chair's arms and legs. At the interrogator's nod, the guards exited, and the door clicked shut after them. Stanton remained still, waiting for T. to move his head under the hood, trying to sense if he was all alone in Antarctica. His own body was insulated by fleece—at least two layers were visible—and boots; a black ski mask protected his face from the cold.

"Nice touch, that mask," said Greta. "T. will think he's among friends."

One at a time, T. tested his restraints, flexed his fingers, tried to stamp his feet. At the sound of Stanton's voice, he went rigid.

"I understand you just missed your flight," Stanton said. "The rest of what you'll be missing is all up to you." He pulled off T.'s hood.

Tariq kept his head down, refusing to show any curiosity about his interrogator.

After a long, rigorous session of questions, threats, and accusations, Stanton had nothing. He took a step back and summed up: "It doesn't matter whether you talk or not, Tariq. We've been onto your cigarette racket long enough to lock you up for life. Smuggling across state lines to avoid the payment of taxes . . . do a Federal crime, you get Federal time. Your drivers will be prosecuted. Your distributors, too."

At that, Tariq's head snapped up.

"And there's that other snag you ran into with those cigarettes. The problem of where you sent all that illegal cash. The charities you contributed to . . . they're nothing but fronts for terrorist organizations."

In a voice thinned by the cold, Tariq spoke for the first time. "Charity is one of the five pillars of Islam. America promises religious freedom. Is that another American lie?"

Stanton hesitated before he took the bait, but at last he had T. engaged. "Religious freedom? The countries your donations go to will throw your ass in jail if you even *think* about any other religion. Or if you don't practice that religion exactly the way they prescribe."

"I am devout. So that is no matter to me."

"It matters to us. Because every one of the charities you support," Stanton went on, "buys a rocket launcher for every dish of rice it doles out to the poor, a Kalashnikov for every bandage it sticks on in a clinic. They operate madrassas where kids learn to hate anyone who isn't their particular brand of Islam. Then those kids are shipped off to training camps where fourteen-year-olds are taught how to blow themselves up and take along as many people as possible."

"Jihad is one of the five pillars of Islam. America promises religious freedom."

"Suicide bombers kill innocent people. How does that tie in with religion?"

"If they are truly innocent, they will become martyrs."

"Too bad they don't get the chance to decide for themselves if they prefer that to staying alive. But I'm not here to argue religion with you, Tariq. The truth is, our interest in you isn't even all that strong. I don't want you to get the idea that you're the only illegal we've got under investigation for smuggling cigarettes and sending the profits to terrorists. The only thing in your favor is that not one of those clowns over at that crapola car service could run it. Without you in charge, the whole operation falls apart. The smuggling stops. The donations stop. So . . . maybe if we deport you on the next PIA flight, and you get home in time to see your mother—that could be a good swap."

"What do you mean, *swap*?"

"An even exchange. We swap you an easy way out for one small piece of information. It's something we're on the brink of finding out anyway, just like we found out about the cigarettes and the charities."

T.'s thick neck braced for whatever was coming with the turtle-into-shell push.

"Tell us who your controller is."

"Controller? I act independently. Always on my own."

"Come on, Tariq! The name of the guy who passes you those surveillance requests at the mosque."

Tariq hissed, "You dared to follow me into the—"

"We know that's where you're getting your assignments."

"Assignments? I run a car service!"

"Who sent your cell after the old gent who lived on West End Avenue? Who gave you the order to toss him out a window?"

"You think we all look alike! You mistake me for someone else who—"

"Don't waste my time!" Stanton barked. "What about your driver, Parlance Lewis? Who gave you the order to send him after the old man's friend—a woman who out-shot him before he could execute her?"

"Lewis? I hired him as a favor, as a fellow Muslim. The man was an American criminal before he came to me! That was nothing to do with me!"

"Take the swap, Tariq—it's a one-time, extremely limited offer. Otherwise, you all go down the toilet. Lewis will look lucky compared to you."

Tariq retreated farther into himself, packed down solid as a brick—the human equivalent of an overstuffed trash compactor. Eyes shut tight, he began murmuring.

"God is great," Zinah translated.

"You can be on the plane leaving tonight, Tariq," Stanton urged. "Everyone in Pakistan thinks you're in Brooklyn. Everyone in Brooklyn thinks you're in Pakistan. No one will ever know."

"There is no God but God," Zinah continued.

"That's okay, Zinah," said August, "I'm familiar with the rest." Pushing a button, he lit a faint light behind T.'s head.

Stanton, still questioning T. over his prayers, said, "You've got ten minutes to think about it." T. continued to pray, not moving even after his interrogator withdrew.

When Stanton joined the group in the viewing room, they could feel the cold rolling off his body. Impatiently, he ripped off the ski mask.

"How do you take your coffee?" August asked over his shoulder. He was at the urn, filling up a cup.

"Light, two sugars, thanks." Stanton's cheeks were a fiery red with what had to be a combination of exasperation and the meat locker temperature. His face, with soft brown eyes and a small, vulnerable mouth, had none of the sharp edges Greta had expected. When August handed him the cup, he warmed his hands around it before he took a sip.

"We've got one hardcore son of a bitch in there," August said to him.

After downing the rest of his coffee, Stanton asked, "How long do you think it's been since he slept?"

"Not long enough," August said grimly.

T., standing, was kept awake with bright lights, bursts of stadium-level amplification, and too few calories to take the edge off his hunger. Every time his legs buckled, a guard slid a baton across the backs of his knees, a reminder to straighten up.

The core team remained onsite, regrouping for the interrogations. Stanton alternated with Kress, whose left outer ear was missing. While she was watching him on the monitor, wondering what he did to hold up his glasses (everyone needed sunglasses now and then), he pulled a pearl-handled knife with a wide blade from his jacket. He'd just asked T. his fifth or sixth question, and while he waited for yet another answer that never came, demonstrated how well-honed it was. The blade flashed as he cut the newspaper he'd brought along into linked shapes—just like paper dolls, except he produced little chorus lines of .38s, hand grenades, and tanks. Every now and then, he held the blade across T.'s throat. Or just behind his left ear. As usual, T. prayed.

When the entire team regrouped, August requested that Stanton ratchet it up.

T. sputtered to the surface, gasping, "Bush . . . is my controller! Every week . . . he comes to my mosque!"

Spitting out water, T. switched from English. "He thanks the interrogator for putting him on the path to Paradise," translated Zinah.

Stanton yelled in T.'s ear, "What's he look like? Where's he from? What's he wear? Does he show up every Friday? Where's the next murder taking place?"

"Allahu Akbar!" was the reply Zinah didn't have to translate.

Rapid fire, Stanton shouted, "I quote the Attorney General of the United States: 'There is no distinction between those who carry out terrorist attacks and those who knowingly finance terrorist attacks.' You are a fucking terrorist, Tariq, and you will give me his fucking name!"

As T. prayed on, Tom got to his feet. "I've got to call in," he said, "I'll be right outside."

Brauner and Rice exited at the same time, answering an urgent request from another JTTF team for backup. Zinah and Greta were left alone, facing the monitor. Greta turned her head slightly and studied Zinah's profile, statue-still in the shadowy light.

Though always helpful, Zinah rarely volunteered an opinion or asked questions. Constantly on alert, never quite relaxed, she was on a scale somewhere between shy and introverted. In the team dynamic, Greta guessed, Zinah made her appear far more outgoing than her own inclination for reticence allowed—not a comfortable fit, since being one of the boys had never been her style. Neither, for that matter, was female bonding—being the only women on the team didn't make for automatic sisterhood.

"You are looking at me," whispered Zinah without turning. "He is praying still. You have a question?"

After a moment's hesitation, Greta replied, "It's not any of my business. I was wondering about how . . . your reaction to . . ."

"Just because that piece of shit and I come from the same part of the world means nothing to me," Zinah whispered. "I know that people in this country group him and me together in their minds. That is wrong. I hate this Tariq. I hate him almost as much as I hate my husband. My ex, as you say here."

"I have one of those," said Greta, unable to suppress a smile.

"I will tell you my story someday, how I became an American soldier. Yours, Greta Strasser, I cannot guess. I am learning much working with you. Much that I like."

"And more that you don't?"

"Oh, no!" said Zinah emphatically. She turned, long enough to say, "Just not for me. Or maybe . . . that I am not ready for."

"What's he saying?" asked August, rejoining them.

"He prays," Zinah answered, "but each time, he leaves off more."

August pressed the control for the signal light in the interrogation room. Stanton waited while the guard resecured T. in the chair. His eyes, rimmed by dark circles, were hard and triumphant.

Greta slumped back against her chair. T.'s controller was still on the loose, orchestrating another murder in another city. When Stanton reentered, she asked, "Any sign that he's softening up?"

"That's being kind," he answered matter-of-factly.

"Your thoughts, Greta?" August asked.

"I've done some interrogation on the job. At this point, I don't think it'd hurt if I gave T. a try."

"A mere woman, trying to intimidate him? Sure, why not?" Stanton warmed to the suggestion.

"What if he recognizes you?" Tom cautioned. "What if T. was the second man in your apartment?"

"It was too dark to see me, and the Seven-Eight kept my photo out of the papers. On the other hand, if he does recognize me," she grinned, "shouldn't he be scared shitless?"

Standing before the door of T.'s cell, Greta took a deep, steadying breath. The most effective way to play it, she'd decided, was to build on that extrovert who materialized by default when Zinah was present. Once in, she wasted no time invading T.'s space, forcing him to look up like a supplicant. The relentless questioning had depleted him. Even so, when he saw a woman interrogator, his anger visibly spiked—he'd already gone through hostility, arrogance, defiance. T. now radiated contempt.

"Shame! You have no modesty!" he protested.

"I'm not the one who's naked," she snapped back. The room had a small table and a chair. She perched herself on the edge of the table. "By the way, there's one thing no one else asked you about, Tariq—that passport of yours, and your visa. The work on them isn't even third rate. Guess your mujahideen figured they'd get you into America, and that was that. And here you are, left twisting in the wind. They didn't expect that you'd be such a good son. That's sad, about your mom. Safia, right?"

"Do not dare speak her name!"

"Right. A man has only one mother, even if she is a woman." Greta crossed her legs, flexing up one foot, so that the sole of her shoe was close to T.'s face.

"How dare you show the bottom of your shoe!"

Greta turned her ankle, as if checking to see if she'd stepped in something, shrugged, and returned it to its former position. T.'s lips immediately drew back in disgust. "What the hell's the matter?" she demanded. *Thank you, Zinah!*

"That is a sign of disrespect."

"Disrespect? After all they've put you through, *I'm* the one who gets the 'disrespect' rap?" Greta shook her head in disbelief. "For a *shoe*? How do you figure you deserve respect from anyone? Your whole life is one uninterrupted pigfest of cheating, stealing, lying, and murder! And whenever you're not doing it yourself, you're clearing the way for others to do it for you!" Bending forward, she added in a low voice, "You know what, Tariq? It's too bad I don't have shit on my shoe—there's nothing I'd rather do than rub your face in it!"

T. lurched against his restraints, desperate to strike at her. "Whore! American whore!" he screamed out.

Greta made a point of looking down and scrutinizing her black pants suit. "Is this what hookers wear in Pakistan? Would it get me stoned?"

"May God grant me the chance to throw stones at you until my arm aches!"

"So you think you're the righteous one here, Tariq? Have you ever counted up all the old people you've killed, all the murders you've set up? The victims are about the same age as your mother. Close your eyes, Tariq, and picture them . . . but with her face!"

"You will burn in hell for speaking of her like that, you—" Confronted by Greta's unflinching stare, he caught himself, as if his scorn had abruptly shifted toward suspicion.

Greta didn't give the sudden silence any time to hang between them. "The man you and your thugs pushed out of a window was my friend. He was a good man, who died trying to help other people who'd survived the Holocaust, just the way he did."

"The Holocaust?" For the first time, T. smiled. "That story the Jews invented to justify Israel?"

Flattening her palms on the table to brace herself, Greta leaned back, then pushed the sole of her shoe into T.'s face, hard enough to make his head snap back.

"So much for the feminine touch," said August. They were all back in the viewing room.

"I do not think he wants to date you," Zinah observed.

Kress, whose knife had just crafted a row of M16s, chuckled softly.

After a long silence, Greta spoke up. "Tom, do we have a little more in the budget?"

"Tell me what you need."

On his next go-round, Kress, edgier than ever with T., repeatedly brandished his knife or held its tip close to the outer corner of T.'s eye.

T. arched his neck back, away from the blade. "You can't keep me here forever," he rasped. "By now, people will know I'm missing . . . they'll find out I wasn't on that plane. Inquiries . . . will be made."

"People? What people?" Kress hissed.

T.'s tongue flicked over his lips. Of all his inquisitors, he was most wary of Kress. "People here . . . and in Pakistan. They will demand action."

"Wow. I'm gonna piss my pants." Kress turned, tossed his knife onto the table, and strode to the door. He spoke into the microphone just under its small window. "Okay, bring it in—that machine we just got today."

T. tensed, not ready to face an ingenious new device he no longer had the strength to resist. When two guards walked in, his eyes darted from one to the other, baffled: both were empty-handed. One walked behind T. Nodding at Kress, the other reached inside his jacket pocket, handed him a mini-cassette recorder, and took a step back.

T.'s relief was short-lived.

Kress held the recorder an inch from T.'s ear. "Okay, listen to this." He pressed PLAY, and Harry-as-Daud filled the room. The sound was surprisingly strong, and had to be loud as a jackhammer so close to T.'s eardrum. "When are you coming back to Brooklyn? Which flight?"

The response from Harry-as-T, interrupted by bursts of static and patches of dead air: "My mother . . . close to death . . . the funeral . . . settling affairs . . . then a trip to the Northwest Territories . . ."

T.'s eyes widened in disbelief.

"I won't know until . . . maybe two weeks . . . but—" The clip ended with a click.

"See?" smiled Kress. "We can keep you here as long as we like. Nobody's worried about you, Tariq."

"Who was that imposter? How did you make it sound like a call from—"

"Pakistan. Exactly! Daud was convinced it was you. So was Guda."

"Those fools! I never spoke those words!" screamed T., slamming his fist into the armrest as hard as he could with his arm tethered.

"Come on! Who the hell can sound exactly like you? And in Pakistani, no less, or whatever language you speak in. No one in the world is that good." Kress sat down at the table and tilted the chair back—the champ, the guy who'd just scored the big breakthrough.

"What did you do to me to make me say that? When did you—?" T. cut his question short and immediately shrank into himself.

Greta barged into the room so fast, the guard who'd delivered the recorder barely had time to get out of her way. "The question isn't when or how," she said. "It's what else we were able to get out of you. You did an amazing job of incriminating yourself."

Doubt briefly clouded T.'s face, but her attitude was too smug to resist. "Again they send in their oldest whore," he taunted, "desperate because they have nothing on me or my people."

"Nothing? I'd say we've got you nailed, Pigface!"

"Filthy stupid slut! Even a leper wouldn't have you! Get out of here with your pitiful lies!"

"You're in no position to talk to me like that!" Greta was steadily advancing on T. "Especially now that we know what your travel plans will be after you put your mother in the ground! I'd say her death has made it pretty convenient for you—great timing for that little side-trip to the mountains! Right on the border between Pakistan and Afghanistan, where cocksuckers like you keep moving bin Laden from cave to cave!" Leaning down, close to T.'s face, she snarled, "When your people saw how he murdered three thousand innocent people, they danced in the streets!"

T.'s eyes were brighter than they'd been for days. He aimed his words up at her, perfectly aimed bullets. "Yes! They danced, they sang, they passed out sweets . . . to honor the glorious victory!"

Like a furnace, Greta's face and chest were sending out red-hot waves of anger. T. flinched when Greta suddenly straightened and lifted her knee. Instead of the kick he expected, she pulled off her shoe. Unable to shield his head, he wrenched it from side to side, raging at the ultimate counter-insult: Greta, repeatedly walloping him in the head with the sole of her black leather pump.

Either one of the guards or Kress said, "Hey, you better stop—"

Dropping her shoe, Greta put up a hand, fingers splayed, and backed off. It only took a couple of steps to hobble backward to the table. Reaching behind her back, her hand closed over Kress's knife. Then, before anyone could anticipate it, she did a one-shoed, running lunge at T. With all her might, she plunged the knife into his gut, burying it underneath his overhanging belly fold of fat. Their eyes locked: hers wild, T.'s full of horror as she lifted up on the hilt.

T. looked down in disbelief. Greta was twisting out the knife. In a gush, blood spurted from his stomach. His body went rigid. The knife in her hand, wet with blood, was about to go in again.

"Stop her!" someone screamed.

The guards rushed her, tackled her, forced her to the floor.

Kress was screaming, "Get a doctor, get help in here quick!"

People T. had never seen before were storming the room. One man in a crumpled suit, yelled, "Why'd I ever let you go with this? Damn it, this was our last chance!"

T.'s body was closing down, his eyes unable to focus.

"Can you still hear, Tariq?" The woman could barely choke out her words from the two-guard press. "Killing you was *my* jihad, you scumbag!"

CHAPTER **TWENTY-ONE**

First, T. heard birdsong, then water—not a running tap, but a lazy gurgling combined with the occasional splatter, just like the music of the ancient fountain at the center of his native village. A wonderful perfume filled the air—a puzzlement, but one he brushed aside. For now, he was in a state of hazy, floating bliss . . . absolutely relaxed, truly joyful. But hadn't he just—?

Soft and low, a woman murmured, "You honor us with your presence, Tariq."

His eyes fluttered open; shining doe eyes were gazing back over a veil. She wore a white chador of a fine, gauzy fabric, and gracefully lowered herself onto a plump silk pillow at his feet. The pillow itself was on a rug of extraordinary quality, its pattern a swirling field of flowers, its dimensions so vast, he could not see the medallion at its center. Instead of the dreadful chair he'd been shackled to, T. found himself on a cushioned throne—jewels, not restraints, were embedded in the borders of the armrests. More pillows were scattered about, in peacock colors of turquoise and rose and purple. Each one was occupied by a reclining woman in a similar pale, gossamer chador. He imagined how beautiful they all must be, and he felt himself swell with desire. Urgently, he glanced down—he had been forced to remain naked for days—to his relief, he was in a robe of magenta silk, his feet in matching velvet slippers dotted with pearls.

Suddenly, another woman appeared—quite incredibly, she glided down before his throne—but from where? Looking up, he saw a pleated silk dome, like a great caliph's pleasure tent. She held a golden tray covered with fruit arranged like an overflowing cornucopia. "For you, defender of Islam," the first woman sweetly crooned to T. "Fruits of all the seasons, fruits of every scattered region, unblemished and perfectly ripe."

Two more enchanting creatures drifted toward him out of thin air. The one on his left offered him kabobs on silver skewers wrapped in a giant green leaf, presented as if they were a bouquet.

"Chicken?" he found himself asking aloud.

"Lamb," she smiled, as if she knew that lamb was his favorite.

From his right, he was handed a cup encrusted with aquamarines and rubies. Tears filled his eyes as he recognized the milky pink color and the scent—cardamom and pistachio—of Kashmiri chai. In two gulps, he drank the tea down, and waited while the bearer refilled his cup from an embossed silver beaker. The woman at his feet held up an enameled plate piled with both *sheermal* and *taftan*.

"Those breads are served at weddings. The tea as well," said T. "Whose fine home is this, and who is to be married?"

"Why none other than you, brave and glorious martyr," said the woman, lowering her eyes. "To all of us! We are all your brides, may it please you . . . I hope to be your first."

"Sure, that's okay," said T., distracted. He craned his neck around. So many women . . . if he counted, would there be seventy-two? Was it a dream? Could it be? Had he truly made it to Paradise?

T. twisted to one side on the throne, away from her eyes. Discreetly, he loosened the sash of his robe and parted the heavy silk. He felt under his belly, where that vicious woman, that ungodly creature, had stabbed him so brutally. No blood, no pain . . . praise God, not even a scar! Angling his head, he lifted the heavy fold of his stomach and examined himself: Sure enough, his wound had miraculously healed! And right under his nose, saluting him like an upheld lance, was his zealot of a penis. He felt a spontaneous smile spread over his entire face. No wonder he felt so elated . . . he'd just taken his own Dream Ride . . . at the wheel of the heavenly equivalent of a brand-new Cadillac!

When he turned back, his Number One Virgin said in a low voice, "Do not be alarmed, noble bridegroom. It is not mere legend that in Paradise you will have the virility of at least one hundred mortal men. Forgive my boldness, but I have been instructed to warn you that your pleasure might be so great . . . there is a possibility you might faint."

Trying not to look around a second time, T. asked, "Besides you, is there any order to follow among the virgins?"

"Oh, not at all. And that was only my own humble desire, which I too boldly spoke aloud. Choose any one of my virgin sisters, whomsoever, whenever you are so inclined. Our virginity will be restored anew each time, a rose that bursts into bloom and then once again becomes a rosebud."

"With no memory of . . . ?"

"However much you wish—or none at all. Words are not necessary. Simply think your desire. Either way, our bodies will perpetually freshen. Ours is the sweet fragrance in the air."

Taking a deep breath, T. gazed around at the waiting brides. Some were still—the most modest brides, perhaps?—while others slowly waved huge plumed fans back and forth over their bodies.

"But first, so we may worship you to the greatest degree possible," his first bride continued, "we beg to hear what great feats you performed on earth in the name of Allah, to gain such an esteemed place in Paradise."

"Yes, yes, noble husband-martyr, how we long to learn of those deeds that will live forever," sang a seventy-two-voice chorus.

T. was so euphoric, he could hardly refuse. His erection was persistent, but he reminded himself that instead of all the time in the world, he now had all the time in Eternity, which was shaping up to be far better than any mortal could dream of.

He sipped his tea, took a slice of sheermal, helped himself to a kabob, and eased back. The instant his spine touched the throne's backrest, another bride-to-be flew to his side with a matching footrest. His mouth full, he lifted his feet and grunted when she positioned it in just the right spot. Getting the hang of it, he swallowed, snapped his fingers, and said, "More tea." The goblet was refilled immediately. In between sips, T. mused,

"Now I comprehend why a martyr in Paradise experiences thirst and hunger . . . so he can be rewarded with all that he wishes from God's bountiful table."

Content, he favored them with a history of his great endeavors: "In 1998, I was sent from a training camp in Afghanistan to Brooklyn, in the Land of the Great Satan—"

At that, many of the virgins made horrified little clicking sounds, many shaking their heads in a show of sympathy.

"—yes, a shameless hell on earth," T. agreed. "In advance, I'd been instructed to pray at a designated mosque, where I would be approached and given instructions. The man who tapped my shoulder was wise in all the ways of the infidels, but he is a true lion of Allah."

The chorus of virgins chanted, "God is great."

"This man and the imam had great respect for one another. After prayers, we were allowed to meet in the mosque's private office to conduct our business. After several months, my American contact—"

One of his brides-to-be gasped, "The imam trusted an American?"

"Yes, but not born in the sewer that is America. However, any stranger observing him would never guess that. Soon he arranged a job for me, driving a car for a service. When I proved I was a capable person and familiar with Western ways, he loaned me money and guided me in setting up a car service of my own. I needed drivers, and he sent men I could rely on until I was ready to recruit drivers myself. Gradually, I built up a cell. Over time, once he was convinced I was too strong to be deceived by our enemies in any way, he taught me how to take a fortune from the American government, smuggling cigarettes."

A collective "Ahhhh!" praised his endeavor.

"After I paid back my debt to him, he showed me how to send charity that would support the jihad against the West. Do you understand this?"

Once again, seventy-two sweet virgin voices intoned, "Yes! Yes! God is great!"

"Your mentor taught you well of their evil ways," said his number-one wife, "and this knowledge was a sword to smite them. Does he live in a great palace in this place of Brooklyn?"

"It was not revealed to me where he lives. Surely not in Brooklyn, because there they do not speak as he does. His tongue was smooth, like the people who report the lies on American radio and television."

"Glorious martyr, we do not know how such a devil would look," a timid voice beseeched.

"Smooth liars, with no stop to their false jackal smiles. Like them, my contact is a handsome man, still with a fine head of wavy dark hair in his fourth decade, neat, well groomed . . . but not in Satan's business suit and tie. Important as he is, what he wears differs little from the other men at the mosque—a modesty that is to be admired."

"Did he deceive our enemies with an American name?" asked a more sultry voice.

"I never learned his name—it was not for me to ask. It was enough that we were brothers in our cause. But I will add that it was easy to tell he was educated in America. Surely he had a university degree. Bright and quick enough to be a success at whatever he chose to do." T. stopped and looked around. "Where is that fruit?" Instantly, he was presented with the platter. His hand roamed over several pieces before he grabbed a cluster of grapes. Holding it aloft, he twirled it by the stem and pulled off grapes one by one with his teeth, aware that his entourage was waiting breathlessly. When he'd had his fill, he continued, "One Friday a year ago, when we were alone in the imam's office, my contact pulled a folder out from under his shirt. My hard work was rewarded with another mission."

A flurry of excited gasps ran through Paradise.

"I was given a dossier of three people, all Jews."

The last word was met by angry ululation.

"My cell was assigned to shadow them all, so my contact could evaluate which of them was to be killed."

"Why not kill all three Jews?" one of the brides behind him suggested.

"Some presented too many obstacles," T. explained patiently. "It was important to select the Jew who presented the least."

"Praise God, how many did you send straight to hell?" asked another awestruck virgin.

"My mission was only to pave the way. Another of the faithful put their miserable lives to an end."

"Upon our husband's command the Jews were beheaded!" an enthusiastic virgin cried out.

"How those died, I do not know," said T. He concentrated on smoothing out his robe, not anticipating that would bring his persistent erection into view. Busily, he gathered it into folds again. "But my role was crucial to the Zionists' extermination. All went along quite smoothly . . . until my contact was informed of a possible intrusion. He quickly traced it to a Jew of particularly evil genius, who was close to unraveling and exposing the entire plan. That Jew I dispatched my men to kill."

"And thus you saved the holy mission!" chanted the seventy-two.

"I died defending its secrets with my life. I gave the Americans nothing! They tortured me, tried to humiliate me, but my faith never wavered! I betrayed no one to them! They are dogs who do not understand how a man can be so strong. It inflamed one of them so"—T. hesitated. It was only a small fib, and he pondered—very briefly—the consequences of telling a lie in Paradise—"that he weakened in my presence. Then, like the coward he was, he killed a bound man who could not defend himself. At my death, I knew that the Jew-killing jihad would safely carry on without me, in cities all over godless America."

"Husband, do you say that there are other cities in America, besides that accursed Brooklyn?" his first bride asked.

"Of course. I know of Los Angeles, Chicago, St. Louis, Boston, Miami, and Dallas. But those are only the starting points—we shall prevail everywhere!"

After demanding more tea and kabobs, T. rambled on, delighting his brides, until he grew sleepy, and his words trailed off.

"Wake up, asshole!" one of his brides called out in English.

T. froze. Was that the hideous voice of the berserk she-devil who'd plunged the knife into him? How could such a hateful infidel pursue him in Paradise? Could it be that one lie he'd told?

"How dare you say a man killed you! *I* killed you, Pigface!"

Horrified, T. watched as one of the brides who'd glided through the air, the one with the wedding breads, ripped off her veil and wrestled free from her chador. It was indeed the mad, ungodly American whore, and now she rose up from the carpet to hover above him, a flying fiend from hell. "Okay girls!" she rallied the others. "It's a wrap!"

All over Paradise, chadors were being torn off. A few women and more than two dozen men wearing heavy eye makeup and earpieces were closing in on T. Without their presence in the foreground, he realized that all the other virgins, once strategically blocked, were mannequins, like the ones in the store windows on Church Avenue.

As his personal Paradise disintegrated, tears brimmed in T.'s eyes. His hand flew to his belly, his splendid feast on the verge of a ghastly backwash. Jackknifing forward, he tumbled off his throne and wound up sprawled across the little footstool.

One of the male brides approached T. He had thick turquoise eye shadow, false eyelashes, and was missing his left ear. "Hey, Sweet Cakes," he growled, "remember me?"

CHAPTER **TWENTY-TWO**

Without the floating virgins and Harry's seductive voices in his local dialect, T.'s personal information spigot ran dry just before his second injection was due to wear off.

The first had been the knockout shot in the back of his neck, administered by a guard at the same time Greta rammed the prop switched for Kress's knife against his gut. (As it telescoped up, it had released an equally phony but very messy gush of blood.) Cleaned up and transported to a Queens soundstage, he'd received a cocktail of Levitra and mood enhancers, which enabled him to star in Greta's big production number. His award-worthy performance, expertly translated by Zinah for participants both on and off stage, had nail-gunned him and all his cell drivers to the wall.

The most valuable news (beyond his confirmation that he wasn't acting independently) was his description of the man calling the shots. Stan and Chris were already poring over mosque footage, on the lookout for a fortyish man with dark wavy hair who favored casual clothing.

While T. had been regaling his mainly male harem with his litany of crimes, reports from the techs in D.C. began rolling in. Updated versions of Theo's money tracking software were picking up dramatically increased activity. With the fund's closing date of July thirteenth approaching, the killers were doing their damnedest to submit as many claims as possible.

Greta's call on the order of cities in rotation was proving accurate. Despite concern that T.'s sudden visit to his mother might have knocked New York out of the lineup, it was anybody's guess how the sequence would be altered, if at all.

As for T.'s mention of St. Louis, Boston, and Dallas, all agreed with Rice's take: "We can't rule out that they struck in one or all of those cities. Maybe it was just more of T.'s bragging to the gals. But at this point, I'd stick with where they had the highest concentrations of hits."

"Then what's next—Miami, Chicago, or Los Angeles?" August asked. "Where do you guys place your bets?"

"I'm putting my chips with Strasser's," said Brauner.

"Mine are on L.A., too," said Rice, and Zinah nodded her agreement.

"Five to L.A. it is," said Tom, and reached for the phone to call Folkestone.

"Well, they say hot weather here, hot weather in L.A. Easier to pack—travel light, yes?" Zinah rolled her suitcase up to the apartment door, next to Greta's. They had to be downstairs in fifteen minutes.

"I was out there once, on vacation," said Greta. "How about you?"

Zinah shook her head. "In the Army, I moved many times. But the state Texas was the most to the west."

"Any place you'd like to go back to?"

Zinah shrugged. "The bases . . . they are very similar."

"Like, seen one, seen 'em all?"

"That is very clever!"

"That's a phrase I can't take credit for, but believe me, it really comes in handy when you're working vice. So . . . you didn't hang around the base all the time, did you?"

"Soldiers on leave go to bars. At first, I went along, to drink a Coke. My English then was even worse. Still, quickly I learned the valuable NASCAR lesson."

Greta smiled. "Which is?"

"The same people who go to races to see a crash go to bars to see a fight. Or to start one."

"Good cultural observation."

"Off the base, I was called Mrs. Bin Laden, Alice Qaeda, A-rab cunt. Some soldiers in my unit tried to stop that. You can guess the rest. It was better not to go out. I saw all over the South the sign 'Jesus Saves.' For me, 'U.S. Army Saves.' It changed my life."

"How long have you been in?"

"Over three years. I have been in this country for eight years. That must make you think, 'This is indeed a stupid woman, to stumble so long with her English!'" She put up a hand to stop Greta's protest. "Remember I said I would tell you? Now is a good time—it is fast." Briefly, she closed her eyes. "A stranger came back to my hometown from Detroit, a seeker for a Pakistani bride. I taught at the same girls' school with his sister. He found out where I lived and arranged everything with my parents. All this, never speaking a word to me. As soon as we were married, back to Detroit. I was not allowed out of our apartment alone, only with him—veiled, of course. He stopped locking me in after I had my first child . . . in case of fire. Three children in less than four years. Down below, I was weak, always feeling like something was pulling my insides down. That did not stop him. Then, a miscarriage. So much bleeding, I had to go to the emergency room. I heard the doctor outside the curtains. First he explains to my husband. Then he warns. I understood none of the doctor's words, but his meaning was clear. The next week, my husband disappeared with the children."

"Disappeared? You mean he kidnapped them?"

Zinah nodded. "A police station was near our apartment. A place we passed by many times. Men and women in their uniforms stared at my veil and my hijab. Their looks were . . . hostel?"

"Hostile. Not friendly."

"Exactly. So I did not wear them when I went to them for help. I feared God would never forgive me for exposing myself, but I was desperate. They brought in an interpreter who helped me make a charge against my husband. All I wanted was my children . . . to get my children back. The next day, a detective came to see me. He had a page printed from the Internet, an Air Pakistan plane in the sky. He raised four fingers, then pointed to the windows where the passengers sit. He shook his head, showing me he could do nothing. Then this man, this stranger, stopped by the door to look back at me. I was shaking from this news. I could not stop shaking. He touched his hand to his heart, and held it there. That was the first kind gesture from anyone in all the time since I left my parents' home."

After a long pause, Zinah glanced down at her watch, "It is not too early to go downstairs now."

"No. There's still time. Tell me the rest."

"I needed money to fly home. I got a dishwasher job in a restaurant kitchen, a job cleaning at the neighborhood clinic, sometimes to help a woman who was a hairdresser in her home. I worked eighteen hours a day, without a veil, without a hijab. I learned some English."

"What about your family?"

"I wrote to my parents, my sisters, my brothers, many times. They never answered. No answer from my sister-in-law—my fellow teacher. By the end of this year living all alone, I was desperate enough to send a letter to an old schoolmate. Her husband works in the town government, and hears much of what goes on. At least she told me the truth . . . what *she* believed to be the truth. As soon as my husband returned to Pakistan, he divorced me. He did this by swearing in public that I am a whore, and how he caught me in bed together with two American men. That made me dead to my family. And if I ever did return, I would be truly dead."

"You mean like one of those crazy honor killings?" Greta blurted out.

Zinah sighed. "I had no hope to ever see my children. A second wife is now their mother. In the place to sign her letter, the woman put instead 'Never write to me again!' The next day I was buying food at a small market. An Army recruiter came into the store. He made a request to the owner to tape a sign to the window. The owner refused. I followed him out. I joined the Army, their program for interpreters—that was what the window sign was for. I barely passed the English, but boot camp made my body strong. I am strong all over. I am still a Muslim. I still pray five times a day. And when I finish, I also pray that I will never again be locked up or used for sex or thrown away like garbage. My modesty comes not from a piece of cloth, but from within. It is up to men to regard me with respect, not for me to hide from men."

Greta opened the door, and Zinah, head high, led the way down the stairs.

As soon as Tom, Zinah, and Greta retrieved their baggage at LAX, August phoned Rice and Brauner, who'd flown out the night before. The team was scheduled to get together with their Los Angeles JTTF counterparts at 6:00 P.M. When they arrived, Tom was greeted by an agent whose dark, weathered skin made his age impossible to guess. Tom introduced him as J. J. Rivera, and they followed him to a conference room where five more agents were waiting. All looked grim.

Rivera took a deep breath. "I don't think any of you have heard about SAC Hernandez. As of this morning, he's out on extended medical leave."

August was incredulous. "Artie, sick? Last time I was out here, he'd just run a marathon!"

"Yeah, he went for his annual physical a couple of weeks ago, and they kept pulling him back for this test and that test. It really pissed him off—you know, the guy's a bull. The latest test was an angiogram two days ago—the results were so bad, they wouldn't even let him go home. They had him in surgery yesterday morning—triple bypass. The surgeon called his wife after, and she called us right away. The good news is that the operation was a success, but it's way too soon for them to predict when he'll be back." Agitated, Rivera shook his head, "I mean, we're talking about a health nut—a guy who picked the cheese off his pizza! It's the job! Total stress!"

August started to speak, but the news had shaken him. After a while, he said, "J. J., next time you talk to his wife . . . please ask her to send him my best."

"You bet. Last day he was in the office, he said he was looking forward to working with you again."

"Next time," said August, still distracted. "Who's filling in for him?"

"Filling in?" J. J. repeated. "Have you ever met Agent Crain?" While

Tom tried to recollect, J. J. said, "You'd remember if you had." A member of the L.A. team coughed. "He was supposed to be here, but he's running late."

"Sure, first full day," said August.

An hour later, without an apology, Crain strolled in. He was wearing a stone-colored linen suit—presumably, it was designed to have a slouchy, crumpled look, unlike August's suits, which took up to an hour to achieve that effect. Since his pale gray shirt didn't have a collar, there was no question of a tie. Thrusting his hand at Tom, he said, "Agent August, I'm Crain . . . Mike Crain." The cadence was spot on with "Bond . . . James Bond." Instead of the stirred-not shaken part, he added, "I guess you've heard that I've been assigned SAC . . . until Hernandez is out of the woods." Except for his eyes and mouth, Crain's smooth face didn't appear to have a single working muscle. He appeared too young for Botox, but that, after all, was the point.

Greta and Zinah exchanged a quick glance. Zinah didn't need a word of English to grasp what Crain was about.

"I wanted to meet with you all face to face," he said, "to let you know that I've discussed this operation with Gary Folkestone, and that he and I will communicate daily. Actually, while we were on the phone, the first estimate came through on how much this operation has wired overseas recently—big, big numbers. And as your SAC pointed out, we'll never know how much more went out before tracking began, or if more is slipping out through another pipeline that has yet to be discovered." After steely eye contact with everyone in range, he drove home The Big Finish: "What we *do* know is the danger every single one of those dollars represents."

All money, no murders—is that the way he's sees it? Greta lowered her head to keep her disappointment to herself. When she looked up, Crain's eyes were locked on her. He seemed to be sizing her up in a way she couldn't quite figure out, except that it had nothing to do with meeting his dating requirements. "You must be Agent Strasser," he said, with enough doubt for two possible interpretations: she'd either fallen short of his lowest expectations, or he suspected her of being an out-and-out imposter. "'That was quite a story, how you and that fellow Appel figured out—"

"'*Story*,' sir?"

"Breakthrough," he backpedaled, "quite a breakthrough."

Reminding Greta of Russell Kim's practiced interceptions, August cut in, "Are we going to be working out of this office?"

"Yes, for the duration of Operation Lonely Hearts."

Among the other members of the New York contingent, there was at least one sharp intake of breath. Greta wanted to smack the smarmy son of a bitch. They weren't in Hollywood proper, but was this guy so starved for material that he already had a cheesy working title? It was a sure bet that he'd write her out of his screenplay after the first act . . . if she even survived his first draft.

"I've given quite a bit of thought to our inter-office assignments," said Crain, "so let's get that ironed out first." He sat down at the head of the conference table; from the look on Rivera's face, he'd appropriated Hernandez' chair. "Oh, by the way, Tom, that list you forwarded, of seven possible victims? Well, we can cross off Tannenbaum. Social Services moved him into a nursing home today. And it's our understanding that this group of killers doesn't do nursing homes." After a pause for laughter that didn't come, he glided right along. "With that in mind, I've assigned six two-person teams to cover the remaining targets. One shift. After all, these are solitary old people, and most live on a limited income. They're hardly running back and forth between tennis dates, drinks, or board meetings. They don't go out after dark. I think we can agree it won't be particularly demanding surveillance."

He passed printouts to the agent on his right. Once they were distributed, he pointed out, "Tom, note that each of your four New York agents will be teamed with an undercover LAPD detective on temporary JTTF assignment. During the day, you'll coordinate activity. We all meet to debrief here every evening." His eyes fixed on August. "About your working concept . . . you're set on having surveillance in place before the killers narrow down the field of victims?"

"That's why we came to Los Angeles. To get ahead of them."

Crain shot back, "Has it occurred to you that your victim list can backfire? What if we wind up watching the wrong people? What if your list doesn't match up with theirs?"

"Good question, since the killers have had the benefit of inside information all along—source still unknown." If August was ruffled, he wasn't permitting it to show. "Granted, it's late in the game, but in the last week or so, we reached out to several Jewish organizations that make the Holocaust their cause. We asked them for help where we need it most— genealogy. As a result, we're confident that our list can match at least one name on the narrowed-down killers' list." He looked around, gradually coming back to Crain. "That way, whichever three senior citizens the cell zeroes in on, we're already there, ready to zero in on the cell. With any luck, they'll lead us to the Los Angeles version of Brooklyn's T. He's the key to the next step: the controller who pulls all the strings, calls all the shots."

Crain, who might or might not have been listening, vigorously thumped the table. "Six teams in place and ready to start tomorrow!" As he stood, he said, "J. J. Rivera will be team leader."

Rivera, embarrassed by the way the stand-in SAC had marginalized August, looked up at Crain. "In that case, I think you'll agree that my first move should be to squeeze one more detective out of LAPD, to give Agent August the ability to coordinate from the field." Crain rested his hands on the back of the real SAC's chair, ready to countermand, but Rivera kept on going: "Field should regroup here tomorrow at six A.M. Oh, and by the way, the twelve of us—I mean *fourteen*—better prepare to work one long shift. Our seniors may not hit the bright lights at night, but this time of year, it doesn't even start to turn dark until after eight."

Late the next morning, Greta's phone rang right after a dark sedan pulled up to the curb half a block behind her and Detective Collier, her LAPD partner. "How's it going?" August asked.

"See the little bodega down at the far corner? Right after we got here, a man with a reasonable resemblance to Mr. Blaustein's last valid driver's license—1992—walked out carrying a newspaper and little white paper bag, like coffee and a roll. He uses a cane, and it took him nearly ten minules to get back to that white brick apartment building. Very determined gent—Collier gave him a round of applause when he finally touched home base. That's it for the last three hours. What's up with the other teams?"

"Interesting morning so far. We've got one little old lady—Nederlander—who's quite the babe. She drove herself to her local library at nine. Turns out she works there part-time three days a week. Besides helping at the circulation desk, she teaches other seniors how to log onto the Internet and surf the Web. An octogenarian stud was overheard asking her out for lunch."

"Did she accept?"

"She told him she wasn't free until next Wednesday, but they've got a date."

"Quite a little fox. Busy calendar."

"Maybe too busy for the bad guys. Then there's Ms. Gershowitz. She left her condo at eight-thirty, walked five blocks to a temple with a very active community center. According to the posted schedule, it runs a preschool and a daily program for seniors, lunch included, until three. We want to see how Gershowitz spends the rest of her afternoon—whether or not she walks out of there with friends. That center could be the sum total of her social life . . . with the rest of each day spent totally alone."

"She could be a possible, then. What about the other three?"

"Ms. Rosen has yet to surface. She's the lady who lives off Pico. Small house, twenty years overdue on maintenance, but she's got rose bushes on both sides of the front door, and somebody's keeping them pruned and watered. Maybe she was out early, before our car showed up. The Dubynoff lady is also a no-show. She lives in one of those apartment complexes built around a pool. One after another, three men came and went after staying about an hour, but the agent couldn't get close enough to verify if those visitors were going to her unit or the one adjacent."

"At seventy-nine, I doubt she's a hooker. Who's that leave? Minchnick?"

"A spiffy white-haired guy in a red sweater. Looks like Santa in a wheelchair. He was pushed to a little park playground near his house by a plus-size black woman in a pink uniform. They watch the kids play, she keeps moving him in and out of the sunshine, they chat a lot. She wheeled him home just a little while ago."

"Minchnick is Rice's, right? Come on, tell me what he said about her."

"That she looks like a defensive end with tits. His take is that if that lady's with him all day, no one's getting past her."

"What about any indication that somebody else is surveilling the vics?"

"So far, we're the only act in town."

While her partner took a break, Greta called Kim, who'd posed as an assistant principal at the Martinez girl's funeral service.

"It was tough, Greta. There were photos of Consuela all around the altar, and so many flowers, they went all the way back to the doors. But the closed casket . . . that said it all." Russell's revulsion over the savagery of the teenager's attackers hadn't diminished.

"The boyfriend is Eduardo Vazquez, goes by Eddie V. You were right—he paid for the funeral, but I also picked him out by the shoulder sling he's still wearing. Remember there weren't any matching gunshot wound reports? Looks like he didn't go to a hospital, and it's taking a long time to heal."

"What else?" asked Greta.

"His gang was all around him, and everyone was giving them space—as much as possible in such a packed church. It was like what happened to Consuela . . . like her disgrace was Blu-Steel's disgrace. And they're expected to avenge it." He paused. "I told the lieu it was your idea to be there . . . it gave us a chance to brace for retaliation."

"The credit wasn't necessary. But the lieu's a good guy. Let's hope you and Cepeda keeping an eye on Vazquez pays off—that he leads you straight to VX."

"Sure—except like the lieu says, 'With VX, you never really know what to expect.'"

That day passed, and two more. The rhythms of the seniors' lives were sketchily established, and the no-shows of the first day came into focus.

Halfway through the second day, they found out that at least five visitors daily were heading to Dubynoff's apartment. The information came from none other than the LAPD. Her thriving business was private Russian lessons, a necessity born of L.A.'s growing Russian mob presence. Cops made up the majority of her clientele, due to her unique incentive rewards: When they came back with all their vocabulary memorized, she taught them a nasty Russian curse word. Dubynoff drove a '75 cream-colored Mercedes convertible. She met friends for dinner that evening in a dramatic black dress brightened up with chunky enamel jewelry that matched her orange lipstick.

As for Rosen, she watered her roses at 6:00 A.M. daily. On the second day, she made another appearance around eleven. She walked several blocks to the closest supermarket, spent half an hour inside, left empty-handed. In the early afternoon, the store's delivery van drove up. Her order filled only one medium carton. The third day was the first time a mailman dropped off mail at her home, pushing it through a slot.

By the end of the third day, bets were on Gershowitz (who did go home from the senior center alone, then stayed put), Rosen, and Blaustein for the short list.

Crain, head down, didn't seem to pay attention to the names. After detailed analyses, his sole question was, "Have you picked up on any tails yet?"

"All false alarms," answered Rivera.

"We've got a lot of manpower tied up in this," said Crain. He suppressed a yawn as he got to his feet. "How soon can we drop those other three?"

"Shouldn't we leave that up to the bad guys?" Tom asked.

"Yeah, yeah. Okay, tomorrow." Clearly dissatisfied, Crain strode out.

Once he was well out of earshot, Rivera said apologetically, "We call him The Headache." The L.A. crew's heads bobbed in agreement, but New York wasn't catching on. "Say it fast: mikecrain."

The fourth day, Greta and Collier were sure it had begun. A Chevy Malibu parked in a spot across from Blaustein's building. After a rough ten years on the street, the near-wreck would've been a perfect fit for Dream Ride's fleet. Only the driver's arm was visible as he puffed on a cigarette, then flipped the butt into the gutter. His short-sleeved shirt revealed olive skin, and he remained in the vehicle, checking his watch frequently. He lit up again. Just as Collier received the results of a DMV search, the man climbed out of the car. Greta, who'd attached the long lens to their JTTF camera, snapped a sequence of pictures. In them, he stretched, hiked up his belt, marched four doors down to a hair salon, and again tossed away the butt. Long before Franco Ponti emerged, hair shorter and generously gelled, it was clear he'd arrived early for his appointment and preferred to smoke outside while he waited.

"Jesus, surveillance sucks!" Collier sighed. "We all need a week with Highway Patrol, just to fucking air out!"

The other teams were equally edgy, equally bored. That night, Crain whined about their lack of progress. August checked in with Folkestone, who told him that he'd advised Crain to hang in, have patience, that very afternoon.

Greta's own reserve tank of patience was seriously depleted: It was impossible to forget that every minute of every day they spent sitting and watching inexorably dragged them closer to the July deadline—a day when, after the last postmark was stamped on the last claim letter, the murderers would become forever untraceable.

Before Greta and Collier arrived the next morning, they'd heard that a driver was sitting in a late-model Chrysler near Rosen's home. They immediately noticed the Audi parked right across the street from Blaustein's building, occupying Franco Ponti's old spot. A man was behind the wheel.

Around one-thirty, August phoned Greta. "Twice a day, I've been driving by Tannenbaum's house—remember, the man Crain crossed off?"

"Right, the nursing home guy. What's up?"

"This morning, a Volvo was watching that address, too."

"That's it? No car on any of the others?"

"So far, nope—hold on, I've got something coming in." When Tom came back on the line, he said, "Strasser, something is way too legit about the registrations and the cars."

"*Too* legit? What's that mean?"

"Apparently, they belong to real people—all above-board—no shell corporations, no warrants, no convictions. And these are all pretty nice cars, late models: an Audi, a Volvo, a Chrysler. Some of these seniors live in rundown neighborhoods, where a Dream Ride car would attract less notice. But hey, who knows? This is Lala Land, where everyone has wheels. Still, something here just doesn't mesh for me."

Shortly after their conversation, a dark gray Honda passed the Audi and went around the corner. The Audi's directional flipped on; its driver adjusted the rearview mirror; its wheels slowly turned to the roadway. The Honda again came into view, pulling up behind the Audi, waiting for it to vacate the spot. Collier was requesting a tail on the Audi before the Honda was parked.

A minute later, Greta's phone rang. "Changing of the guard," reported Tom. "Yours was the second to go—a Buick just replaced the Volvo. Looks like the Chrysler is next. Sit tight—I'll let you know where those guys are headed as soon as it comes in."

Collier leaned toward the phone, so August could hear. "The bad guys get away with a half-day shift! There's no justice in this world!"

Just as darkness fell, the Honda and the other two replacement cars headed back to the same destination as the earlier surveillance cars—exactly as expected.

At that night's meeting, Crain didn't utter a word. While energized agents noisily shared and pieced together the glut of new information the day had delivered, he found himself increasingly marginalized. Not only had his own skepticism and thinly veiled disinterest in the operation nearly prevented the discovery of a cell in his own city, but his criticism of the JTTR list of potential victims had been a glaring misjudgment: It shared an optimal three matches with the cell's list. Even worse, one of the names on it was Tannenbaum, whom he'd so breezily dismissed.

The stakeout cars (all, as August had ascertained, legitimately owned) had all been driven back to Tortello's Auto Body. The four-bay shop was a registered business one Joseph Tortello had sold to a Syrian, Gadil Ikhtiyar, back in 1994. Ikhtiyar was in the country legally. He and his wife, Abella, lived near Tortello's in a modest single-family home.

"Apparently, Tortello's came with a decent reputation," August explained to the group, "and Gadil was careful about keeping it up. It's preliminary, but I'd say that he runs the cell. The tails who followed the morning shift cars back to the shop saw him go right out when each watcher drove up. Then he'd march the guy into the office for debriefing—heads down, like they were whispering. All we know about the six surveillance guys is that they—along with four other men who worked in the shop all day—appear to be of Middle-Eastern origin." With a small smile aimed at Collier, he said, "They put in a long day. They bang out dents and replace bumpers when they're not watching the potential targets. We'll be on them all around the clock. Back in Brooklyn, T. had drivers who weren't involved in cell smuggling or surveillance, and it's only a matter of time before we figure out whether that applies to those four other guys."

Rivera explained the auto body angle: "From this afternoon's activity," he began, "it looks like the business provides enough volume for a different fleet of surveillance cars every day. All six cars on the street today were completed body jobs—cherry-picked so that nothing was too flashy, top-of-the-line, or expensive. LAPD has no record of any accident reports filed by the actual owners, so we're surmising these vehicles were involved in some sort of minor fender bender—fixing something like that is never cheap, but reporting it to your insurance company, you know how that goes. After you pay your deductible, what do you get?"

"A big fat rate hike on your next premium," Rice observed.

"Exactly," Rivera wrapped up. "So when the customer drops off the car, he or she is advised that it'll be ready in four or five days. If that's a problem, the customer's probably told that the shop is backed up, or a part or the paint needs to be special-ordered. Meanwhile, the work is done ASAP, and the car goes into the day-tripper pool. In case it's stopped, it's just out for a test drive. But they hardly do any driving around tailing Rosen or Blaustein, and they don't even know Tannenbaum isn't home."

August turned to Crain, whose perpetually unworried face betrayed neither regret nor resentment. "Tomorrow morning we can start turning things around a little. We watch Tortello's, see how many cars they send out, and where they go. Just to be sure."

"Is that really necessary?" asked Crain petulantly, shot down but not yet ready to give up calling the shots.

No one took the time to reply.

The next day, three newly restored cars showed up in the same three places. Shortly after 10:00 A.M., a Realtor's FOR SALE sign went up in front of Tannenbaum's house. Less than two hours later, the surveillance car returned to Tortello's. By three, no replacement car had arrived. August and the LAPD detective he was partnered with paid the real estate office a visit.

At the evening meeting, the detective reported what had happened there: "I asked if she'd had any calls on the Tannenbaum house, and she said only one, from a man with a heavy accent. His first—and, it turned out, his only—question was about 'availableness.' As soon as she told him the house was available *and* unoccupied, he hung up. She couldn't identify the accent, but we were able to trace the call back to Ikhtiyar."

"That sign did you a big favor," said Crain, and for once, everyone nodded in agreement. "What about the cell members?"

Rice, whose surveillance of Minchnick had ended, spoke up, "We think the same four guys stayed in Tortello's today. Hard to be sure exactly who, because Tannenbaum had no afternoon replacement. All of them except Icky—Ikhtiyar—could be illegals. Breakfast and lunch is take-out at the shop. They live in either closet-sized apartments or fleabag motels. Nobody went out last night. Work, eat, sleep, no chicks. Maybe a dream about blowing yourself up is better than sex."

"Sounds like we should start planning the next phase," said Crain.

As if getting one step ahead of Crain were an infraction, August confessed, "When you're out on a stakeout, it's tempting to think about that." Crain glanced at him, without a glimmer of curiosity about what those thoughts might be. Tom went on speculating, anyway. "I'd say to J. J.," and he looked right at the agent, " 'J. J., tomorrow morning, what if you go to Mr. Blaustein's apartment and offer him a choice of ten days in Hawaii or an Alaskan cruise, all expenses paid'?" August turned back to Crain, "And J. J. might say, 'Mmmmmm. That'll keep the old guy pretty much incommunicado and out of harm's way, especially after the way Icky's guys dropped Tannenbaum. They'll cross off Blaustein as soon as he gets into a taxi with a couple of suitcases and heads for the airport.' "

All eyes were on Crain. "Exactly. Our objective is to narrow the field. I'll work that out with Folkestone right now." He left the office, full of purpose.

After details were worked out on Blaustein, Greta asked, "So we're forcing their hand to choose Rosen?"

"She and Blaustein both ranked high on the solitary scale, both are regular in their habits, and neither goes out much." August produced a series of surveillance photos, blown up to an eleven-by-fourteen format. "But between the two, we're much better off in a house than an apartment building."

One after the other, he held up the pictures. The first one showed Rosen's home from the street, the second had the owner in view, walking out the front door. She had short, curly gray hair and wore a rose-print bathrobe. In the next four, she watered the roses to the left and then the right of the door, took a pair of clippers from her pocket, then walked back inside with a few flowers. The following shot was tight on the upper floor, probably a converted attic—it had windows, and the windows had curtains. "Rosen's second floor provides us with space for a communications setup. Plus, we can pack more agents inside her home. Here she is, Day Two of our surveillance, the only time she went out—to buy food."

In the next photos he held up, the eighty-year-old Rosen was wearing a light-colored blouse and dark slacks. Without the bulky housecoat, she was slimmer than expected. The robe had also concealed a back severely out of line. As she walked away down the block, she listed to one side.

"She has trouble walking, no?" Zinah asked.

"Yes, a pronounced limp," August replied, as he held up another set of photos. They showed the rear of Rosen's house and another street with bungalow-type homes similar to hers. "We can get access through her back door from the backyard of the neighbor to the south. Someone going in that way can't be spotted from the street."

While Tom stacked the blowups together, he looked around at the team. "We should keep watching Tortello's, stick to Icky like glue, keep the surveillance team outside Rosen's in place, and put three agents inside with her. We should also start someone on Mrs. Icky, just in case." He responded to Greta, who was holding up a hand. "You have a question?"

"No, a problem. Even if you put twenty of us in that little house, Rosen's still bait for these bastards. You're getting Blaustein out of harm's way to narrow down the list. You've got to get her out, too."

Collier immediately replied, "But if they don't see her, they'll either pull a Tannenbaum, or start all over again."

Greta pulled the second photo out from August's stack. For a split second, Mrs. Rosen, early morning gardener, melded with Paulina Kantor. "They'll see exactly what they're looking for," she said. "I'll make good on that."

CHAPTER **TWENTY-THREE**

"What do you mean, Strasser?" Rivera asked.

"First let's all agree," said Greta, "that our problem is how to keep Icky's cell focused on Rosen as their next victim . . . without exposing her to danger." Her voice was breathy, hopefully not quavery enough to betray the nervous flutter in her chest. Because she hadn't had a chance to think her proposal all the way through, she could only go on her gut that it would play out, gaining cohesion as she went along. "Okay, no argument on that," she said, more to reassure herself than the others. "What I'm proposing is the placement of a female agent with extensive undercover experience in Rosen's house ASAP—tonight, actually. With professional help—hair, makeup, the type of clothes Rosen wears—this agent simulates the physical look and mannerisms of the real Rosen. Collier, we're not that far from Hollywood, right?"

"Neither literally nor figuratively." Collier's eyes locked on her, very interested.

"The agent," she continued, "has to be familiar with the Holocaust scam—she'll have to coach Rosen through all the questions on the claim form, and, along the way, gather even more details. We need background, credible background. Next step, we pull out Rosen, and the agent follows her daily routine. Then we wait for the cell to pass its report to the controller." Greta took a deep breath, waiting for a reaction, nearly sold on the viability of the scheme herself.

"Unfortunately," said August, "that creates an equally dangerous situation for this theoretical agent."

"Theoretical?" frowned Brauner. "Didn't you hear? Strasser just volunteered."

"Too risky," August snapped.

Greta fired back, "Actually, we have plenty of control. The killer has to convince the Rosen-agent to open the door, to sit down and listen to an explanation of the fund's concept and its process. That's complicated under any circumstances, but when you're dealing with a senior citizen, it has to be spelled out, maybe more than once. After all, it brings back horrific nightmares . . . flashes of your family ripped away, death all around you, a war going on. Worse, this happened when you were young . . . just a child, or hardly in your teens. The killer has to make a show of sympathy and compassion . . . rush through any part of it, and all credibility's down the tube.

"As a counterbalance, the Rosen-agent projects suspicion, distrust. She's so skeptical, convincing her to fill out the application will take time. The form itself is long, complex . . . emotionally exhausting. But the killer can't strike until it's completed."

She looked around at the other agents. "If I'm dragging this out, it's to make the case that our team will have, at the very least, an hour and a half to intercede. Played out, two and a half hours isn't unreasonable. That reduces the risk dramatically."

"Okay, you're not opening the door to someone pointing a gun at you," said Tom, "but I have a totally different concern."

Greta, with no clue as to what was coming, remained silent.

"Professionally, you took a lot of flack for your follow-through on Paulina Kantor's murder. And your friend, Theo Appel," Tom continued, "makes it personal for you. It's hard to forget how—" He put the brakes on whatever he was going to say.

Had his mind just rerun the crazed way she'd lunged at T.? Her bloodlust histrionics had stopped everyone in their tracks, especially when she'd plunged the trick knife into his gut. Did Tom—who had some convincing thespian chops himself—wonder if she'd crossed the line, that it was more than a damn good performance?

Calm and steady, she replied, "I thoroughly understand what's at stake. The JTTF objective is taking the killer into custody. And I have every intention of staying alive while that's accomplished."

With his eyes on her, August said, "To be honest, I can't imagine anyone else who'd be able to carry it off. But no agent should be in there alone. If you go in, I go in with you."

Rivera made the call. "Sorry, Mrs. Rosen, I know it's late, but this call is to inform you that a burglary took place in your neighborhood earlier this evening."

"I didn't hear anything."

"That may be, but I'm calling to alert you to the presence of detectives on your block, going house to house for information."

"You think I'm so sleepy or so stupid to believe that? For all I know, you could be the crook yourself, Mister." No one who'd seen the surveillance photos of Rosen was quite prepared for what was coming through on the speakerphone.

"I'm not a crook, Mrs. Rosen. And you can request a look at their credentials."

Unconvinced, she asked, "They'll come in a police car?"

"Detectives usually travel in unmarked cars, ma'am."

"Then make sure they come with someone in a uniform, with a radio and all the rest of the stuff they carry around these days. Otherwise, forget it." She clicked off.

"Damn! That was supposed to be the easy part," said August. "No way we risk a patrol car, even with Icky's guys all tucked in for the night."

"I have to notify the precinct anyway," said Rivera. "We'll get a beat cop to prepare Rosen for the so-called detectives. Tom, Greta, let's get going. I can start moving the right people to Rosen's place en route. We need communications set up before morning, and all support people up and running tonight."

"That's *if* she cooperates," said Tom.

"Yeah, that too."

They parked several houses away from Rosen's, and the three of them speed-walked down the block in silence.

As they turned onto the short path leading to her home, Rosen opened her door wider than expected. "First I want to see your IDs," she said, holding out her hand.

When she brought the three JTTF identification cards into the light pooling out from the doorway, she stiffened. "You said they were police detectives," she said in a confidential, cautious voice.

"I do apologize, ma'am." The reply came from behind a rosebush. "They're like . . . well, partners with the LAPD. I personally vouch for them. And ma'am, I really have to go now—I'm not supposed to be here."

"So go." Rosen appeared irked, but placated. "And watch out for the thorns." The uniform took off toward the sidewalk, discreet enough not to turn and look at Rosen's visitors. "Okay, you might as well come in."

As the old lady handed back the IDs, Greta felt a pang of anxiety; she stood about five inches taller than Rosen.

They didn't have far to go. The entrance led directly into a small living room. The walls were a very pale pink, the sofa a deep rose, and the two white wicker side chairs had cushions covered with pink and mauve roses. Real roses filled a vase on the coffee table. Facing the rear, a staircase with a coat closet built in under the risers was to the right, a partial wall with a TV on a cart in the center, and left of that, in deep shadow, an opening led to the back. Rosen limped to one of the chairs, indicating that her uninvited guests should take the sofa. Instead of letting her squeeze them into a row like naughty triplets, Greta took the other chair.

Further demonstrating that she was anything but timid, Rosen was the first to speak. "Starting maybe in the Seventies," she began, "hardly a day went by when someone didn't stroll down this block with some kind of loot on his shoulder—an air conditioner, or a TV. Then came those videotape machines. Now, computers. Did I ever once see anyone trying to catch them? No! Not even back when I still called the police!" She wagged an angry finger. "You're not here for a burglary. You're not even police. You're terrorism people."

Rivera leaned toward her, his hands locked together on his knees. "Mrs. Rosen—"

"Miss," she snapped.

"Excuse me. Miss Rosen, I'm afraid you're at the center of an extremely dangerous situation."

"I know. I live in Los Angeles, and I'm over thirty."

"Miss Rosen," August cut in, "some time prior to or during World War II, a relative of yours made a deposit in a Swiss bank."

"What? That?" Surprisingly, she didn't register much more than mild annoyance, slightly tinged with disappointment. "My grandfather's so-called *fortune*? I found out all about that years and years ago. That Swiss bank account was a fairy tale."

At the edge of her chair, Greta asked, "What makes you so sure of that?"

"The bank had no record of it. My uncle came to America before the war, and I was the only other Rosen from our family who survived. After the war, he brought me here from Europe."

"So your uncle contacted the bank?" Rivera asked.

"He sent letters to Zurich, at least a dozen, with the account number and the date the account was supposedly opened. I remember he always made me seal the letter and put it in the mailbox—you know, for good luck. Eventually, the bank sent their reply. It was a printed form with the bank name on top. The form was for accounts that they had no record of—I saw it with my own eyes. I know Uncle Jackie did everything he could, because he was completely broke."

"Is your uncle still alive?" asked Greta.

"Oh, no. He died in the early Fifties."

"And since then, you never tried to get any information?"

"Why bother? Like I said, it was there in black and white. Official."

"Miss Rosen," said Greta, "I assure you, there actually was such an account. The bank that lied to your uncle isn't the only Swiss bank that lied to Holocaust depositors or their heirs." Rosen began to protest, but Greta put up a hand. "No matter what you were told, the Swiss banks made a settlement. Your money is waiting to be claimed."

Biting her lower lip, Rosen turned her head toward the darkened archway. "That would be very good news, if I could believe it." The toughness was gone, her voice thin and wobbly as the tail end of an echo. "Even if I did . . . well, it's late for me, isn't it? Really, really late." After a while, she turned to face them. "The Swiss bank, this 'danger,' that agency you work for . . . I'm very, very confused."

"Let us try to explain," Greta suggested.

After her condensed version of Theo's discovery, August outlined the impending operation. Rosen followed what they said with fierce concentration.

The room fell silent except for the battery-driven click of a little plastic clock on the coffee table. Shaped like the top of a grandfather clock, its face had a garland of roses above the roman numerals. Outside, a car swooshed by. "Memories," Rosen whispered at last. "You think you can retrieve the one you want, like switching television channels . . . but it's more like playing Russian roulette, isn't it? Because, like the bullet, there's always the chance your mind will go to something you couldn't bear to remember again." Maybe it was the empathy in Greta's eyes that made her turn to her and ask directly, "Tell me, if I lived through the Nazis, do you think I can live through this?"

Greta hesitated. "You don't mean this particular operation, do you?"

Slowly, sadly, Rosen shook her head. "All the terrorists. All their hatred. If they're coming after *me* . . . are they everywhere?"

"Miss Rosen," said Tom, "I want my kids to live to see the world free of them. But for that, we need all the help we can get."

She replied without hesitation. "Then I'll put myself in your hands."

"Thank you. Considering how we've walked in here, so out of the blue . . . your trust means more than you can imagine."

Trust was a word, Greta had noticed, that Tom never used lightly. For him, it meant fair exchanges, promises kept, the step beyond respect. The importance he attached to it reminded her of another equally determined slogger, another veneer-in-reverse . . . Hank Strasser.

"You said you have to begin immediately."

"Yes, Miss Rosen. Our plan is to pull you out tomorrow night, some-time after dark. Between now and then we'll be doing a lot of talking, but what we should discuss first is where you'd like to go until it's safe to re-turn home. No matter where you choose, you'll have round-the-clock protection." He mentioned the destinations offered to Mr. Blaustein.

Rosen considered for a moment. "Could it be someplace closer?"

"Of course, depending on the risk factor. Where do you have in mind?"

"My first day here in California, my uncle met me at the train station. He picked me up in a car his friend loaned him for the day, a beautiful baby blue convertible. We drove around Los Angeles, all the way to the Pacific Ocean. On the way back, we went by The Beverly Hills Hotel. I'd never seen anything like it—the palm trees, all the flowers—it looked like a tropical paradise." She raised her eyebrows expectantly. "What do you think? I can't imagine terrorists staying there, can you?"

The communications techs were on standby, their van on the street be-hind Rosen's bungalow. Along with their own gear, they brought black-out drapes for the entire house. After a quick overview of the layout, they moved their equipment to the second floor, taking over the smaller of the two bedrooms. On the first floor, the dark area off the living room turned out to be a dining area. It opened onto both a narrow sunroom at the left and a kitchen at the rear. The kitchen had a door on its right that ac-cessed the backyard; because there was no basement, a utility closet was located in its left corner, adjoining, but not connected to, the sunroom.

Unfazed by starting his workday so close to midnight, the hairdresser greeted everyone with good cheer as he was led in through the kitchen. As soon as he called down that his portable workstation was set up, Greta and Miriam—she'd insisted on everyone using her first name—climbed up to her bedroom to join him.

"A wig is the only way to go for you," he said to Greta. "All those gray curls—even up close, it'll look like the real deal."

"Agreed. And what about changing Miriam's look?" Greta asked. This was a tactic she'd suggested to August, to help Miriam hide in plain sight.

She slipped off the chair, and Miriam eased onto it, confiding, "Once upon a time, this mop used to be light brown."

"Thick gray is better than thin anything—you're lucky." He smiled back at her reflection in the mirror and bent to examine one of her curls. "A dark honey shade will be lovely, and we'll frost it—that'll bring more light to your face. It's too short for much styling, but maybe—" Grabbing a brush, with a few strokes he brought some hair down onto her forehead. "Yes! Softer! Do you like that as much as I do?" Miriam nodded enthusiastically. "Excellent! I'll be back around ten tomorrow morning, with the old gray wig for Greta, and the hot new color for you."

"Are you tired?" asked Greta, as Jenna and her assistant took over.

Miriam whispered in her ear, "Having your life threatened is too exciting to get tired." Nevertheless, she dozed off on a folding table while the makeup artist fabricated latex molds of her face.

Fascinated, Greta watched while impressions of her own teeth and hands were taken. When Jenna gently rocked her shoulder, her watch read ten after two. "I'm done," the makeup lady whispered. "Wardrobe is waiting downstairs. I'll see you tomorrow, around noon. Applying all this stuff can be tricky, so be prepared to spend some time while I do a trial run. I'm not quite sure what you had in mind for Miriam."

"Miriam is going to . . . to a resort. I was thinking some makeup to go with hair that's going to be dark honey. Frosted."

"A resort? Good for her! Definitely sunscreen, or she'll burn to a crisp, she's so pale. I'll put a little makeup collection together. Understated, natural."

"I'm too old for anything but lipstick," Miriam insisted, as the assistant helped her down from the table.

"Only the lipstick will show," said Jenna. "The rest is magic. We're never too old for magic."

Wardrobe went quickly. Mai, a pretty Asian woman dressed in heavily appliquéd jeans and a sheer white blouse with a black bra underneath, measured Greta and Miriam from head to toe. She examined the shoes and clothes in the bedroom and packed some up in a garment bag. "I wish I had a little more time to have copies in your size sewn up," she told Greta, frowning. "I'll check my costume houses, but I know I'll have to find some new stuff and age it. I'll be back around four tomorrow afternoon."

"So we're done for now?" Miriam asked. The predawn hour had finally slowed her down, and she thanked the young woman before excusing herself to go across the hall to the bathroom. She paused with her hand on the doorknob, troubled about something. "Dear, do you know that your bra is showing?" Mai nodded. "That's the style?" Another nod. "Okay," said Miriam, shaking her head as she walked away.

As soon as they were alone, Mai said to Greta. "I'll bring padding for your hips and a kind of pillow to give you the look of that sway Miriam has in her back. Oh, and something for your left shoe—a constant reminder for you to walk off-kilter."

"Any suggestions about my being taller than she is?"

"I wish." Gathering up her bags, she added, "Actually, another reason I'll be so late is that one of the guys downstairs said Miriam needs new clothes for a vacation. I'm supposed to ask you for details."

Groggy as she was, Greta managed to blurt out, "Oh, think the Hamptons. At least ten days' worth."

Greta bunked down on the living room sofa, while Tom slept on the recliner in the sunroom. At six-thirty, Rosen came down the stairs in her rose-printed robe and slipped out to take care of her roses. When she tiptoed in with a bouquet wrapped in a towel, the closing door woke Greta. Greta asked if she'd seen anyone in a car watching her.

"No one that I saw."

"Miriam, your roses are beautiful. But promise me you won't go outside again today, okay?"

"I just wanted make sure they won't have to be pruned for another weck. The watering is only a minute with the hose on each side." She looked worried.

"I promise to faithfully water them every morning."

From the kitchen, Tom's voice called out, "Better show me how to work your coffeepot, Miriam." In his shirtsleeves, not much more disheveled than usual, he was holding up a plastic filter cone. "Last night while you gals were upstairs, we had all sorts of stuff brought in to fend off starvation—juice, muffins, bagels, et cetera."

Miriam stared at the gun in his shoulder holster. "You sleep with your gun?"

"Yes, but we're in love," Tom replied, petting his weapon.

"You too?" she asked Greta.

In reply, Greta unbuttoned her jacket.

Miriam instinctively took a step back. "I'd say that makes everything very real, doesn't it? I mean, last night—the hairdo, the makeup, the clothes—I have to admit that was . . . well, fun. Now we're very serious. So serious, that if Greta and her friend Theo hadn't stuck with it, I would be next, wouldn't I?"

Bleary-eyed as Greta had been, breakfast revived her. While a second pot of coffee was brewing, she assembled the CRT survivor's claim form, pens, blank paper, her notebook, and a portable recorder. "I guess the best way to get started, Miriam, would be for you to give me several copies of your signature. As Miriam complied, Greta added, "And before we get to the claim application, we need an overview of your life before the war. I know it's going to be stressful, but—"

"I can handle it, Greta," Miriam cut in. "The whole truth and nothing but the truth."

"You're not under oath."

"Oh, yes I am. I am strictly under oath . . . to my family. That's what this is all about, isn't it? Go on, turn on your recorder. I'm ready." Tom refilled her coffee cup, she took a sip, and, inclined slightly toward the machine, she began:

"I was born and grew up in my grandfather's house in Bremen, a city in northern Germany. His name was Samuel Rosen, and he was the owner of a factory that made metal into containers—cans for food, barrels for gasoline, things like that. He had two sons, my father Maurice and my uncle Jakob. My two aunts died from the influenza when they were teenagers. Jakob—Jackie—was the younger son, and he got into some kind of trouble . . . maybe over a woman, maybe gambling. Definitely unfit for my young ears, and bad enough for him to leave home. He hopped all over Europe for a while, then he did the same thing in America. Every month or so, my grandmother got a letter from him. She kept it secret from my grandfather, but the rest of us always knew when he wrote, because she cried for days afterward. The last letter she received was from Chicago. He said that was going to see the Wild West, on his way to Los Angeles.

"Now, bear in mind that in those days, women and children were pretty much sheltered from any business matters, so I can't be sure of the how or when or why of what happened. All I know is that my grandfather sold his factory immediately after Hitler came into power. Eventually the Nazis seized all Jewish-owned businesses."

"Sure," Tom observed. "They would've snapped it up right away—what he manufactured would be an important part of the German war machine."

"So I've learned," Miriam agreed, "but at the time, I didn't understand anything—not even when the SS dragged us out of our home. In less than ten minutes, we were standing on the street." She sat back in her chair so she could put an elbow on the table, then rested her head in the cup of her hand and closed her eyes. As soon as she heard Greta click off the machine, she said, "Please, put it back on. I stopped because . . . for me, that moment was the end."

The end of family, the end of childhood, the end of life as she knew it, the end of home as a haven. Greta kept her head down, struck by the image of a curly-haired girl on a cobblestone street, encircled by soldiers.

When the tape began to roll again, Miriam resumed. "Remember last night, I told you about the bank's letter to Uncle Jackie? He figured that whatever my grandfather deposited from the sale of the factory was used up trying to get the family away from the Nazis. In fact, we did run all across Europe—what Jackie did for pleasure, we did out of desperation. Eventually, a collaborator betrayed us in Paris—he got a hundred francs a head for Jews. The last time I saw my family was when we got off the train in Auschwitz." Miriam took a deep breath, then shook her head vehemently. Except for dates, unless it's absolutely necessary, I don't want to talk about the camp. I was nineteen when it was liberated."

"Understood," said Greta. The recorder was still running. "Did your uncle know about the bank account before he left Germany?"

Miriam didn't have a ready answer. "We still had the factory then. But my grandfather disowned Jackie—cut him out of his will. Saying his name in the house was forbidden. On the train to the camp, my grandmother had to be thinking that the only member of the family who would survive was disinherited."

"Do you think she mentioned the account in her letters?"

"Maybe. But like I said, my grandfather was so furious, he would have made sure the bank knew he wasn't an heir . . . I have no idea how that's done." She shook her head. "What do I know from banks? I used to say hello to the teller when I handed over my paycheck, and that was that."

Tom's phone rang, and Greta clicked off the recorder while he took the call. "A Pontiac fresh from Tortello's just pulled up," he announced. "We can't take a look because we have to keep the blackout curtains on until tomorrow morning. Miriam, I'm sorry we had to put you through such an upsetting session. We can move on now, go over your daily schedule, your neighbors, anything of a day-to-day nature that occurs to you. We can just take notes."

"If it's okay with both of you, I'd prefer to keep recording," said Greta. "Miriam has just a trace of an accent. I'd like to get as much as I can on tape for reference,"

Miriam shrugged her shoulders. "Fine by me."

As Rosen provided the current information, Greta tried to recall a half-formed question that had occurred to her just before the phone interruption. She knew it was about Miriam's uncle, but its precise nature escaped her.

They were finishing up the Holocaust fund application when the hair-dresser walked into the kitchen through what he dubbed "the cloak-and-dagger portal." By the time the tear-inducing odor of hair color drifted downstairs, Tom was sealing the completed form in an envelope.

The rest of the day rushed by, with Greta piling on the decades and Miriam happily shedding them. By the end of the afternoon, Rosen, wearing the little black dress Mai had selected for her, watched Jenna's finishing touches on the latex masterpiece glued to Greta's face and neck. All she said was, "That's too much like looking in a mirror."

"Not anymore," Jenna replied. "I want you to take back that remark about just lipstick last night. And wait until that moisturizer kicks in—five days, and you will be totally amazed."

Tom was called in. "Hi Greta," he said to Miriam.

"Tomorrow should go much faster," Jenna told him, "but for the first few days, we'd better allow about an hour in the morning." She was enough of a pro not to blink when Tom told her that meant 5:30 A.M. While she removed the Greta-into-Miriam creation—another long, careful process—Greta remembered the question that had eluded her that morning.

"I want to ask you something, Miriam," Greta said after Jenna's departure. "It's nothing essential as far as the application. It has to do with your uncle."

Miriam nodded. "I saw that look this morning. It's about the adoption, isn't it?"

"Sort of. You and your uncle were one another's only family. But you were twenty-one when you came here."

Miriam nodded. "I wrote him right after the Allies marched in. I wanted him to know that he had at least one relative still alive. A soldier put my letter in the mail pouch, but no one had any idea how long it would take to get all the way to Los Angeles. The idea of adopting me was

In my uncle's first letter back—ten months later. There were millions of displaced persons in Europe. Being adopted . . . once it finally went through, it was like I'd been pushed to the head of the line."

Greta nodded. "I was just curious. Thanks."

"You're wondering how long it took me to catch on why my uncle adopted me . . . or maybe if I was naïve enough to even catch on at all. Am I right?"

Intrigued as she was, Greta held back a reply.

"Greta, you're talking to someone who survived a concentration camp. For that, you have to be shrewd. You have to be ruthless. I didn't remember my uncle much from when I was a girl. But as a survivor, I could see right through him. He was handsome, fluent in five languages, charming, but the man had no heart. What kind of person asks his mother for money while she's trying to outrun the Nazis?

"Somehow, he convinced the woman who was keeping him to help him bring his poor little war orphan niece to America. The problem was, she was expecting a ten-year-old kid. One look at me, and she kicked him out.

"Sure, my grandmother sent Jackie the account number. What it all boiled down to was that Jackie was betting if he wrote to the bank—using my name—presto! a check would be on its way. I was too embarrassed to say that before, in front of you and Tom."

"You shouldn't—"

"No! I owe you an explanation. All the while the bank dragged it out, my uncle was scrambling for cash to live on. He went out every night, all dressed up, and plenty of times he showed up the next morning looking like a truck ran over him. I didn't want to be around if the same people came looking for him at home. I had no money and hardly any English. But the whole world knew Hollywood was where movies came from, so I tried to find work at the studios. As an extra, I didn't have to speak. I certainly didn't need any help looking skinny and needy. I rioted for bread in the French Revolution. I schlepped water for the slaves building the pyramids. I played a ghost, a zombie, and I was near the front of the crowd running away from flying saucers."

"I guess after what you lived through, that was a piece of cake," said Greta.

"Nothing to it," Miriam agreed. "One day, I was in my costume—tattered rags—looking for a seat in the studio commissary. A man at one of the tables called over to me, "Hey, kiddo, how well do you know the alphabet?" He managed one of the back lot offices, and noticed my SS tattoo when I passed by. His file clerk had just quit, and that was that—I was hired. Right about the time I saved enough money to move out on my own, the letter came from the bank. By the way, *my* name, not Jackie's, was on the envelope—no account, no money. I was of no further use to him. Two days later, he disappeared."

"Did Jackie really die in the early Fifties?"

"Yes, down in Mexico. The woman who was currently covering his expenses found him in bed with her daughter." Pretending she had a gun in her hand, Miriam pulled the trigger several times. "I got a letter, asking me to come down and claim the body. I never replied. My past was already full of unclaimed bodies."

Shortly after the second surveillance car of the day returned to Tortello's, the female agent assigned to Miriam for the rest of the operation arrived in a dark sedan.

Tom put his arms around the old lady and kissed the top of her head. "You look great," he said. "Just remember, avoid talking to strangers for the next week or so, except if they ask you 'What would you like to drink, Miss Bloom?' or 'Shall I move your chaise into the shade, madam?'"

Greta and Miriam embraced, hugging each other hard. Miriam stood on tiptoe, and whispered into Greta's ear, "One more hug, Greta dear, and one for the memory of Mr. Appel—he's my friend, too."

Immediately after they drove away, Collier slipped through the kitchen door with supper. It wasn't even 10:00 P.M. when Tom nodded off on the sofa and Greta collapsed on Miriam's bed. She fell asleep to the sound of Miriam's voice on her headphones. Collier pulled the recliner halfway into the darkened dining area, keeping watch.

Cutting through the back, Jenna arrived at five-thirty the next morning. The JTTF car was in position by six o'clock. Jenna exited, the blackout drapes were pulled back, and a car with an impeccable Tortello's paint job pulled up a little before seven. Greta, bent over in a flowered robe, watered the roses and performed make-believe snips with Miriam's clippers. Through binoculars, the JTTF lookout watched Icky's guy keeping her in focus through binoculars of his own. Later that morning, Greta, crouching to offset her height, limped down the block and returned about an hour later. Roughly an hour after that, she tipped the agent who delivered her groceries in the supermarket van.

The next day was Sunday. Although that was the only day Tortello's was closed, a shiny black Chrysler exited its lot and arrived near the Rosen house at six forty-five.

All through the previous week, Rice had been watching Icky. Virtually all his waking hours were spent at his body shop, just like T. back at Dream Ride.

Early that afternoon, Tom, who spent each day out of sight in the kitchen, spoke to Greta from just inside the dining alcove. "Rivera just called. At nine-thirty, Rice saw Icky and his wife get in the family car. He tailed them to Hollywood. There's a farmer's market set up there every Sunday. I've been there. Big crowd, all different types—something like Union Square in Manhattan. It's jammed in the morning, because the best stands sell out fast. Mr. and Mrs. Icky buy some fruit, Middle Eastern bread, and then they look at their watches and split up. By the time they meet up again, they've got so many plastic bags wrapped around their wrists, it's impossible to see their hands."

"Meaning no one saw a drop?"

"Correct. But why rule one out?"

"As in why else drive to Hollywood?"

That evening, everyone participated in a conference call between the L.A. and New York SACs.

"They have everything so fiendishly compartmentalized," Folkestone stressed, "that we can't assume anybody knows anybody else. That's the reason we couldn't go much farther than what we pulled out of T."

"You must be thinking what I'm thinking," said Crain. "That the controller here isn't necessarily the same controller from N.Y."

No one contradicted him, but they all nodded at what August said next:

"Someone has to be in charge," said Tom. "Someone, somewhere."

Monday was totally routine. Jenna was down to twenty minutes of A.M. Rosenizing Greta, ten of P.M. de-Rosenizing. Tuesday started out according to schedule. Tortello's latest morning surveillance car was outside. Just after ten-thirty, Miriam's phone rang. Since they'd taken up residence, only about a dozen phone calls had come in: telemarketers, a neighbor with a missing cat, wrong numbers, a friend. For that lady, Greta had complained about a summer cold in a raspy, barely accented voice. Coughing, she promised to call back when the laryngitis was gone. But this call was different.

"Miss Rosen, I'm Rabbi Sackler's wife from Beth Shalom, a congregation in The Valley." The woman's voice had a soothing, reassuring quality. She sounded well-educated, neither particularly young nor old.

"Do I know you?" Greta asked, straining to sound calm, disinterested.

"Oh, no, I don't think so. I'm calling because the rabbi and I are area coordinators for the Survivor's Fund."

"I'm on Social Security. I have nothing left for contributions."

"I'm not asking for anything, dear. Just the opposite, actually. I have information about a deposit your grandfather made long ago in a Swiss bank."

"My grandfather?"

"Yes. Oh dear, I just lost my place. Here it is—Samuel Rosen. Of course, this was so many years past, you must have been a child."

Greta, astonished at how easily the senior victims had been played, felt fury rising in her throat. She let it go, not as a scream, but as a sob.

"I'm so sorry," said the woman, "I've upset you. Believe me, I know, I know. My own great-grandmother . . . her entire family."

Greta was still fighting down her rage, straining to sound vulnerable and confused. "I don't understand . . . all so long ago . . ."

"This isn't right, discussing such a matter over the phone." The woman was sympathetic, apologetic. "I'm only a few blocks away." She quickly shifted up from tentative to urgent: "Can you make time for me if I stop by?"

Greta put the phone down. She heard the dining area floorboards creak as Tom approached from the kitchen.

"We just got a call," he said. "The car from Tortello's just drove away . . . without the usual afternoon replacement." He studied her face. "What about *your* call? Did Icky rush his pigeon back to the roost so he wouldn't get a look at who turns up next? Was that our boy?"

"No," Greta replied. "That was our girl."

CHAPTER **TWENTY-FOUR**

Minutes later, tucked behind the entrance to the dining area, August fed her the stream of information coming in on his earbud: "A dark blue sedan was standing on the street behind us for fifteen minutes, engine running. It's now on the move."

Greta walked to the small mirror hanging next to the entry coat closet. She forced Miriam's face into a smile, and Jenna's dental prosthetic, modeled in a dull, stained yellow, grinned back at her.

"Surveillance sights it coming around the corner . . . going past . . . now circling the block." With a thumbs-up, he added, "Confirm a woman behind the wheel. Coming around again . . . another pass—nope, she's parking. Two houses away."

"Here we go," said Greta, as the mirror caught Tom's head and shoulders leaning into the living room behind her. His reflection gave her a thumbs-up. A moment later, a door closed; he was in place in the kitchen utility closet.

Greta sat on the edge of one of the rose-patterned chairs, her right foot tapping out a jittery SOS. Strange, but she felt more exposed in Miriam's living room than in any of her past undercover setups—nearly every one a sting directed at a man with a reputation for brutality. Had she been incredibly brave back then, or just unbelievably stupid? Why so apprehensive of this particular adversary, a phony rabbi's wife not yet put to the test by someone under the age of seventy five? How much of a threat could she pose against a cop with an entire JTTF crew as backup?

Greta moved to one of the windows, stood to the side, and studied the blue sedan. Two doors, inconspicuous, the typical economy-priced rental. The woman behind the wheel waited several minutes before getting out, like a person who didn't want to be the first to arrive at the party.

As she came around the hood, Greta figured her for a woman about her own age, medium height, medium build, with precisely cut and highlighted brown hair. Everything about her was subdued but stylish. Her two-piece navy outfit had a boxy top with understated white detailing at the neckline and cuffs. The skirt was slightly flared, not too short, not too long. Halfway down the front walkway, the fabric came into focus as a light bouclé knit. It had a crisp, new look, as if the rabbi's better half had just walked out of a Bloomingdale's dressing room, minus all the tags. The heels of her matching pumps were a sensible height, two-and-a-half or three inches. Good legs, well-defined calf muscles.

The first *What's Wrong with This Picture?* was the cheap car . . . definitely not picked from the unlimited fleet of Audis and Volvos provided by Icky-Tortello's. Tom had guessed right about the compartmentalization.

The second *What's Wrong?* was a pair of outdated, oversized—as in Jackie O.—sunglasses that covered half her face. However, as soon as she set foot on Miriam's front walk, she switched her no-nonsense briefcase to her left hand and slipped them off and into her shoulder bag. The woman now standing face-to-face with the front door was a humanitarian with class, a still-youthful kosher fairy godmother to elderly Holocaust survivors.

"The bell doesn't work." Greta cracked the front door only a few inches, just enough to let her I'm-not-exactly-thrilled-to-see-you tone drift out. "I saw you from the window." Opening the door wider, she grumbled, "As long as you're here, you might as well come in."

With a big smile (teeth bleached sparkly white), she sailed inside without the slightest hesitation. Her eyes darted around the room; Greta was sure they were absorbing hundreds of details she'd failed to notice during her nearly week-long stay. "What a lovely room! Roses, roses, roses! Everyone's favorite flower!"

"Unless you have an allergy," Greta responded, invoking Miriam Rosen at her most cantankerous. She gestured toward the sofa. "Have a seat."

The visitor held up her briefcase. "It would be easier if we could sit at a table, where I can spread out the papers I've brought along." Catching sight of the dining area, she inclined her head toward it. "Now, *that* would be perfect."

"All right," Greta shrugged. "I had some water on the boil for tea when you called. Maybe you want a cup?"

"If it's not too much trouble, I'd love to join you. Call me Linda, please."

"Have a seat, Mrs. Sackler," said Greta, pointing to a chair.

While Greta puttered in the kitchen, her guest seamlessly segued into a condensed explanation of the Claims Resolution Tribunal. An efficient multitasker, she draped her handbag over the back of her chair, put her briefcase on the seat of the adjacent chair, flipped it open, and placed neatly stacked forms and ballpoint pens on the tabletop while she spoke. Seconds after Greta returned with two mugs, she punched up the pressure, stressing the here-before-you-know-it July thirteenth deadline.

A little shiver ran up Greta's spine—how many times had this witch rattled off the same deadly spiel, to deliver it so flawlessly? "Just a minute, Mrs. Sackler," she said, and returned to the kitchen. She hobbled back in with a plate, pushed aside the precisely aligned pile in the center of the table, and set it down. It was covered with Pepperidge Farm cookies, Paulina Kantor's favorites. "Go ahead, take one," she urged.

"Oh, thank you—I really love these!" the woman crooned, head down, her hand briefly hovering over the plate as if she'd just been forced to choose between brain cancer and AIDS. "But no—I have to be strong! I'm on Weight Watchers."

"You don't look fat to me," said Greta with a shrug, then sat down heavily on the chair across from her. "Listen, I tried to warn you that coming here was a wild-goose chase, but you insisted. Too bad I don't have the letter to show you, from years and years ago. The bank wrote that there was no account . . . nothing."

The response was a deep sigh—polite confirmation that the bank had been less than honest. "Believe me," she said, "if your grandfather's name is on this list, you have a check coming." From one of the piles, she selected an artfully worn sheaf of papers, several bent staples barely holding them together. "This was the rabbi's idea—the man is absolutely *tireless*—to speed up the search for matches in the greater Los Angeles area." She leafed through to the "Rs," and to Samuel Rosen.

After a little gasp of recognition, Greta asked, "You think that's really him . . . my grandfather?"

"Absolutely. But as I said, the time to file a claim is running out. I'm here to help. And you don't even have to pay for the postage stamp—our congregation has generously established a little fund for any incidentals." She held out a pen.

Miriam's mouth turned down at the corners, but Greta's hand accepted the pen.

"Bear in mind that you are the claimant, and your grandfather the account owner—sometimes that can be confusing. Make sure everything is printed, and in capital letters. Don't rush—take as much time as you need." Dangerously close to sounding like a proctor at the start of an SAT exam, she quickly reverted to Hallmark condolence card mode: "These questions will stir up unhappy memories—that's why I'm here with you. No one should have to go through this alone."

The form's first part, Claimant Information, requested a copy of a driver's license, passport, or other photo ID. "'Please do not send originals,'" Greta read aloud. "I still have a driver's license, but I'll have to go out to get a copy made."

The rabbi's wife put up a hand. "Of course not! That can be taken care of back at the synagogue office. I'll personally return it tomorrow."

"No big hurry—where am I driving? It's over a decade since I owned a car."

"Maybe you'll buy one when your money arrives!" Maybe Linda was a cheerleader back in high school.

"Yeah, sure. One of those little kiddie cars, with pedals." Slowly, Greta rose and made her way to the sideboard, where she'd stowed the vintage purse Mai had come up with, thick plastic printed with a basket weave. After she dropped Miriam Rosen's California license under the woman's nose, she sat again, shifting her hips with discomfort. "What about this next part? 'Alternate Contact'? Most of my friends have moved away or . . ." A sigh, then another uneasy adjustment in the chair. "Should I just fill in your name and address?"

"Just leave it blank, dear." As her visitor flipped ahead to the Family Member Information section, Greta noted that she wasn't the only one in the room wearing a wig. "Any other relatives who'll be part of the claim?"

"I'm it. The only one who made it out of Europe."

Her visitor's mouth shaped itself into a small "O." It was a credible attempt at a look of surprise and sympathy, considering that the bitch wouldn't have been sitting there if Miriam had a roomful of relatives. "Then please, just check 'No.'"

The next few pages, mostly questions dealing with previous or separate claims, went by quickly. For Account Owner Information, Greta filled in Samuel Rosen's name. "But this part," she frowned, "I don't understand all this power of attorney baloney."

After listening to a rudimentary explanation, Greta said emphatically, "The account was for the family, nobody else." After a moment's thought, she backed down. "Well, there was my disinherited uncle. They have a question somewhere about that?"

The slightest glint of annoyance flared up in the woman's eyes. "I don't understand. Your uncle—is he still alive?"

"No, but—"

"Families always have one of those, don't they?" was the comeback, breezy, but relieved. "Well, let's move on to the next part, 'General Information about the Account Owner.' These answers are easier with a parent than a grandparent. Do you know Mr. Rosen's date and place of birth?"

"How would I *not* know?" Greta bristled. "We all lived in *his* father's house. Four generations lived there! My grandmother always gave him a birthday party, with a beautiful cake, decorated with roses." She filled in the dates Miriam had supplied. "And these answers? The day and place he died? They're easy, too. The same day, the same place I got this." She pulled back her sleeve, exposing part of Miriam's SS tattoo.

Perilously close to over-the-top, the woman's hand flew to her heart. "So brutal! I can never see one of those horrid things without . . ." After waiting a few beats, she resumed, still breathy with emotion: "Section Twelve. 'Account Owner's Address Information.' They need all the places your grandfather lived after the account was opened, up to his death."

"We ran all over Europe, trying to get away from the Nazis. There aren't enough spaces for all the places we lived." She scanned down the rest of the page, tracing her index finger along questions whose answers were locked in her memory. "Thirteen—did we ever have an address in Switzerland? Those bastards wouldn't even let us in! Fourteen—any connections to Switzerland? Another joke! This one, Fifteen, asks if my grandfather was a victim of Nazi Persecution. Tell me, does being gassed qualify?"

Before the woman could respond, Greta lowered her head and concentrated on filling in the blanks, just as Miriam had. Then she flipped to the next page, where Sixteen requested 'any other relevant information related to the Account Owner's circumstances and fate' 1933–1945. Carefully, she printed, "My grandfather was stripped of his family, his home, his health, his business, and the clothes on his back. When they took his life, he had only one thing left. His dignity."

After that, she let her coach guide her forward, stopping her only to ask, "What's this Twenty-three? They want me to draw a family tree?"

"There's a blank form at the very end, a chart with little boxes for the names of everyone in your family. Do you want to skip ahead, and do it now? The rest is mostly signatures, and a checklist and review. I already filled out the acknowledgment postcard that they'll send you when your packet is received." She held up the postcard and dropped it into a large manila envelope addressed CLAIMS REGISTRATION OFFICE, CLAIMS RESOLUTION TRIBUNAL, P.O. BOX 1279, OLD CHELSEA STATION, NEW YORK, N.Y. 10113. Miriam Rosen's address was in the upper left corner.

"I'll go in order," Greta replied. She plowed ahead, then painstakingly inserted names in the blank rectangles of the genealogy chart. With finality, she put down the pen and rubbed her wrist. "I can't remember the last time I wrote so much."

"Sorry, but you're not quite done—even though you're very, very close to the finish line." After that display of perverse humor, she flashed a saccharine smile. The claim form disappeared into the envelope.

"What are you talking about? Wasn't that the last page?"

"Yes, but we still have to set up the bank account where the money can be sent."

Greta strained to keep in character while she played back the task force's theories about how new bank accounts—the stepping-off point for the offshore wire transfers—had been set up. She herself had been convinced that forged documents were used, in lieu of active participation by the senior victims. But that, she realized, was par for the course in a scam devoid of any moral boundaries. With more than a tinge of insult, she asked, "Mrs. Sackler, you think because I'm old, I keep my money under the mattress? I had a bank account before you were born."

"Oh, I never doubted it for a second! Every one of the seniors I've helped so far has had direct deposit for Social Security checks. But the point is," she added in a confidential whisper, "you have to take steps to prevent the government from viewing your settlement check as taxable income. Naturally, that's not the case. But any large amount, they'll go right ahead and tax your Social Security income. Or worse."

"Worse? Like what worse?"

"Like cutting it off."

Greta leaned forward, gripping the seat of her chair in alarm. "Social Security! They wouldn't!"

"Oh, you'd eventually get it back. But the burden of proof would be up to you." She lowered her eyes while she delivered the nastiest part of the threat. "I've heard it takes at least two trips to the Social Security office. In person."

As if she'd just taken a direct punch to the gut, Greta recoiled. "That's always an entire day! Getting there, waiting in those miserable plastic chairs, no eating, no drinking, then coming home at rush hour!"

"Terrible, yes. And after that, it takes at least sixty days until they re-activate the monthly payments."

Duly motivated, Greta picked up the pen again. "What do you need?"

"Just these forms." From the smallest paper stack, she handed Greta three white cards. Each had underlying copies in blue, pink, and yellow. The bank's name, unfamiliar, pegged it as regional. "I took the liberty of filling these out with your name and address. All you have to do is sign them and fill in your Social Security number."

"My Social Security number? But isn't that exactly what the problem is?"

"Yes, yes, I'm afraid so, but it's still necessary to open any kind of account. Remember, the best way to avoid the situation I described is to keep the money separate. Not only in a separate account, but in a separate bank, as well. What you don't want to do is mingle the funds."

"Mingle? That's what they kept telling us to do at the senior center! How do you know all this? It's so complicated!"

"Believe me, this isn't my forte at all. But several top accountants are members of our congregation. This is the expert advice they gave the rabbi and me. The last thing we wanted to do was create a headache by acting from the heart." Having already touched that vital organ for emphasis, she didn't repeat the gesture. "Sign next to the Xs. Be sure to press hard with the pen."

As she had on the claim form, Greta scrawled out her practiced facsimile of Miriam Rosen's signature, required twice on each card. It was impossible to miss the blank line for a cosignor signature below each X'd line. Centering the second card, she blurted out, "Maybe this isn't such a good idea."

With her eyes locked on the two yet unsigned forms, her visitor asked, "What could make you say such a thing?"

"I can walk to my Bank of America branch," said Greta. Her pen rattled as she dropped it on the tabletop. "This bank isn't in my neighborhood."

"Oh! Didn't you know? Their newest branch just opened, only two doors down from yours! They were still hanging the sign when I picked up the forms there. Go for a walk tomorrow, you'll see."

The woman was a turn-on-a-dime liar, and the knowledge that her victim wouldn't be around to expose her lies certainly gave her an edge.

"Well, that's better," said Greta. "In that case, I'll drop these cards off in the morning. I have to do my weekly grocery shopping, anyway."

"Oh, I already told the officer who's setting everything up that I'd drop them off today. A very nice lady, a Miss Zimmerman. She'll have everything ready for you tomorrow. And don't worry that you'll miss me coming by to return your driver's license. I won't be here until after the bank closes." She glanced at the two remaining forms.

Greta once again reached for the pen. While she completed the second card, the woman blurted out, "Oh, no!" She was staring at her wristwatch.

"Did I make you late, Mrs. Sackler?"

"Not yet dear," she said gently, as she began to gather the papers into one neat pile, "but I'm afraid I will be if I don't get a move on. A Hadassah meeting at the temple."

Taking the hint, Greta poised the pen over the third card.

"Do you mind if I freshen up?"

"The bathroom is at the top of the stairs."

"Thanks, but I don't need to powder my nose, just fix my lipstick," she said with a smile. As she got to her feet, she smoothed out her outfit and brushed away invisible crumbs from the cookies she'd never touched. Hoisting her handbag off the back of her chair, she placed it on the table and rooted around inside, coming up with a lipstick and a small mirrored compact. As she rolled a raspberry shade over her lips, Greta was sure her eyes weren't on the mirror, but on the last card—verified when she sang out, "Mazel tov! You are officially done!"

With a little flourish, Greta dropped it on top of the stack.

Using both hands, the woman made a little show of putting the lipstick and mirror back in their proper places. As if making a discovery, she brought up a gold-plated cylinder, slightly longer and wider than the lipstick. Her left hand remained in the purse. "Oh, I almost forgot I had this! They were handing out these samples at Macy's last week—the newest fragrance from Chanel." She brought the sprayer up, about three inches from her nose, and sniffed appreciatively. "Lovely!"

Suppressing any shift of her shoulder, Greta reached under the table-top and pulled the PPK from the holster taped to its underside.

"Here, try it!" As she rounded the table, something white entered Greta's peripheral vision—fluttery cloth, possibly a handkerchief. It was in her left hand, mostly out of sight behind her back. The woman's right arm was coming up, extended out straight.

In one fluid movement, Greta pushed her chair back hard and sprang up, assuming a shooter's stance. "Freeze! Federal Agent!" she yelled.

The woman, her finger poised to depress the sprayer, blinked at the agile eighty-year-old woman who was now pointing a gun at her heart. Except for her eyes, she could have been a movie frame paused on a DVD player. Soundlessly, August came up directly behind her. "Move and you're dead," he said. She flinched at his closeness and at the menace in his voice, but the finger above the sprayer didn't move.

"Drop the sprayer," Greta shouted. "Now!" She guessed she was too close to survive whatever lethal dose it contained, but it was too late to take a step back, too late for any distraction at all. August had her. If Greta failed, August would put an end to the murders.

It was obvious that the assassin had entered a state beyond mere denial. So polished, so smart, she had to be struggling not so much against the reality of being trapped, as the absurdity of it—as if being caught had never been even a remote possibility.

Shuffling sounds drifted in from the sunroom's open windows. Agents were converging in the alley, cordoning off the house.

A muscle tremor ran through the extended arm holding out the sprayer, but the finger remained absolutely rigid.

Car doors slammed outside, sirens bleeped, and the kitchen and front doors slammed open simultaneously. The bungalow was filling with agents. Greta sensed a ripple of instability run along the old floorboards from their accumulated weight; the assassin had to feel it as well.

"I'm not Miriam Rosen," she said. "You gain nothing by killing me. But unless you drop that sprayer now, I will shoot."

Returning from wherever she'd been, the woman said, "I want to live." She bent her arm at the elbow, opening up the space between them by at least two more feet. In the next split second, with a flick of her wrist, she sprayed herself full in the face. The golden tube clattered on the floor. With her last lie still on her lips, she collapsed.

August screamed, "Get a medic!"

The woman's body went into convulsions, and her hand grabbed at the fabric over her heart. Greta bent to whisper to her, "You watched them all die. I hope your pain is unbearable. I hope it follows you all the way to hell. May it never stop, through all eternity."

CHAPTER **TWENTY-FIVE**

"You're sure?" August asked the medic.

"Whatever that stuff was, it worked fast. She's dead, definitely dead."

August looked around the bungalow. Minutes before, nearly two dozen JTTF agents had stormed in. To make room for the medics, they'd pushed back into the kitchen and living room. Crowded together, they stood shoulder to shoulder.

Rivera told the medic, "Hold off. We have to speak with the agent in charge."

It was almost two, a quiet time in the neighborhood, with plenty of time before school let out and the early-shift workers began their trek home. Nevertheless, the sudden influx of agents had brought people out of their houses, or at least to their windows.

"Okay, thanks to all of you," said Rivera as he ended his call. Keeping his voice low enough not to carry outdoors, he added, "Quick response, tight coordination. At this point, we're ready to downsize to our core team. Agents who were positioned to our rear, exit first, the way you came in. Remaining agents, as soon as they clear the kitchen door, out through the front. Not a word to anyone, not even a 'No comment.'"

While the backup agents filed out, August and Rivera huddled on the bottom steps of the staircase. During their hushed conversation, both glanced repeatedly at the corpse. Rivera made his phone call, then gestured for the two medics to come closer.

"No body bag—the corpse goes out on a stretcher," Rivera instructed them. "Put an IV in her arm and an oxygen mask over her face. Wheel her out in a big hurry. Emergency lights and siren until you're out of range. You know where the lab is?" One of the medics nodded. "They're expecting you at Bay Two."

Rivera made another call, somewhat longer, then snapped his phone shut. He and August approached Greta, who'd stepped away from the body only when the medics had rushed in.

"Greta," said Rivera, "you can reholster your weapon now."

She looked down, startled to find the PPK still in her hand. She clicked on the safety and watched August stoop to peel away the duct tape holding the holster to the table. He held it out to her, dangling tape and all, and she eased the gun into the leather and handed it back.

A voice came from one of the wicker chairs. "They say this job ages you, but you're taking it to an extreme, Strasser." Although not always the voice of reason, Brauner definitely had a knack for bringing everyone back to reality.

August, she suddenly grasped, was the only agent who'd seen her disguised as Miriam Rosen. No longer concerned about damaging the latex, she ripped away her nose, chin, and cheeks. Slack-jawed, the medics stared, bracing themselves for the next layer to be peeled away. "That's it," she said to the room at large, as she picked off a clump of adhesive clinging to the corner of her mouth. "Only forty years at a time."

She positioned herself behind the head on the gurney and eased off the corpse's brown wig. The pinned-back hair beneath was blond, sprouting dark roots. The assassin had been close to either a touchup or a complete color change. Her wig had concealed a narrow line of bare skin running along her hairline. Olive-toned, it stood out against the considerably lighter makeup covering the rest of the face and throat. "Might as well go out in this, bitch," said Greta as she pulled off the Rosen-wig. Between the blanket stretched up to the oxygen mask and the tight gray curls, no neighbor could imagine that anyone other than Miriam Rosen was being wheeled away to the hospital.

A few minutes after the ambulance siren trailed away, Rice and Zinah walked in. "An Express Mail envelope is on the passenger seat of her car," said Zinah. "On the backseat, a small bag—a nylon carry-on type."

"Too many neighbors poking around right now to bring them inside," said Rivera. "Besides, Crain wants us downtown, so follow us back to headquarters in the rental. When we get there, we'll bag and remove those items, plus anything else in the car."

"Who's got the keys?" Rice asked.

"They're in her purse, over on the table," said Greta. "You have an extra pair of gloves, Zinah? I'll get them."

Rivera touched his head, as if he forgot something. "I'd better call to make sure there's someone waiting in the garage to shoot her car over to Impound for tests. Note the mileage and the gas gauge before you leave the curb."

As soon as his call was completed, Rivera assigned one agent to bag everything on the table, another to drive Greta downtown right after she changed into her own clothes. She handed Rice the keys and was starting up the stairs as Rivera added, "While you're waiting for Strasser, get in touch with the agent minding Miss Rosen over at The Beverly Hills. I doubt either of those ladies will have a problem staying there an extra few days . . . we have to give her enough time to fully recover from the terrible seizure she suffered here today."

"I just got off the phone with Folkestone's office back in New York," Crain announced, as he strode into the conference room. "He's chairing a meeting that just began, so our conference call is off." He looked around. "So what exactly is the issue? Something about an Express Mail envelope?"

"It was in the rental." Rivera pointed to the blue and white cardboard envelope at one end of a long evidence table. Sackler's manila envelope was next to it. His arm swept over the other items on display: the contents of the purse, plus those of the briefcase and the carry-on. "All the rest can be addressed later. Right now, top priority is getting that Express

Mail envelope to the post office before it closes at five, so it can get an L.A. postmark dated today."

August took it from there: "Strasser watched Sackler put the claim form into that manila envelope addressed to the Claims Resolution Tribunal in New York, with Miss Rosen as the return address. Note the regular postage stamps. In contrast, the Express Mail package has prepaid machined postage, the type you buy from a post office clerk. All Sackler had to do was slide the manila envelope inside and drop it in an Express Mail box. She had plenty of time before the five p.m. cutoff for next-day delivery." Pointing up at the wall clock, which read 4:10, he added, "Unfortunately, we don't."

Crain peered down at the large envelope. "From" was filled in with Miss Rosen's address. However, the "To" was not the Claims Resolution Tribunal. "That's interesting—a post office box. Stamford, Connecticut."

"That post office box is in the main post office, in the Stamford city center. It closed five Eastern, and it looks like we have to wait until tomorrow morning for the clerk in charge to locate the box owner's name and address. Everything points to Sackler dropping the packet off en route to the airport. A plane ticket in the inside flap of her purse was for a roundtrip Boston–L.A. flight, arriving here at three-fifteen p.m. yesterday, departing today at five forty-five. To avoid any suspicion that Sackler didn't carry out her assignment, we need to mail it *now*. A surveillance team will have that Stamford post office covered before it opens to the public tomorrow. The red-eye should get us back East a little after six a.m. That gives us a big cushion, because the ETA for an L.A.–Stamford Express Mail package isn't until between noon and three. Then—"

Crain's eyes narrowed. "What red-eye? Tomorrow? When did I authorize that?"

"We tried to reach you as soon as we saw the post office box address," August replied. "You left the building and weren't taking calls, so we called SAC Folkestone."

Teeth clenched, Crain snarled, "*I* was with the *mayor!*"

"So was he."

Despite his perfectly smooth face, Crain's eyes and body language emitted several conflicting signals: Short-lived relief (he'd wanted August and his manpower-sucking operation out of L.A. from Day One), indignation (out of L.A., but only with *his* permission, and certainly not before the case was cleared), and arrogant confusion (Crain's usual state).

"We don't have to be at the airport until eleven," August assured him, "so we can do a preliminary check of the evidence with Rivera. But—"

Crain cut him off. "By all means, get the damn letter to the post office. Done. Now, moving ahead, any results on the dead woman's prints?"

"Nothing so far," Rivera replied, "but there's more to the Express Mail issue. A point Strasser raised after we spoke to Folkestone."

Crain, thoroughly exasperated, asked, "What more can there possibly be?"

Rivera replied, "We need you to sign off on including Miss Rosen's driver's license in the manila envelope—"

Crain waved his hand—dismissing it as a no-brainer.

"As well as," Greta jumped in, "those three bank signature cards."

"What about them?" Crain was strangely wary, as if Greta were no more to be trusted than the assassin.

"Collier contacted the bank's main branch, and a vice president confirmed that Sackler was lying about that new branch. No record of any Miss Zimmerman, either. She also explained that someone—not necessarily the account holder—has to go to the bank in person to *open* an account. To actually *activate* it, those signature cards can be mailed in. The banker volunteered to e-mail the entire staff about any pending Rosen application, but the bank closed while she and Collier were on the phone. It's doubtful whether any results will surface before tomorrow."

"Banks and post offices," Crain muttered impatiently, "unreachable after closing hours."

Greta watched August and Rivera exchange a glance, no doubt about Crain's unreachability *during* working hours. "While we examined Sackler's things on the evidence table," she resumed, "I kept thinking about how many times she'd gone through the application process . . . more precisely, how many times she'd *killed,* to make it such an effortless exercise for her. Relaxed, no qualms, no hesitation—the woman had to be a hired gun, period. Signing the blank cosignor lines and dropping off the cards at a bank would've given her access to the account."

Rivera picked up from there. "And *that* would've been a serious breach of the operation's scrupulous compartmentalization policy. Look at the way she's *mailing* the packet, not passing it along. It points to Sackler only having a single contact in L.A.

"That contact had to be the person who received Icky's surveillance specs—probably dropped Sunday morning in the crowd at the farmer's market. He or she subsequently okayed Rosen as the victim—we forced his hand, sending Blaustein on a cruise, and by then they knew that Tannenbaum was in a nursing home. The next steps were to go to the bank to get the Rosen account started, arrange for Sackler to fly in, and then to review Rosen's profile with her when she arrived in L.A. At that meeting, this sole contact also gave Sackler the signature cards and the postage-paid Express Mail envelope. Oh, and Sackler had to commit to a scheduled time when she'd show up at Rosen's house, so Icky's boys would drive away without ever seeing her. Compartmentalization, once again."

Rivera concluded, "That contact might or might not be the person picking up the Express Mail packet in Stamford tomorrow. Regardless, we didn't want to include the cards and the license without running this by you . . . in case you see something we missed."

Smart enough to catch the sarcasm, but unable to fault the logic, Crain muttered, "Sure. Include them."

All eyes were on J. J. while he slid the license and signature cards into the manila envelope, dropped it into the Express Mail packet, sealed it, and handed it to an agent.

"That's out of the way," Crain sighed, while the agent raced out the door. He gestured toward the evidence table. "What about all the rest of this?"

August shot a go-ahead look at Brauner. In his straightforward manner, he replied, "We've been concentrating on the plane ticket, Avis agreement, and motel receipt we found in her purse. All three were in the name Maria Terle, as well as a MasterCard and a Delaware driver's license. She had Sackler ID, as well. One piece of luggage was checked on her flight from Boston—we doubt it was the carry-on. Strasser's suggestion that it was a garment bag with Sackler's outfit makes sense.

"Between the time she left the Avis lot and checked into her motel, four hours are unaccounted for—three hours, allowing for drive time and traffic. During that period, she could have met her contact at any one of hundreds of motels, bars, restaurants, or fast-food outlets en route to her motel. For that matter, she could've parked the rental a stone's throw from LAX, and waited for the contact to pick her up. Three hours seems a reasonable amount of time to review surveillance photos, learn Rosen's background and routine, study maps of the neighborhood. Dell Rice did the math with the beginning mileage on the Avis agreement and the mileage he recorded when he left the Rosen house. Pretty close to the exact distance between there and the airport.

"The motel receipt shows that she checked in at 8:25 last night, paid cash in advance—$58.60 for a single, plus a three-hundred-dollar security deposit. Her signature as Maria Terle acknowledges that the deposit was returned in full when she checked out this morning. Agents were still on their way to the motel about fifteen minutes ago. At this time of day, they might be able to interview both day and night managers—if they haven't already switched shifts.

"Only one other item of interest in the purse." Brauner swept his hand over the rest of what had been removed from the handbag, which included makeup, contact lenses, nonprescription glasses, the big sunglasses, an Altoids box stuffed with ten one hundred dollar bills, tissues, pens, and spare change.

Crain blinked. "This?" He leaned forward briefly to scrutinize a knife with a five-inch handle and slightly shorter blade.

"It's an ordinary kitchen knife," Brauner replied. "This brand is sold in supermarkets and discount stores. She probably bought it somewhere along the highway. We figure it's a backup, just in case the spray doesn't work."

Greta summed up the rest. "As far as the briefcase goes, you won't see anything other than what she used for the application. The carry-on had an auburn wig, more makeup, a pale pink knit top, a black jersey top, black slacks, and black shoes. None of it was up to the quality of the Sackler outfit."

"Tell Crain your take on that," J. J. urged.

"She checked one piece of baggage in Boston, probably left it in her car overnight, and changed—in the car—from Terle to Sackler on the way to Miss Rosen's house. The change would've been reversed on the way back to the airport, with Sackler's stuff tossed in a Dumpster."

"Well *that* never happened." Crain's tone had a strange edge. "What an invaluable asset she would've been . . . if she was still alive."

"What's that supposed to mean?" Greta stared at him. No reply, just a stare in return. Again, notched up several decibels, she demanded, "What the hell is that supposed to mean?"

"Well, we *were* aiming for an arrest . . . not a suicide."

"Are you saying I fucked up because in an entire two or three seconds, I didn't read her mind and figure out what she was going to do and stop her? Or was my big mistake not letting her kill me first?"

"I'm only saying it was a lost opportunity. So much effort, such an ambitious setup . . . She could have moved us up at least another level, gotten us closer to the masterminds at the top. Wasn't that the intended result?"

"Fuck the intended result! We saved Miriam Rosen's life!"

Before Crain could retort, Rivera's phone rang. "It's the guys at the motel," he said, putting up a hand for silence. Greta looked at Tom, who gave her an almost imperceptible shake of the head, a "Cool it."

Rivera mostly listened, then said, "No, we don't need a copy, we have it here. Just follow through on the room, then. Thanks . . . right, that should do it." He sighed as he clicked off. "The night manager followed protocol— with a cash deposit, he had to copy ID before handing over a key. He said she looked pretty much like the Maria Terle license photo, just a little older. His description matches the wig and clothes found in the carry-on. Fortunately, her room wasn't rented out after she left, and the agents on site had it sealed. They're checking for prints, et cetera, but apparently she wiped it down and left nothing behind, not even a Kleenex. So far, no one on the motel staff saw her or any other person entering or leaving her room. No additional luggage was noted by either manager, just the carry-on. When she left in the morning, she was wearing the pink sweater."

Acting as if there had never been a blowup, Crain made calls on the other side of the room. Meanwhile, the agents continued to sift through the evidence.

August whispered to her, "Engaging with people like Crain only feeds their egos. I know what you're thinking—Crain and Quill, one bullet. It's not worth it, Strasser. Meanwhile, Rivera thinks you're smart as a whip, and that you're secretly a spunky Latina. Believe me, he's the guy who matters."

Half an hour later, Rivera's phone rang again. The lines on his face deepened as he listened. When the call ended, he announced, "Maria Terle was a real person reported missing over a year ago in Delaware. Her body was discovered four weeks ago. Looks like Holocaust survivors aren't this killer's only victims."

CHAPTER **TWENTY-SIX**

"You didn't get any sleep, did you?" whispered Zinah, as they edged past the fresh-lipstick smiles of the flight attendants.

"It sounds like a bad song," Greta replied, "but I couldn't get that woman out of my head."

"Bloody cold . . . that is how you would describe her?"

"What you want is 'cold-blooded.' I'll use it in a sentence: She was one of the two most cold-blooded pieces of shit I ever met." To answer Zinah's questioning look, she added, "The other one is a drug dealer in my precinct—a thug who fired his gun across a playground full of little kids . . . and killed a young woman in a wheelchair. Unlike Miss Chanel, he was still alive the last time I spoke to my partner."

"Cold-blooded," Zinah whispered, locking it in.

A van was waiting for the team. Outside the terminal, the early morning air was tainted with jet fuel. Along with the subway's dank blended bouquet and bus exhaust, it was an essential element of eau de New York—noxious, but oddly comforting in its familiarity. Greta, Zinah, August, Rice, and Brauner piled into a waiting van.

Although Greta had remained incommunicado during her JTTF assignment except for Kim, the brief exchange with Zinah reminded her that he was at the top of her short list of people owed a phone call. Schuyler, the detective from the Seven-Eight, had left several messages. They always ended "I know you can't call back, but what the hell." And the law office of one Maurice Yablonsky—did her smarmy ex have a new lawyer?— had been annoyingly persistent. They'd all have to wait.

In the glare that followed a July sunrise, their driver made it up Interstate 95 to Stamford without hitting too many traffic snags. Folkestone, either up all night or an early riser, phoned to welcome them back.

"I've been in touch with the top at the Connecticut State Police," he told Tom, "and we agreed that our best interface is their Bureau of Criminal Investigations. Ron Todaro is our lead officer. He's already with our advance people in Stamford. Todaro will be responsible for coordination with the local cops, in Stamford and any other municipality involved. He'll also provide additional backup as needed."

As they rolled down the exit ramp, a call came in with the latest tracking update on the Express Mail envelope. It was due to arrive at the post office by one-thirty that afternoon and wind up in the post office box approximately an hour after that.

After check-in at their hotel and a chance to freshen up, they regrouped in a meeting room. An agent apparently known to everyone but Greta handed her a sheet of paper that had just chugged out of a desktop printer. He introduced himself as Waylon—whether that was his first or last name wasn't specified, but he was young enough for his parents to have been country music fans in the late Seventies.

"Meet our post office box holder, Jules Bersonne," Tom announced. "For once, T. was actually telling the truth—he really is a good-looking guy in his forties."

Greta glanced down at the blowup of Bersonne's Connecticut driver's license. Not bad: a full head of wavy dark hair, neatly combed back; amused eyes; a curvy mouth caught close to a smile. Enough space was left at the bottom of the photo for a hint of jacket and tie, with the collar of a white shirt setting off either a fading tan or dusky complexion. Date of birth, 04-25-61. Brown eyes, 5'8". Home address, Darien.

"Waylon here was lying in wait for the postal clerk when she showed up for work this morning," Tom continued. "Turns out that leasing a post office box not only requires several forms of ID, but they also send out a certified letter that requires a signature—an on-premises verification. The box in question is in the name of a bona fide Stamford business. That business is owned by Bersonne."

"Our agents fanned out immediately, both at Bersonne's home and his business," Waylon began. He clicked a desktop computer off screen saver. "All e-mailed reports from the field are coming in on this computer. Actually, we can get started right now, with his office building."

They all moved in closer while a slideshow worked through photos of a two-story corner brick office building on a wide through-street.

"The post office box holder is SISS, a corporation. Jules Bersonne, the CEO, has sole access to the box. SISS stands for StoneWall Internet Security Systems. According to its Web site, they have a perfect track record for protecting small to midsize online businesses from fraud."

A low chuckle rumbled from Rice. "Fraud? Talk about the fox guarding the henhouse!"

"You'd think so, but it's Chamber of Commerce-legit, not a shell. This is its only bricks-and-mortar location, roughly a mile from here—the street is US-1. SISS is in Suite 2F, on the second floor. Nine other businesses are listed in the lobby directory." He hit pause for a shot of a sign affixed to the building; it advertised available office space. "Two suites are currently unoccupied." Next up was the front entrance, with double doors and a metal canopy. "This is the only public entrance. A fire door's at the rear and an exit is on the side you can't see from this view—it opens directly into the building's parking lot. Here's Bersonne, arriving at 8:36."

The next sequence of shots showed a black car pulling into the parking area. "2003 Lexus, registered to the business," Waylon noted. Bersonne, carrying a slim leather briefcase, emerged and punched in a code at the side door. In his dark suit, he projected a purposeful-business-owner attitude. "Unless anyone wants a second run-through, I'll show you what we've got on his home."

After a glance around, August said, "Go ahead."

The young agent clicked his way to another slideshow featuring a handsome white colonial perched on the crest of a gentle rise. An expansive lawn sloped down to a low, hand-stacked stone wall. Straight in some spots, sagging in others, it marked property lines that might have been obsolete for centuries.

"Literally a stone wall?" Greta wondered out loud. "I mean, as in SISS? Was I the only one thinking more along the lines of Stonewall Jackson, the Stonewall Riots . . . or maybe just the attributes of being obstinate and stubborn?"

"Personal traits no one here would ever associate with you, Strasser," sniped Brauner. "But I was absolutely with you on that." He nodded at Waylon, who started a quick tour of Bersonne's neighborhood.

"As you can see, Darien—certainly this part of it—is pretty upscale. It's just a short ride up I-95 from here. Okay, this car pulling out of the garage? A 2002 BMW, also registered to SISS. The woman behind the wheel is Bersonne's wife, Maureen. Those shots of Bersonne arriving at SISS? They're time stamped at just about the same time as these of Maureen leaving the house."

Maureen L. Bersonne's driver's license filled the screen. She was a blue-eyed blonde with a round, fading-pretty face. Greta noted that she was two inches taller and five years older than her husband.

"No signs of anyone left inside the house, and school's been out for a couple of weeks," Waylon was saying. "There's a basketball hoop around the back, and kid stuff stacked near the pool, so we're checking on kids. On to the Stamford main post office?"

"Sure," said Tom. "I figure it's not too far from here?"

"Not at all. By way of orientation, you drove here on I-95. The I-95 overpass is visible from the post office, looking south. Looking north from there, you can also see U.S.-1, a block or so away. The main post office has one public entrance, on Atlantic Street. It sits on the corner of Atlantic and Federal."

Waylon guided them through exterior shots of the post office, a dignified structure with a brick and limestone façade and Spanish tile roof. Double stone staircases swept up to a line of three doors, each set beneath one of the building's many soaring arched windows. The front was guarded by two colossal lights of glass and oxidized copper. Their shape was an amalgam of coach lantern, Greek urn, and lighthouse beacon.

"They don't make post offices like that anymore," said Rice.

"About a hundred years old, landmark status," agreed Waylon. "Our surveillance also includes this USPS truck lot on Federal." The lot shot was followed by a stark modern concrete structure. "This garage is right across the street on Atlantic. We've sealed off its top level. From up there, you can observe everyone approaching the main entrance without being seen. Any questions on the exterior?"

When no questions were forthcoming, he continued, "Inside, the space open to the public is smaller than you'd expect—a lot goes on behind the scenes."

August whistled. "What are we looking at? Over a thousand post office boxes? That sure narrows down the space."

"All together, fifteen hundred," Waylon replied. "The majority's massed right there, opposite the entry doors—not much more than a hallway, with just the boxes and a couple of tables for filling out forms. Here we turn right after entering the building, then left—as you see, there are the clerks, way back, behind a counter at the far end. Think of it as L-shaped—except the L is flipped backward."

"And those are the remaining boxes, along that inside wall where you're facing the clerks?" Rice asked.

"Correct, but the one we're watching is to the extreme left when you walk in."

"As far away as you can get from the clerks and people buying stamps," Brauner noted, "completely out of their line of sight. That clerk you met with this morning might be the only one who's actually had contact with Bersonne."

Waylon frowned. "Unfortunately, that's not the case. She was transferred here last year, and SISS has had that box since 2000. Take a look at the shots of the target box section. The boxes come in different sizes, with the smallest, for regular business envelopes, generally on top. Closer to the bottom, they're bigger, for small packages—or an Express Mail envelope. Here's the SISS box, so low Bersonne has to stoop down to open it. Even if she stooped down at the same time, she wouldn't necessarily see—"

The computer chimed for an incoming e-mail. It came from Stan and Chris in Brooklyn, still actively watching the T.-less T. team. Waylon opened a video clip. It began with a daytime surveillance shot all too familiar to Greta: the exterior of the storefront mosque where T. met his contact.

The sun-splashed sidewalk was deserted until a few men meandered out, scattering in different directions. T. emerged next, looking all around, one hand up to shield his eyes. He stopped, put on sunglasses, and passed out of frame. After an interval, a long-bearded group emerged, all dressed in loose white shirts, wide white trousers, and sandals. They were followed by a steady stream of men, exiting singly or in pairs. Suddenly, a knot of five burst out, all extremely animated; they appeared to be involved in a friendly disagreement. Another man hurried from the mosque, catching up with their group. He did not participate in their discussion. His dark beard was short and neat. The scene froze.

Next, the sandaled brigade's exit was repeated. The camera zoomed in on a blurry mass lurking just inside the right side of the mosque's doorway, then rolled forward again. When the Arguing Guys walked out (only two of them fit on the left side of the enlarged frame), the blur moved to the center. It was quickly reconstituted as Tidy Beard Guy, caught waiting for the best cover. The rest of the scene played out, this time close on his face. As the visual information was refined, a big cheer went up from the group clustered around the monitor.

"My main man, Jules!" crooned Rice. "The Bersonne Personne! Lookin' good at the mosque! Pussy on yo' chin!"

A split screen appeared, with Tidy Beard's enlarged image on one side, Bersonne's Connecticut license photo on the other.

"You're grandstanding, Flatbush!" Tom yelled at the screen, but with both thumbs up. "Okay, that's a confidence builder," he grinned. "Now, back to the post office—Waylon, how many agents inside at present?"

"One behind the real clerks at the far end, sorting through dead letters. A second is out of sight in the area directly behind the box. Later, when the Express Mail arrives, we'll have two more filling out forms, one in each part of the L. They'll be refreshed with agents from exterior surveillance every twenty minutes. Enough, you think?"

"As long as you maintain a lock on the exterior," August replied. "Do we have ears in Darien yet?"

"Should be finished by noon," Waylon replied, "and the office by tonight."

"Good. Let's dig deeper into Bersonne—some background we can mull while we're sitting in that parking garage." August rolled his shoulders, then pressed his shoulder blades together a few times. Greta looked around at a room filled with people who, more than anything, could use a few hours of uninterrupted sleep.

Waylon shrugged apologetically. "We need more time to fill in the blanks on a complete profile. He's been living at his current address in Darien since 1996. His first known appearance in Connecticut was in 1993, applying for a driver's license. Showed Motor Vehicles an Illinois license he'd held four years, Chicago address. Prior to that, he drove in California—L.A. '86–'89, San Francisco '85–'86. His first California application listed a dorm at a North Carolina State college as his previous address. That meshes with a report from Immigration that he entered the U.S. on a Belgian passport in 1981, student visa. Right before we began, an agent was camped out, waiting for the N.C. State registrar's office to open. I was hoping to have heard from her by now."

"I'm just being greedy," Tom smiled. "Great job. We'll get it as it comes in."

During their vigil in the parking garage, Greta kept imagining the Express Mail packet in the SISS box, propped up and tilted to one side, waiting. Bersonne didn't leave SISS for lunch. Without him in play, everyone in the van took turns at stretching their legs for ten-minute breaks, pacing back and forth through the top level's empty parking spots.

Near the end of Greta's first tour, a big man in a suit strode right up the middle of the ramp. He was wearing the skinniest tie she'd ever seen, thin as a pencil. Greta stopped short, about to shoo him right back down to the next level, until the obvious gave him away: he still walked as if he had motorcycle boots on.

Hand extended for a shake, he called out, "Hi, Ron Todaro, State Police. You must be Agent Strasser, but I don't believe you were expecting me." His voice was deep and clear, as calm as the TV voices that urge Americans to buy pickup trucks. "I guess you weren't in the van when I called."

"I guess not," she said, shaking his hand. "Interesting tie."

"Required, but no size restrictions," he smiled. "We were pretty busy this morning, so I couldn't meet up with you folks right away. I wanted to connect the names to faces."

"Vice versa," she said, and escorted him to the van.

"I got a look at the wife earlier," Ron reported after introductions. "On her way out of the real estate agency where she works. Drove a couple to one of her listings. The sign had one of those extra hangers attached. Her name's on it, 'Maureen L. Bersonne, Diamond Circle of Excellence.' Guess she sells a lot of houses."

Todaro was smart enough to leave the surveillance van before he got as twitchy as the team.

"Blood from a stone!" burst angrily through the speakerphone—it was the agent in North Carolina, hours later than expected, and mightily riled. August and Brauner immediately swiveled toward Greta, as if they'd just discovered her long-lost twin.

"I spent the morning being accused of trampling on civil rights! You won't believe the fuss they made over a twenty-year-old yearbook!"

Once she caught her breath, she went right to early Bersonne: "Three years at NCS—they accepted all his credits from a year at the University of Liège, in Belgium. He graduated in 1984, cum laude, major in engineering. Lived on campus, no political affiliations, just math, chess, and French clubs. I wasn't going to leave with just that, and I was sure I was missing something. It was hell getting them to make a copy of the transcript from Liège, but I refused to leave without it. It took all this time to check out, but listen to this: First, the address on the transcript isn't the university at all, but a small shop near the university. Six different owners since. Second, Bersonne never attended Liège. Third, that was because he never existed—except on the passport he used to enter this country. I was amazed that the college never picked up on it. Then I thought about what a different world it was in 1981 . . . no e-mail, no Internet . . . calls to Europe must've cost a fortune. Did we even have fax machines back then? It makes you wonder how many Bersonnes weaseled their way in like that. Think about it—a small state college attracting a foreign student— must've made them feel like they were in the Ivy League."

Hours of watching the ebb and flow of postal customers had them doubting if Bersonne was ever going to show up.

"He's cutting it close," said Greta. "The post office closes in twenty minutes."

Five minutes later, the voice of their communications coordinator filled the van: "Bersonne just exited through the parking lot door . . . walking to his car, taking off his jacket . . . in no hurry pulling out." After a brief interval, she reported, "We have two cars on him, headed your way on U.S.-1. Traffic's heavy, but moving at a steady pace."

"Okay, we've got him in sight," Tom informed her. The van's clock read 4:53.

"Half an hour ago, no parking spots on Atlantic so near to the post office," observed Zinah, as Bersonne's Lexus glided up along the curb. "Most cars now are gone. He times it to take this advantage."

Bersonne slid out of the Lexus and, with no indication of haste, climbed the stairs leading to the post office entrance. The afternoon was still and hot, and he hadn't bothered to put his jacket back on. His tie was loosened.

"Straight to the box," said an agent inside the post office. "Removing envelope. Exiting. Gone. Never looked at the label."

Two cars parked on Federal became Bersonne's new tail. Communiqués came in as he continued on to I-95, eased into the bottleneck at his Darien exit ramp, and finally came to a stop in the three-bay garage next to his wife's Beamer. An empty third slot could accommodate the missing five-year-old Range Rover registered to Maureen.

Back at the hotel, the team spent the evening sorting through information gathered earlier in the day. For starters, Bersonne's home in Darien was now owned solely by Maureen, inherited from her first husband, William Lafferty. Four children had been born to the Laffertys: two daughters, twelve and sixteen; and two sons, nineteen and twenty-one, both college students. Several telephone calls had come in for the boys and the older girl. Maureen patiently told their friends that "the gang" had driven up to their grandparents' summer house in Maine for two weeks, and that the area was a cell phone dead zone.

"One Land Rover accounted for. Hoo-rah." Slouched down in a chair, head tilted back, Brauner added, "You've got to hand it to Bersonne— marrying old Maureen was one hell of a coup. Just like Zinah pointed out about the parking spot, he timed it to his advantage. It delivered instant family, instant lifestyle."

"Add instant pillar of the community to that," said Tom. "He's only been in this area twelve years—for pillardom, that's the fast track."

The more the team dug, the more impressed they were by the way Bersonne had so thoroughly insinuated himself into his privileged little corner of Connecticut. His name came up on a number of community Web sites; he was variously listed as a board member, committee head, and/or elected officer.

Waylon had turned up an online industry newsletter with a short article on SISS. It quoted Bersonne's tribute to the fledgling tech company that had hired him when he first arrived in Stamford. "Their receptiveness to fresh ideas inspired me to create a business of my own."

"And inspires me to gag," Brauner sighed, "but it sure looks like the guy is bulletproof in this town."

"Waylon," Greta asked, "could you go back to that split screen Brooklyn sent this morning?" He obliged, and everyone stared at her staring at Bersonne. "As soon as I saw that license, you know what I thought? That the person behind the camera at the DMV had to be a woman. See that look? The guy is flirting with her! And Belgium—do they speak French there?"

Rice was nodding. "Some parts do. Liège sounds like the French part."

"Remember those clubs in college? One was the French club," said Waylon.

"There you go," said Greta. "Combine that with the name Bersonne and his lie about the university in Liège—that's a lot to risk unless you're fluent in French. Maybe he speaks English with a sexy French accent."

An embarrassed silence followed, a group *Where the hell is she going with this?*

"Come on, where else do they speak French?" She quickly added, "I mean, where in the Middle East?"

"Lebanon," Zinah called out, "but not officially. I am seeing your direction, Greta—you are after trouble spots. North Africa, you have Algeria and Morocco. Several countries more all over Africa."

"Got it!" said August. "Absolutely no reason to peg Bersonne as a Belgian. Impressive deductive reasoning, Strasser . . . with a sprinkling of feminine intuition."

"I'll take the deductive reasoning part," she shot back, "but I was really pissed when all of you started looking at me like I wanted to date the slimy son of a bitch."

CHAPTER **TWENTY-SEVEN**

At eight-fifteen the next morning, Bersonne's Lexus pulled up to an Express Mail Box outside a post office on U.S.-1. Without leaving his car, he dropped something in.

Before Bersonne's short commute ended at SISS, the Mail Box underwent an unscheduled emptying. The Express Mail envelope was on its way to one Shimon Schlechter, a resident of 18G in a building on Olympic Boulevard in Los Angeles.

Agent J. J. Rivera was alerted immediately.

Later that morning, Greta studied surveillance shots of Maureen walking from her car to her office. Her print wrap dress showed off great legs, but the seams of her linen jacket strained across her back. The stiff hairstyle hadn't changed since her last driver's license photo, nor, in all likelihood, since the one before. "What's the consensus on Maureen?" she asked. "Is she involved? What does she know? Does she even suspect him?"

Rice answered right away. "She's lived in the area her whole life. She's a mom. A 'yes' to any of those questions would put her kids in harm's way. I just don't see that."

After nervously shuffling through some papers, Zinah spoke up. "I have also been curious about Maureen. I searched Motor Vehicle records, and her maiden name was McBride." Her hands were rolling and unrolling the papers into a tube that became narrower and narrower. "Familiar, this name, but from where? I went through everything twice. Then I saw who gave Bersonne his 'inspiring' first job in Stamford."

Tom checked his copy of the newsletter. "Good work, Zinah! 'Polk, *McBride*, and Jensen!'"

"This firm is no longer in business for several years, thanks to—as a newspaper described it, 'a handsome buyout.' But that McBride— Terence—is six years older than Maureen. From DMV, their first licenses show the same address, so we may assume they are brother and sister, yes? From there, many opportunities for Bersonne and Maureen to cross paths can be imagined."

She stopped and looked around, her dark eyes widening with the realization that her solo investigation had her colleagues greatly intrigued. "A year and a half after Bersonne comes to Stamford," Zinah resumed, "Maureen's husband is on a train delayed very late from New York because of a heavy rain of ice. When he leaves the station, the ice is thickly on everything, and still falling. His car makes it over the top of a steep hill, then skids off the road. It flips over going down. By ten-thirty, Maureen is so worried to call the police. They do not find the car until morning. Lafferty is inside, dead. Their report gives brake failure as the cause. This storm was predicted in the newspaper three days before. Lafferty's car sat in the train station parking lot all day."

Zinah tried to flatten the papers on her lap. "Here is Lafferty's obituary, from 1994." As soon as she placed them in their outstretched hands, the papers curled up again.

The local newspaper had run a two-column obituary, complete with photo. The dignified, Karsh-like portrait was provided courtesy of Lafferty's employer, a firm described in the second line as "Manhattan's top-billing advertising agency." William S. Lafferty ("known to all as Billy"), 41, had steadily risen through its ranks to Executive Vice President. His accounts were listed in order of billing dollars: one of the Big Three auto manufacturers; the nation's largest brewery; the top soap manufacturer; a pharmaceutical giant. Next, it was pointed out, Billy had been instrumental in "recently shepherding" his firm from private to public owner-ship.

"I see a guy with a shepherd's crook looking up at the star of Bethle-hem," said Brauner. "Under his robe, he's in wingtips and a pinstripe suit."

After a long list of Billy's clubs and civic and charitable affiliations—more than Bersonne's, but many the same—it was noted that the Lafferty family had lived in the same Darien home for over a century. Maureen and their four children, ranging from three to eleven, came first among the survivors.

"I bet if his life insurance company was one of his accounts, they would've slapped their logo on his coffin," said Greta.

"Maureen is a widow at thirty-eight with four young children," Zinah summed up. "Not a number one choice for a man seeking a wife—except for the fat wedding purse."

"Count on it," said Tom. "Count on Bersonne picking out a wedding ring for Maureen the day he met her, too. What a romantic guy! Maybe six, seven months after Billy literally gets iced, he makes one of those thinking-of-you calls, just to see how the lonely widow is coping. Before you know it, he's whispering to Maureen—in ze sexy French accent—that she's his dream girl . . . that her genius children can do no wrong . . . that her house belongs in *Architectural Digest*. All this from a hottie who's spent the last three years knocking himself out for her brother. How could she say no? Zinah, when did you say the brother's business was bought out?"

"The handsome buyout is 1999."

"That either put Bersonne out of a job, or passed him along to new people who were of no use to him whatsoever. But just like that ring, he's been ready to spring his concept for a new business for a long time."

"Right, a business that uses his true management skills," said Rice, "like getting his sleeper cells staffed and ready. SISS makes the perfect cover for all the traveling he plans to do. Which reminds me—any up-date on that travel history, Waylon?"

"Still incomplete—I'm on my way to see if I can give them a push . . . no, a shove." Waylon stood up. "But I'd just like to add a thought on Agent

Strasser's question—about whether Maureen Bersonne knows anything? Lafferty's obit makes it pretty clear that the guy had to be one hell of a workaholic—all those big clients, scattered all over the country. Why wouldn't Maureen see a schedule that's heavy on airplane trips as Business-as-Usual, Husband-as-Usual? Bersonne could care less about putting her and her kids in danger. But the guy has the whole city fooled—why not his wife?"

Just before 4:00 P.M., two phone calls came in from L.A.'s JTTF in rapid succession, both from Rivera. The first was a bulletin about Schlecter's address on Olympic Boulevard. "Put me on speakerphone," said J. J., a little out of breath. "First of all, it's not an apartment building . . . even though that's the intended illusion. We're talking about a so-called suite in a small office building, one of those places that has a receptionist out front and a wall of mailboxes in the back. An address like 18G is used by people looking to pull a quick scam and even quicker fade. That's how the suite owners can ask for—and get—three months rent in advance. Anyhow, the mailman stopped there a little after ten. Maybe an hour later, the guy with 18G's key shows up. If I say late twenties, jeans, scruffy beard, he sounds hip—he's anything but. Nothing was in his box. He leaves. He drives to two more locations, same phony setup as 18G. Maybe he visited a few others before he got to Olympic—we'll find out tomorrow. Anyhow, nothing was in those last two boxes, either."

"Sounds like his daily rounds," said Dell.

"No doubt," Rivera agreed. "After that, he drives to Valencia, a long ride. He lives in a little shit box, like every one you've ever seen explode when a stoner turns up the burner under the meth too high. His car is registered to Nabil Barhoun. No surprise that the registration address is also a phony mail drop. We'll be waiting for him tomorrow, when he picks up the Express Mail, but at the same time, during his long drive down to L.A.—"

"Definitely," agreed August, "find out what's really cooking in Valencia."

The second call began, "Speakerphone again, guys. I've got very good and very strange news. The good news is short: "The bank officer with a pending Rosen account, Ms. R. Jenkins, was out sick yesterday, so she couldn't reply to the e-mail until today. One look at Bersonne's license photo," Rivera explained gleefully, "and she's sure he's the guy she met, if you added a beard and glasses. Teeny accent, big flirt."

With a small celebration breaking out behind him, August had to yell: "That's great news! What's the strange stuff, J. J.?"

"Open the e-mail we just sent you. We just caught a match on aka Sackler's prints."

"What's the source?" asked Tom.

"Israel has her in their 'presumed dead' category—too dangerous to be written off without irrefutable proof. They're patient, though. This the first time anything's come up on this little honey bun in years."

"Were they willing to share?"

"Beyond willing—they had to suppress their elation. Our assassin went by the name Fahada. Half-Syrian, half-Palestinian, orphaned at fifteen. One of Hezbollah's first female recruits. They picked her out of a refugee camp in Lebanon . . . you'll see why."

Two images appeared on the monitor: On the left, a man and woman in a restaurant, unaware of the camera, their faces close, his hand on hers. On the right, a blowup of the woman's face, framed by her long, dark hair. She was a knockout. Fine-boned, about twenty. Take away the youthful softness, and she could be the future Miss Chanel.

"That restaurant picture was taken in London," J. J. explained. The guy was an Israeli agent—not nearly as undercover as he should've been. He bled to death in an alley a few doors from the restaurant, not just knifed, but—" Rivera searched for the right words. "Let's say she left her signature . . . and it wasn't 'Love, Fahada.'

"Same MO with two other covert op Israelis, one in Damascus, the other in Marseilles. After the attacks on the Marine barracks and the U.S. Embassy in Beirut, she got bolder. Popped up in a Jerusalem hospital in

'84. Two injured members of Hezbollah were being treated and held there after a botched bombing. The soldier guarding them got suspicious when a nurse he never saw before came out of their room. The soldier didn't survive, but he screamed loud enough to force our girl to take off without the knife she stuck in his gut—her prints were all over it. Somehow, she'd managed to sneak in and kill the two bombers—either they knew too much, or the political capital Hezbollah could gain from pinning their murders on Israel far outweighed their value.

"After that, her assignments were mainly top-ranking Hezbollah members suspected of treason—naturally, Israeli spies were blamed whenever possible. To sum it up, for her line of work, she had a long career. She married at least twice. Her first husband was killed in a mortar attack in '86. She was with the second one when their unit set up a bomb-making plant right next to an elementary school in '93. Some Gaza villager who was afraid his kid would get blown up ratted them out. The Israelis evacuated the school, then blew up the factory. Fahada was believed to be the only woman inside. A badly burned female torso was found in the rubble. She obviously carried a spare."

"Fahada," said Rice. "Fahada what?"

"One name, like a rock star," Rivera replied. "Arabic for leopardess. I guess that's the closest they could come to Nasty Bitch with Knife."

"She certainly was adaptable," said Brauner. "Her initial weapon of choice didn't exactly fit the plan to make the Holocaust victims look as if they died by natural causes. But it explains the kitchen knife in her purse. These days, a girl can't be too careful."

"She certainly didn't mellow with age." Greta didn't have to close her eyes to relive how Fahada had moved in on her, looming larger and larger as she rounded the table, the sprayer at the end of an elastic arm that seemed capable of stretching to any length, like an Olive Oyl balloon run amok from the Thanksgiving parade. "She got away with so many murders over so many years, she couldn't accept that she'd been trapped in Rosen's little dining room. Committing suicide—one more escape, wasn't it? It all makes you wonder when, where, and how she linked up with Bersonne."

"Yeah, Bersonne," said J. J. "The Israelis I spoke to did a quick check on him. Nada. But Belgium's been the go-to place for phony documents for a long time. They told me about a scandal with thousands of blank official Belgian passport forms winding up in the wrong hands. That's a source Bersonne might still be tapping into—just for starters, think T.'s and Icky's boys." After a sigh of frustration, he ended with, "That's it, guys. Tomorrow's going to be a busy day."

"She's a scary piece of work," said August. They'd spent nearly an hour discussing the chilling details of Fahada's life, and the inevitable question of whether Bersonne employed more than one assassin.

"I'll bet no guy ever had a chance to ask her if he could date her sister," said Brauner. "Well, any association with her is definitely another shovelful of shit to heap on Bersonne."

"Absolutely," agreed August. "The case against him is definitely building. We've got that Express Mail to L.A., which should contain the countersigned bank signature cards for our Ms. Jenkins, along with Miriam Rosen's CRT application. Obviously, Bersonne worked on the claim form last night and sent it back to Nabil for an L.A. postmark. Running this op in multiple cities the way he does, he couldn't risk somebody at the CRT wondering about an unusual number of claims mailed from Stamford."

"Damn smart, using the post office like that," Rice added. "Even junk mail is legally sacrosanct. Plus, in the scheme of things, you couldn't do it faster or cheaper."

"Speaking of smart," said Greta, "let's back up—how do you think he changes the CRT application? That 'legal or other representative' always hit me as a possible angle."

August rooted around for a blank form. "Here—page fourteen: 'Name of Legal/Other Representative Filing Claim on Behalf of the Claimant,' which then requires 'Power of Attorney,' page sixteen. He's got enough copies of Miriam's signature to pull off a forgery—with or without a computer."

"Speak of the devil," said Waylon. The computer had just signaled an incoming e-mail. "At last! Get ready for Bersonne's travel records."

Just under an hour later, August summed up, "So far, we've isolated eleven suspected murders in three cities that pretty much follow the same pattern: Bersonne arrives two to four days prior to each of the murders, always departs the night before. Using our experience in L.A. as a template, his first morning in town he receives the surveillance reports from his local Icky type. He spends the rest of that day reviewing them and selecting the victim. Also, he contacts Fahada. The next morning, he goes to the bank. To justify this as a business trip, it's a sure bet he meets with SISS clients for lunch. He meets Fahada that day or the next, hops the next flight home.

"Unfortunately, as Waylon pointed out, there are far more murders than this report accounts for, since Bersonne didn't have to fly into New York. And that led to Dell's suggestion about Boston and Philadelphia— also well within driving distance of Stamford—cities where we haven't even scratched the surface."

The next morning, a JTTF agent in Manhattan called to report that he'd received written confirmation that the CRT had received and sent off to Switzerland the genuine claim form that Miriam Rosen had completed with Greta. While they waited for news from L.A., Greta checked in with Kim.

Since the funeral of the Martinez girl, Kim and Cepeda had kept tabs on Eddie Vasquez. Though not Blu-Steel's leader, twenty-year-old Vasquez was regarded as having a lot of muscle in the gang.

"The kid's no fool," said Kim. "He learned from all the mistakes that sent him up for juvie time. No record except what's sealed, which is pretty remarkable. Tough, wiry guy. The sling's off, but he favors his right shoulder. The street vibe has Blu-Steel members dissing VX as a coward who kills girls and kids but doesn't have the balls to face a man. And then they ask where the hell he's hiding."

About 1:00 P.M. Eastern, J. J. called in from Valencia. "Nabil left the house right after eight o'clock, about when we expected. Sitting down?"

"No, we're all standing," Tom replied. "That means you've been inside the house two hours—what the hell's in there?"

"For starters, a locked room with two windows, but they're boarded up on the inside. A desk is against one wall, with a fairly new computer. But then there's this shelf right above the desk, with six identical cell phones, all lined up like little soldiers. They're all activated, all charged. These phones are basic, uncool Nokias: no flip, no video, not even text-capable. One of the agents said it's the exact same prepaid phone her grandmother takes along in her car for emergencies. You can pick it up at chain drugstores. Buy a hundred minutes, and they throw in the phone and a year's service.

"Five of the phones have a name taped underneath, on the edge of the shelf. The names are David Stein, Jack Fairstein, Lev Zellkind, Aaron Cooperman, and Shimon Schlechter. The sixth phone—no name. The desk has a deep drawer that was locked. Inside, five file folders. The Schlechter folder is empty, but all the others have a copy of a completed CRT claim form. Those names taped to the phones? They aren't the actual claimants' names. Instead, they come up on the application once, on page two."

"Page two?" August scrambled for the blank claim form, shaking his head.

"Yeah," said Rivera. "First thing one of my agents did was a side-by-side check against our copy of Miss Rosen's own original application. Nothing was filled in on her page 2, number 2. Are you looking at it? This appears to be the only place where Bersonne might have changed something . . . *added* something, to be precise."

"'Alternate Contact Information,'" Tom whispered, then read aloud: "'Please provide the name and address of a contact person in the event that the CRT cannot reach you.'"

"Exactly," said Rivera, "with spaces to fill in last name, first name, mailing address, et cetera. No relationship required. No signature. Like it could be anyone."

"*'No signature. Like it could be anyone,'*" Tom repeated, incredulous. "That easy." He stared at the blank form. "And? What was filled in, J. J.?"

"Those arrogant bastards are using the addresses of the four other drops Nabil checks on every day. Same setups as Schlechter's. Those alternate contacts are filled in with the numbers on these phones, and— hold on, I think Olympic is Nabil's next stop. So far, he's left the first two empty-handed." He excused himself, then flashed back on. "Yes, he's headed for Olympic."

"What about the Holocaust survivors themselves?" Greta asked. "Are they—?"

"I waited for their status before I called. I'm afraid all four are dead, their deaths attributed to natural causes."

"When were they killed?"

"Starting almost a year ago. Two females, two males. From the looks of this place—smelly, sticky, a mess—Nabil lives here alone. Ergo, all male alternate contact names for if and when the phone rings."

"Did you find out when 18G was set up?" Brauner asked.

"Too much risk that the receptionist might alert Nabil," J. J. replied, "but I did check the Schlechter phone activation against the Bersonne travel records you e-mailed yesterday. They dovetail exactly: the same day he flew out of L.A."

"The same day Fahada flew in?" asked Brauner.

"Yup. The phone had to be activated so he could get the number he needed to fill in the alternate contact page as soon as he received his Express Mail in Stamford. So that's what no-name phone six is there for: the incoming call from Bersonne. We have five phones with names, five drops, four murders. Looks like Nabil is standing guard to field any calls until the money comes in. Of course, he's also checking those drop boxes every day for a CRT check. What do you think? You agree we have enough?"

"Tell your agents to put that piece of shit Nabil out of business the second the Express Mail envelope is in his hand."

CHAPTER **TWENTY-EIGHT**

Just before three that afternoon, preceded by two unmarked State Police cars and with two City of Stamford police cars at its rear, the team van moved in on SISS.

In the lot, one JTTF car already blocked Bersonne's Lexus, another, the exit door. Two more took opposite sides of U.S.-1. Inside, uniformed officers positioned themselves at the exterior doors, main stairs, fire stairs, and along the length of the second-floor corridor. The elevator was dispatched to the basement, out of service.

It was hard to miss STONEWALL INTERNET SECURITY SERVICES on the last door of the second floor, all in individual imitation brass letters. With Zinah and Waylon taking either side of the door, August was first into a reception area so small, three straight-back chairs and a narrow coffee table filled it completely. A wall with a door and sliding window apparently had cut the original waiting room to a fraction of its original dimensions. The window skated along on its track, and a woman asked, "May I help you?"

The receptionist seated on the other side was a young brunette in her late twenties. She wore a blue sweater set, the cardigan draped over her shoulders against the air-conditioning. At first, she'd seen only August, and she startled when a woman, a large black man and a third man with a severe buzz cut followed him in. "No soliciting allowed in this building," she said nervously. "I'm surprised you made it all the way up to the second floor." She reached for the window.

"All we're soliciting is Jules Bersonne," said August, his hand stopping the progress of the glass. Clasped between the thumb and forefinger, his ID came within three inches of her nose. "Open the door. Now."

Greta glanced sideways to confirm that the icy voice she heard truly belonged to Tom August. It had already drained all color from the receptionist's face. The cardigan fell from one shoulder as she hit the control button for the inner door.

The office, a busy place unaffected by the torpor of the July afternoon outside, had an open floor plan. Half a dozen secretaries sat at workstations perfectly aligned right down the middle. Right and left, partitions formed nearly a dozen small cubicles along each side. Only one of the women in the center took the time to glance up, and not a single head poked up over the segmented walls. There were two doors at the rear; a sign indicated that the one on the right was the conference room.

Behind a T. Rawley nameplate, a woman hunkered in front of the closed door of the corner office on the left. Her desk was the only one set apart, out of the secretarial chorus line. Representing the safest choice imaginable for personal assistant to the boss when the boss's wife has five years on him, T. Rawley was gray-haired and square of brow and body. She didn't even look at August's ID. Her finger was rapidly jabbing at a button on her phone.

"If Mr. Bersonne wasn't on the phone, I would've alerted him that you walked right in, without an appointment. I don't see why you couldn't have—"

"Because we don't have to," said Tom, moving past her. "Stop buzzing him."

"But you can't go in until I let him know that—"

"We're going," snapped Tom. "Close it behind us," he said to Brauner, as he thrust Bersonne's door wide open.

The Pillar of the Community was ensconced behind a massive U-shaped mahogany desk. He was half-turned away, hunched protectively over a cell phone, anxiously speed-whispering in an unidentifiable language. When the door slammed open against the wall, his head snapped up. The windows behind him didn't look out on anything more scenic than the parking lot, but a swivel of his chair could have alerted him that an unusual number of cars were converging there. Betraying no emotion, he quickly took in his three visitors: August in the center, business card in hand, his worn-out appearance barely masking his fierce determination; to his left, Rice, who resembled an advancing tank even when standing still; Greta on his right, hands fisted at her sides.

"Thanks, I'll get back to you later," he said in unaccented English, clicking off. While he twisted around to face them, Bersonne's expression was one of put-upon bemusement. He took Tom's card, read it, then bestowed a smile on Greta, full of the same calculated flirtation that radiated from his driver's license. His eyes darted warily at Rice and Tom, but always found their way back to the lone woman in the room. Suddenly, they shifted to the doorway, and the sound of the door closing confirmed that Brauner was keeping their meeting private.

Bersonne rested his head against the back of his tall leather chair. As if it had just occurred to him, he asked, "Is something going on? Is someone dangerous in the building?"

"Only you," said August.

"Me?" Holding August's card aloft, he turned it around to face his visitors. "I'm in the same business as you, protecting the security of others."

"Your business is wholesale murder and larceny, Bersonne. The game's over."

"I'm afraid you're terribly, terribly mistaken." Briefly, he brought up his palms, upturned to telegraph his inability to set this misguided trio straight. Regret and concern for all their wasted time washed over his face.

Tom reached in his jacket, withdrew the warrant, and began to Miranda him.

Bersonne instantly switched gears to thinly controlled outrage, "This is now absolutely preposterous. I'm calling my lawyer."

"You'll get your call as soon as you're taken into custody. If you have any doubts, Miss Rosen's doctored claim arrived in New York today, and we have proof that you sent it."

"Miss who? What claim? You're talking nonsense!"

"Oh, and that Express Mail to Schlecter? Nabil was arrested before he had a chance to re-mail what was inside."

"Nabil? I've never met anyone by such a name!"

"I'm sure that's true—so far as never in person. And I'm sure that his name is no more Nabil than yours is Jules. But whatever it is, we're taking you in."

Bersonne snapped back, "There's no reasoning with you—let's just get this over with. Be advised that I have friends of influence in this community. Far-reaching influence." He began to rise. As soon as the gun he'd concealed on his lap cleared the top of the desk, he fired.

"Gun!" August yelled, violently shoving Greta right. She crashed into a visitor's wing chair. The chair thudded into a credenza, knocking down a lamp. Ceramic shards crashed around the top of her head. Partially shielded by the half-overturned chair, she grabbed for her gun. Above her, shots were being exchanged, glass shattering. A roaring suddenly flooded her ears, blotting out all distinguishable sound. Rising onto one knee, she broke cover and fired at Bersonne. His mouth flew open in a silent gasp, but he nevertheless pivoted around, aiming at her. She ducked, and the chair shuddered as his return fire passed through wood and upholstery. She glanced in Tom's direction, hoping to see his shoes, reassurance that he was still standing. Instead, he was down, sprawled on the floor. Beyond, a crouching Rice was firing from behind a large bank of file cabinets. As he drew back from Bersonne's return volley, Greta popped up, surprising Bersonne before he could spin around at her again. In a split-second, he was slammed back against his throne-like chair, jerking with mechanical spasms that matched the speed of Brauner's entire clip as it emptied into him.

Greta crawled toward Tom on her hands and knees, into the warm blood pumping from his neck. "Ambulance!" she screamed, even though her voice sounded too far away for anyone to hear. "Emergency! Get a doctor! Now!"

Tom's face was ashen, growing grayer. "Don't you dare die on me, August!" she yelled. "Talk to me, talk to me, talk to me now—damn it, talk!" She clasped his hand in hers; it was sticky with blood, and there was no response. Rice had stripped off his shirt to staunch the bleeding. When he moved Tom's head to apply pressure, more blood, pooling at the back of his head, was revealed. The rest of the team had closed around them. Greta bent close to his ear. "We're here, Tom, all of us, and you don't want to piss us off. Come on, talk to us!"

CHAPTER **TWENTY-NINE**

Accelerated by her ceaseless pacing, the blood saturating Greta's clothes had dried and stiffened. Somewhere in her brain, a busted flip-switch jolted her back and forth from numb to wired.

The team was quartered in a simulation of a living room, identified by a door plaque as The Family Room. Even with its formal New England decor, it provided far more physical comfort than the usual ER molded plastic bolt-downs. Instead of glaring fluorescents, the slanting light of the summer evening filtered in through a bank of oversized windows.

Brauner faced the center window, his hands in his pockets. Back in the SISS parking lot, when Tom's gurney had been transferred to the ambulance, its open doors and milling EMS workers had completely blocked him from view. The moment they sped away, he was exposed, bent over the roof of a car, sobbing into the crook of his elbow.

Only the team was in the room; apparently, all the day's scheduled surgeries had been completed. After the screams and shots and sirens of the crime scene, the room's quiet was profound, but it was a silence without peace, an acoustical block of the frenzy at the far end of the surgical wing.

A nurse opened the door, startled to find the room occupied. She shut it quickly, but not before a doctor in scrubs hurried by. Head down, he was doing his best to duck the questions that could come flying out of The Family Room like shotgun pellets.

First, do no harm; second, give no false hope.

Tom's warning of "Gun!" still reverberated in Greta's ears.

Long before they met, she'd been convinced that her turn to pull the short straw was long overdue. Surely, Tom's unlucky pick had been slated for her, the final scene of the movie she'd been watching for over forty years. One film per customer, one ticket, no sneaking across the multiplex lobby into another theater.

Tom had to know that his swift, violent lunge into Greta would place him directly in the path of Bersonne's second bullet. He should've been sitting up in a hospital bed, calling to tell his wife that he was A-OK, no need for her to drive all the way up to Connecticut. "Gun!" was what he'd given Greta, a gift so great, its weight was unbearable; a gift so undeserved, it shamed her.

Small consolation that Tom would never have to learn the outcome: The man who'd shot him wasn't just dead, but a dead end . . . exactly like Fahada. Bersonne's license-smile was taunting them, mocking them: Go ahead, close down every one of my carefully compartmentalized cells, and you'll still be stuck on your own ineffectual, compartmentalized Square One.

Folkestone had arrived by helicopter and rushed to the hospital. Even he hadn't been able to extract any news from the staff about Tom's chances.

"Not one of you will like what I'm going to say," he announced, "but right now we're at a critical point, and it's crucial that we keep pushing on every front. Momentum is what it's all about. We've got it, and we've got to keep it going. Otherwise, what we're closing in on will disappear faster than ice cubes in hell. Difficult as it is for all of us, that's what Tom would want."

His head briefly tilted toward the door, as if he could hear August's shout of validation rolling down the corridor.

"That said, effective immediately, Rice will be filling in as team leader. Brauner will be the direct link to Rivera in L.A. As you know, Waylon is acting as liaison with all the techs back at the crime scene, and—excuse me." Turning away, he answered his cell phone.

Rice and Greta made eye contact, exchanging identical takes on where momentum should be shoved, as well as the amazing speed with which indispensable morphed to replaceable in the workforce. Brauner retreated to his window. Zinah concentrated on the carpet's pattern of laurel crowns, tracing and retracing the same unclosed circle with the toe of her shoe.

Folkestone snapped his phone shut; he was frowning. "Since Bersonne was on a cell phone and connected with another cell phone in Paris, all we're going to get is whatever the room bug picked up—only one side of the conversation. Whoever he was talking to was moving along the Rue de Rivoli—in a car, a taxi, possibly walking at a good clip. Alerting the DST—our counterpart in France—would be like them asking us to track down every person talking on a cell phone who walked through Times Square today."

Just then, an agent Greta recognized from the New York office led a pe- tite and very pregnant woman into the room. Rice jumped up and wrapped her in a hug. The agent, immediately comprehending Folkestone's slight lift of the chin, slipped right out. Next, Brauner grabbed both the woman's hands in his; without a word, their heads shook in denial, refusing to ac- cept where they were, and what they were waiting for.

"For those of you who don't know this lady," Rice explained, "she's Tom's wife, Cassie. Cassie August."

"Mrs. August." Folkestone solemnly shook her hand. "Tom is still in surgery. We flew up a specialist from New York . . . he's supposed to be the best there is."

Zinah stepped up to her. "I'm Zinah, and this is Greta." She gently hugged Cassie, and Greta awkwardly followed suit, taking a quick step back when she realized that she might be smearing Cassie's yellow summer shift with her husband's blood. No stain, but as if she'd sensed it, Cassie was swaying slightly.

Rice guided her to a wing chair so deep, her toes barely reached the floor. She thanked him, then Brauner, who handed her a bottle of water. She drank quickly, one hand pressed to her chest, tracking each swallow on its way down to the baby.

"When Agent Davies came to drive me to Connecticut"—she looked around, only then realizing that he wasn't there—"When he told me about Tom, I couldn't help crying, right in front of our boys. Ryan's four, and James is only two . . . we had to wait for my mother to drive to our house to stay with them. That must have been hours ago . . . and Tommy's still in surgery."

Folkestone said, "Proof that he's a fighter. That's a good sign."

Without any hesitation, Cassie said, "I don't understand how this could have happened."

"The subject was a businessman with no history of violence," Folkestone replied.

As if he hadn't uttered a word, Cassie continued, "Tom started wearing those baggy suits when he made detective in Philly, so his gun and all the rest wouldn't show—the vest, the phone, the radio, the cuffs, the ammunition, the notepad . . . all that stuff . . . all that protection." She put the cap on the empty water bottle and gave it a little twist. Then, looking directly at Folkestone, she added, "A terrorist is a terrorist, even in a white collar."

The sentence hung in the air, part warning, part rebuke, part epitaph.

Cassie's heart-shaped face was pale, and her eyes had fixed on some distant point. The case had kept her and Tom apart since the team had left for L.A. Even back when they were working out of Brooklyn, he'd been such a constant presence that Cassie must have already put in a long time missing him. Abruptly, she cried out in panicky desperation, "I have to see him—it has to be now, while he's still alive! I don't care if he can't see me, or doesn't know I'm there! I've got to touch him before he dies!"

———

After 9/11, it was predicted that the rubble would smolder for months, that the cleanup would drag on for at least a year. The fallen towers had been cleared far more swiftly than expected. But inside Greta, the charring, the hollowing-out by fire, was still going on. It had begun with the urgent, primal need for physical contact that had overwhelmed her that September morning. To touch Bram, if only for an instant, would mystically and furiously weave an invisible adamantine shroud around him, his shield against a cold and starless eternity.

Cassie bolted. Her dash down the hall ended immediately, in an unavoidable collision with a doctor in scrubs. Tall and solid enough to easily absorb the impact, he held up his hands in mock surrender, as if the little lady presented a dire physical threat. He even smiled briefly, until he caught sight of her pregnant belly. All apologies, he gently attempted to steer her back into The Family Room.

"No, let me go!" She squirmed, trying to shake him off so she could resume her wild race to the corridor's end. "I've got to get to my husband!"

Caution clouded his face. "What's his name?"

"Tom! Tom August!"

As she struggled, he put his hands on her shoulders, more to restrain than comfort her. "I'm so sorry. I was coming to tell you that we . . . I'm afraid we lost him, Mrs. August. You'll be able to see him in a little while."

"Too late, too late!" Cassie moaned. Her arms dropped limply to her sides.

Greta stepped forward, with a look that made the doctor back off. This time there was nothing awkward about the way she embraced Cassie. Each in her separate time, they had arrived too late at the edge of the void.

CHAPTER **THIRTY**

By early the next morning, an avalanche of new information faced a team in shock over the loss of Tom August. Every time Greta turned to his usual place at the conference table, she was hit by the sucker punch of reality. Concentrating on the smallest detail was a struggle. The translation from the Arabic of Bersonne's part in the Stamford-to-Paris cell conversation only fueled the anger consuming her.

> BERSONNE: *This call is a heads-up. Just now I was retrieving a file from a cabinet near a window that looks out over the parking lot. I spotted several plain dark cars driving in. They were followed by a dark van with satellite equipment on the roof.*
>
> SILENCE DURING OTHER PARTY'S COMMENT
>
> BERSONNE: *That is possible, but I am sure they have come for someone else in the building.*
>
> SILENCE DURING OTHER PARTY'S COMMENT
>
> BERSONNE: *No, no. I'm the last person they'd ever—*
>
> SILENCE DURING OTHER PARTY'S COMMENT
>
> BERSONNE: *Of course, every precaution has been taken.*
>
> TWO BUZZES—SOURCE: SECRETARY'S PHONE

> BERSONNE: *Yes, all in place. This call is simply the required alert, according to our protocol.*
>
> ANOTHER BUZZ—SOURCE: SECRETARY'S PHONE
>
> SILENCE DURING OTHER PARTY'S COMMENT
>
> BERSONNE: *That buzzing? My annoying secretary. I'm confident that—*
>
> SILENCE DURING OTHER PARTY'S COMMENT
>
> BERSONNE: *Betrayed? Not a chance! If I suspected anyone, that person would already be dead.*
>
> OFFICE DOOR OPENS. (FOLLOWING IN ENGLISH)
>
> BERSONNE: *Thanks, I'll get back to you later.*
>
> CELL PHONE CONNECTION CUT. OFFICE DOOR CLOSES.
>
> BERSONNE: *What's going on? Is someone dangerous in the building?*

Rice whispered the next line, Tom August's reply, "Only you."

No one had to read any further.

Waylon broke the silence. "Rawley, Bersonne's secretary, claims the way she buzzed Bersonne was a procedure he'd insisted on: 'Do not ring, cut in, or walk in—only buzz, because *nothing* is important enough to interrupt me while I'm speaking with a client.' That ties in with the way we found his office phone—off the charger, turned on, no number dialed. Had to be his routine for creating the illusion he had a client on the line whenever he used his cell phone."

"Ensuring he'd never be disturbed—or overheard—during an overseas chat in Arabic about how much cash their last assassination netted," said Brauner.

Folkestone, who'd remained overnight in the Stamford hotel, held up his copy of the translation. "Interesting, the way Bersonne starts out with a straightforward report to Paris. It doesn't take long for that smugness of his to seep through: 'I'm too damn smart to be discovered, too intimidating for any of my underlings to give me up.' The first time I heard the recording, with no idea of what he was saying, it was pretty obvious that he was pissed when he let loose with that 'would already be dead' line."

One of the agents sifting through Bersonne's office had turned up a laptop stashed at the back of a locked four-drawer file cabinet. It had spreadsheet software, but no data. An unopened pack of blank discs was in the same drawer, but so far no disc with data had turned up in his office or his Lexus.

"The cells in L.A. and Brooklyn alone—no one could keep that much in his head," said Waylon. "It had to be saved somewhere. But his office was swept three times yesterday. We tore down every ceiling tile and ripped up the carpet. Nothing."

"This is a hiding-away place too clever for anyone on the office staff to find," mused Zinah. "But easy for Bersonne to get to."

"It has to be in his office," Greta agreed. "I've been going over every square inch of it in my head—whenever I'm not wondering if his boss in Paris has a boss . . . with a whole damn pyramid of bosses over him." She left out the accompanying image of innumerable Bersonnes, falling one by one, and forming a large, dead heap.

Late morning, Brauner stood up and stretched after spending almost an hour on the phone with Rivera. It hadn't exactly been a conversation— every time Greta looked over, he'd been scribbling notes furiously, stopping only to read something back for accuracy or ask a question. Nabil had been in custody nearly twenty-four hours, and his small house in Valencia had been thoroughly searched.

Folkestone called over to him, "Eric, how about an update?"

"In brief, Nabil said nothing until he saw the photos starring him at all the mail drops. The news that his phones and files were evidence softened him up even more. He didn't fold in record time, but fold he did."

A brief, thin smile passed over Brauner's face, definitely the first of the day.

"Something amusing we should hear, Brauner?" Folkestone asked.

"At first, Nabil told the interrogator that the six phones were for his personal use—one for each of his girlfriends. His story was that he had to label them, so he wouldn't get the jealous American babes mixed up. When the agent pointed out that David, Shimon, Jack, et cetera, aren't girls' names, he tried to slug him." He looked around, biting his lower lip, and they all knew it was exactly the sort of story Brauner and Tom would spin out, playing Nabil-the-great-lover the rest of the day.

Rice didn't leave him hanging. "What was inside the Express Mail envelope?"

Brauner, clearing his throat, replied, "Five pieces. Two copies of the phony application Greta filled out for Fahada—one for Nabil's file cabinet, and one to go to New York." Brauner referred to his notes: "Folded prepaid Express Mail envelope addressed to CRT in New York. Stamped business envelope addressed to bank, 'Attention: R. Jenkins.'" Looking up, he added, "No surprise, the bank signature cards were inside— Shimon Schlechter as cosigner. J. J. pointed out that his address is now officially *Apartment* 18G, on Olympic. And, last but not least, a USPS Change of Address form—it's printed on a postcard, no postage necessary. Filled in as a request from Miss Rosen to forward her mail to Apartment 18G, effective immediately."

Shaking his head, Brauner said, "Rivera read me the warning on the postcard. 'False information is subject to a fine, imprisonment or both.' J. J. found out that the verification process is a letter sent to the old address. Basically, it says, 'We hear you've moved. If you do not reply to this letter, your mail will be forwarded to the terrorists.' Only if someone gets back to them and says, 'Bullshit, I'm still here!' does the USPS investigate. So the interrogator pushed Nabil on that. If he'd had the chance to put the postcard in the mail, the next day his daily route would've included the mailbox at Miss Rosen's house, too—until the verification letter arrived. Since his only other stops were those phony drops, we can assume he intercepted all the other USPS verifications."

"Mail *and* phone," Folkestone observed. "Turning Nabil into a pipeline that fed any communication from the CRT straight to Bersonne."

"By the way," said Brauner, "I heard parts of Nabil's interrogation tape. His English is good enough to field a call from the CRT if or when one of those phones rings."

"'If or when'? I'm still puzzled about *why* the CRT would call," said Greta.

Rice jumped in. "My bet is, A: that they'd send a letter if the claim is denied. They're lawyers, so they're not going to waste time arguing about money unless they're the ones demanding payment. B: if they need more information, they'd have to request it in writing anyway. So it was Bersonne, playing it ultrasafe."

"True," said Greta, "especially with an expert like Fahada filling out the application. That wouldn't leave much for the CRT to call about, unless they check to see if a claimant's passed on since he or she mailed in the claim form. That's cold, but off the top of my head, I can't think of any other reason."

"If they don't get an answer, or if the phone service was cut off, they might write . . . or call Schlechter," Rice said grimly. "Either way, Nabil's got it covered." Switching to an upbeat, friendly voice, he exclaimed, "'You're looking for my best friend, Mimi Rosen? I just spoke to her this morning—she's up in San Francisco, coming home tomorrow. You want to leave a number so she can call you? No? Bye.'"

Greta sighed. "The check is mailed to Miriam's house, but it winds up being forwarded to Olympic Boulevard. Nabil Express Mails it to the box in Stamford. Bersonne endorses it as Schlechter, Express Mails it back to Nabil. Nabil sends it on to the bank with an L.A. postmark. When the check clears, Bersonne wires the money out of the country—it's off on its merry way, flipping through a zillion offshore banks."

"This time," said Folkestone, "payday was canceled."

Rice nodded. "And when Waylon's team digs up Bersonne's files—and they will—we might get to see the day Tom always talked about. Eric, you know what I mean?"

"Yeah," said Brauner, "the day we run out of handcuffs."

CHAPTER **THIRTY-ONE**

A small stack of data CDs turned up in Bersonne's office, neatly concealed in the circular brass base of a ceramic lamp. It was the same lamp that shattered when Tom pushed Greta from harm's way. Even shoved back in a corner, the jagged earthenware was a hazard—it had slashed through an agent's trousers, leaving a scratch along the length of her calf. When she picked it up to throw it in a trash bin, the base—loosened by the crash—started to twist open. Just as Zinah had predicted, it would have been an easy-access hiding place for Bersonne.

In the course of the next month, the hidden CDs provided what they needed to dismantle cells in six U.S. cities. Rice was on-site to coordinate each sweep. From Chicago, he called in to report that the operation there was even more extensive than anticipated—briefly, they actually did run out of handcuffs. On that day, Cassie August gave birth to a baby girl.

About the same time, Maureen Bersonne was cleared of any involvement. Due to her late husband's meticulous deception, she could only guess at the scope of his crimes, but being investigated by the Joint Terrorism Task Force had thoroughly shaken her. In interviews conducted by Greta, it was evident that in Maureen's mind, whatever Jules Bersonne had done to break the law paled in comparison to his ruthless exploitation of her and her children. Trembling with rage, she'd railed against the extreme danger to which he'd so unconscionably exposed them.

As for the crushing humiliation he'd subjected her to, Maureen's first counterpunch came with the funeral arrangements.

The service and cremation were scheduled to begin at nine o'clock on a Monday morning—not the most convenient of times. Even more incommodious was the location, a city in New Jersey her second husband had probably never heard of, home to both an oil refinery and a chemical plant. Despite all of Jules' community affiliations, not a single mourner made the effort to rise before dawn after a lazy summer weekend and brave fifty miles through pollution and rush hour traffic.

Maureen herself spent the entire morning in a Darien law office, setting in motion the legal process that would change her name back to Lafferty.

Miriam Rosen's voice came across the phone as feisty as it'd been at their first meeting. "In twenty-three days I'll be living at the Thunderbird Oasis," she announced.

Surprised by the possibility that Miriam would even consider giving up both her home and her independence to enter a nursing home, Greta asked, "Is it in L.A.?"

"Nope. It's a senior condo community in Arizona. A fellow I met at The Beverly Hills told me all about it. Then he took me online," she said with a little giggle. "It's wonderful."

"Going online, or the Oasis?"

"Both!"

Mrs. Rosen's role in exposing the Holocaust scam might have expedited her claim; it had been approved in a fraction of the usual time. She was excited by how quickly everything else was going, as well: her L.A. bungalow had been snatched up after only five days on the market. "I describe it as rundown," she explained to Greta. "The real estate agent says it's Arts and Crafts—who was I to argue?"

Greta closed her eyes, wishing Paulina Kantor could have been Miriam's new condo neighbor. "I'm happy your stay at The Beverly Hills worked out so well."

"It was exactly the way I dreamed it would be," Miriam confided. "Lounging by the pool, fancy meals, a massage whenever I wanted . . . all that was great. But you know what the best part was? Realizing that I couldn't go back to the way I was—an emotional hermit. With all that you're involved in on a daily basis, I know you might not understand, but I don't want to be closed off for the rest of my life."

And Greta whispered back, "I do understand, Miriam . . . I do."

Compared to the grinding surveillance in Brooklyn, L.A., and Stamford, Greta's first week at Fed Plaza passed quickly.

For the first time in months, she was back in her own apartment—it was still home, but in many ways she felt like a stranger there. After the break-in and the wrenching loss of Molly, she'd thrown away not only the rubble and old clothes, but everything that could remind her of that night—which didn't leave much. During her absence, the floors had been refinished, the bullet-pocked walls spackled and painted, the shattered windows reglazed, every surface cleaned. The place exuded the domestic equivalent of new-car smell. It would've been a pleasant little extra, except that it was canceled out by the lonely echo of her footsteps.

After checking in with Kim and finding that Blu-Steel was having no more luck finding VX's location than the NYPD, Greta reluctantly punched in the number of the attorney, Maurice Yablonsky. His office had piled up eleven unreturned calls.

The person who answered the phone at the law office put her on hold after rattling off the firm's name—Yablonsky was first in a string of four partners. After a brief wait, Yablonsky himself came on the line.

"I can't believe it's Greta Strasser . . . at last!" he exclaimed. If he was, as she suspected, another scheming lawyer working for her ex-husband, he certainly sounded friendlier than any of his predecessors. "Your precinct told us you were on a special open-ended assignment, but we kept trying."

"That's right," she answered, trying for neutral. "What's this about?"

"A client of mine, who also happened to be my dear friend, died some months back." After a deep intake of breath, he said, "Theo Appel."

Greta could still see Theo sitting across from her at The Hungarian Club, astonished and amused by her threat of imminent arrest. "My dear friend, too," she murmured.

"Theo and I had a meeting here at my office just before he . . ."

"There's no need to be diplomatic," Greta snapped. "Except Theo didn't kill himself. Any friend of his would know that."

"Since you're a detective, it's a . . . a solace, to hear you say that. You see, there was no way I could accept his death as a suicide. Even though I'm not a criminal attorney, I did make inquiries on my own. The homicide detective assigned to—"

"Oh, I could probably quote him verbatim," she said bitterly, "but—" Abruptly bottling up the rest, she said, "Mr. Yablonsky, this isn't something I can discuss. I'm truly sorry, but it's an ongoing investigation."

"That wasn't at all how that detective described it. As a matter of fact, he was quite adamant. He said the case was closed."

"It's not. Believe me."

"I want to, I truly do." After a low grumble, more confusion than protest, he resumed, "No matter how Theo passed, regardless of any misgivings I hold, the fact of his death is the reason I've been trying to contact you."

"I don't understand."

"Some years back," Yablonsky explained, "after his wife, Estelle, died, Theo made a new will. The purpose of that last meeting of ours was to make its first and only revision. He'd called me in a great rush, asked me to fit him in that same day. I was surprised when he insisted that the change had to be made immediately. Under most circumstances, I advise my clients never to make such decisions in haste, but he pressed me to have it revised, signed, and witnessed on the spot."

"What kind of revision?"

"Some personal property was designated for you."

"I . . . I don't know what to say. I'm honored that he considered me." It took her a few moments before she could speak again. "I'm back in Manhattan. I can stop by your office, and . . ."

"Oh, the property isn't here, Detective Strasser. It's in storage, pending delivery to your home. I'll put my secretary back on, and she'll make arrangements. We will accommodate any day or time that fits your schedule." After a pause, he added, "Clearing that wrong against Theo's memory . . . if your investigation is successful, will you kindly let me know?"

The following Saturday morning, Greta rose early and went for a run. She was envious of every person running or walking along Prospect Park West with a dog. After a dash down to Seventh Avenue to buy groceries, she was home before eight-thirty; the window she'd been given for both of her deliveries was nine to three.

The first to arrive, in several compact cardboard cartons, was her new bed. While she assembled it, attaching the hoses and pump that would fill it with air, Greta looked forward to stretching out and adjusting the mattress's firmness control. The same shape and size as her TV's remote, it was the feature that had clinched the deal in the store.

The remote was by her side when the doorbell roused her from three hours of deep, dreamless sleep. Despite being jolted into consciousness, Greta's back already felt better as she made for the bay window at the front of her apartment. Below, a big box truck was double-parked in front of her building. The name on its side panel was the company Maurice Yablonsky's secretary had given her, but she'd been expecting a van.

"I'll be right down!" she shouted into the on-again-off-again intercom.

By the time she opened the brownstone's front door, a man was standing in the street at the rear of the truck, arms outstretched for whatever was being lowered from its loading platform. Wrapped in thick padding, it was unwieldy, and he handled it gingerly, taking care to prevent any contact with the street. He slowly navigated the curb, sidewalk, and stoop, constantly darting his head around the side of the package. When he reached the front door, he guided it past Greta, through the vestibule, and into the hallway. With a grunt of relief, he propped it up against the little balcony—in her mind, no longer the Juliet Balcony, but the Parlance Lewis Balcony—and turned back toward the door.

"Wait a minute!" Greta called out, "I don't think I can get this upstairs by myself!"

"Lady, there are four more in the truck, plus a little box. I'm gonna get all five offloaded first. Then me and my partner move 'em upstairs. Don't worry—you don't have to do nothin'!"

While she waited, Greta tried to peel back the padding for a peek, but it was girdled with far too much duct tape. Suddenly, she panicked— what if this supersized mystery shipment, even if did come from Theo, turned out to be something she wouldn't like? Not likely, but a possibility she'd have to deal with before these guys left.

As the mover steadied the fifth piece in place, the back of the truck ratcheted shut. His partner, an older man, hauled his heavy body up the stoop. A cardboard package about the size of a book was tucked under his arm. "This is the sixth piece, Miss," he said, as he gave it to Greta. Removing a pen and papers from his work shirt's pocket, he added, "After we set everything up in your apartment, you have to inspect the delivery and sign this form. Press hard. You keep the yellow copy on the bottom."

Greta raced upstairs to prop her door open. She fished a tip out of her wallet and stuck it in the back pocket of her jeans, hoping it would be the right amount.

Once the movers had the five pieces propped up against one of her blank living room walls, the senior man produced a box cutter and severed the tape holding the padding of the item tagged with a bold #1 in magic marker. In tandem, the two men pulled back the padded blanket. First, there was only a glimpse of lavender. It became a sky dotted with silver stars. Then there was Sarah Bernhardt, luminous as Camille . . . until her image blurred through Greta's tears.

"You okay?" one of the movers asked. "You want we should go ahead with the rest? Want 'em, like, all around the room?"

"That would be great," she managed to rasp, "thanks."

"Whoa!" the senior mover cried out when #2, *Medée,* was unveiled. "When my wife looks at me like that, I get out of the house fast!"

"I'll be right back." Greta put the little package and the paper forms in the middle of the empty floor and hurried back to the bedroom. She paced back and forth, doing her damnedest to compose herself. When she returned, she held the package up to the elder mover so he could slice open its clear plastic tape. Moving to the windows, she peeled back the flaps. Inside was a boxed DVD collection of Greta Garbo classics. On the cover, a tragic Garbo was in a costume from *Anna Karenina. Camille, Grand Hotel,* and *Ninotchka* were the other films in the set. While she cradled the plastic box in both hands, she watched Bernhardt as *Gismonda, Lorenzaccio,* and *La Samaritaine* emerge. The posters glowed against the freshly painted white walls.

After the men departed, she slowly turned in the center of the living room. "Thank you, Theo," she whispered, as the incomparable Sarah shifted from role to role. "How could I have doubted any gift coming from you?"

Waylon, Brauner, and Zinah were scheduled to leave JTTF NY on the same Friday in late August. Zinah, who'd successfully retaken an English test that had held her last promotion back, was being transferred to D.C.; the others were on loan to a special unit in Miami. Rice was back, Rivera was in town, and Folkestone assembled them all, plus Chris and Stan, the now-separated surveillance duo from Brooklyn, for one last team lunch together. They'd been assembled once before, at a memorial service for Tom August, and not one of them failed to glance toward the door, as if any minute he might arrive . . . a little late, tired but smiling, in one of his wrinkled suits.

Greta was scheduled for a meeting with Folkestone at two, right after the lunch. Since they'd returned from Stamford, he'd approached her twice with an offer to join the JTTF on a permanent basis. Both times, she'd been able to reply that she was so involved in the case, it was tough to reach a decision before it wrapped up.

When she walked into the SAC's office, he hit her with his secret recruitment weapon: the assurance that any time remaining to qualify for twenty-year NYPD retirement (the countdown was down to weeks) would be cut to zero. The frosting on that cake was: "Tom and I discussed hiring you on several occasions. He took great pride in your performance, and justly so. He was amazed that the NYPD didn't value you a fraction as much as we do."

Before she could respond, Folkestone barreled along with, "You're smart, you're innovative, you can handle the pressure. We need people like you."

"Sir, I appreciate that, but you're making it sound like I was working alone. It was a great team, and we accomplished a lot together. I only wish we could've netted more."

"More?" Folkestone sat back against his chair. "The cells in Miami and Chicago alone—"

"I know," Greta cut in, "from cigarettes to counterfeits." Dell Rice had hauled in truckloads of faux Rolexes, Nikes, Vuitton bags, even phony prescription drugs. "It's like we hit the Hezbollah piñata, and all kinds of goodies are still spilling out. Call me greedy, but I wanted—I still want—more than that. I want to close down Bersonne's boss in Paris."

Folkestone shot back, "The man was a stone's throw from the Seine. I guarantee you that his phone hit the river before you took a single step into Bersonne's office. We have no link to him, nothing."

"How about going back to all the cash that was doing the loop-de-loop along Theo Appel's money trails? If that could be traced to—"

Folkestone stopped her with both hands up. "Hold on. Bersonne's files gave us the victim names we needed to alert the Claims Resolution Tribunal. Once the CRT stopped payment on those doctored claims . . . well, don't you see? After that, there was nothing left to track!"

That stopped her short. She'd never considered the cost of success. "That doesn't change the fact that every claim that Bersonne did push through—and we'll never know how many there were—every one was a murder."

"Yes, of course, Greta, but we can't prosecute some phantom in Paris. Those six cells are an amazing coup. But we can't lose our focus on all the other crazies doing their damnedest to blow up bridges and power plants, poison our water, and pull the plug on our economy."

"Those 'crazies,' sir—isn't it essential to expose the banks that are funding them?" Her attempt to mask her exasperation was failing.

"*Funding?*" Folkestone's eyebrows shot up. "Wasn't Mr. Appel investigating offshore banks engaged in *laundering* money?"

Greta hesitated. The two had melded in her mind. The interconnection seemed so logical, she was puzzled as to why such a distinction mattered at all. Replacing emotion with caution, she said, "The last time I saw Theo, he'd just discovered that at some point, all the Caribbean money trails passed through one bank—call it Bank A; he didn't tell me its name. After that, it kept on splitting and flipping, but half the original CRT payout amount eventually reentered Bank A."

"'Half'—so that led him to suspect that the money landed in two banks at the end? A fifty-fifty split?" asked Folkestone

"Exactly, yes. His next step was to identify Bank B. He was murdered before we had a chance to meet again."

"Did he mention whether or not Bank A operates in the U.S.A.?"

"He wasn't able to locate a branch in this country."

Folkestone didn't use the moment to say "That's not my department," but she could hear the laundering-versus-funding question thud as it fell through the floor. Theo was former CIA, and he'd reached out to his old colleagues there. An effort to untangle the financial web of the smashed Bersonne network would require going back to the CIA for help. So far, the JTTF had racked up six destroyed cells, more than a hundred good arrests, and fifty-eight unchallenged deportations. Been there, done that, and if you looked back, you'd get slammed by whatever new domestic terror plot was about to come chugging around the corner.

Greta took a deep breath. "Sir, I'll be blunt. Indecision, someone sitting on the fence—just like I'm doing now—that's always driven me crazy. But at this point in my life, it's no longer only between the JTTF and the NYPD. I can't stop thinking about what it would be like to walk away from all of it . . . to start a whole new life. As much as I hate to say it, I'm afraid I need more time. Please, just a few more days."

———

When T.'s guys had vandalized Greta's apartment, they smashed her TV and DVD player. She'd taken her time replacing them because she dreaded not only shopping for electronics, but the whole intuitive-versus-the-manual setup headache. Earlier in the week, once she'd eventually cursed her way through the process, she wanted the first film she played to be something lighter than Anna Karenina throwing herself under a train, so she'd picked *Ninotchka*. That Friday night, after a quick decision not to wrestle with her future until the next morning, she settled down with her all-time Garbo favorite, *Camille*. Not exactly a story with a happy ending, but impossible to resist.

Halfway through the titles, the screen went black and the music stopped on a screechy violin note. Greta groaned. *Why, of all four films, did this have to be the one with a defective disc?* She fumbled with the unfamiliar new remote, searching for fast forward, hoping the glitch affected only a few opening frames, and not the entire film. Then she heard a voice she never thought she'd hear again.

"Hello, Greta. When you see and hear this, I'm afraid I'll be dead."

Her head snapped up. Theo was onscreen, sitting at his long kitchen-dining table.

Pulse racing, Greta scooted to the foot of her bed, barely two feet from the TV, her face and Theo's image eye to eye. She dug her thumbnails into her finger pads to make sure she wasn't dreaming.

After a wry smile, he continued: "I apologize if I've upset you, my dear friend. Let me begin by assuring you that Maurice Yablonsky knows absolutely nothing about our joint investigation.

"Obviously, my inquiry into the banks and money trails sparked an Internet alert of sorts, because I've just spotted the second unsavory character of the day in a beat-up car parked below my window—I believe they're taking turns keeping an eye on me. I can hear you scolding me right now: 'Theo, how many times have I warned you that these guys are dangerous—be careful!'

"I admit, I flattered myself that I had them outsmarted by never staying online too long, then dashing on to the next wireless connection before they could pinpoint my location. But just a couple of days ago, I waited a very anxious hour and a half just to get into an oncologist's examination room, only to wait on an extremely hard table for what seemed like another eternity for my test results. Without even stretching out my arm, I could touch the doctor's computer. My own computer briefcase was right below the table. I was so close to that bank break-through . . . I felt like an addict desperate for a fix. So . . ." He shrugged sheepishly, "I connected. I kept an eye on the clock, shut down after half an hour. Ten minutes later, the doctor gave me the news—the *good* news that I'm eminently treatable, get to keep my hair, get to keep my lunch down. And we spoke for a while about next steps.

"I convinced myself that luck was on my side, and that I'd finally get to the end of the money trails on my next try. But the following morn-ing, when I logged on at the Lexus dealer, I discovered I'd been totally blocked. I made some frantic attempts to resume at an earlier point . . . then my screen went black. They had me tagged at the doctor's office. Too bad he can't switch my good news over to someone who didn't fare as well.

"Right now, I'm splurging on a town car to go to and from my appoint-ment with Maurice. Along the way, all three computers—hard drives al-ready removed and bashed with Estelle's heaviest rolling pin—will be disposed of. Maurice's office will send the flash drives and our notes to my D.C. colleagues. Once I'm back, I'll call you. If not, consider what follows to be my swan song:

"You won't be surprised to learn that what I referred to as Bank A is based in Switzerland, where it's been operating for five generations. When the Nazis came into power, Bank A attracted a large number of Jewish accounts—I base that on the disproportionate number of Holocaust claims that were filed against it. Why so many Jewish depositors? My guess is that the bank brought them in with promises it never intended to keep—promises of account confidentiality, good interest rates, excellent security, whispered hopes for Hitler's defeat.

"At the same time, Bank A was thoroughly involved with the Nazis: It accepted illicit Nazi deposits of gold—gold that was stolen from both the central banks of Europe and concentration camp victims. The same can be said of several other Swiss banks, which, like Bank A, recipro-cated by extending credit to Germany—their way of rooting the Third

Reich on to victory. After the war, those unpaid loans had to make staying solvent quite a challenge for Bank A. The reason they didn't go bust? An ingenious bailout plan: simply confiscate their so-called confidential Jewish accounts—all of which had been conveniently tagged 'J' for *Juden*.

"And so Bank A survived, under the tight control of a long line of heirs. The latest CEO, like his grandfather and father before him, was at the forefront of every roadblock the Swiss set up to stall the investigation of Jewish accounts. Their bank led the fight for more than fifty years . . . until Senator D'Amato pushed the CRT fund through in 1998.

"Bank A was hammered with a huge involuntary contribution to the Holocaust fund. They were vulnerable once again, this time with no J-accounts left to raid. Their predicament drew considerable notice from a group of international investors—most of them from the Middle East. Many of them were associated in one way or another with Al Taqwa Bank, based in Zurich.

"Two months after 9/11, Al Taqwa was shut down by both the U.S. and the UN because of links to terrorist groups. Before the end of the year, Bank A was renamed Bankers Alliance Zurich. The CEO retained his position. His name is Anton Wolfram."

After spelling out Wolfram and Al Taqwa, Theo said, "It's time to leave for my appointment with Maurice. Thank you, Greta dear, and the very best of luck. I must admit that, in a strange way, I was pleased when you thought I was dangerous enough to be a con artist. We knew one another only a short time, but I treasure you as one of my closest and truest friends."

For a moment, the screen was black. Then *Camille* resumed, the second or third scene along. Greta folded herself into a shape as tight as a clenched fist while she mourned Theo as if for the first time.

Eventually, throat sore, nose stuffed, in need of air, she made her way out onto her bedroom terrace. She began to pace back and forth, only to ache for the sweet Molly who would've been glued to her side—if she hadn't been ripped away by the same bastards who were responsible for the cold-blooded murders of Theo and Tom August and Mrs. Kantor and countless others.

In essence, Folkestone saw walking away as the best strategy for staying ahead. But for Greta, walking away wasn't an option. Especially when the latest incarnation of Al Taqwa was part of what she'd be walking away from.

Back in her bedroom, she hit rewind and played Theo's message over and over. It became clear that T.'s crew had spotted her saying goodnight to Theo the night of his fateful doctor's appointment, and that she'd been followed home on the subway. Two days later, while Theo was with Yablonsky, they'd broken into his apartment, lowered the blinds, and searched for any possible links to their Holocaust scam—computers, printouts, discs, flash drives. They'd taken great care not to toss the place; it would be convenient for his murder to appear to be a tidy senior's suicide. When their search failed to turn up anything, they resorted to torture: all the bruises and shattered bones they'd surely inflicted on Theo would be difficult to differentiate from the trauma of a seven-story fall.

Still desperate to find out how much had leaked, they went after the only person who'd visited him, convinced that he'd either passed or e-mailed Greta information. To control the breach, they'd terrorized and kidnapped a child, killed Molly, and planned to torture and kill Greta as well.

Folkestone had been right about one thing: forget the guy in Paris . . . for now. First, she was going to find out all there was to know about Al Taqwa Bank, Bankers Alliance of Zurich, and one Anton Wolfram.

CHAPTER **THIRTY-TWO**

Lieutenant Geracimos was at his desk, head down, filling out a report.

"Hello, Lieu," said Greta, barely above a whisper.

When he looked up, a broad smile spread across his face. "I've been expecting you. I've never seen an evaluation like the one you got from that guy Folkestone down at JTTF! Why didn't you let us know you can walk on water?"

She shrugged. "Hard to do when you're on desk duty."

"Which brings me to my next question, Detective Strasser." She walked into his office, and he gestured for her to close the door. When it clicked shut, he turned deadly serious. "Greta, why the hell did you come back?"

"A little boy, a young woman in a wheelchair, a fifteen-year-old girl."

"There is no doubt," he said, studying her face, "that you are your father's daughter." After a few measured beats, he added, "But I'm pretty sure you know that Kim and Cepeda are already—"

"Let me be the third wheel," she cut in. "I'll cover everything else you put me on."

Geracimos drummed his fingers on his desktop. "I'll be honest. I couldn't decide whether or not to discuss your . . ." After consulting the ceiling for guidance, he settled on ". . . your *status* with Quill. Long story short, I just let it ride. That's never been my style, but after all, squad assignments are my call. I'm putting you on unrestricted duty. If he wants to make an issue out of it, and deny an understaffed unit a sharp, seasoned professional, he can take it up with me."

"'Sharp' and 'seasoned' . . . nice. Much better than 'recipe for disaster.'"

"Let's hope so. You put Kim on the right track, shadowing Vazquez with Cepeda. And Manny, aside from the fact that one day his wife is going to cut off his right cajone while his girlfriend cuts off his left, is a thorough investigator. Like Kim, he's full of energy, very dedicated. Plus, in case you haven't noticed, unlike Kim, Cepeda comes from a Puerto Rican background, same as Vazquez. So when and if he finally talks, we'll be sure we're getting more than a literal translation. That said, my plan is to pair you with a detective who's being transferred in from Queens tomorrow, and have you both jump in on VX–Vazquez as needed."

Comfortable as she'd been working with Kim, Greta had serious concerns about the Strasser Stigma rubbing off on him in the Two-Four; now she had one less thing to be anxious about. "That sounds good," she said with a nod. "Who's the new guy?"

"Malcolm Fergusson."

"Promise me you'll have a talk with him if he shows up in a kilt."

"Welcome back, Strasser."

Greta plopped down in Cepeda's empty chair opposite Kim. With a sigh of relief, she announced, "Paperwork completed!" and gave him a thumbs-up. Kim, who hadn't seen her in person for months, was studying her intently. "What?" she asked.

"I don't know. You look different. I can't explain exactly how. It's like when my girlfriend looks at some actress and says, 'Oh, she definitely had work done, but it's so good you can't see it.'"

"The only change is to what you can't see because I'm sitting on it. All that surveillance, all those meetings and deli sandwiches—I've been running an extra five miles every week to work it off." She swiveled around, checking out the squad room. "What's with those desks over by the wall—Donovan's and Miller's? It doesn't look like they're using them."

"You're right." His phone rang, and he pointed to Cepeda's desk. "Okay, swing by in ten minutes. Yeah, she just finished checking in. I'll let her know." After clicking off, Kim said, "Manny says he's glad you decided to come back." Kim quickly signed the DD5 he'd been working on. Without looking up, he added, "I'm glad, too, but—may I speak frankly?"

"You think I'm either crazy or a masochist."

He stood and buttoned his jacket. "Actually, both."

"You're probably right." She smiled. "Okay, Kim, you've got to go. But tell me fast—what happened with those two?" She tilted her chin toward the deserted desks.

Russell, who rarely took interest in office gossip or intrigue, said matter-of-factly, "I guess it wasn't too long after you left that Donovan and Miller were put under review. Last week, they were split up, reassigned to other precincts." His eyes emphatically darted right and left.

"That's too bad." She glanced at her watch. "No wonder I'm hungry! C'mon, I'll walk down with you. Meanwhile, fill me in on the latest on VX and Vazquez."

Once they were out of earshot, Russell whispered, "There were complaints . . . like they refused to issue burglary reports unless the vics produced serial numbers and receipts. They delayed a stolen car complaint over a month." He patted his jacket right over his gun, a nervous habit she recalled. "And there was a businessman who was slammed bloody against a brick wall and rolled—that was entered as a 'lost property.'"

"A 'lost property'? How?"

"The basis was he never saw his attacker. That one really sucks."

"Shit like that, and they were just reassigned?"

They'd reached the lobby, and Russell opted for silence as they passed Quill's door.

When they were out on the sidewalk, she answered her own question. "But if you're one of Quill's boys, you write it up however the hell you want, and you're reassigned. That's not much more than a slap on the wrist." Cepeda wasn't in sight, so she asked about VX for real.

"No sightings," Kim replied. "I still keep going back to Tyrel's family and every regular who brings kids to that playground where he was shot. In one way or another, they all tell me to let poor Tyrel rest in peace. I tell them, 'We want to prevent another kid from resting in peace before his sixth birthday.' They hang up on me, or slam the door in my face, or just grab their kids and walk away.

"As far as street dealing, Blu-Steel seems to be in permanent retreat inside its old boundaries. But Vazquez's guys have been sneaking back to offer free samples in exchange for information on VX. That's not working—even the most hardcore junkies can't forget what happened to the Martinez girl, so whatever they're offering about VX is worthless. I doubt Vazquez is having any more luck than we are."

Cepeda pulled up, sweet-talking his wife or girlfriend on his cell. Greta returned his big smile and wave as he drove away with Kim.

As she walked away, she considered how, a few minutes earlier, she'd found herself scrambling to deflect Russell's observation that he sensed some kind of indefinable change in her. He'd guessed right: She actually had changed—was continuing to change—but not in any physical way. She hadn't lied to him about running harder and farther, but she'd long since burned off her extra L.A. pounds. The truth was, she was running after something *inside* her, something intangible and troubling that had never figured in any past stages, phases, or evolutions of the current Greta Strasser.

Even before returning to the Two-Four, she'd been wrestling with her conscience about playing Kim, an earnest kid who probably trusted her unconditionally. Although her part in all things job-related would remain one hundred percent legitimate, her motives were now questionable at best.

It was weird, going undercover as Greta Strasser, and weirder still, not knowing who she might become.

Fergusson didn't talk a lot, but by the last afternoon of their work week, she knew that he lived on Long Island and had three sons in high school, all of whom played basketball. He'd showed her the family photo they were going to send out for Christmas—the boys were tall and ropy like their dad, but with considerably more red hair on their heads. She couldn't resist the old ploy of asking if the only female in the picture was their older sister; he'd proudly told her it was his wife, Moira.

He became a cop, he told Greta, because "When I worked for the IRS, everyone loathed and feared me."

"What's so different about being a cop?" she asked.

"Now I'm loathed, feared, and respected," he'd replied.

While they double-checked statements and filed reports, Malcolm, like Greta, did his best to be thorough and avoid shortcuts. He was also reluctant to put off anything that could be wrapped up right away. However, for the first time, he was covertly glancing at his watch.

"Fergusson," Greta said without looking up, "you're about to be late for something, so go—it won't take me long to finish up."

"My oldest has a big game tonight."

"Right, so you'll make it up to me. Get out of here."

His departure left Greta with a clear view of the squad room, where four other detectives were tapping away at their computers. Now that she was ensconced at Donovan's old desk, right up against the wall, no one—short of coming around and stooping down to peer over her shoulder—could see her screen. She'd already made considerable progress at home, with ever-broadening Google searches that began with Al Taqwa Bank. NYPD access had taken her even deeper, not only into Bankers Alliance Zurich, but Anton Wolfram, as well.

Al Taqwa Bank, translated as Fear of God Bank, (a name Greta wanted to counter with Baby, Burn Your Burqa Bank) opened in 1988. Most of its founders were leaders of the Muslim Brotherhood, which publicly promoted itself as peaceful, religious, educational, and charitable—even though its ultimate goal was a worldwide Muslim caliphate. "Peaceful" hardly applied to the terrorist organizations pursuing that same goal by infiltrating and overthrowing Western governments, yet the bank had strong ties with several such extremist groups. In 1997, it passed $60 million to Hamas alone.

Under the guise of an institution where Muslims could invest within the strictures of Islam (which forbids charging interest), Al Taqwa developed an intricate framework capable of obscuring financial finagling, like money-laundering and tax evasion. Besides its Swiss headquarters, it had branches in Italy, Liechtenstein, and the Bahamas. Two months after 9/11, the United States and United Nations accused it of being al-Qaeda's largest financial supporter, and shut it down.

Of great interest to Greta were the ties between several of the bank's founders and the Nazis. Its chairman, Youseff Nada, was allegedly recruited by the Third Reich's military intelligence branch as a young man. Another director, Ahmad Huber, a Swiss convert to Islam, reportedly spent decades forging ties between neo-Nazi and radical Muslim groups and had portraits of Hitler and Osama bin Laden displayed side by side in both his home and office.

The most notorious Al Taqwa founder was François Genoud, a Swiss lawyer-banker. Invariably, his name came up as the man who paid for the legal defense of both Adolph Eichmann and Klaus Barbie.

Greta was fixated on Genoud's most offensive quote ("Hitler was a great leader, and if he had won the war, the world would be a better place today.") when Lieutenant Geracimos, about to go home, called over, "Hey, you working late again?"

Greta quickly minimized the open file and looked up from her computer screen. "Time to face the reality of life after forty, Lieu. If I don't record everything that went down during the day, I'm in trouble."

"How's Fergusson working out?"

"He's a pro."

"Takes one to call one."

The following Monday, Greta and Quill crossed paths in the lobby. Ever since her return, he'd refused to acknowledge her existence. Markedly haggard and distracted, he no longer even bothered to smite her with his silly death-ray stare.

Semi-monthly, Quill was one of the seventy-six NYPD precinct commanders forced to endure intense pressure in the fierce CompStat derby at Police Plaza. CompStat had its critics, but its usefulness in tracking crime trends and zeroing in on local problems and vulnerabilities couldn't be denied. Precinct commanders bore direct responsibility for those weak spots, and consequently, they all vied for the lowest Seven Major Crimes

Index scores. (Murder, rape, assault, burglary, robbery, grand larceny, and grand larceny auto—although they didn't quite match up with the Seven Deadly Sins, the thought was there.) At the least, the PCs were subjected to intense scrutiny; humiliation in front of peers and lower-ranking officers was always a possibility, as was the sudden, ruthless derailment of a decades-long career.

However, none of the Two-Four's indices had risen, and two were even down, so Greta suspected that whatever was gnawing at Quill might be something other than precinct affairs. Embracing her Invisible Woman status, she kept her head down as she hurried out into an early morning downpour to catch up with Fergusson. Best not to be a moving target . . . especially when she was tracking a target of her own.

When Greta returned in the early afternoon, she became aware that she wasn't the only detective doing unofficial Web searches. Vin Giraldi, another Quill-ite, was totally locked into eBay. Unaware that Malcolm was still out of the office, Giraldi was back to back with his empty chair—affording Greta a direct view of the way he was tearing through listings. The items that popped up were weirdly all over the lot—from digital cameras to pearl necklaces, from autographed baseballs to designer sunglasses—but the guy was definitely a quick study, stopping only to jot down notes on a legal pad.

Less than fifteen minutes later, on what was becoming an exceptionally busy day, Greta was called out to meet up with Fergusson, leaving Giraldi alone in the squad room. As soon as she stepped out into the hall, the lieu barked out, "Giraldi, I still need you out on the street—ASAP."

"Yeah, well, ASAP is when the chief's expecting this rush analysis." As an afterthought, he added, ". . . *sir.*"

Long after the end of their shift, when Malcolm and Greta dragged themselves back into the Two-Four, Greta got a quick glance of Giraldi speed-scrolling away on another site, scrutinizing antique silver flatware. After they finished up, Greta told Malcolm she'd be staying, waiting for a call from a friend. As soon as he departed, Greta went online. Not long after, Giraldi made a call.

Voice low, he recited a string of numbers. *Was it one digit short of a case number, or two numbers run together?* "No more than eight hundo nine five," the detective continued, his tone a mix of boast and belligerence. "And without the receipt, not a prayer proving those earrings are anything but fifteen-buck knockoffs." Another possible case number mumbled, then a disappointed, "Fifteen hundred . . . nah, it's top-of-the-line, three gig, still too new to be discounted anywhere." A pause, while he consulted his list. "Yeah, Christie's, only seven-fifty. Right—even cheaper than eBay!"

The next day, Giraldi and Greta weren't in the squad room at the same time for more than twenty minutes, but that was all it took to establish that his good news was always a price under a thousand dollars, his bad news anything over. She was dying to rub the little toady's nose in his own gloating satisfaction when it hit her: A thousand dollars was the threshold amount that escalated a theft from a misdemeanor to grand larceny— one of the seven index crimes so integral to CompStat.

Giraldi's mission—Quill's "rush analysis"—was checking every relevant Web site until he found a price lower than the value provided by the victim of a crime: $999.99 would remove it from CompStat inclusion. (Greta bristled at his last search, aimed at knocking down the value of someone's kidnapped Yorkshire terrier puppy.)

The rest slid right into place: Detectives Donovan and Miller had similarly downgraded crimes, reducing assault and robbery to lost property and notching down unreceipted burglaries to criminal trespass. They'd delayed complaints (perhaps even destroyed them, betting on the chance they'd get lost in the system) until the current CompStat score was low enough to absorb their impact. With a shudder, Greta wondered if some murders had actually been written off as suicides or accidental deaths.

Quill had succumbed to the temptation of cheating the numbers on CompStat, coming up like a winner because he appeared to be beating down crime in his precinct. She wanted to think that his lackeys had been whisked away to the NYPD equivalent of Siberia with their pensions intact simply to put him at ease, leaving him to continue his dirty scheme while Police Plaza surveillance built one hell of a case against him.

Maybe Quill looked the way he did because he'd figured out it was time to stop, but feared that the sudden spike in precinct crime resulting from the *real* numbers would expose him even faster than any covert investigation. Internal Affairs would have Quill for lunch, the New York City Commission to Combat Police Corruption would serve him up for supper, and, just in time for breakfast the next morning, the press would skewer him all over the front page.

It was a moment to savor, but Greta was torn: She came from a cop family, and in days, her own service would hit the twenty-year mark—even longer than her dad's. No matter how savagely and tirelessly Quill had tried to disgrace her, she wasn't wired to be a rat. It made you small, dirty, and tainted, and the stink never washed off.

Wishing she could stare holes into the back of Giraldi's giddily bobbing head, she struggled with the problem of finding a way to stop their dirty game without losing the ability to live with herself.

What she came up with might not have a "happily ever after" attached, but it was, she decided, good enough.

CHAPTER **THIRTY-THREE**

"I'll always be thanking you for something, Theo," Greta whispered. Once seriously computer-challenged, she found herself working furiously to put together a Two-Four puzzle that had been deliberately designed not to fit.

The pieces were a virtual treasure trove of stolen objects, all representing victims whose complaints hadn't been filed because they couldn't furnish a serial number, a receipt, or, in some cases, a simple photograph. Barely scratching the surface, she'd compiled a list that could keep a dozen cops busy for weeks.

Before she left for home, she returned to Al Taqwa's François Genoud, a criminal who would have been quite a challenge for CompStat to fully define.

Besides the qualifying acts of accomplice to murder and grand larceny, Genoud—in addition to terrorism, war crimes, sabotage, hijacking, defamation, smuggling, and extortion—had managed to get away with crimes beyond any category in the NYPD lexicon. In fact, the one constant of his life was the way his shadowy allies always dashed in to rescue him from prosecution at the last minute.

Greta pasted together the defining moments of his life in chronological order:

In 1934, Genoud joined the National Front, a popular Swiss pro-Nazi group. Not long after, he was introduced to the grand mufti of Jerusalem, Amin el-Husseini, the religious and political leader of the Palestinians and also a strong Nazi sympathizer. They remained close for nearly forty years.

During the war, Genoud was enlisted by the Abwehr, the German intelligence branch. Postwar, using his Swiss bank contacts, he was instrumental in setting up ODESSA, a network which transferred German marks into Swiss banks and bankrolled the relocation of top Nazis.

He went on to open the Arab Commercial Bank in Geneva, which financed the Algerian National Liberation Front. It also covered the legal fees of the three members of the Popular Front for the Liberation of Palestine who blew up an El Al plane in Zurich. Genoud was linked to the hijacking of a Lufthansa 747; he was instrumental in funneling a $5 million ransom to the PFLP.

The combined influence of the grand mufti and Hitler had formed a creature who regarded Arab terrorists as the logical successors to the Nazis in the spread of anti-Semitic violence. Greta suspected that Genoud regarded Al Taqwa Bank as his crowning achievement. A 1995 article described it as "the most important financial structure of the Muslim Brotherhood and Islamic terrorist organizations."

As another shift of detectives straggled in, Greta put her desk phone to her ear and kept repeating "Okay . . . okay" while she read an account of Genoud's last days:

In 1996, after a half-century of implacable resistance, Swiss bank executives yielded to Jewish groups demanding an examination of secret bank and government files by an outside commission. The Swiss government launched its own investigation into the Nazi plunder that flooded the country during and immediately after the war. 1996 was also the year Senator D'Amato's campaign against the banks began. In the wake of those three probes, a new Swiss law was passed, a law that trapped Genoud in the homeland that had never once denied him safe haven. When a warrant was issued against Genoud for racial incitement, his Get-Out-of-Jail-Free card finally expired. Emulating Hitler right up to the end, Genoud committed suicide with poison.

Forcing out an upbeat "First thing tomorrow!" Greta hung up, shut down, and nodded at the new arrivals as she headed for the door.

The next morning, Greta, never so anxious to get to work, arrived at the Two-Four an hour before her shift. When Geracimos showed up, she followed him into his office.

"Lieu," she said, "a call came in about a stolen car report—it should've been filed weeks ago. I couldn't find it—maybe a glitch in the system. The vic was really stressed out—said it's the fourth time she's called, so it sounds like someone should see her before it escalates. I might've calmed her down a little, so maybe Fergusson and I . . ."

"Sure, go ahead."

"If anything else like that comes up . . . ?"

"Hey, I'm all for anything that'll boost community support."

Over the course of the next week, no less than three grand theft auto reports were filed by Fergusson-Strasser. Footage from a surveillance camera that Donovan and Miller had either missed or ignored not only transformed their lost property report into assault and robbery, but also led to an arrest.

Her greatest satisfaction came from fielding complaints from seniors who'd been denied burglary reports because the cops found "no evidence." Still seething over the implication that they were suffering from dementia, they wasted no time acting on Greta and Malcolm's advice: contact merchants for receipts; request delivery records from carriers like UPS or FedEx; sort through holiday or birthday photos taken with the stolen Chiparus bronze in the background or the pilfered Cartier watch on the wrist that was cutting the cake; dig out the will with the bequest for the three missing Tiffany favrile vases; get proof from the rug service that they'd cleaned a small silk antique Kashan. Assault, burglary, robbery, grand larceny, grand theft auto: five of the seven CompStat major crime categories that had been downgraded, delayed, or erased suddenly spiked in the Two-Four.

As Quill's next CompStat meeting neared, the pouches under his eyes grew noticeably darker and puffier; his nose appeared to be a darker purple against his sallow cheeks. If Greta came into range while he was conferring with someone in the lobby, he'd cut off the conversation to turn toward her, hands knotting into fists, upper lip curling back. Invisible Woman no more.

"What's his problem?" Fergusson asked, convinced that Quill's rot-and-die look had been aimed at both of them. "Any other PC would be handing us commendations after all the complaints those two transferred detectives dumped on the precinct."

Since that was more or less the way she'd explained it Malcolm, she had to mumble, "Don't hold your breath on that."

When the countdown had only a few days left to go, Quill's door was closed more often than not, but even an underground bunker wouldn't have muffled mad-scene rants so intense that they reached all the way up to the squad room. During the PC's all-too-brief respites, his shirtsleeved minions, clutching file folders and spreadsheets, would race up and down the stairs in blind panic.

In the meantime, work had the challenge of Greta's old undercover days—in a sense, she *was* working undercover again. At no time in her twenty years on the job had she racked up so many arrests in so short a time frame—thanks not only to Malcolm's professionalism, but also to the slapdash arrogance of Donovan, Miller, Giraldi, and their ilk.

Quill returned from the CompStat meeting just as Malcolm and Greta were leading an uncooperative perp across the lobby. The PC's face was masklike, his movements robotic. He was so closely flanked by two resolute strangers, they appeared to be steering a blind man by the elbows—except neither was actually touching him. One was trailing a tipped-up hand truck that held several large cartons, folded flat and secured by wide plastic straps.

The shackled prisoner, an addict whose hoodie was splattered with the blood of the bodega owner he'd shot and killed, was spewing nonstop curses at Malcolm and Greta, ignoring his Miranda-ized right to remain silent. His escalating harangue snapped Quill out of his trance at the very same moment Greta stepped into his direct line of vision. Less than ten feet separated them, and the mirror image of another prisoner being led by two cops—one of them Strasser—froze him in his tracks.

For a moment, he appeared to be weighing the impulse to make a wild run at her against its cost: being tackled and cuffed facedown on the floor of his own precinct house. The hand truck clanged down. Restraining hands immediately wrapped around his upper arms, canceling out both the action and its consequence. In lockstep, he was propelled toward his office. He twisted his head back to glare at Greta, and a burned-out ceiling bulb and the bill of his dress uniform hat turned his eyes into two black holes.

"Would you say he had a bad meeting?" Malcolm asked as soon they'd put some distance between themselves and Quill.

"Those guys . . . you think they're from Internal Affairs?"

Malcolm shrugged. "If they are, they work fast."

Greta thought back to her conclusion about Donovan and Miller: Police Plaza's transfers—barely punishment at all—might have been a ploy to keep Quill complacent enough to keep his subterfuge in play. That would give them time to build a case against him . . . right up to the next CompStat meeting.

Later, when Greta and Malcolm headed up to the squad room, it was hard to miss the computer on the floor just inside Quill's office door. The hand truck already had two cartons stacked on it, and the man who'd wheeled it in was easing on a third carton. His partner crossed the office to hand him a file folder, and when he lifted the top flaps, he had to force back what looked like the contents of an entire file drawer to make it fit.

Upstairs, Quill's boys were nowhere to be seen. At the end of the shift, the lieu came out of his office and made an announcement to both exiting and incoming detectives. "I don't know what rumors you've heard, but all I'm going to say is that there's a cloud over the precinct. We're all going to have to cope with shift-shuffling until staffing returns to normal—which," he explained sourly, "currently means somewhere between seriously understaffed and decimated." A sense of relief was palpable in the squad room when he added, "Our top priority remains fighting crime, not numbers."

After months of trying, Cepeda finally got Vazquez to agree to a meeting. Naturally, the first proposed site, the Two-Four, was rejected immediately. They volleyed back and forth between public spaces, bars, the back room of a nail salon run by a Blu-Steel member's mother. Cepeda grinned at Vazquez's next suggestion. "Sure, I know the Rios Botanica." Later, he translated his own follow-up remark for Greta and Kim: "With all the saints in that place, we'll be in deep shit if we fuck with one another. How about if we meet there at three?"

That gave them just over an hour, a time short enough for Vazquez not to suspect an elaborate setup.

Greta figured she'd passed the Rios store a thousand times, but never once had been inside. F W Woolworth was incised in its concrete cornerstone, so the store had been a five-and-ten back when they dotted the city as the go-to-for-everything local emporium. She'd arrived first to back up Cepeda, dressed as a shopper in a black wig, glasses, and red lipstick—all she'd had on hand in her locker, besides the black knit poncho she wore to work that cool October morning. Kim was listening with a translator in a nearby van.

Inside, the botanica was cluttered, but it was well lit and alive with salsa music, pungent aromas, and a faint undercurrent of horror-movie vibe. True to Cepeda's remark, nearly a third of the space was crammed with statues of saints, from dashboard-ready plastic stick-ons up to three-foot ceramic models. There were also thousands of candles and countless varieties of incense to burn before them. No barrier separated the Catholic zone from the assorted peacock feathers, horseshoes, dried scorpions and bats, coyote skulls, and amulets. Greta's gaze lingered over the pincushion dolls she silently dubbed Voodoo Barbie. The botanica also sold herbs, roots, bark, tea, oils, soaps, sprays, and perfumes. Printed or implied, its entire inventory came with a promise: Every item was a different way of praying for wealth, health, love, revenge, or anything in between. Behind the checkout counter, a waving American flag sign offered to PACK AND SHIP YOUR SELECTION TO YOUR SOLDIER'S APO. However, *Any statue over 15 inches excluded* had been handwritten across the bottom—perhaps to avoid any liability if carried onto the field of battle.

Vazquez walked in and headed right for the saints. Greta, earbud in, positioned herself out of sight in the adjoining aisle, sniffing bath salts. A minute later, Cepeda joined Vasquez, whispering a greeting in Spanish.

"English is better in here," Vazquez replied, his voice low.

"Okay." Cepeda readily acquiesced, eliminating Kim and Greta's translation delay.

"Your face is familiar. I've seen you before."

"My partner and I were at Miss Martinez's funeral. Quite a crowd . . . obviously a lot of people loved her. My condolences."

Vazquez didn't waste any time. "I know where he is."

"You mean Ernest Flowers . . . VX?"

"Whatever the piece of shit's name is, yeah. It took me a long fucking time, and I don't think you'd be here if you had any information of your own."

"That's right," said Cepeda, "and you wouldn't be here if you didn't want something for it."

There was a long pause, and Greta could imagine Vazquez and Cepeda staring one another down.

"I want to kill him."

"Kill him, you go to jail. Let the police take care of him."

"I'd be doing the cops a favor taking garbage like him off the street. I've got a clean record. I know you can put in the fix."

"Nobody fixes Murder One, Vazquez. Not even if one of these blessed santos is holding the gun."

"Yeah, well I made an oath to kill him. I didn't come here so I can watch you arrest him and let him go free the same day."

"Never going to happen!" Cepeda protested, trying to keep his voice down. "Not when he's being held for three murders!"

"Three nothing! You don't have a single witness! He'll walk."

"Not true. The wheelchair girl downtown had a witness who—"

"Come on! Some fancy college student! Even I couldn't blame her if her memory goes blank on the stand . . . if she stays alive long enough to walk into a courtroom in the first place."

Cepeda looked over Vazquez's shoulder. Greta wasn't supposed to be in the script, and the kid's head whipped around to see who was coming up behind him when he saw the surprise on the detective's face. "Who the hell is she?" he demanded.

Taking off her sunglasses, Greta introduced herself and pulled her ID from her poncho. "And," she added, "I'm not only the second witness to the murder down on Broadway, but I was in pursuit of Flowers when it happened. I *will* be there."

Cepeda explained, "Detectives Strasser and Kim—my partner—worked the Tyrel Dobbs case. That's another reason she's here. Kim's right outside. He has a kid sister the same age as your girlfriend—he's totally committed to getting scum like Flowers off the street."

"I'd like to kill him, too," Greta said softly, "but he's not worth going to jail for."

"You're a cop—they're not gonna lock you up."

"If I executed him, which is what you want to do, I'd be in jail in a heartbeat. Except for not getting that concept, you're pretty damn smart. You got your equivalency diploma when you were in juvie. Tested high."

Vazquez shrugged and tilted his head, like it was no big deal.

"You're not even twenty. Ever think about turning your life around?"

Cepeda jumped right in with, "Why would he want to do that, when he can't wait to go to prison and wind up somebody's bitch?"

"I told you, I took an oath to kill him for what he did to my girl. And to Blu-Steel."

"Sure," said Cepeda, "joining a gang is a lifetime commitment. Good, you'll have people to write to when you're inside . . . it's just a question of who outlives who."

"Send Flowers to prison," Greta urged in a low and compelling voice, "and you will guarantee that every day of the rest of his life will be a living hell. Not only a child-killer, but the coward who murdered a young woman in a wheelchair—that'll make him his cell block's favorite date. Consider that over mercifully ending his miserable excuse of a life in two or three short seconds."

Vazquez looked down, not ready to compromise, but not arguing the point.

"And while he's rotting in prison," she continued, "we can get you out of here, get you in a good place . . . like starting college upstate . . . a new ID, a new life."

"What, like witness protection? I'm no witness, and you're not the FBI."

"It's been done before," she pressed on. "It's not a free ride. You'd have to work part time and get passing grades. And stay away from the city."

Vazquez slowly shook his head, but he took plenty of time before he answered: "If I tell you where he is, I go in with you."

"Absolutely not," Cepeda snapped.

"Think about it," Greta said.

"*You* think about it," Vazquez shot back.

That evening, Greta wrapped up her research.

Any progress Switzerland had made in transparency, at least on the Holocaust accounts, kept being canceled out by its alarming record on terrorism. Since 9/11, the United Nations had criticized the country on several issues, among them its failure to stop Al Taqwa Bank executives from funding terrorism at new or renamed Swiss financial institutions. (Bankers Alliance Zurich was exactly such a reinvention.)

More recently, *The Washington Post* reported that Taqwa funds, under multiple corporate disguises, were still being moved by chairman Nada. (Mysterious infusions of new capital had substantially boosted the most current financial report of Bankers Alliance Zurich, whose predecessor-bank had been perilously close to being drained dry by the CRT.)

Switzerland's half-hearted attempts at taking an international stance against terrorists had been unsuccessful. Only the past summer, the Bahamas had flatly refused to release any information to Switzerland about transactions at their Al Taqwa Bank branch office. And Saudi Arabia, which had received all the transferred records of Al Taqwa's Swiss headquarters, adamantly rebuffed attempts by Swiss prosecutors to return them.

To all this, Switzerland's response was astounding.

Its three-year investigation of Al Taqwa Bank was suspended.

Switzerland simply walked away.

The October evening was unexpectedly nippy when Greta left the Two-Four, but her cheeks remained flushed with outrage—not only at Switzerland's ongoing accommodation of terrorists, but also at the unruffled manner the rest of the world had turned to look the other way.

CHAPTER **THIRTY-FOUR**

The officious female gatekeeper rattled off "Allo," a bit of rapid-fire French, and ended with "Monsieur Wolfram." It took her very little time to detect that the caller had not only sneaked past the initial defenses of Bankers Alliance Zurich, but ascended all the way to the assistant to the CEO. Mightily displeased, she was poised to hang up.

"Connect me to Wolfram immediately!" Greta snarled in heavily accented English.

"What? Do you know who you're speaking—"

"Tell him a Genoud is on the line, and don't waste another second of my time!"

A click sounded, but only to put the call on hold. After four failed attempts to get through, Greta's last bet had paid off: Why not assume, despite their smug arrogance, that Swiss neo-Nazis would follow commands with the same unquestioning obedience of their original German role models? An authoritarian tone, coupled with the Genoud name, seemed to have done the trick.

A man's voice, brimming with respect, said, "Madame Genoud, je suis—"

"English!"

Without hesitation, Wolfram made the switch. "I am honored by your call, madame. Please accept my apologies. The girl has absolutely no concept of who you are. Kindly tell me how I may be of assistance to you."

"Listen to me, Wolfram. My name is Fahada. We have a mutual acquaintance in Paris."

"Then you're not a relative of . . . ?" His voice turned sharp. "Who is this? What the hell are you talking about? Never mind, I could care less. This call is finished."

Feeling as if she were jumping in front of a speeding car, Greta blurted out, "The J-accounts operation."

Thousands of miles away, Wolfram's breath caught in his throat.

"I was recruited by your man in Paris . . . as a facilitator."

After a pause, Wolfram countered, "Ridiculous! I have no 'man in Paris'!"

"Shall I jog your memory with the all the particulars over your bank phone? I certainly hope your 'girl' is listening."

"No, no!"

"Then give me your cell number, and I'll call you back."

As soon as they were cell to cell, Wolfram, sounding a bit shaky, asked, "What did you say your name was, and what exactly do you want?"

"The contact number I had for Paris seems to be permanently out of order. Same for my contact number here in the States. I didn't receive my fee for the last job, and I've lost all patience with waiting. Basically, all you need to know is that I'm not the kind of person you scratch off the payroll, Anton Wolfram."

"Don't say my name!" he hissed. "They've found a way to listen in on these damn things!" He was beginning to pedal harder. "Listen, I have to make inquiries, verify what you're saying. You can't expect me to agree on your say-so and send you a check."

"I don't take checks. I take direct deposits. And by the way, while you kept me hanging for the money that never came and the assignments that dried up, I had time to do some research. Here's a quick recap: While you were sitting looking out your window at the Alps, I was risking everything to make you even richer from that 1.25 billion payoff to the Jews. So I'm raising the stakes. I want more than a paycheck. I want what the Americans call a 'golden parachute.' I've had my fill of doing dirty work for people like you." Lowering her voice, she added, "Bear in mind that if your offer insults me, I know exactly where to find you. I'll call you back in an hour."

"An hour!" Hard as Wolfram tried for irritation, desperation overrode it. "Impossible! I need a couple of weeks at least! I can't pick up a phone and get through—this isn't like calling to order a case of wine!"

"I don't drink," Greta snapped. "One week. To the minute. I'll call you on this number."

Wolfram picked up on the first ring. Greta pounced before he could say a word. "Are you going to continue this stupid pretense of not knowing what's going on?"

"Please," he protested, "I was never included in that part of the loop, I swear it! You must be aware that's what we have to do to protect one another . . . keep each sector separate." He took a deep breath. "Fahada, I deeply regret that we got off on the wrong foot. I've been informed that few are more dedicated than you." The pauses, the syrupy tone, all clearly indicated that a very nervous Wolfram was reciting lines as canned as Del Monte peaches. "I thank you for all your contributions over the years. And I want you to know that the fund you spoke of isn't earmarked for personal gain, but to support the same worldwide struggle you yourself are committed to."

"Right. Bullshit for whatever's left after you take your cut. I'm touched. Now what about the compensation I have coming to me?"

"I'm going to be in New York on business in less than two weeks. Can we meet then?" he asked nervously. "For lunch?"

"I keep the number of people who see my face to a minimum. Send it, like that bastard should've done, before he broke communication with me."

"I fear that avenue of payment had to be closed."

"You're a banker! Open a new one!"

"That's already in progress. And please take this advice: It would be safer for both you and the bank if no further transfers were made to your offshore deposit account." Without giving Fahada a second to reply, he added, "If you permit me to arrange a new one, I'll have it all set up and ready to accept the ID and password of your choice."

"And the deposit?"

"Bring your cell phone, and the funds will be transferred right before your eyes. No verification, no tedious paperwork . . . the way Swiss banking used to be," he said wistfully. "I'll make a reservation at—"

"Forget it. I'll be the one who picks the restaurant. What's the date?"

He sighed. "As you wish. Call me at this same number at eight a.m. on the Monday the fourteenth. Your restaurant at noon."

An NYPD database did not list Wolfram as a person of interest. However, for the previous four years, he'd traveled to New York at least once annually. Doubting that he was an Autumn-in-New York kind of guy, Greta did a search of upcoming finance-related conventions and conferences. A symposium on offshore banking was scheduled to take place the week of November fourteenth at the Marriott, offering networking sessions, workshops, and lectures by several keynote speakers. Greta's jaw dropped at the some of the topics: Unnecessary Due Diligence and Swiss Banking, Tax Avoidance Schemes, Compliance and Anti-Money Laundering, Penalties Relating to Foreign Trusts, and International Anti-Avoidance. She double-checked, but they'd left out All You Need to Know About Funding Terrorism.

On November tenth, Greta called Bankers Alliance Zurich once again. Reaching its travel department was certainly less problematic than contacting the lofty CEO.

"Hi, I'm Madeleine at Floraganza in New York, and I'm calling about a floral delivery for a Mr. Wolra?"

"That would be Monsieur Wolfram," said the bank's travel lady, and spelled it out slowly. In a far more pleasant tone than Wolfram's assistant had used, she asked, "Do you need the bank address?"

"I wish it were that simple," sighed Madeleine-Greta. "No, it's to be delivered here in New York. I can't reach the sender, and the person who took the order was so busy, it appears she botched the delivery address— can it be a conference room at the Marriott? Since Mr. Wolfram isn't booked there as a guest, I'm desperately calling Switzerland!"

"Actually Mr. Wolfram will be at the Marriott next week, but only to attend a symposium. He prefers to stay at the St. Regis."

"Lucky him! If I were a tourist here, that would be my hotel of choice, no contest! Well, thank you, now I can—" Greta stopped short. "Oh, did she at least get the date right? Arriving on the thirteenth?

"Yes, late afternoon. Who's sending him the flowers?" asked the obliging lady, openly tit-for-tat.

"Not his wife," giggled Greta, as she hung up.

Just after noon on Sunday the thirteenth, Greta was helped into the St. Regis lobby as she struggled—in heels—with a large vase, two paper-wrapped bouquets shaped like giant lollipops, a shoulder bag, cellophane-wrapped twigs and ferns, and an oversized tote bag. A young man rushed from behind the registration desk to assist her, while a bellman caught the vase just as she faked losing her grip on it.

This was the year the fashionistas decreed that the most fabulous way to look was like Audrey Hepburn—or at least Audrey Hepburn as Holly Golightly. Greta's brunette wig was pinned in a Fifties French twist. The sunglasses, tiny triangle of cloth tied under her chin like a babushka, and the little black dress had been easy, but not the white swing coat. That hadn't turned up until the fourth thrift shop, but the ten-buck price— there was a stain on the front that only the huge tote could conceal— made the hunt worthwhile.

"We'll bring these up to your room, Madame," said the young man. He was blond, moved elegantly, and no doubt awoke each morning from wonderful dreams of being discovered.

"My room? Oh, I wish!" purred Greta. "Madeleine, from Floraganza," she said, loosening her grip on one of the bouquets just enough to wiggle her fingers at him in lieu of a handshake. "As if you couldn't tell!"

The previous week, Greta had scouted Floraganza, society's florist darling of the moment. Earlier, she'd roamed the Sixth Avenue flower district, picking up everything she was juggling at one quarter of Floraganza's retail. The paper and ribbons matched the Madison Avenue boutique's purple and pink color scheme.

"We're closed today," she whispered to Prince Charming, "but someone took this order without checking with *me,* and it *has* to be delivered this afternoon, which could only be *now,* because I'm due to set up a bridal shower on Park and Sixty-second at two, and a dinner party just up Fifth Avenue by five—can you imagine? Tomorrow they'll be sending flowers to my very own funeral!" She gave her head a little overwhelmed half-roll because he couldn't see her roll her eyes behind the sunglasses. "Do be a darling, and have someone help me carry all this gear up to Mr. Anton Wolfram's suite."

"No need. I'll get a bellman to bring it up for you."

"You are too dear!" she exclaimed. "But who would know what to do with all this?" I create the arrangement—The Romance in the Vase!" She extended her tote—not too far to reveal the stain—brimming over with ribbons, two spritzer bottles, and small boxes. "You'd blush if you knew," she winked. "I only need half an hour."

He glanced over his shoulder at his colleague behind the desk, her head down as she patiently marked a map for an elderly Japanese couple. Two other guests, one with a bill in hand, were lining up for service. Turning back to Greta, he confided, "Someone is supposed to remain with non-guests, but we're short-staffed today, so I guess . . . I'll have a bellman let you in, but make sure you don't step out of the room—otherwise the door will lock automatically."

"I usually call Housekeeping when I'm finished, to take away the paper and vacuum up the snippings—okay?"

"Very considerate of you," he said, hurrying back to his station.

On the Fourteenth, Greta called Wolfram's room at eight a.m. He answered immediately.

"I'll be calling you with the name of the restaurant at eleven forty-five," she said. "It's only a few blocks away from your symposium."

"Who told you about that?" he asked suspiciously.

"You should hardly be surprised that I take every possible precaution," she retorted. "The reservation is in the name of Mrs. Foster. Be warned that anyone who gets there before me or who walks in after you will not escape my notice. Unless you're alone, I'm a no-show. And if that happens, you'll never stop looking over your shoulder . . . without even knowing who to look for."

Greta had five essential restaurant criteria, and no food critic was likely to award a single chef's toque or golden fork for any of them: no bar, a ladies' room close to the entrance, a medium-to-small dining room, a walk of four or less blocks from the Marriott, and cuisine that excluded the need for servers to converse in French, German, Italian, or Arabic—languages an international banker might rely on to leave her in the dark. Mrs. Foster would be lunching at a Thai restaurant.

Just prior to entering at eleven forty-five, she called the banker with the address. As she'd hoped, she was the first customer of the day. After hearing her apology for her early arrival—how she'd intended to spend the morning at the Metropolitan Museum, only to discover it was closed on Mondays—the maitre d' jokingly offered Greta her choice of any free table. From eating there the week before, she knew exactly where to sit for the widest view of the room.

At noon, three tables filled with business types. Regulars with barely an hour to spare, they ordered without menus as soon as they were seated. Five minutes later, the maitre d' reappeared with a man in his fifties, whom he pointed toward Greta. At the moment, no one else was waiting to be seated.

Anton Wolfram was of medium height, medium build with a pronounced gut, and thinning light brown hair. His appearance would be unremarkable if not for the way his shoulders hunched forward, pulling neck and head along in the same arc. Threading his way through the tables, he turned to one side, revealing that his long, narrow nose turned down sharply at the tip.

The week before, Greta had read a newspaper article about a businessman who spent his country weekends hunting with hawks and falcons. What had caught her eye was the accompanying photo of a hawk bent over its downed prey, wings expanded like a hood. This, the caption explained, was a warning to all other predators to back off. Nothing was written about the terror a writhing animal trapped in the darkness under those wings would feel. Wolfram's bowed head and shoulders and beaklike nose evoked that same savagery.

Three women burst in just after the banker, New York loud, their armfuls of shopping bags brushing every diner they passed. When one lady's bag skimmed Wolfram's elbow, he pushed it back at her with undisguised belligerence.

True to her expectation, Wolfram did not reach out to shake her hand. Even though she imagined her telephone attitude had led him to expect someone younger, leaner, meaner, and certainly not so dowdy, his eyes registered distaste more than surprise.

The Audrey Hepburn wig was now pulled back behind Greta's ears, kept in place by a brown felt beret that rode low on her forehead. Briefly, she'd considered the Sackler-rabbi's wife look, but opted instead for the added coverage of a mainstreamed Muslim woman—a brown and green paisley wool dress with a high neck, long sleeves, and a very long skirt. Brown contact lenses, dark foundation, and black eye makeup (heavily applied so it would smear into raccoon circles) completed the look.

The restaurant was already half-full, and a waiter approached with menus. "You have some kind of quick salad?" asked Wolfram, who turned his attention to the waiter while he recited four offerings. Without any pretense at politeness, he ordered a shrimp salad and a bottle of sparkling water for himself.

"I'm really not hungry," said Greta, "so just iced tea with a slice of lemon and lots of ice, please." As the waiter hurried off, she quickly scoped the room before leaning toward Wolfram. "You requested this charade of a meeting to give me what I'm due," she fumed. "Well, here I am. Hand it over."

"Our mutual friend in Paris and I are prepared to offer you two hundred thousand dollars." Indignation at the sum crept into his voice as he asked, "Is that parachute golden enough for you?"

"Does that include the last job?" Greta-Fahada asked.

"Yes and no."

"What the hell is that supposed to mean?"

"It's inclusive of all your assignments to date . . . but not the bonus payment for one last favor he'd like you to . . . execute."

Mind racing, Greta tried to grasp what could be behind this unexpected request. The Claims Resolution Tribunal deadline had passed several months back . . . did Wolfram have an inside man supplying them with the names and addresses of survivors who were about to receive a check—their same hateful plan, only in reverse? Was it a hit against one of their own—some cell leader, a T. type, who'd betrayed them? Or was it an ambush for a greedy assassin who'd outlived her usefulness? Striving to appear completely disinterested, she replied, "I'll pass. I'm about to retire. Give me what I came here for."

The waiter cut between them with the drinks and Wolfram's salad. Greta lowered her head longer than necessary while she squeezed the lemon into her glass.

In a low voice, the banker continued, "You don't even have to travel. The location isn't far from JFK. You can hop right on a plane, twenty-five thousand dollars richer. Two hundred twenty-five thousand total."

Greta's head bobbed up. "You don't think I can add? Forget it. I already swore I'd never do another job in this city. More cops than cockroaches."

"All right. You walk away with two-fifty."

Wolfram was too damn relaxed. Maybe arguing about money, buying and selling a human life as if it were Microsoft shares, had put him in his element. But no, he'd been that way right from the start—he'd walked in minus any of the panic she'd heard on call to Switzerland. The fear was gone. Now it was her own gut's turn to churn.

"Pay the bonus in advance."

"Half the bonus in advance." With his eyes fixed on hers, he took a cell phone from his breast pocket, dialed a number, conversed briefly in German, and clicked it shut. Before replacing it, he took two folded pieces of paper from the same pocket. Printed on the first, besides the non-U.S. phone number, were: ID: FEMME01 and PW: LIBERTE01. "Go ahead," he urged. "Call and log in. Then change the ID and password through Menu."

Greta dipped into the unwieldy handbag hanging on the back of her chair for her phone. After making the call, she was prompted to enter the ID and password. DEPOSITED 14.11.05: $225,000.00 came up, and AC-COUNT TOTAL, with the same amount. MENU brought her to CHANGE ID AND PASSWORD. With the phone in her lap, Fahada's first husband and the year he died became the ID; husband number two was used for the password. Shutting off and restarting the phone, she dialed the number again, and logged on with the new ID and password. $225,000 still came up. She reached out for the second paper. It was blank, folded around a passport-sized photo of a thirtyish Middle Eastern man who looked as if he hadn't slept for about a year. A name and address were neatly written on the back.

"Call my cell to collect the balance upon completion," he said, as if she were starting a paint job.

"Any preference?"

Wolfram had speared his first shrimp and was deciding which of the two small bowls of dipping sauce to try first. "For what?"

"What the hell do you think? Accident, suicide, mutilation? Hand, tongue, or his testicles stuffed in his mouth?" Wolfram put down his fork. Grabbing her bag, she snapped, "Make up your mind before I come back from the ladies' room."

The restroom had two stalls; she headed into the wider of the two, sized to accommodate a wheelchair. After pulling off the beret and wig, she wriggled out of the ugly dress, ripped off the inflatable vest that had plumped her up about thirty pounds, pulled out its four gaskets, and unfastened the Velcro bands that held up her slacks.

With sweat running down her forehead and torso, she threw the contact lenses in the toilet, squeezed a small tube of cream over her face and wiped it and the makeup away with toilet paper while she stomped the rest of the air out of the vest. Someone in clickety heels hurried in; Greta silently cursed and whisked up the nearly deflated vest, pressing it flat against her chest.

The sound of peeing came from the next stall while Greta pulled on a black sweater as clingy as her black slacks. The other occupant flushed and left without washing her hands. Less than five minutes had passed by the time Greta wrapped a colorful scarf around her damp hair like a turban. She kicked off the low brown flats—the only comfortable part of her disguise—and slipped on four-inch heels. She flushed the toilet, flipped the reversible bag from brown to mustard, and stuffed it with everything except the clunky shoes, which she dumped in the sanitary napkin bucket.

Loose and swingy, she ambled out the restaurant's front door, adjusting small rectangular sunglasses against the midday glare. A town car was waiting outside the restaurant, engine running. A man in a leather jacket leaned against the small window that displayed the restaurant's menu, smoking a cigarette. He wasn't the man in the picture, but he could have been his brother. He never turned her way.

CHAPTER **THIRTY-FIVE**

Within a few hours, Greta was driving around the same Queens block for a second time. The address on Wolfram's slip of paper was in a neighborhood where half the homes were in poor repair, the other half freshly renovated or undergoing the process. Some had two bells by the front door, but they'd all started out as cookie cutter one-family, two-story structures back when Queens passed for a suburb. Bare, gnarled trees towered over yellowed mid-November front yards only slightly larger than a regulation Ping-Pong table. Every now and then she caught a glimpse of bright corduroy slacks and fleece tops, little kids at play in backyards sealed with sturdy cyclone fences.

The target house was just about at the middle of the block. Though not the most rundown, it had patches of peeling paint and missing roof shingles. Two dying azaleas, their leaves the color of burned toast, did even less for its curbside appeal. There was no indication that anyone was at home.

Greta methodically checked out the neighborhood, making the house the center of a simple square maze. The local public school was four blocks to the east. Three blocks west, she passed a Catholic church with a rectory on one side and an adjoining parochial school on the other. Continuing west and north two blocks each, she hit the commercial strip, where apartment buildings rose four stories above street-level storefronts. Its sidewalks were plied by women pulling their groceries home in folding carts after stops at the small Key Food, the fish market, the combination butcher-produce shop, or the bakery, where the display window featured a dusty plaster wedding cake surrounded by loaves of fresh bread. Greta spotted only one nail salon and real estate office within a five-block stretch; besides a computer repair shop, the only other sign of change was a corner mosque with abundant parking—the building still resembled the gas station it once had been. Three cars were parked in its lot, facing signs with stern warnings that vehicles of nonmembers would be towed at their owner's expense.

Parking was scarce on the shopping street, but one spot—tight, but an excellent vantage point—freed up. Over the course of twenty minutes, Greta watched as the owners of the three cars, each coming from a different direction, hopped in and drove off. It was an easy guess that they were locals who knew which days or hours the tow-away threat could be ignored.

Daylight dimmed, pedestrian traffic increased, lights appeared in the apartments above the stores. Greta pulled the photo of Omar Saleh from her pocket, a final look before darkness fell. For at least the hundredth time that afternoon, she tried to construct a strategy that would encourage the dour young man's trust. What did he know, what had he done, that made his death worth fifty thousand dollars to Wolfram? (And, no doubt, to the man in Paris, as well?) Had Saleh betrayed them? Failed them? Did they suspect he'd stumbled upon privileged information? Whatever the reason, something was happening right here, right now, on American soil. Whether it was part of the ripple effect spreading from the shutdown of Bersonne's network, or a totally new security threat, there was no question that it would be necessary to notify the JTTF. While her focus was on Wolfram, Saleh's activities could be the key to so much more. But she first had to verify that he was at the Queens address.

At the moment, however, she was once again submerged in the most tedious—and dreaded—of all passive pursuits. Her forty-year-plus back ached at the prospect of more surveillance. Hours sitting in a car loomed like a life sentence. Even worse, the cold would only make her have to pee in a cup more often—to be tidy, an act performed only by dint of the most excruciating contortion. Wolfram had made her too antsy and too angry to even contemplate another round of surveillance, but there was no way around it: She had to discover how many people were inside the house, whether or not Saleh was among them, and how to get answers without endangering either him or herself.

She turned on the engine and headed back to his house. Downstairs, lights and the unmistakable flicker of a TV leaked through closed venetian blinds. Passing by slowly, she took note of the spotlights created by the block's streetlamps and private anti-intruder lights.

Anticipation of her meeting with Wolfram had put her on edge for weeks, and the tension was ballooning. She'd have to rush to buy all she needed for the next few days before the stores closed. On Tuesday morning, she'd start her surveillance early, and in earnest.

Even the Brooklyn-Queens Expressway didn't have much traffic at 5:30 A.M. Saleh's house was dark when Greta pulled up a few car lengths away. The sun still hadn't come up, but more and more lights were popping on, piercing the inky grayness. She drank some coffee from her giant thermos, warming her gloved hands on the cup, and ate Cheerios right out of the box. Except for the Saleh house, the neighborhood gradually came to life. The whine of jets in takeoff and landing patterns became a constant. As dawn broke, Greta picked up the pad she'd positioned on the front passenger seat. Using a blue marker, she drew a crude sketch of the block, with an oblong indicating every parked car on each side of the block. Switching to a pen, she filled in each oblong with the car's color, make, and (if legible) license number. Whenever a vehicle left, she noted the time, plus any additional information, like the plate number, model name, and the driver's characteristics. Although her primary objective was to determine which car, if any, was Saleh's, the drill also kept her awake and alert.

Even though passersby could barely see her through the car's tinted glass, she instinctively slumped down and turned her face away whenever a pedestrian approached. Men and women headed to work, teenagers to high school. About an hour later, mothers shepherded kindergarteners and older children to their classes. After that, the street quieted considerably, except for the UPS van and a plumber who carried a tool case and piping into a house undergoing renovation. With one earbud, Greta listened to the news on a tiny transistor radio; she couldn't risk turning on the engine. In the late morning, a mailman wheeled his cart down the sidewalk, but he didn't stop at the Saleh house. About one, Greta could no longer put off the siren call of the peanut butter and jelly sandwich she'd packed. More coffee. She'd brought plenty of cups.

So far, four vehicles had arrived in the proximity of the target house: three were driven by moms ferrying toddlers, all headed for the same playgroup; the fourth driver was a priest calling on a white-haired lady in a caftan who needed a walker to make it to the door. All, recorded by green markers, had since departed. Purple would be for replacement of replacements, then red. Once again, time and identity were duly noted. Six of the original blue oblongs had yet to move. *Was one Saleh's?*

Mid-afternoon, she drew a fifth green oblong on the opposite side of the street. A man in a black hoodie and jeans slid out from behind the wheel and briskly walked her way. His head was down low enough so that he couldn't see Greta; consequently, she couldn't see much of him, either. Not only did his short, stocky build not match up to Saleh's gaunt face, but he quickly turned left, his destination somewhere around the corner.

Yearning to throw open the car door, stretch, and run up and down the block forty or fifty times, Greta stayed put, her only distraction brief interludes of listening to her radio. In reverse order, children, teens, and adults began the trudge home. A song that was popular when she and Bram met was playing, a song she really wanted to listen to with her eyes closed, but the damn surveillance wouldn't even let her blink. It was already getting dark, the temperature was plunging, and her only comfort was remembering the way his eyes had met hers, the way one corner of his mouth turned up slightly when he smiled . . . as if he, like Greta, marveled at their exceptional good luck in finding one another.

———

At the time, she hadn't worked undercover regularly for several years. However, she'd occasionally be tapped to take on the role of an "age-appropriate female"—crass, but it provided a welcome break from the day-to-day precinct routine.

In the two months the case was building, Viv The Interior Designer became a regular customer at a Brooklyn warehouse that specialized in custom tables, sinks, counters, shower enclosures, and decorative objects crafted from exotic imported stone. Huge sheets of marble, onyx, and granite were suspended for viewing in its cavernous showroom. Dramatically veined and shaded, they were also so heavy and unwieldy that they provided perfect cover for anything sandwiched in between while in transit.

The screech of power saws and polishers back in the fabrication area intermittently drowned out conversation while Don, the salesman, walked Viv down an aisle hung with the green onyx she'd asked to see. It wasn't the first time he'd pestered her with "C'mon, what's your Manhattan markup?"

Her reply was always a brittle "Enough to cover the cab ride here." While she vacillated between green veined with tan versus green veined with ochre, the owner appeared with a younger man in a tan leather jacket opened to display a pastel argyle sweater, its V-neck filled with thatchy chest hair. As they hustled toward the door, an overstuffed satchel had Tan Leather listing to one side. Greta twirled back to the green with ochre, the slab that would obstruct most of Don's view. "Let's use this one," she said decisively, and reached into her portfolio. On her "Here's my sketch" go-ahead, cops rushed the showroom. While the owner began screaming, "What the fuck is this about?" her hand slid out of the portfolio with a Glock aimed at Don.

"Don," she announced, no longer the unashamedly slumming Viv, "I'm a police officer. You're going to turn right slowly, hands in the air, and not try anything stupid."

Protesting, Don nevertheless turned. He found himself facing the uniform who'd silently moved down the aisle behind him, gun drawn. Without another word, the salesman complied with Greta's order to assume a kneeling position. While she bent forward to cuff him, Greta glimpsed a pair of shiny black men's shoes under the next row of marble slabs. "Listen, asshole in the wingtips, my gun can shoot right through this shit, so stay exactly where you are!"

"Unless you're holding a howitzer, that's absolutely preposterous," responded the indignant voice above the shoes. "I have no idea what's going on here. I'm only a customer—a customer who was waiting for an estimate on a conference table until that salesman saw you and totally forgot about me . . . not that I blame him. Can I at least slide my wallet under this tombstone to prove my identity?"

From the very start, the year they'd shared had been the best of her life.

The sun was setting, briefly pouring neon orange light over Saleh's block. What Greta saw in the instant before it faded had the impact of a grenade shattering her windshield.

The car parked by the man in the hooded sweatshirt, the man who'd gone around the block without returning, now had a man sitting in the driver's seat—at least, the silhouette of a man. In reaction to the sudden flash of sun from the west, his left hand had shot up, visor-like, over his eyes. Then he disappeared, obscured by his tinted windshield.

Greta was positive that no one else had approached the car, a gray Chevy Malibu. In a panic, she checked her pad while she could still see. Same car, same license plate. With the workday winding down, six other cars had filled all the empty spots on the street since the Chevy had pulled in at 3:15.

Only two had left: One was an Acura, from a spot it occupied barely five minutes; a man had parked it, and a woman wearing a long quilted coat over white pants and shoes had driven it away. Greta had seen the woman walking a boy and girl dressed in the Catholic school's uniforms to and from school. Now she looked like a nurse heading for a night shift as soon as her husband took over the kids for the evening. The second departure, at 3:30, was a beige midsize Ford. Greta had been keeping an eye on the kids returning from school—most stuck together in one big noisy pack, followed by a few stragglers—to see if any would run into the

Saleh house. All the children walked right by, but the distraction made her miss whoever had entered the Ford. She'd turned as soon as she heard an engine start, only to watch it pull out immediately.

Maybe that nurse wasn't the only one working a shift.

The Ford had been there when Greta arrived, before dawn. It very well might have been occupied by someone on surveillance for ten or twelve hours, someone smart enough to depart under the cover of the grade-schoolers' commotion. And the man who'd hurried away from the Malibu was a smokescreen who gave the impression of leaving an empty car.

Clearly, someone else was watching Saleh.

Maybe these Chevy-Ford guys were protecting him from Wolfram. On the other hand, Saleh might be a threat so toxic, they might represent an entirely different group that he'd pissed off. Third possibility: they could be JTTF, or another Homeland Security organization already investigating whatever strategic value Saleh possessed.

As the first-floor lights came on in the Saleh house, a fourth scenario, and by far the most dangerous, simultaneously clicked on in Greta's head:

Maybe they were watching *her* watching Saleh.

Had they caught sight of her? Were they watching Greta Strasser, or were they on the lookout for Fahada? If they were after the woman Wolfram met at the restaurant, that gave her some wiggle room, but not a hell of a lot.

Shielding her cell phone screen with her hand, she dialed the offshore account Wolfram had set up for Fahada. The money was still there, but she'd never doubted that the Swiss banker had come to New York with a plan. Now, Greta figured, it would go like this: Fahada eliminates Saleh. For $25,000 or so, the Hoodie hoods eliminate her—just like a supermarket's Buy One, Get One Free sale. After a simple chargeback, Wolfram returns to Zurich with $225,000 he never intended to spend.

Despite the cold, Greta broke out in a sweat. She had to get to Saleh ASAP, get him out of that house. Only after that could she deal with Wolfram. The TV started to flicker through the blinds of the Saleh house. Crossing her arms around her chest for warmth, she stared out into the night, trying to work out what the hell to do next.

CHAPTER **THIRTY-SIX**

A few minutes after nine, a faint glimmer filtered through the drapes of Saleh's second floor windows. One by one, the downstairs TV and lights were turned off. Fifteen minutes later, Greta drove away. After three blocks, she found a parking spot, killed the engine, and called the number she'd preset for the local precinct.

"There's this car parked outside my house since this morning." Her tone was agitated, only a notch away from a whine. "All day, there's a man sitting inside. I could see him staring at the kids when they came home from school, watching where each one lives. Tell me, who sits in a car that long unless he's up to no good?"

"What kind of car?" the duty cop asked.

"A gray Chevy. My husband says it's a Malibu. It's right in the middle of the block. I'm telling you, the guy's a creep!"

"We'll have a patrol car check it out," the cop replied. "Stay inside. Let us take care of it."

Greta twisted around to retrieve the canvas rucksack she'd stowed on the floor between the front and back seats. As soon as she was out of the car, she began to run, slowing to a walk only before crossing the final intersection. Two houses away from Saleh's, only one house away from the rear of the Malibu, she ducked down behind the dwarf pine that had been in her line of vision all day. It came to a severely pruned point five feet from the ground, but its base flared out wider than its height, and it was dense enough to provide cover for someone in head-to-toe black in a low crouch.

A few minutes later, a patrol car rolled up next to the Malibu. After the two uniforms did a double flashlight search of the car's interior and asked a few inaudible cop questions, Mr. Silhouette was asked to exit the car. Shoulder to shoulder with him, the cops hustled him out of the shadows and into the street, next to their cruiser. Now that he was closer to Greta's position, she could see that he was medium height, his build camouflaged by a puffy down jacket. A wallet was in his right hand, and his fingers fumbled while he worked his license out of a slot.

The cop who took it swept a flashlight over the man's face for a photo match. As he'd done at sunset, the guy flinched, his hand flying to his forehead.

"Insurance? Registration?" The cop flexed his fingers impatiently, gimme mode.

"Glove box," the man replied.

The other uniform removed a small folder from the glove compartment, studied it, and stepped back to check out the car. It had to be a rental, with insurance included in the agreement. He took the license from his partner and reentered the patrol car to run the documents through the system.

The suspect, ratcheting up from sullen to steamed, began to vent at the cop who unofficially had him under guard. "This is crazy! I have right to park here! Free country! I only wait for friend! What if bad news happening to him?"

While he played his starring role in the roadway, drapes parted on both sides of the street. Greta burrowed into the little tree.

The other cop climbed out of the car, countering, "If that's the case, Mr. Anwar, there's really no reason for you to hang around here waiting for him to come home, is there?" As he handed the documents back, he added, "I could write you up for loitering. Instead, do us all a favor and get in your car, drive away, find a well-lit place to park, and do what everyone else does: Use that phone on your front seat to call your friend."

Anwar, his hands balled in fists at his sides, stood his ground.

"Ever seen a Western movie, Mr. Anwar?" his partner asked. Not waiting for an answer, he continued, "The part where the sheriff rides behind the troublemaker until he's far enough away not to be a threat to the townsfolk? This is how it goes." Both cops got back in their car, put on their flashers, and split the night's calm with a distinctly unfriendly *whoop-whoop*. Cold, tired, and stiff as she was, Greta wanted to applaud.

Unable to ignore the hint, Anwar slid behind the wheel and wasted no time pulling out. The patrol car initiated a sluggish pursuit—slow enough to keep the rental to a nerve-wracking fifteen miles per hour. The bright, strobing lights in his rearview mirror would have him blinking all the way to the closest entry ramp of the Van Wyck Expressway.

Several minutes after the last of the onlookers retreated from their windows, Greta proceeded with her primary objective—getting to Saleh. Her plan had been to cut through the adjacent backyard and right into his—until she ran up against his next door neighbor's fence. Her only option was to duck behind the cars parked along the curb and then sprint down the narrow driveway separating the two properties. A break came in the shape of the van parked in the drive; it was wide enough to shield her while she squeezed her way past Saleh's side entry door, small frosted bathroom window, and two bashed-in metal garbage cans.

As she stepped around to the rear, strangely spaced Stonehenge-like columns stopped her cold. No lights were on at the back of the house, but a high-wattage anti-intruder beam several houses down helped her make out the remnants of a stockade fence. Broken pikes were scattered across the packed dirt of the yard, partially concealed by drifts of leaves. The bottom of the first window she came to was only a few inches above her head. Once she got it open, she'd be able to grab the bottom of the casement and pull herself up and in.

With all the B&E arrests that she'd made, Greta possessed firsthand knowledge of the essential tools of the trade. The previous night, while waiting to pay at Home Depot, she'd wondered if the most chronic burglars (like the incurable mutts she'd hauled in as many as five times) had the nerve to use the contractors-only register.

A small crowbar was the first indispensable item she pulled out of her rucksack. On tiptoe, she positioned it under the window's middle sash and pushed up. There was absolutely no give. After tries at a number of points, she moved on to the next window, which was larger and not so high off the ground. Even though that put more muscle into the effort, it failed to budge. Two small tilt-out basement windows were directly under the upper two. One was boarded up, and ripping the wood away with the crowbar would be far too noisy. The flat tip of the crowbar was too thick to wedge under the frame of the other window, so she tried to slide her new flat-tipped screwdriver underneath it instead. No yield at all—this was concrete masquerading as wood.

Straining to hear the sound of any vehicle, any footfall, she flattened her body against the house as she rounded its far side. Advancing, she tested every window she passed. All four were either locked or swollen in their frames.

In the distance, a car approached. Greta hit the ground, holding her breath until its engine faded. Seconds later, the screech of brakes signaled another car, cutting around a corner too fast. With her chin and forehead pressed into the dirt until it sped by, she once again ruled out any attempt on the house's two doors—the risk of being spotted in the sweep of headlights was too great. Besides, judging by the windows, her limited skill with a lock pick would be no match for Fortress Saleh.

She was down to only one window option . . . the filthiest and nasticst of all.

The area houses all had narrow front porches, not much more than railed-in aprons for sitting outdoors in warm weather. A number were bedecked with the all-purpose gourds, pumpkins, and cornstalks that were supposed to celebrate the season between Labor Day and Christmas. Originally, wood latticework had covered the three or four feet between the porch floor and the ground. Starting beneath the entry stoop, it ran along the front and wrapped around the side wall for five feet, in tandem with the porch. The refurbished houses were refitted with white plastic slats, but the Saleh porch, gourd-free, still sagged over the original wood crisscross.

The lattice concealed two swing-out cellar windows like the ones at the back; relics of the pre-dehumidifier era, they were designed more for ventilation than daylight. The only way to access them was by lifting away a small square hatch on the side of the porch that fit into a corresponding frame in the lattice. With her screwdriver, Greta gently pried all around the hatch. As it loosened, the rotten wood cracked and splintered, never again to snap back in place. No matter . . . Greta would get Saleh to safety, away from this house.

The crawl space was filled with a deep, oozy layer of wet leaves and dead insects and rodents—the accumulation of seven decades. As she wriggled through the tight opening, it slammed her with a rot-sewer combo that was less odor than toxic gas. Because she had to keep her head down to protect her eyes from a thick tangle of spiderwebs, all she could do was breathe through her mouth and keep a lid on the gag reflex. Slogging forward on her knees—the damp decay immediately soaked her jeans and gloves—she edged up to the first window. Her cramped position afforded little leverage as she twisted to insert the screwdriver under the window frame. Again, for a rickety little house, this place was unyielding. Next window—last window.

The sound of a car crawling along with the jerky stops and starts of a parking-spot-hunter froze her in mid-scuttle. Greta stayed put, anticipating a desperation search all around the block. Sure enough, the driver returned, braked, reversed, and straightened twice to wedge his vehicle into a tricky spot on the other side of the street. With the block's layout imprinted on her memory, Greta knew that his rear had to be blocking part of the driveway diagonally opposite. He killed the engine. Five minutes passed, with no sound of a car door opening. Was he a replacement for the guy the cops had run out of Dodge? If so, as long as the driver remained in the car, there was no way he could spot her—hell, he could stand a foot away in Saleh's front yard, and never suspect she was there. That was the good part. The bad part was that there would be no good part if she flipped on her skinny little penlight to orient herself in the total darkness.

Greta advanced to the last window. To her surprise, the screwdriver slid in; a push earned her an inch. She pressed the tool up against the bottom of the frame and withdrew it slowly. Groaning, the window followed. Alternating left, right, and center, Greta repeatedly nudged the screwdriver under the frame, each outward yank producing a small advance and many splinters. Once the edge of the frame passed the sill, Greta concentrated on one all-out tug. The force pried the window free, but as it swung out, open and horizontal, something snapped. A musty aroma escaped while her finger searched the glass—a fracture, deep enough to be felt through her glove. She passed her hand up and down in the space between the glass and the upper casement frame. Making an estimate of how much room she had was tricky in the dark. Fifteen inches? Eighteen? Was that enough to wiggle through into the black void of the cellar? Of course, actual wiggling over the window itself was out, since the strength of the frame could hardly be trusted any more than its cracked pane.

Greta rummaged through her rucksack, found her figure-eight twist of rope, and repacked the screwdriver and crowbar. She threaded the rope through the sack's drawstring and fastened it to her wrist. A shove left it about two feet right of the window.

Briefly, she weighed whether or not it was time to switch to night vision. The only way to enter was to tilt her head back, stretch her arms forward to grip the top of the casement, and kick her legs straight out. During her head's carry-through, there was a chance that the upper casement might knock off or damage her bulky, outdated goggles, a pair she'd used during a search in the marshlands around La Guardia. Technically, they were still adequate, but current models were far more compact. She decided to keep them safe for their primary purpose . . . moving through Saleh's dark house.

Greta rolled her shoulders and flexed fingers stiff from the November chill. After locking onto the casement and a silent one-two-three, her legs lunged forward. She was braced to endure a short fall—floor to ceiling, the cellar couldn't be much over six feet, and the window and the upper wall had to cut that in half.

In a split second, she discovered that the darkness before her wasn't empty at all: Her feet smashed into a barrier that, huge as it seemed, offered minimal resistance—it tumbled away on impact, followed by a series of dull, bumping thuds. A fall of less than two feet left her unhurt, but her body reflexively scooted away from the blunt object pressing into her spine. That movement hauled down the rucksack, which must have been teetering on the edge of the window frame. More muffled thumps rolled out, followed by a descending musical scale—silvery tinkles, like a shower of ornaments plummeting down from a Christmas tree.

She hoped Saleh was fast asleep two stories up, that the small chaos she'd unleashed hadn't been loud enough to rouse him. Not quite steeled for the sound of feet pounding down the upper staircase, she didn't dare move.

The wind found its way through the latticework, bitter enough to make her shiver. She shivered again when her ears picked up a faint grinding—or was it a clawing? Something was inching along the wall above her, stopping and starting, gaining momentum . . . or getting bolder. This wouldn't be the first time a rat—potential trailblazer for a whole army of rats—had followed her into a building, but it was the first time one was so close to the top of her head. As she reached inside her jacket for her Glock, a very un-ratlike shifting and shuddering made her instinctively roll left. The next moment, the undefined menace wrenched away from the wall, whooshed past her cheek, and smashed into the cellar floor with a clatter as sharp and loud as a rifle barrage.

Unless he was stone deaf, Saleh had just been jolted out of bed. As for the guy parked outside, his car window would be closed. And even with the cellar window open, it would be difficult to pinpoint the exact source of the crash . . . until Saleh's lights flashed on and the shouting began.

Greta chambered her gun, reeled in the rucksack, and grabbed for the goggle case. Night vision revealed no immediate danger—she was sprawled over a heap of large cartons. Careful not to disrupt more of them, she hopped to the floor. The other front window was still blocked by three neat stacks of smaller boxes, in contrast to her entry point, where she'd toppled all but the two base cartons. In between the windows, several stacks of upended wood planks leaned against the wall. Some were painted, some varnished, none matched exactly in length or width, as if they'd been scavenged for some rough carpentry project: One stack, splayed out on the floor; was what had hurtled down with such explosive force, apparently set in motion by the falling cartons.

Turning around, she saw that the rest of the cellar was an undivided room with stone walls and floor. A decrepit furnace was on the right wall. The corner beyond was taken up by a crude work bench, a pyramid of dented paint cans on one end. Above it, a Peg-Board with hooks held a few tools, paintbrushes wrapped in aluminum foil, and a pack of sandpaper. An open staircase ascended in the other corner.

So far, not a single sound had filtered down to the cellar. Greta warily advanced toward the stairs, still not quite believing that she'd made it inside. Had Saleh simply blocked the last window with cartons, assuming that no one was fool enough to slog all the way to the end of the slimy pit of a crawl space? Or was the final window just as tight as all the others, but simply no match for an attack fueled by sheer desperation? Maybe some secret power did come into play when you were down to betting your last chip.

Gingerly, Greta placed a foot on the bottom stair. There was no banister, every riser was concave from wear, and the entire structure shook with her every step. For ten minutes, she held her ear to the door next to the top step, waiting and listening. All along she'd assumed that Saleh was alone in the house, but now she pictured every male relative and cohort imaginable gathered on the other side of the door, a mob poised to strike with knives, clubs, and guns.

Another ten minutes passed without so much as the creak of a floorboard. She twisted the doorknob, expecting the door to be locked. Instead, it swung open too easily, and she swiftly grabbed it back, nearly slamming it shut. Through the narrow opening, her goggles swept over a kitchen with an ancient refrigerator and stove, empty shelves, and a sink that looked like the first model produced after hand pumps went out. Partially visible in an alcove at the far side of the room was a washer or dryer. Other than the lingering whiff of cat, no sign of life. Freezing for an entire minute after each noisy groan of the floorboards, she crossed the kitchen.

The next room was bare, except for an empty bookcase and a sagging daybed.

It was the room at the front—the one that had emitted such a warm and cozy glow while she froze her butt off in the car—that stopped Greta in her tracks.

Directly ahead, a TV was centered on a Formica kitchen table. A crooked floor lamp and two table lamps on plastic milk crates were spaced as if an invisible sofa and armchair separated them. Each was connected to its own timer device.

Greta momentarily squeezed her eyes shut, not ready to accept the crude mechanics of illusion, or how thoroughly she had been deceived. So far, she'd seen her mission as straightforward: get Saleh out of the house and learn why Wolfram was paying Fahada to kill him. But Saleh was no longer here.

Clearly, the house had been abandoned for some time. Saleh could have discovered it, holed up in it, and taken all necessary precautions to keep out unwanted visitors. Apparently, he'd made a speedy exit, giving himself a lead on his pursuers—and Greta—by tricking them into thinking he was still inside.

Just in case, the second floor still warranted a quick search. She began to head for the stairs, but once again stopped short. As for that surveillance unit outside, she could now pretty much rule out anyone trying to protect Saleh, and going by the watchers she'd seen so far, cross off a clandestine branch of the government.

As she turned toward the newel post, something about the front door caught her eye. Even with night vision minimizing its distinctive silvery gleam, Greta knew she was looking at duct tape—lots of it. In a wide X big enough to stretch across the entire top half of the door, it supported something that was roughly where a wreath would be hanging on the outside. She blinked several times to register what she was looking at. Stunned, she retreated, stumbling backward into the staircase. A cell phone was wired into a mass of C4 spiked with nails, metal fragments, and ragged stone chips. She'd been in enough seminars, plus two real-life situations, to know it had the potential to blow away everything within a range of twenty feet on both sides of the door. Fahada, who'd killed so ruthlessly and so ingeniously, was not a target to be taken mano a mano.

Saleh hadn't skipped out. Saleh had never existed.

The first signal Greta's brain sent out was to run really fast and really far—no stopping for at least a mile. The second was to back away very slowly.

For the first time, she noticed the narrow door next to the stairs. It was ajar. Her mind replayed her dash to the back of the house . . . the small frosted window, the side door . . . Peering in, she saw a toilet and sink; the alcove with the washer was the sole way to get to the side entrance. Retracing her steps, she found that the door was completely boarded up with vari-colored planks, just like the ones in the cellar. No exit.

Greta backed into the kitchen. She was trapped in a house that could explode at any moment, needing no more than a remote signal sent to a cell phone detonator—*she* was the pathetic prey trapped under the hawk's wingspan. That stinking turd of a Swiss banker had outmaneuvered her. And as much as she loathed his greed and callousness, she had her own gullibility to blame for winding up in this mess.

While she flipped the heavy goggles back onto the top of her head, she dropped, cross-legged, onto the linoleum floor. After peeling off her wet and filthy gloves, she blew on her fingers to warm them, then hugged her arms around her knees.

As she struggled to regain focus, she decided that she might not be so hopelessly cornered after all. Assessing, reassessing, and recharging, Greta lost track of time. With a hand cupped over her wristwatch, she flicked the button that illuminated the face. Not bad—only half-past midnight.

Her easiest conclusion had been that the tool she now needed the most hadn't been on her Home Depot shopping list. Shifting onto one hip, she pulled crime scene gloves from a pocket of her jeans, snapped them on, and got to her feet. Goggles back on, she did a quick check of the kitchen drawers for a substitute. The only knife she found was too dull to cut butter. As she tossed it back, she remembered the workbench in the cellar and raced down the stairs.

Every tool on the Peg-Board—handsaw, wrench, hammer, and several pliers—was badly rusted. She plucked off the one pair of pliers that might prove useful. It wouldn't move without catching, and was in dire need of a squirt of WD-40. The only available stand-in was a grubby rag that still carried the tang of turpentine. Several minutes of intense rubbing had the pliers moving—if she squeezed hard. Continuously flexing the tool in her hand, Greta ran back up the stairs and toward the front door.

Hardly breathing, her face inches from the bomb, she found it impossible to control the body-wide tremors that seemed to both begin and end in her right hand. Clenching her teeth, she held up the shaking pliers and concentrated on lining up the cutting edge with the wiring that extended from the cell phone. With all the speed and force she could muster, holding her breath, she snapped the rusty, resistant tool shut. In the same split second, her eyes closed instinctively. When she opened them—and resumed breathing—she discovered that the pliers had done the job, clipping right through the wire. For a few seconds, she just stared, amazed that it was actually severed.

Back in the kitchen, careful not to snag the plastic gloves, she ran her fingers over the bottom of the first window she'd tried. Several nail heads poked up out of the frame. The other rear window was also hammered shut; there was no reason to check the rest.

When she finally got to the second floor, as expected, there was a setup like the one downstairs, with two lamps on timers flanking a space the size of a double bed.

Greta made a beeline back down to the cellar, where she carried two paint cans from the workbench to the entry window she'd worked so hard to open. After she stood on them to pull it closed, she rebuilt the carton tower until the window was once again fully blocked. The fallen wood planks were upended.

Tucking the hammer from the Peg-Board in her waistband, she dragged the workbench a few feet and positioned it under the back window that wasn't boarded up. She climbed up and set to work prying out the nails with the back of the hammerhead. Extremely resistant, they had her perspiring in her layered surveillance clothes in no time. Another exasperating ten minutes went by before she dropped the last nail into her jacket pocket. With no small satisfaction, she flattened her hands against the left and right sides of the window frame and proceeded to thwack it with all her might. After several tries, gloriously fresh and cold air rushed onto her overheated cheeks. When the window was fully open, she hopped down, lugged back the workbench, and grabbed her two paint cans. They provided enough of a boost for her to hoist herself up; she used her stretched-out foot to kick them over so it would look as if they fell from the paint can pyramid. Finally, she crawled through the open window into the backyard. She turned and used both feet to shove it closed.

The adjacent yard to the rear had no fence, and she passed through its shadows cautiously until she made it through to the next street. Then she began to run toward her car, going all out, reveling in her resurgent freedom

The next day, Wednesday, Greta slept in until seven, Googled Kmart locations, changed to another car, and arrived at the stakeout shortly after ten a.m. The surveillance team had a different vehicle as well, and it took her a while to figure out that a man in a white Pontiac was watching her watch him. Just before two, she drove off, rented another make and model, and returned just before the after-school switch. She parked in the middle of the next block, keeping an eye on the Pontiac in her rearview and side mirrors. A blue Taurus pulled into the last empty spot on Saleh's block. The driver who left the Taurus was wearing a gray hooded sweatshirt. The Pontiac drove off about ten minutes later.

Hanging back, Greta tailed the white car. It drove three blocks before stopping at a bus stop to pick up a man in a gray hoodie. The Pontiac stuck to major avenues and boulevards, never exceeding the speed limit. It turned at every sign pointing the way to JFK, no shortcuts. About two miles from the feed into the airport, the Pontiac's right blinker activated. It slowed and turned into a motel entrance. Greta kept on going, then doubled back and pulled into the gas station directly across the street. Of its four pump islands, she chose the one where a big Suburban was still a car away from being served. Across the road, the Pontiac was parked at the southernmost end of the motel. While the Suburban's tank was guzzling, a man walked out of the motel's central passageway, the type that sheltered vending machines and the stairs leading up to the second floor rooms. Through her binoculars, she could see that he was in his late twenties and had a patchy dark beard. As he walked along the row of doors, she noticed that his left foot dragged as it caught up with his right. His arms were full of soda cans, snacks, and a plastic ice bucket, so he couldn't knock on the door three parking slots north of the Pontiac. Instead, he kicked it with his good foot. Greta caught only a glimpse of the man who opened the door, but he bore a strong resemblance to the man who'd been waiting at the bus stop.

It was dark when she left the closest Kmart with two cell phones, a roll of duct tape, wire, and a big-faced digital watch. Before she left the parking lot, she set the watch's alarm for 11:15.

An hour or so before the timers were due to sequence off the second-story lights in the Saleh house, Greta parked on the street to its rear. After climbing into the backseat, she slouched down to avoid being sighted by passersby. Her mind raced, making it nearly impossible to remain still. She'd been caught up in plenty of threatening situations, but never one as sinister as this: The faux-Fahada she'd created was marked for death because, by tracking down Wolfram, she'd cracked the compartmentalization of the terror-funding network. Assassins were primed to kill the network's star assassin in order to restore that compartmentalization. The cycle would repeat when they themselves knew too much. The scariest part was that Greta Strasser had been sucked right into their deadly game.

The watch alarm took forever, but it finally pinged.

Channeling a teenage boy looking for trouble, face grim under a baseball cap, shoulders squared up against a heavy backpack, she came up on the blue Taurus from behind and memorized the plate number. Two blocks down, she headed back to the street where she'd parked, and returned to Saleh's house via the same backyard and basement window.

———

First the UPS truck, then the mailman: both of them whistled as they did their morning rounds. Thursday, one week before the big Thanksgiving holiday, was the rare November day—sunny, dry-cold, and windless—that made being outdoors a delight.

As soon as the mail cart was off the block, a car slowly drove around the block twice, finally choosing a spot where the guy in the white Pontiac couldn't miss it. A woman eased out of the driver's seat: resembling a giant potato, she was in drab brown, from her felt beret to her long wool coat, all the way down to her thick brown boots. If someone was snapping her picture with a digital camera and e-mailing the image to someone who'd recently met Fahada, there'd be no question of a positive match. She reached across to the passenger seat and dragged out a large brown handbag. As soon as it was over her shoulder and next to her right hip, she slipped her right hand into her coat pocket. When she withdrew it, it was concealed by the purse. Her arm remained bent at the elbow. Wearing the purposeful smile of someone going to visit an ailing friend, she strode briskly along the walkway and up the steps to Saleh's front door.

Using her left hand, she pressed the doorbell, waited, pressed again. After a third ring, she cocked her head, straining for a response or footfall from within. Next, she knocked, paused, and knocked some more, pulling her fist back as if she were really pounding the door. More listening, then her big brown form slid sideways onto the porch, face-to-face with the nearest front room window. Tiptoeing up and down, she tried to peek inside, but the drapes gave up nothing. A quick study of the next window met the same result, and she returned to the door. One more ring, one more knock, and she retreated down the stoop, pausing on each step to turn, crane her neck back, and search the second floor windows for some sign of life. When she reached the sidewalk, she spun around quickly to face the house. Again, her head twisted right and left and up before she resolutely headed back to her car and drove away.

Greta made the first left she could, pulled into a driveway to turn around, and positioned her car close enough to the corner to see and not be seen. The door of the Pontiac swung open. The man who emerged had a cell phone in his hand, and he pointed it at the Saleh door, then jammed it into a pocket. He did his best to hurry across the street, but a limping left foot slowed him down.

Like a magnet, the front door of the Saleh house pulled him closer and closer. Both his hands were balled up in rage against a squandered opportunity, and by the time he stepped up onto the sidewalk, his head was shaking in disbelief and exasperation.

As soon as he began stomping up the walkway, his back to the street, Greta pulled around the corner. Inching along, she managed to come up directly behind him just at the moment he began to jab a key at one of the door's locks. She had a cell phone of her own in her lap, and her index finger was poised directly above the option she needed. She simultaneously pressed the keypad and slammed down hard on the gas pedal. After the few seconds it took to speed dial the area code and number, the steering wheel trembled in her hands. A single clap of ear-piercing thunder, totally unexpected on such a bright morning, rolled across the neighborhood. As she drove through the first intersection, she glanced at her rearview mirror. Assorted chunks of debris, trailing flames like comets, dropped from a great height onto the roadbed.

By the time she reached the area's commercial street, now a blonde in sunglasses, a fire engine was barreling toward her in the opposite direction. She steered as far to the right as she could and stopped, giving it as much leeway as possible. While the red blur passed her, she checked her watch. 11:34 A.M. Fifteen minutes later, she left the deserted parking lot of a nearby multiplex, where the movies didn't begin until after one on weekdays. Fahada's gear, neatly folded, was in shopping bags on the backseat.

At four minutes after noon, half an hour after the bomb exploded, she phoned the same precinct she'd called on Tuesday night.

"That explosion! I saw the guy who set it off! I was in my car, and I saw him run into a car, and I followed them!" Breathless and shaky, she blurted out the words between gasps.

"*Them?*" the cop interrupted.

"Yeah, there was another guy, the driver, waiting in the car. I couldn't stop until now—I didn't want to let them get away!"

She panted for a moment, giving the duty cop a chance to ask, "Where'd they go?"

"This motel—it's just before you get to JFK." She gave him the information he needed, including the license plate number of the blue Taurus. The cop asked for her contact information. "No way—he looked like one of those damn terrorists! I got three friends serving in Iraq! I don't want one of those crazy bastards coming after me here!"

CHAPTER **THIRTY-EIGHT**

While Greta hid in the closet of the Wolfram suite, she found it hard to believe that only five days had passed since Madeleine of Floraganza had furtively sketched every detail of its layout.

One wall of the silk-papered living room was dominated by a fireplace with an extraordinary marble mantel; above, a crystal Niagara of a chandelier was suspended from a ceiling at least twelve feet high. Multiple seating groups of sofas, settees, chairs, and tables in some Louis-the-umpteenth style were clustered about, with plenty of room left for a bar and cupboard that opened onto a flat-screen TV and sound system.

The bedroom, in addition to two separate seating areas of its own, had a king-sized bed, dresser, and a mirrored armoire perfectly positioned to reflect the swags of blue silk that cascaded around the bed's heavily embroidered headboard. The adjoining marble bathroom had double sinks, a massive tub, and separate shower.

That past Sunday, as promised, she phoned Housekeeping after she'd finished the diagrams . . . in between jamming flowers, ferns, and branches into a vase.

"I've made a bit of a mess! Sorry-sorry!" Greta-Madeleine had gushed to the maid dispatched to tidy up. "Please, I'd love you to have these for the trouble." One by one, she dropped small boxes of chocolates, two miniature stuffed animals, and a spray of roses into a paper gift tote.

With a big smile, the young woman said the gifts would make her daughter very happy.

While Madeleine gathered up the rest of her gear, she sighed, "I'll be lucky if I get home by midnight tonight." Just as she'd hoped, the maid volunteered that her workday wasn't about to end that soon, either—not until eight. Once that was established, it was easy to chat about the time she started to turn down the beds for the evening, how long each room took, and if this suite was the very last one. No, next to last, so from the time the maid walked in here, she had only twenty minutes left before she punched out.

Just after seven-fifteen, Greta, to avoid being pinpointed by the elevator surveillance camera, got off three floors below Wolfram's. She'd climbed the stairs and waited by the door to the hall, watching the maid's cart advance toward his suite. The same young woman was on duty, but that was no problem: Fahada bore no resemblance to Madeleine.

The maid knocked on Wolfram's door, listened for a response, then used her card to enter, leaving the door ajar to access her cart. As with the previous rooms, she did the bathroom first, carrying out used towels, then heading back in with fresh replacements and a plastic carrier filled with scouring brushes and spray cleaners. Greta casually made her way to Wolfram's suite, strolling in as if she were the paying guest. Once inside, she cautiously approached the open French doors that led to the bedroom. The maid was humming in between bursts of running water. Flattened against the wall, Greta slid to the armoire. It held only one suit—more room to hide, but very little cover.

A little after eight, Greta emerged to find the bed turned down, the room softly lit by matching lamps on matching gilt-edged nightstands. Greta switched off the one closest to the bathroom. She reached into her coat and withdrew the final edition of the *New York Post*. The explosion had

STEALING FROM THE DEAD

made the top of page three: "Deadly Terror Bomb Destroys Queens Home" ran above a photo of charred ruins. So far, there was one confirmed death, victim not identified. No further casualties had been reported. The bomb had all the hallmarks of the roadside improvised explosive devices used against American soldiers in the Middle East.

As for the cratered-out house itself, the reporter had discovered that the title was held by an unnamed man with dual Syrian-American citizenship whose property taxes were overdue. According to various neighbors, he "kept to himself" and had not been seen for "a really long time." They described the house as "really rundown—like abandoned." It had suffered so much structural damage that a NYFD demolition order was expected to be carried out as soon as the investigation wrapped up. Greta folded the tabloid with the article on top and placed it on the foot of the bed.

The TV news channels had been covering the bombing all afternoon and evening, but there had been no mention so far of an anonymous tip to the police, or of any suspects in custody.

Wolfram's offshore banking symposium had been slated to wrap up with a luncheon at the Marriott. She had no idea where he was at present, or when he'd return to the hotel. That he'd stopped there several hours earlier was evident from the printout on the dresser. A Swiss International e-ticket for the next day, JFK to Zurich, had been e-mailed to Wolfram at three-ten that afternoon. A suitcase packed to the max sat next to the dresser. Another, with very little room left, was open on the luggage stand. Patches of gift wrap showed between the dry-cleaned shirt, tie, underwear, and socks neatly lined up on top. One by one, she lifted them to get a better look at the four small gifts beneath, each labeled with a different recipient's name.

All along, Greta had been sure what the banker's initial move would be after hearing the news that confirmed—as far as he was concerned—Fahada's final fadeout. Reserving a seat on the next plane to the Alps had never been at the top of his list.

The money came first. For Wolfram, the money *always* came first.

Early in the afternoon, she started to monitor the account he'd set up for Fahada on her cell phone, compulsively checking every few minutes.

She pegged the exact minute he heard the news as 1:57—simply because at 1:58, every penny was cleaned out, and not a trace of the account remained. Not only was there no access, but no record that it had ever existed. She was positive that the banker never would've risked shutting it down if he'd believed there was a chance that the unidentified remains in Queens belonged to anyone else.

The two guys at the motel would've been picked up by the cops before the news hit. And they'd never know that their buddy hadn't had a nanosecond to discover that, as the recording went, "The number you have dialed has been changed."

Greta dropped onto one of the two chairs with high oval-shaped backs that stood near the foot of the bed. Once again, the fabric was silk; the pattern was wide blue and gray stripes pleasingly separated by a quarter-stripe of pink. She glanced up—another chandelier. Two thousand a night for the suite? Three? No big deal—Wolfram had just stuffed $225,000 back into his fat cyberspace wallet.

As she waited for him to return to the suite, her thoughts drifted back to the two choices she'd eventually struggled with the night before, while she was hidden on her car's backseat.

The first was to drive home and get a good night's sleep in her own bed. The next afternoon, she'd watch the changing of the guard and identify the car doing surveillance, phone the bomb squad, and point the way to the rest of the crew at the motel. Even if that meant giving up her best bargaining chips, she would've still had this chance to confront Wolfram.

But the second alternative—sneaking back into the house and taping one of her new cell phones to the C4—had been the one she'd taken. That the weapon used was the very same device intended to blast her to bits made not a speck of difference—it was still an act of premeditated murder, a crime that would go against everything she'd spent her life defending.

Even worse, it would permanently erase any vestige of what had differentiated Greta Strasser from Fahada.

Perhaps Fahada hadn't committed suicide after all; perhaps what appeared to be the assassin's last breath had transposed her twisted essence into Greta: that fearsome disconnect from the rest of humanity, the cold fire that drove her to kill.

Blame it on Fahada then, blame that hellish bequest for forcing Greta out of the car with that new phone. And blame her yet again, for Greta's return that morning to hit speed dial. One little movement of her finger and, right along with the limping man, she'd blasted whoever she once had been to Kingdom Come.

Through a crime-scene glove, Greta traced the stripes of the oval-backed chair. Pretty, but stiff, and not particularly comfortable. With a wry smile, she reminded herself that if she'd played it according to the book, the off-shore account Wolfram had set up would still be active—traceable evidence against the Swiss banker. But that was for the now-abandoned Scenario Number One. Number Two would play the account's disappearance quite another way.

Several times she asked herself if any of the people who'd made a difference in her life would have approved of her choice.

Theo? Too gentle a soul, too decent a man to condone what she'd done.

Tom August? Maybe in theory, but he wouldn't have wanted her to tell him any of the details.

The scam's victims? Paulina Kantor had been angry enough to snatch the application form out of Fahada's hands, tenacious enough to hold on to that last little scrap of paper. But Greta suspected that Paulina had suffered too much, lost too much, to be anything other than a self-defense only, righteous-kill lady.

Bram? He would've tried to fathom her action and her anguish. But how could she expect him to see her the same way again? On several occasions during their too-brief time together, he'd joke about hitting the brick wall of her "ingrained cop-think" on certain topics. No way to laugh off assassin-think.

A deep sigh rolled out of Greta's chest. All those extraordinary people . . . If they hadn't been murdered, she wouldn't be here, and Greta Strasser would still be able to live with herself.

Just past 10:30, the suite door opened. Someone entered, marched across the living room and banged open the double-doors of the expertly antiqued home theater cupboard. Impatient channel surfing commenced, a rush through jingles and gunshots, volume ratcheted up for a female voice introducing political sound bites, sports, hyped-up shortages of the hottest new Christmas gifts. Beneath the cavalcade of eager voices, clinking sounds came from the suite's well-stocked bar. Ten to eleven, local news, volume up even higher, the better to hear the faux-concern of a male reporter. "Unidentifiable," "terror," and "peaceful neighborhood" were repeated twice in his thirty-second cameo. TV off, glass thunked down, silence.

Without switching on the chandelier, someone walked into the bedroom and headed directly for the bathroom. Light seeped into the bedroom from the partially closed door. A man was taking a leak—an extremely long leak, followed by a sigh of relief, toilet flushing, hand washing, bathroom light clicking off. A silk tie landed across the back of Greta's chair and over her right shoulder as Wolfram, whistling merrily, moved directly to the nightstand. He let go a loud, unapologetic fart—still unaware another person was in the room. Back turned to Greta, he switched on the lamp she'd turned off and emptied his pockets onto the nightstand.

The whistling halted abruptly when she asked, "Where is my money?"

Her four words had been low, not quite down to a growl, but she was positive that for Wolfram, they were powerful enough to reverberate throughout the entire suite. She twisted to face him in her chair just as he twirled around. Even in the low light, she saw his eyes widen at the sight of her.

"I did the job." Greta pointed at the bed, where the *Post* was on display. "There it is in the paper. You just saw it on the television."

"But . . . you . . . you didn't call." He had to be shuffling his deck of lies, excuses, escape routes, and bribes. The physical resemblance to a hawk was still jarring, but now that he'd been trapped by a dangerous assassin, his arrogance had been brought down considerably. "You were supposed to call after you—"

"Yes for the—how did you put it?—'Balance upon completion.' Something told me to check my account first. And guess what I found?" She paused a beat; no reply from Wolfram. "Nothing! The whole account—wiped away!" Her flattened hand flew across her throat—never a reassuring gesture, especially from a hired killer whose CV was rife with knifings. "Gone—as if it never existed! Tell me, what was the point of calling you? Do you take me for the type of person who uses a telephone to whine and beg?"

"Impossible!" he sputtered. "Right after I heard the news, I paid in the extra money! Someone must have hacked into—"

"Don't insult me with your lies!" She lifted the silencer-fitted .22 that had been out of sight on the chair next to her right hip. "My first husband advised me, 'Never aim a gun unless you plan to use it.'" With the faintest of smiles, she aimed it at his head.

Wolfram's Adam's apple began to bob up and down. Transfixed, he stared at the pistol as if he'd never seen one before.

"Admit it—that assignment you handed me wasn't for Saleh, it was for *me*! I can just imagine how you were looking forward to the news—your go-ahead to grab every penny of my money! Go ahead, show me this deposit you say you made—easy enough, since you already logged into my account today!"

She chucked her cell phone at his chest. He only flinched, too panicked to either avoid or make a catch for it. "People all around the world trust me with all their money," he protested feebly. "I never tampered with an account in my entire life."

With a disgusted laugh, she hurled back, "*Never*? What about all those forms I forwarded to Bersonne? You think I was too stupid to figure out that charade? Don't waste any more of my time. Pick up the damn phone!"

A fleeting glance at the phone, then back to the mesmerizing .22. "That event in Queens . . . I had nothing to do with any of it . . . I only passed along a photo and address."

"Listen to the poor innocent go-between, how he insists his hands are clean!" she mocked. "Why, who would imagine that a banker—a Swiss banker, no less—could have the slightest connection with something nasty enough to draw blood?" She sat back a little, taking his measure, making it obvious that she found it lacking. "I knew exactly what I was putting in motion when I first contacted you, Wolfram. I put you on notice that someone was out there who could not only track you down, but could also bring your secret partners and dirty business to light. Your type has never been able to stomach the constant threat of exposure. As far as you were concerned, I couldn't get dead fast enough."

Sweat began to bead on Wolfram's brow. "Of course I was afraid of you . . . yes, for all those reasons. Now . . ." His chin indicated the gun. ". . . even more. But you heard the news—they keep saying no one can be sure exactly who or even how many people died. So whoever set it up—"

"*Whoever?*" She nearly spit the word back at him. "As if it wasn't *you*?"

"Please, please, be reasonable," he pleaded. "You know *I* didn't build that bomb, no less set it up to explode. I'm only trying to make you understand that the person who was responsible has no way of knowing that you escaped. And I swear, I'll never tell a living soul." He paused, searching her furious face. "Don't you see the benefit? You're safe! You're free! No one will ever go after you again!" His eyebrows shot up, anticipating a joyous reaction to the freedom his promise carried.

Instead, she stood—not only taller than Wolfram, but, in her coat and padding, a far more imposing figure—and glowered at him.

In reaction to her menace, his hands flew up, palms out in surrender. "I'll give you enough to retire very comfortably, to disappear from all your enemies." Excited, nearly breathless, he said, "Double what we agreed on." Realizing that she hadn't ordered him to raise his hands, he lowered them sheepishly, furtively wiping off the sweat on his trousers.

She took a step toward him. "Will it miraculously appear in that same account? Just like the magician's trick—'Now you see it, now you don't'?"

Suddenly chilly, he shot back, "Before you reject my offer, just stop and consider—kill me, and you get nothing."

"Thanks to you, doesn't that describe exactly what I have right now? Wolfram, money may be the most important thing in your life, but not in mine. I don't have to get a penny to make a little visit to your beloved wife—Anne-Claire, correct? After we ladies have our lovely tête-à-tête, I'll meet your children—Simone and Guillaume." She tilted her head, as if considering. "Better yet, perhaps I'll warm up by popping in at Maman Wolfram's first. Sweet old thing . . . but getting on in years, isn't she?" As if in a preview of the peril his mother would face, she moved closer . . . the .22 all the nearer to the banker's heart.

"Damn bitch—you'll never get near them!" he cried, as he lunged for the gun, both hands twisting around her wrist, his unaccustomed recklessness fueling his strength. In his struggle to wrest it away, he succeeded in sidestepping just enough so that her flailing left arm was punching at air. Applying all his might, he forced her gun arm into an unnatural angle. Pain shot all the way to her shoulder, an urgent warning that bones were near their snapping point. As her fingers peeled back from the .22, she found herself stumbling backward, onto the bed. When she righted herself into a sitting position, Wolfram was standing over her, the gun pointed at her face.

CHAPTER **THIRTY-NINE**

"If you shoot me," Greta gasped, "you'll have to call the police. You'll have them crawling all over this room!"

"So what?" he cried triumphantly. "You broke into my room and tried to kill me! I grabbed your gun and shot you in self-defense! This time your death is guaranteed!"

Shaken by his determination, she worked to keep her voice level. "I have friends—friends who'll find you and kill you!"

"According to Nizar, assassins work alone. And besides, what sort of moron makes a friend of an assassin?"

"So you say it was . . . Nizar . . . behind the operation in Queens?"

"Of course. Not only do you know too much, but our little encounter proves that you've outlived your usefulness. Before long, you'd be going after your victims on a walker." He snickered before driving the next insult home: "Isn't it obvious? After all, I'm no professional, and who's holding the gun?"

Shamed, she hung her head. In a low, confessional voice, she replied, "I drove out to Queens Monday afternoon, but something . . . it just didn't feel right." She stole a quick look up at the gun. "I made it my business to follow you when your conference ended every afternoon . . . in and out of this hotel, the best restaurants, all those luxury shops. I couldn't stop making comparisons of your life and mine, and thinking about all the time and energy I've wasted hiding and running." She massaged her temple, as if that could rub away a throbbing headache. "But back to this morning—your last day at the conference. I had to act. You still weren't booked on a flight, and—"

"How the hell did you know that?"

Taking her time, she tilted her head until she was staring directly up at him. "Easier than it was for you to hijack my account. Anyhow, it took me no time to pick up on the Saleh surveillance, but I couldn't take the chance I'd be walking into the middle of a police or intelligence operation—either spying on Saleh or protecting him. So I called an agency that sends out health care aides. I said I was Saleh's wife, that I couldn't handle him by myself after his stroke any longer. They sent a woman right away, and . . ."

Outraged, he huffed, "You turned an innocent woman into a guinea pig!"

She shrugged. "I don't look at it that way. It could just as easily have been a salesman, or someone asking directions, or coming to read the meter . . . she only got what was meant for me. And before you get hysterical over her, you and Nizar paid me to murder old people for their money. Doesn't that bother you?"

Without a moment's hesitation, he replied, "Absolutely not."

"Then don't be a hypocrite." He was a creature devoid of humanity. Like the hawk hunched over its prey, he kept guilt at bay, as if conscience itself were a rival predator. "What about his split of the money?" she probed. "Ever wonder where it's going?"

"No concern of mine."

"Really? Then I'd advise you to ask Nizar exactly where he's planning his next attack before you visit New York again, or take your family on a vacation, or go to London or Paris or Amsterdam on a business trip."

Wolfram didn't reply.

"And by the way, who actually fed you the name of 'Nizar'?" Her eyes narrowed as she pressed, "Did that come from him, or from the person who first put the two of you in touch?" Wolfram was standing close enough for her to sense the slight frisson—as the floor subtly began its shift beneath his feet. "My bet is on the man who introduced you . . . near the top of Al Taqwa Bank . . . before it was shut down."

"Who told you that?" Wolfram snapped.

Without blinking, she said, "Theo Appel, of course."

"Who? Appel? Never heard of him."

"No big surprise. The man you know as Nizar Hashmi had him killed."

"Hashmi?"

"Hashmi, Kazemi, Husseini—pick one of those, or from a thousand other aliases! By now, I hope you've figured out that his real name will never be revealed to you." Still holding his eyes, she scoffed, "And he probably told you that he'd be moving around a lot—always a new cell phone number, always—"

"Enough! He leads a dangerous life, so what?" He pressed the gun against her upturned forehead. "I'm sick of listening to you, you miserable—" He pulled the trigger, body braced in anticipation of the kickback.

Even though the gun was equipped with a silencer, the hollow click wasn't what he'd expected. Wolfram's brow furrowed. Astonished, he stared down. Relentlessly, but ineffectually, his finger kept pulling back the trigger, over and over again.

The clean, metallic snap of a bullet being chambered made him flinch.

Once again, it was Wolfram who was being held at gunpoint.

Greta, whose hand had surreptitiously slid down into her right coat pocket, had suddenly brought up her Glock. "Back off! Now!" she ordered.

Wolfram moved away from her so fast, he crashed into the nightstand.

Rising to her feet, she moved in reverse as well, inserting additional space between them. "You know that sorry excuse for murder—we've all heard it hundreds of times—'I didn't know the gun was loaded'? I hope you appreciate how neatly that was turned inside-out on you, Wolfram." She jutted her chin in the direction of the dresser. "By the way, your e-ticket will come in handy. It'll take no time to convert it into my free flight to Switzerland. Weren't we discussing your family in Zurich before you grabbed my gun?"

"I swear you'll get it all—half a million dollars!"

"Is that all their lives are worth? Wife, son, daughter, mother?"

"A million!"

"And what about Nizar? As soon as I walk out of this room, you'll be on the phone, squealing, 'She's alive! Fahada's alive! Please, aka Nizar, try to kill the bad woman again!'"

A hand shot up in protest. "No, no—I'd sound foolish, calling him a second time, after I already thanked him."

"You did *what*?"

"I thanked him for—"

"Idiot, I don't care what you *said*!" Stunned, she muttered, "You spoke to him? He thinks *you* are alive?"

"Isn't that . . . isn't that the way it ought to be?"

"Show me your phone . . . show me your call." Her foot was tapping nervously. "The exact time you made it," she demanded.

He turned and snatched his cell phone from the night stand. He quickly selected call history and held it out to her. "It's the one right before Swiss International," he said as she snatched it out of his hand.

Moving away from him again, she scrolled down to the international exchange number. "Shit!"

"I don't understand. Why shouldn't I be—"

"Alive? Because Nizar hired me to kill you!"

Wolfram's mouth moved, but no sound came out.

"Are you so simple, you can't figure it out? After I killed you, I was supposed to get paid at the Saleh house—*my* turn to be killed! I saw what those amateurs were up to immediately. And you were too much of a moving target, so I turned the order around. This visit here tonight would have worked—Nizar doesn't follow the local news in New York. Now your damn call has made a mess of everything! I'll work it out so I'll get paid for killing you. And then I have to work out a way to kill him before he can order another hit on me."

"But . . . but . . ." Wolfram was incredulous. "Why would he want to kill *me*?"

"All you can think about is yourself! You're so gullible, he has you thinking you're on the inside, nice and safe. A key player. You accused me of outliving my usefulness? Look in the mirror!"

"You're insane! My bank is essential to—"

"Essential to nothing! The fund deadline passed months ago, and now you're not only just another Swiss banker, but one who knows far too much about Nizar's agenda. He can have his pick of younger, smarter men who'll work cheaper, faster, and more innovatively than you. You certainly ought to know—you just came from five days of being in the same symposium with hundreds of them!"

Seething, she kept rapping the cell phone against her hip until it attained a rhythm of its own. She stared at him, looking him up and down several times, until something frightening flickered across her face. "Okay, Wolfram," she said matter-of-factly, "kick off your shoes and lie on the bed. On your back."

He didn't move until she said, "I'm not going to repeat that. No reason to, since I remembered to bring along a knife."

In seconds, he was shoeless, one knee up on the bed. "What . . . what are you going to do?"

"Like I said, I have to honor the deal I made to kill you. Then, after my little stopover in Switzerland, I'm going to kill Nizar—what name did you say he's using now?"

"I didn't." Wolfram hoisted himself up onto the bed, then leaned back, every muscle tensed, tears starting to stream down his cheeks. "Stay away from Switzerland, and I'll help you find him much faster. I'll pay you anything you ask to kill him—to just put an end to this!"

"Name and location," she said evenly.

"I swear, I wasn't lying. I only know him as Nizar . . . Nizar Zahir. He's in Syria."

"I can figure that out from the number," she bluffed, "so you're not giving me much at all."

"Swear you'll kill him!" he groaned, "Swear!"

"Oh, I'll take care of him," she whispered, "if it's the last thing I do. But since you're still holding back, Wolfram, my first stop is Zurich."

"Okay, okay! His split . . . it eventually landed in an account in Damascus . . . in the name of a charity. I'm not supposed to know that, but . . ."

"But," she picked up, "doing business with a terrorist, no matter how lucrative, made you uneasy. You needed a safety net, Wolfram, and used your banker's bag of tricks to turn one up. Sit up, and use the pen and pad on the night table. I have no doubt you've memorized the name, number, and password of the account. After you write down all that, plus the bank name and branch, you can sit back against the headboard and relax."

After Wolfram had put down the pen and settled himself more comfortably, he asked, "How much do you want?"

One at a time, she counted off on the fingers of her left hand: "Back pay, retirement pay, the lost fee from Nizar for killing you, the upcoming job on Nizar. It adds up. Two million. Much more than what Mrs. Kantor was supposed to receive." Before he could ask who Kantor was, she said, "Paulina Kantor. Doesn't ring a bell? She was murdered. By the real Fahada."

Wolfram jackknifed forward. "The 'real Fahada'—what the hell are you talking about?"

"Fahada is dead. The only way she could wriggle out of the trap we set for her was by committing suicide. We'll never know how many people she murdered."

"*We?* What is this? Who are you working for? Who the hell are you?"

"My name is Greta Strasser. I was a New York Police Department detective before the Joint Terrorism Task Force recruited me. Nizar's man, Bersonne, killed one of our best agents . . . a good man . . . a good friend." After swallowing down her anger, she continued, "Our team shut down the tail end of the scam you had going with Nizar. Unfortunately, it was too late to save Theo Appel—that man you never heard of—who was another friend of mine. You're in deep shit, Wolfram."

"I was thousands of miles away—I never committed a crime in this country! How can you arrest me?"

Raising her eyebrows, she asked, "Who said anything about arresting you?"

"I just told you everything I know about Nizar, more than enough to track him down. I'll pay you the two million to let me board that flight back to Switzerland."

"You have a big problem, Wolfram," she said as she edged closer to him. "You were born into blood money. Every penny you've ever touched is blood money. It never lost the stink of the murder machine your father and his fellow Swiss bankers kept going sixty years ago in Europe, and now you're doing your damnedest to recycle it into more death and more terror and more misery all around the world. I'd give my last breath to expose what you've done."

"This is entrapment—I demand to speak with your superior! You're sworn to protect people, to follow the rule of law!"

"My retirement papers arrived weeks ago—my days of obligation to protect garbage like you are over."

"Clever as you think you are, there's nothing you can do to me."

"Right, your type never gets caught. I spent more than twenty years watching scum like you stroll out of court, laughing and slapping your lawyers on the back. I'd just sit there until no one was left in the court-room, trying to figure out what flaw of evidence or testimony I missed . . . but that wasn't it. The blame goes to the bastards who get around the system. And to the system itself." Still slowly advancing, she lifted one shoulder in a self-deprecatory shrug. "Hey, if you don't blame someone or something, then it's just you, alone and humiliated." She sighed as she reached the nightstand. "One last thing—do you know how Fahada got away with killing all those elderly people you robbed?"

"I don't give a damn—let them all rot in hell!" If she hadn't been stand-ing directly above him, the accompanying spitstorm would have hit Greta directly in the face.

"You have no idea, do you?" Her left hand reached into her coat pocket. The white handkerchief drew no reaction from Wolfram; his face was still twisted with contempt. "I'd like to show you how Fahada operated. She always carried a spare."

With lightning speed, she dropped the Glock into her right coat pocket and whipped out the small gold perfume sprayer. As soon as he saw she was no longer holding her weapon, he propped himself on his left elbow and extended his right arm, his hand grabbing a fistful of her coat. By then, she'd pressed the handkerchief to her face like a surgeon's mask and was hitting Wolfram straight in the face with the second of three rapid bursts of the sprayer. On the last spurt, his right arm went slack. She be-gan to back away.

Enunciating carefully to get through the haze and panic that were flooding his brain, she said, "All your victims died of cyanide poisoning.

You're younger, so your agony might last longer—but not long enough." Before she reached the door to the living room, Wolfram was lying still on the bed. "Oh, and make sure you hook up with Fahada in hell. The two of you will make a fun couple."

When Greta returned to the bedroom, Wolfram was perfectly positioned, his hand clutching at his chest. Reaching into her pocket again, she put the safety on the Glock, then removed two foil-covered alcohol towelettes. She used one to clean around the dead banker's open mouth, the other to wipe around his nostrils. After a quick suite check, she opened the door just enough to check the hallway, then walked to the stairway at a leisurely pace, the *New York Post* under her arm. Three flights down, she took the elevator to the lobby.

The doors had just parted when a crowd of twenty or so pushed in from the street. All of them appeared to be in their middle-to-late fifties, out-of-towners. They were dressed up for the evening, the men in suits and topcoats and the women in dark fur coats. Nearly every one of them was clutching a Playbill for *Jersey Boys*, and their faces were rosy—maybe a combination of the chilly November night air and drinks during intermission.

The musical about the rock 'n' roll group The Four Seasons had opened earlier in the month, an unexpected hit. A knot of women kept singing "Big girls don't cry-yi-yi," while a few of the men backed them up with, "They don't cry!" A rival group came back at them with snippets of "Rag Doll." Laughing, they dueled back and forth with their favorites until a petite blonde at the center silenced them all. Her pure, untrained voice rang out:

> "Oh, what a night!
> You know, I didn't even know her name,
> but I was never gonna be the same. . . .
> What a lady, what a night!"

Greta had no choice but to walk straight through the group, but with all eyes fixed on their star soprano, no one noticed her at all.

> "I got a funny feeling
> when she walked in the room,
> as I recall, it ended much too soon. . . ."

While Greta wended her way to the door and out, the sweet voice trailed after her:

> "Why did it take so long to see the light?
> It seemed so wrong, then it seemed so right. . . .
> Oh, what a lady, what a night!"

CHAPTER FORTY

Fergusson looked up at Greta. Makeup couldn't hide what the last week had cost her. More concerned than casual, he asked, "How was your vacation?"

With what she hoped was an ironic smile, she replied, "It was one of those vacations that's more work than work. You know, running around taking care of stuff you can't get to otherwise. I'm beat." Greta scanned the squad room before whispering, "What should I know?"

Malcolm leaned across his desk. "Word is that Quill's still here—but that's unverifiable. His door's always closed, and nobody's seen him since they took his computer and files—that had to be more than a week before you left."

"That's about right." Greta flipped on her monitor. "I guess they don't make snap decisions when it comes to—" Her phone rang, and she picked up.

Her caller said, "I want to talk to you. Not to Kim and not to Cepeda. Can you meet me at the botanica right now?"

She hesitated. Vazquez must have called while she was away, got the voice mail message with the day she'd return, and called first thing. "Twenty minutes. I'll have someone outside."

"So will I."

There were no open parking spots, so Fergusson pulled up next to a hydrant diagonally across the street from the Rios emporium. "You shouldn't go in alone," he said for the third time.

Greta adjusted her black locker-wig, then smoothed out her blouse over the wire. "Like I said, the fact that he didn't waste any time means he's got something important to say. Let's not spook him."

She found Vazquez in the aisle of saints. Instead of saying hello, he gestured toward a small statue of a man dressed like Zorro, minus the mask and cape. His hair and skinny moustache were a high gloss, shoe-polish black. "This is Jesus Malverde," the young man said, as if formally introducing him to Greta, "the patron saint of drug dealers. He's known as the narco-saint."

"Whose side is he on?"

"You pray to a saint to protect you, but sometimes the best way is when they protect you from yourself."

"Okay, I'm all for that side." Greta was impressed . . . and interested. "Are you taking his advice?"

"Maybe." Vazquez, who looked like he worked out, was Greta's height (both were wearing low-heeled boots). Unlike the majority of gang members she'd encountered, he maintained strong eye contact. "First, I want to know how you're going to make good on what you talked about."

"You mean a chance to get out?"

"Yeah. College. Moving upstate. All that start-over crap."

"I had to wait until you approached me. Now I can speak to someone at the top about relocating you and getting you new ID." Greta stole a glance at Malverde, wishing he could instantly replace Quill with any other precinct commander in the world—someone who'd make an effort to help this kid so they could finally nail the most lethal criminal in the precinct. "There's also the reward for information that results in the capture of VX."

"What reward?" Vazquez sounded surprised. "I never heard about any reward."

"There was supposed to be a press release about it. But that was right about the time I left town on a temporary assignment, around six months ago. Maybe we both missed the paper that day." She frowned, but went on, "It was offered by the mother of Abigail Conklin—the girl in the wheelchair—because the police weren't making any progress on VX. Twenty-five thousand dollars."

"All that time, all that money, and nobody had the balls to finger him?"

Greta took a chance. "I thought that after Miss Martinez's death . . . I really thought that anyone with a daughter would be scared *not* to come forward." Vazquez's mouth twisted slightly as he gave a small nod of agreement. "But some things happen for a reason, and Mrs. Conklin would probably find some comfort, maybe even some justice, if you were the one who . . ."

She let it hang right there, until Vazquez broke the awkward silence that followed. "That's more than two years tuition and board at a state college. And you were right—two of those schools are more than four hundred miles from here."

"So you've been checking it out. Glad to hear that."

"Yeah. Well, don't get too happy. Me giving you VX's location isn't going to happen unless you deliver what I want."

She sighed in exasperation. "That's never going to change from the last time, Vazquez. The NYPD will never be party to an execution"—the words seared, acid on her tongue—"no matter how many crimes a person's committed."

Vazquez squared his shoulders. "Last time we were here, that was the first point you made. I thought about it, even more about the rest of what you said. My oath is to kill him, but your way—one day at a time, every single day of his fucking life, without giving up my own freedom—that's why I'm here."

All too aware that she still hadn't cleared the minefield, Greta probed. "So . . . what is it you want?"

"To go in with you. Yeah, yeah, no weapon. But that way, I'm still part of it."

"An absolutely essential part," Greta agreed, "but there's no way I'd ever get permission for that. And to be honest, I'd never even ask."

"Then why should I believe all the rest you promised?" He cursed in Spanish and turned to walk away. "Forget it."

"Stop the bullshit drama, Vazquez!" she hissed. "What you're asking . . . it isn't like sneaking into the movies. Even if we turn you inside out with a weapons check, if you make one false move—even unintentionally—a cop could get shot, or the entire operation compromised, or both."

At least she got him to turn around and pay attention; actually changing his mind seemed hopeless. "Hold on," she said suddenly, "what type of place is he hiding out in?"

"Are you crazy?"

"Come on, I'm not asking you for an address! Small apartment building, high-rise, brownstone, store, cellar, church—"

He stopped her with, "Like a high-rise."

"Have you been inside?"

Two elderly women shoppers had entered the aisle. With a light touch on Greta's elbow, he steered her away to a back wall that had an odd mix of incense, household cleaning items, and small spray bottles. "One night about a month ago, we spotted VX's top lieutenant," he confided, "but no VX so far. We've followed this guy to the same building about three times a week. Always around midnight. Doesn't stay more than a few minutes. Building's got a doorman and cameras. Plus, we don't even know what floor he's going to. So we can't . . ."

"Break in on your own. Oh-so-gently, of course."

"Yeah. You should see how the doorman opens the door for this dude— just a little bit, not wide, like for the regular people who live there. Like the guy may be cleared to go in by one of the tenants, but he still doesn't like letting him inside."

"Got the picture. So he goes up and comes back by elevator?"

"I'm giving too much away without getting anything back."

"We're not in one of those little towns four hundred miles away from New York, where there'd only be one or two high-rises. How many elevators?"

"Two that we could see."

Greta thought for a moment. "Give me the address. We should be able to target the apartment he's visiting. I'll do my best to get you inside the fire stairs on that floor."

"You're fucking with me, right?"

"No, I'm one hundred percent serious. I'm not taking any chances with you. Body check, a cop covering you at all times. You may be a good student, Vazquez, and you may have a clean record and a real desire to make a new life, but you're a self-acknowledged member of a gang that deals drugs. What I'm offering you is a chance to truthfully say that you went in with us." After the briefest of pauses, she added, "I want your answer right now—final offer."

Vazquez tilted his chin toward the display in front of them. "The beginning of every year, my mother went through the same ritual . . . she'd light special candles, pray, then she'd rip through the whole apartment with these cleansers—we're not talking Mr. Clean, she'd already done that. This stuff is supposed to clean away bad spirits, any kind of negative shit. After that, she'd use good luck sprays and special incense. All it did for me was to make my eyes burn." Rubbing his hand across the light stubble on his chin, he said, "New Year's is just a few weeks away—let's see if you can get better results than this magic potion crap."

After he gave her the address, they agreed that he should leave first. Greta lingered by the display, to give him plenty of time to exit. She studied all the bottles, especially the cleansers, but she didn't see any specific enough—or strong enough—to get rid of her own negative shit.

Back at the Two-Four, Geracimos waved in Kim and Cepeda, then closed his office door and kept the volume low while they reviewed the tape. After a second playback, the lieu said, "Good work. And Strasser, hard for me to blast you about Vazquez on the fire stairs—otherwise we wouldn't be having this meeting." Looking from face to face, he said, "Ernest Flowers will be the Two-Four's most significant arrest in all my years here. This thug has terrorized the entire precinct for so long, it's a total embarrassment. That said, the four of you make a very strong team, and I'm confident that you'll bring him in."

He took a deep breath. "At the same time, my gut is warning me to keep this operation top secret. There's a lot of distrust in this house, and, off the record, it's justified. For now, let's keep this to the five of us, with Strasser as the unit leader." He sat back in his chair, satisfied with his decision. "However, if the need for more of a presence or even a SWAT team is indicated, Strasser, let's play it safe and reevaluate immediately." He turned to Malcolm. "You drove past the building on the way back. Anything unusual?"

"Not really. A medium-sized high-rise, tallest building on the block, mid-block. Quiet street, nearly all residential, relatively well maintained."

"VX in a *nice* neighborhood? That's a surprise."

Working mug shots with Vazquez had turned up a positive ID of the man he and other Blu-Steel members had followed. Justice Jefferson, who more than lived up to his name by having been brought to justice four times in his twenty-six years, was currently wanted for drug trafficking. He'd narrowly escaped arrest just the past summer—what must've been a sloppy arrest went along with even sloppier record keeping; no details were in his file.

Although the day doorman drew a blank, both the evening and late night-shift doormen recognized the man in the photo. Both stated that whenever "Mr. Winston" was announced to the tenant—they called her Miss Geary—he was immediately granted permission to go right up to 5N. Quizzed on when and how often her guest usually showed up, their answers indicated that he was timing his visits to alternate between the end of one doorman's shift and the beginning of the next—between 11:00 P.M. and 1:00 A.M. Consequently, neither saw him more frequently than every fourth night or so.

None of the doormen had much to say about Geary, but shakes of the head and "night owl," "zombie," and "skeletal" filled in a lot of blanks. Thought to be in her early twenties, she was never seen without sunglasses and usually wore a leather jacket and matching pants—all covered up, even in the summer.

Kim had asked all three men a key question: "What about food deliveries?"

The day doorman had replied, "Gristedes." Pressed to be more exact, he replied, "Hard to keep track, because a lot of the tenants order their groceries from there."

"How much? A bag? A carton?"

"Usually a carton."

To that, the evening doorman had added, "Take-out. Lots of take-out. Yeah, she's a rail, but she's not the only one of those throw-up chicks we have in this building. They're so skinny, they can cover everything they got with a Band-Aid."

The building manager's floor plan showed 5N to be an undersized one-bedroom apartment. Its two-year lease was made out to Kristen Geary, sole occupant, who'd lived there barely half a year. The manager had not met her personally; he explained that it wasn't unusual for the paper-work and background check to be handled by the listing Realtor, who delivered the first month's rent and two months' rent security deposit, in addition to collecting her own commission, equal to fifteen percent of the annual rent—a hefty amount to cough up before getting the key.

The apartment was back-to-back with a similar, but much older building. As far as room height and facing windows, the fifth floors didn't line up, but those differences weren't what ruled out surveillance from there: No one with a view of 5N could remember the last time its heavy burgundy drapes had been opened.

On their first night of watching, Mr. Winston-Jefferson showed up at 1:00 A.M. As tall and muscular as VX, he'd approached the building with the same swagger Greta had seen down on Astor Place. He was admitted after the obligatory call upstairs and was out of the building in less than five minutes.

"Allowing time for the elevator, too quick to have sex," said Kim.

"Wait until you get married," snapped Cepeda, as he took off after Mr. Winston.

Cepeda tailed him to a club in Harlem, then back to what was supposed to be an empty tenement in the precinct, slated for demolition; it was two blocks from the playground where Tyrel Dobbs had been shot.

Minutes after Jefferson departed, Geary also left, wearing a skin-tight dark green leather jacket and matching pants. Emaciated enough to be a model, she fell short by about ten inches, but she certainly had the vacant gaze that stared out from the pages of fashion magazines. After slinking in and out of clubs in the meatpacking district, she returned to 5N just after 6:00 A.M.

Later the same day, the team regrouped with Geracimos. Since they didn't expect Jefferson to show, they planned to get into position that night and play out a dress rehearsal of sorts: Greta would follow Jefferson into the elevator after alerting Kim and Fergusson that he'd entered the building. They'd be waiting in the building's other passenger elevator, locked on the fifth floor with an OUT-OF-SERVICE sign. Greta would exit the elevator on the fourth floor, sprint up the fire stairs, and wait by the door where Cepeda would be babysitting Vazquez. On the signal that Kim and Fergusson were leaving their elevator to follow Jefferson into 5N, Greta would proceed to station herself just outside the apartment as backup.

The following night, all was going according to plan. Jefferson hadn't even glanced at Greta, who, taking a cue from a nearby hospital, was wearing a doctor's scrubs, stethoscope, and thick-soled cross trainers. Her hair was pulled back severely, and she wore no makeup. She waited inside the fire stairs until Kim's voice whispered, "Now, Greta!"

Quietly gliding along, Glock in hand, she saw the door to the apartment open. Apparently, it didn't swing in all the way—Jefferson had to angle sideways to enter. Kim glanced back at her, nodded, then whispered to Malcolm, and they pushed forward into 5N.

As she caught up, Malcolm was saying, ". . . even think of doing anything stupid. There are eight more cops on this floor alone, so let's get this over with. Both hands behind your back, *now!*"

"Call him," was Jefferson's ultra low-key order to whomever had opened the door. That person—presumably Geary—was now concealed by his own and Fergusson's backs. Meanwhile, Jefferson complied, calmly offering his hands behind his back. Kim had him cuffed instantly.

"What the fuck are you doing?" a shrill, indignant female demanded. Two nights before, Greta had overheard Geary cursing out a bouncer; it was the same voice.

"Who else is in this apartment, Miss Geary?" asked Malcolm.

"Who the fuck are you?" she shot back, without a trace of trepidation— on the contrary, she sounded outraged. "Don't you stupid shits know this place is off limits? Both of you—get the hell out!"

"Just call him," urged Jefferson, now minus a lot of his cool. "What the fuck you waiting for? Pick up your damn phone and *call* him."

Ignoring her rant, Malcolm continued, "We have warrants for a search of these premises and for the arrest of—"

Russell shot Greta a quick look, and she stepped inside to cover Jefferson while he moved around the cuffed man's right. Peering out from behind Jefferson's massive left shoulder, she could see that Malcolm had been advancing on Geary; Russell swiftly joined him while Geary backed away on a leftward diagonal, snatching a cell phone off a lamp table. She hit one of its buttons as she continued on her path toward the bedroom, her eyes flitting from Malcolm to Russell while she screeched, "Daddy! *Daddy!* Why the hell are cops here? Who sent these stupid goddamn—?"

Just before Geary could sidestep into the bedroom, an arm shot out and reeled her in. Startled, she resisted, stumbled, then disappeared inside, her voice trailing a pathetic "Daddy!"

In seconds, she reemerged in the grasp of VX. Nearly twice her size, his left arm was wrapped around her throat, his large automatic pointed at her right temple. Her legs were pedaling furiously to make purchase with a floor more than a foot out of reach. Her sudden silence and frantic, bulging eyes signaled that VX's huge forearm was pressing on her windpipe.

"Who the fuck sent you?" VX snarled, eyes darting from Malcolm to Kim. Both faced him in a standoff with their weapons drawn. "What dumb-ass cop was stupid enough to—"

At that moment, he caught sight of Greta's head, tilted out behind Jefferson. He reacted by jerking hard on Geary's neck—definitely a surrogate for Greta's—with enough force to raise her even higher off the floor.

"It's you, you fucking bitch!" he growled, as he turned his gun from his captive's head and aimed it at Greta.

Good, cocksucker, go for me. And before I hit the ground, Malcolm and Russell will leave gaping holes where your kneecaps used to be.

Meanwhile, Jefferson, unaware of Greta's presence and believing VX had just mistakenly sized up the situation and accused him of betrayal, turned to run. When he found himself blocking Greta—the real bitch—and her Glock, VX's bullets were already ripping into him. Cuffed, he toppled straight forward, fast and hard. Barely escaping a crushing, total-body press, Greta hopped to her right.

Experiencing a strange tunnel vision that excluded all but VX, she raised her arm and fired at his shoulder, a split second before VX—encumbered by his now-limp hostage—twisted to adjust his own aim.

VX's weapon skittered along the floor, right to Malcolm's feet. Greta's eyes followed an unconscious Geary, splattered with blood and bone; abruptly released, she crumpled to the floor. Nearly tripping over Jefferson, VX was headed for the door.

For the briefest moment, Greta saw him sprinting down an endless Broadway, escaping into a darkening evening. Then she snapped back to the trailing rivulets of blood, to the broad back with a hand cradling an arm so minimally attached to his torso it was unbelievable he was still on his feet and moving as fast as he was. As she took off after him, she shouted—not sure if her words were coherent because of the reverbera-tion in her ears—"Malcolm—make sure no one else is in the apartment! Kim—two ambulances! And get that goddamn phone!" Next: "Cepeda—Jefferson's dead, Flowers is seriously wounded, fifteen feet from your posi-tion, no weapon—shit! No, he has a gun!"

VX was turning, a small pistol in his left hand. He had to be in shock; the hand was shaking hard. Greta, picturing Cepeda and Vazquez di-rectly behind the fire door, fired.

A little shaky herself, she'd gone for his left arm. There was a fine red spray—not much of a hit—but the gun fell to the floor. Bending from the waist, VX made a feeble reach for it, then lurched around, going for the fire door. "Cepeda, I winged him, no weapon, approaching your position.

Flowers, halt!" she shouted, as she kicked his gun toward the wall. "You're under arrest!"

"I'm behind you, Strasser!" It was Malcolm, minimally audible in her ear.

With what seemed to be his last reserve of strength, VX kicked at the fire door. It swung open, and he stumbled onto the stairway landing. Cepeda was waiting, weapon drawn. Vazquez was right behind him, transfixed by the sight of VX's right arm and fragmented shoulder. "Stop it right there, Flowers!" Cepeda shouted. "You're not going anywhere."

Perhaps drifting beyond seeing and hearing, Flowers came to a standstill; his left hand jerked out for the handrail, but it failed to make contact, and he staggered. Cepeda instinctively moved a half step back.

Even in those fleeting seconds, blood had pooled on the cement floor and was flowing toward the stairs. VX staggered again, and Vazquez's boot kicked out as he yelled, "Fuck! Brand-new boots—and this cocksucker's blood just ruined them!"

Before he finished, VX, all two-hundred-plus pounds of him, was hurtling down the concrete fire stairs, head first. Cepeda raced down to where he'd come to a stop, sprawled on the next landing.

Greta's eyes locked with Vazquez's. Was he reading that she understood exactly how free and exultant he felt . . . as well as the warning that it wouldn't last long? Or, more likely, did he suspect that, as the lone witness to what he'd just done, she had yet to decide whether or not to use it against him?

"If you see brains all over and he's not breathing, he's dead, right?" Cepeda shouted up.

CHAPTER FORTY-ONE

The cell phone's owner, alias Kristen Geary, became the centerpiece of the Internal Affairs hearing. She verified that it was her personal phone. She confirmed that the envelope presented as evidence was the same one Justice Jefferson had handed her the night of his murder. She also identified its contents, packaged in glassine packets labeled Bliss (with a rough sketch of a naked postcoital woman sprawled across a four-poster bed), as heroin.

Was she was addicted to the drug? "Probably." Asked who introduced her to it, she named Ernest Flowers, whom she later described as "the coolest guy . . . at first." When did they meet? A true romantic, she pinpointed a day early in the year: That first "date" occurred two days after Greta and Russell heard the scared little girl who'd been Tyrel Dobbs's friend cry out about "the shiny-head man." By then, of course, a spate of hoodlums with shaved heads were roaming the Two-Four.

And what were the circumstances of her move into 5N? She explained that in June, Flowers had phoned from out of town—he'd been away on a business trip for a really long time, but he'd made sure that Mr. Jefferson "looked after her." During that call, he'd asked her to find an apartment in the precinct "right away."

Not East Side or West Side? Not a neighborhood? Not a street? A precinct? *The* precinct? Yes, *the* precinct. The Two-Four.

Background information for her lease indicated she was employed at the time—could she state her place of employment? No. Did Mr. Flowers pay the rent? No, her father did. So Mr. Flowers joined you after you moved in? Yes. Did he go out much? No. Did he conduct business in your apartment? Maybe on the phone. And just before Mr. Flowers shot Mr. Jefferson, who did she call? Her father. Was that the man she called "Daddy" on the cell call? Yes. The man who made her apartment "off limits" to the police? Yes. Did she see him in the room?

She pointed to Quill.

It turned out that Malcolm (whose real name was Jake Murray, and who had neither a family nor a drop of Scottish blood) had been dispatched to the Two-Four by Internal Affairs. When Greta confronted Lieutenant Geracimos in the corridor during a recess in the hearing, he vehemently denied knowing that Jake was an IA plant. Still, she had her suspicions.

Geracimos had shrugged it off with, "Hey, you've got to admit that the two of you made one hell of a team. Real serendipity. A: all those civilian complaints didn't add up with the CompStat numbers, so they sent someone in to . . . observe. B: that was exactly when you began to sniff out where the stink in the precinct was coming from."

"Quill's guys were turning people into double-dip victims," Greta halfheartedly agreed. "I couldn't look the other way. But the last thing I wanted to look like was a rat, Lieu, and there I was, partnered with a guy from Internal Affairs!"

"Murray was doing his job, and you were doing yours. You never dropped the dime on anyone. You cleaned up what they did wrong by doing something right. Besides, Greta, what's going to be remembered out of all this isn't anything about you—it's all about how easy Flowers played Quill.

"When the Dobbs boy died, Flowers was smart enough to figure out that he and his gang couldn't silence everyone in the precinct forever. Word was out that Quill's daughter was a cokehead. She already had quite a reputation for being wild—she didn't drop out of college, she was *kicked* out for doing blow. I never heard of anyone getting expelled during freshman orientation—the kid literally never set foot in a class-room. She probably thought Flowers was quite the novelty—ultracool, dangerous, all that shit that eventually turned her into a junkie. All Flowers had to do was threaten to pimp her out and Quill was his. And no matter how corrupt our peerless leader was before, he had to scramble for ways to look good while Mr. Most Wanted ran a thriving business from his daughter's apartment."

Movement in the corridor signaled that the hearing was about to resume. As they walked back in, he whispered, "What I love about you, Strasser, is that you're too disgusted to gloat."

The hearings took two days. The outcome could go several ways: In the past, precinct commanders found derelict in their duty had been transferred, suspended, or reassigned to other duties—i.e., demoted. Some had resigned—the word implied a voluntary act, but there was little doubt that more than one resignation had been forced. To even consider sending a PC to prison, no matter how serious his crimes, was anathema; the disgrace it would bring on the Department was unthinkable.

Quill resigned immediately; an NYPD press release had him "opting for early retirement after breaking the violent hold of Ernest Flowers and his gang on his precinct."

Before the end of the week, Vazquez was four hundred miles from New York City, enrolled for the next semester at a two-year state college. Somehow, the requirement of SAT scores for admission had been waived. He thanked Greta in an e-mail; *straightaaa* was his user name. She printed it out and brought it into Geracimos' office.

"You know what? I really believe he's gonna get straight A's," he said.

"You don't think he's going to feel the pull to come back?"

"Nah. The guy was smart enough to listen to you. Not too many of us get a second chance like he did. You ever hear of a third chance? No! Because people who screw up their second chance don't get another one."

"I hope you're right, Lieu." She hesitated, then said, "Lieu, there's something I've been wanting to ask you for a long time. My dad . . . all I come up with was that he was shot in the line of duty. Do you know any more about what happened?"

Geracimos' face darkened. "We were in the same precinct, down in Marine Park. But why are you asking me now?"

"When I was with JTTF, our team leader was shot in the line of duty. I had a lot of respect for him . . . always will. And . . . he saved my life. I should've been the one to save his. He left two little boys, and his wife gave birth to a baby girl just a few weeks after he died. He was only thirty-six."

"Same age as Hank. Way, way too young."

"When we were working together, he kept reminding me of someone . . . like one of those wisps-of-memory things." She gave up trying to maintain her customary reticence. "It's really tough to match up impressions you had of your parents as a little kid with the way you'd see them with a forty-something brain."

Geracimos got up and looked out his window. Mid-afternoon, mid-December, it was already dark enough for him and the room behind him to be reflected in the glass. "It was summertime," he began. "There were all these big fish markets at the south end of Flatbush Avenue, where people used to stop on their way back from the beach to buy seafood—God, I haven't been back there in decades. They had giant tanks filled with lobsters—that was the big draw, because they had the lowest prices anywhere in the city, and the prices were all fixed, to the penny. No surprise that they were all controlled by the mob—this was the middle Seventies.

"Your dad was on patrol with a rookie. They always put him with rookies—I'd been one of them myself. I guess it was because he had this instinct, this knack for how to handle himself, handle a situation. What I'm trying to say is that he knew how to do it by the book, and he knew how to get the right results. So they're in the car when they see all these people running like crazy out of one of these lobster joints. Hank and the rookie—I forget his name, a Nam vet, a good kid—they run in, but there's water and glass all over the floor, because one of the tanks was shot out. There's the main lobster tank right in front of them, water so full of blood, you can't see the lobsters, but you can see the top of a man's head bobbing on the surface. All of a sudden a guy pops up right behind the tank. Your father yells "Gun!" and jumps in front of the rookie. Hank got the son of a bitch, and the bastard got him. I was in the precinct house when the kid gave his statement. He couldn't stop crying. Nobody could."

In the silence that followed, Greta whispered, "Thanks, Lieu."

When he turned around, she was gone.

Eric Brauner's number was still on Greta's phone. They spoke for a while, and she asked if he'd been in touch with Zinah and Dell. He'd had lunch with Zinah in D.C. "She's already been promoted, and she's less . . . reserved, I guess. And it looks like Rice and I are going to be teamed up again after the holidays."

"How about Cassie August?"

"Busy with the baby and the boys. She e-mailed me some photos of the kids. It's going to be a tough Christmas for her." After a deep breath, he asked, "And what about you, Detective? Still back on the beat?"

"Can't seem to give it up." She paused. "Brauner, you remember the outfit that gave J. J. the background info on Fahada?"

"If you're thinking of applying for a job with them, I don't think you'll fulfill the basic requirements."

"Too much of a commute anyway. But I've come up with a little way to thank them for their help. How about if you give them my number?"

"Why not?"

An hour later, her cell phone rang. "Darling," a woman's voice breathed out, "can you meet me at Zabar's in twenty minutes? Cheese counter—I have no idea what to bring tonight, and this place is an absolute zoo. Don't be angry—I'm wearing that navy beret with the little white anchor that you love to hate."

———

"...so I'm afraid I've been sitting on it for nearly a month," Greta summed up. They'd been walking quite a way, and had just crossed Fifty-seventh Street. "I was trying to figure out some way to pursue it myself, but things heated up at work, and—"

"Right. That Flowers thug."

"Your intel's up to date. Know what I had for lunch?"

"We have to be on top of things. Anyhow, good for you. And by the way, you would have been an absolute lunatic to even go near Damascus." The woman, a redhead about Greta's height in a peacoat, jeans, and matching navy suede boots—she'd pocketed the silly beret the minute they walked out of the store—suddenly doubled over with laughter, as if they'd been best friends since kindergarten.

Greta shook her finger at her, and flattened her hand across her chest, as if it ached from too much laughing. "Do you have any idea who he might be?"

"Well, we've got a good soup going between Al Taqwa, Bankers Alliance Zurich, Paris, and Damascus. Sounds like he might be the person who got them in touch with Fahada in the first place, then tried to get rid of her when she wasn't submissive enough."

They both nearly keeled over with that. For real.

"Our taxi is coming up right behind me," the redhead said softly. "Good luck to us both. Air-kiss and shalom."

"Greta, am I disturbing your Christmas Day? It's Cassie August."

"Not at all. I'm at work, and it's turning out to be a quiet day. How are you doing?"

"Hanging in. I want to thank you for the gifts you sent the kids. They love them. I know the boys do, because they're fighting over them, and the baby's been taking a nice long nap in her new sleeper suit."

They spoke barely a minute more, and then the baby woke up, hungry.

Greta sat with the phone in her hand, wishing she could have found a way, without getting weepy or weird, to tell Cassie how Tom reminded her of her father, and how she'd looked up to both men.

For the past week, her thoughts kept going back to the way the lieu had described her father: ". . . he knew how to do it by the book, and he knew how to get the right results." Her initial impression had been that the right results had to follow—could only follow—proper procedure. But it suddenly occurred to her that he might have been signaling the opposite: that Hank Strasser had taught those rookies that doing it strictly by the book could sometimes bring the wrong results . . . or maybe no results at all.

Whatever Geracimos knew, or only guessed at, he could not have offered her a greater consolation than that of being her father's daughter. She couldn't have asked for a better point of return.

The phone rang again.

"Merry Christmas," said Schuyler.

Greta heard shouts in the background. "Are you at work or in a bar?"

"At work. The guys who stay up assembling toys until four A.M. shouldn't be walking around with guns. What about you?"

"I'm at the Two-Four. Crime doesn't stop for Christmas."

"Speaking of crime, I heard your precinct commander got the boot. And that you nailed that piece of shit you were after all year. I'd say that calls for a celebration. And I have a celebration rain check."

"Consider it about to be redeemed."

ABOUT THE AUTHORS

Al and Jean Zerries, husband and wife, write together as A. J. Zerries. Their first novel was *The Lost Van Gogh*. Al Zerries has won national recognition as a portraitist.